I0823756

TALES OF HEROES, GODS & MONSTERS

BABYLON & SUMER

MYTHS & LEGENDS

FLAME TREE PUBLISHING
6 Melbray Mews, Fulham,
London SW6 3NS, United Kingdom
www.flametreepublishing.com

26 28 30 29 27
1 3 5 7 9 10 8 6 4 2

ISBN: 978-1-83562-260-5

Cover and pattern art was created by Flame Tree Studio, with elements courtesy of Shutterstock.com/svekloid/Zvereva Yana. Inside ornaments courtesy Shutterstock.com/Rustanto 69.

Judith John (General Glossary) is a writer and editor specializing in literature and history. A former secondary school English Language and Literature teacher, she has subsequently worked as an editor on major educational projects, including *English A: Literature* for the Pearson International Baccalaureate series. Judith's major research interests include Romantic and Gothic literature, and Renaissance drama.

A copy of the CIP data for this book is available from the British Library.

Designed and created in the UK | Printed and bound in China

Represented in the EU for product safety and compliance by Authorised Rep Compliance Ltd., Ground Floor, 71 Lower Baggot Street, Dublin, D02 P593, Ireland. Contact at www.arccompliance.com

COLLECTOR'S EDITIONS

TALES OF HEROES, GODS & MONSTERS

BABYLON & SUMER

MYTHS & LEGENDS

FIONA COLLINS
& JUNE PETERS

Introduction by
PROFESSOR MARTIN WORTHINGTON

Further Reading & Glossaries of Terms

FLAME TREE PUBLISHING

CONTENTS

CONTENTS

CONTENTS

TALES OF HEROES, GODS & MONSTERS
BABYLON & SUMER
MYTHS & LEGENDS

SERIES FOREWORD

Stretching back to the oral traditions of thousands of years ago, tales of heroes and disaster, creation and conquest have been told by many different civilizations in many different ways. Their impact sits deep within our culture even though the detail in the tales themselves is a loose mix of historical record, transformed narrative and the distortions of hundreds of storytellers.

Today the language of mythology lives with us: our mood is jovial, our countenance is saturnine, we are narcissistic and our modern life is hermetically sealed from others. The nuances of myths and legends form part of our daily routines and help us navigate the world around us, with its half truths and biased reported facts.

The nature of a myth is that its story is already known by most of those who hear it, or read it. Every generation brings a new emphasis, but the fundamentals remain the same: a desire to understand and describe the events and relationships of the world. Many of the great stories are archetypes that help us find our own place, equipping us with tools for self-understanding, both individually and as part of a broader culture.

For Western societies it is Greek mythology that speaks to us most clearly. It greatly influenced the mythological heritage of the ancient Roman civilization and is the lens through which we still see the Celts, the Norse and many of the other great peoples and religions. The Greeks themselves learned much from their neighbours, the Egyptians, an older culture that became weak with age and incestuous leadership.

It is important to understand that what we perceive now as mythology had its own origins in perceptions of the divine and the rituals of the sacred. The earliest civilizations, in the crucible of the Middle East, in the Sumer of the third millennium BCE, are the source to which many of the mythic archetypes can be traced. As humankind collected together in cities for the first time, developed writing and industrial scale agriculture, started to irrigate the rivers and attempted to control rather than be at the mercy of its environment, humanity began to write down its tentative explanations of natural events, of floods and plagues, of disease.

Early stories tell of Gods (or god-like animals in the case of tribal societies such as African, Native American or Aboriginal cultures) who are crafty and use their wits to survive, and it is reasonable to suggest that these were the first rulers of the gathering peoples of the earth, later elevated to god-like status with the distance of time. Such tales became more political as cities vied with each other for supremacy, creating new Gods, new hierarchies for their pantheons. The older Gods took on primordial roles and became the preserve of creation and destruction, leaving the new gods to deal with more current, everyday affairs. Empires rose and fell, with Babylon assuming the mantle from Sumeria in the 1800s BCE, then in turn to be swept away by the Assyrians of the 1200s BC; then the Assyrians and the Egyptians were subjugated by the Greeks, the Greeks by the Romans and so on, leading to the spread and assimilation of common themes, ideas and stories throughout the world.

The survival of history is dependent on the telling of good tales, but each one must have the 'feeling' of truth, otherwise it will be ignored. Around the firesides, or embedded in a book or a computer, the myths and legends of the past are still the living materials of retold myth, not restricted to an exploration of origins. Now we have devices and global communications that give us unparalleled access to a diversity of traditions. We can find out about Native American, Indian, Chinese and tribal African mythology in a way that was denied to our ancestors, we can find connections, match the archaeology, religion and the mythologies of the world to build a comprehensive image of the human experience that is endlessly fascinating.

The stories in this book provide an introduction to the themes and concerns of the myths and legends of their respective cultures, with a short introduction to provide a linguistic, geographic and political context. This is where the myths have arrived today, but undoubtedly over the next millennia, they will transform again whilst retaining their essential truths and signs.

Jake Jackson
General Editor

TALES OF HEROES, GODS & MONSTERS BABYLON & SUMER MYTHS & LEGENDS

INTRODUCTIONS
& FURTHER READING

INTRODUCTION

BY PROFESSOR MARTIN WORTHINGTON

Humans must have been telling stories for as long as we've been able to talk. One of the first places in world history where we can access these narratives is Ancient Mesopotamia (modern-day Iraq). There, in the birthplace of writing itself, the cuneiform script was inscribed onto clay tablets, one of the most durable writing supports ever used. If the earliest records date to before 3000 BCE, and chiefly consist in administrative documents, by about 2500 BCE the uses of writing had expanded to embrace stories. And from about 1800 BCE, in the 'Old Babylonian period', we have them in large numbers – in both Sumerian, a language with no known relatives, and Babylonian/ Assyrian, two very similar languages related to Hebrew and Arabic, and often known by the umbrella term 'Akkadian'.

For these stories to reach modern readers, they have gone through many different steps: first, of course, they had to be composed – a process about which we are very little informed; then, someone had to decide that they were suitable for writing down (there were probably multiple filters that interposed between the body of stories that existed, and those we get to see); often, they were copied and recopied. Then, millennia later, the tablets had to be excavated, and their inscriptions deciphered by specially qualified scholars (philologists), who produce scholarly editions.

Often, this is where the process stops. It is a remarkable feature of the present volume that it goes one step further: it is the work of two professional storytellers who have for decades immersed themselves in the thought-world of Ancient Mesopotamia and brought the riches of Mesopotamian literature to modern-day audiences, in venues as far afield as the British Museum in London and the Iraqi Business Council in Amman.

June Peters and Fiona Collins do not claim to be specialists in the languages in which the stories were written, though they have often consulted such specialists. Nor do they aim to capture, word for word, what the clay tablets say. Instead, they use their long experience of performing these stories orally to capture what they see as the spirit of them, and to express them in a form to which modern readers will find it easy to respond. In doing this, they are bringing the stories back to the life they surely enjoyed in Mesopotamia, where they were no doubt told with different intents and sensibilities and, why not?, changes to both language and plot.

An example of how the literal sense has been changed by the current authors is provided by the first line of the poem 'Atra-Hasis'. The sense of the original 'inūma ilu awīlum' is debated: some opt for 'when the gods were man', others for 'when the gods were like man', others still for 'when the gods in place of man [taken with the following line]'. Taking a lead from the famous opening of the Hebrew Bible, June and Fiona have opted to simplify the opening of 'Atra-hasīs' to 'In the beginning'. This gives the audience the sense of primordial time, and allows the narrative to move on to the (quite lively) action.

Another feature which has been consciously changed is to give way to prose. The originals were written in syntactically complete lines, with various features that mark them as poetry in any reasonable definition of the term. In keeping with their focus on the stories as stories, June and Fiona have opted to tell them in prose.

Most of the characters in the pages which follow are gods (known by both a Sumerian and an Akkadian name, e.g. Inana/Ishtar), or humans with a special proximity to the divine. 'Ordinary people' are few. It would be easy enough for the lay reader to assume that people in antiquity were obsessed with gods and told stories about little else. But I think it is likelier that the preoccupation with gods reflects the biases of the available sources and their institutional background: 'The Poor Man of Nippur', where the gods scarcely get a look-in, is probably the tip of an iceberg otherwise unknown.

The gods perform a range of actions in the stories, and do not always come out of them terribly well. They can be cowardly, petty, ineffective and unimpressive – as well as majestic, awe-inspiring, wise and clever. Nowhere is this clearer and truer than for Inana/Ishtar. When, in one story, she marches off to the Underworld, she comes across as naïve and spoiled. But when, in another, she confronts her rapist Sukaletuda, she maintains composure and power. She is a figure onto whom the largely patriarchal world of our narratives seems to have projected all manner of fascinating contradictions.

How far any of this reflects what individuals really 'believed' about them is very hard to access. We do not, so far, have documents equivalent to the Inquisition records which enabled Carlo Ginzburg in *The Cheese and the Worms* to reconstruct the thoughts of a fifteenth-century Italian miller, whose cosmology would otherwise never have been known. Thus what people thought about the gods' roles in the stories, and in what senses they perceived the stories to be true, is, in my view, a mystery to us as deep as whether there were people in Mesopotamia who denied the gods' existence altogether.

Another striking feature of the present volume is that it sometimes spells out what the story only said by implication, making the translations read more smoothly than the originals. For example, where in the 'Poem of Creation' we hear with reference to Tiāmtu's (Tiamat's) children that *šunūti igammila*, or 'she spared them', this volume has 'she loved them nonetheless', giving the intention which underpinned the action. This is an interpretation; one of which many lay readers will be glad.

The sources (clay tablets) which ultimately underpin the volume come from dozens of sites all over Iraq, and sometimes further afield. There are three principal groups: learners' manuscripts of the Old Babylonian period, inscribed as an exercise and often bearing only extracts a few lines long; Neo-Assyrian manuscripts, chiefly from the Libraries of Ashurbanipal, at Nineveh; and later Babylonian manuscripts, some of which date all the way to the Common Era.

How far there are connections between Ancient Mesopotamian literature and that of the Middle East today is hard to say. Some scholars see continuities in the use of four groups of poetic lines, or the 'quatrain', which is common in Mesopotamia and standard in Arabic. Perhaps the strongest case for a connection concerns the 'debate poems' or 'disputation poems', well known from the Sumerian world, while Akkadian examples are more fragmentary. In these, two similar entities, such as Bird and Fish, debate their rival merits. The genre is still alive in the Middle East today.

A final point worth making is that the literature of Mesopotamia is in constant flux, with new discoveries by the year: the dialogue between the two women ('And Are You a Woman?') was edited for the first time in 2021. Who knows what the future may bring? But, as the following pages show, we already have a great deal to enjoy and ponder.

Professor Martin Worthington

INTRODUCTION

BY THE AUTHORS

We have been telling the stories of Mesopotamia for over thirty years. We worked with Zipang, the storytelling group founded by Fran Hazelton as part of The Enheduanna Society's work to popularize the literature of ancient Iraq. Fran gathered stories from the Electronic Text Corpus of Sumerian Literature and from current research. We began dipping into these vast resources to shape our own versions of the stories. Fran suggested we call our group 'Zipang', the Sumerian word for breath. She said, "We'll be breathing new life into the old stories."

We have told Mesopotamian stories in the October Gallery, the British Museum, the Poetry Cafe in Covent Garden, and Aberystwyth Arts Centre, among other venues elsewhere in the UK and in Jordan. One night in the Kufa Gallery, at the end of a performance of *Gilgamesh*, an audience member rose to his feet. He lifted his hand to pause the applause and said, "I was born in Babylon on Christmas Day eighty years ago, and I liked these stories."

A group of Iraqi teenagers living in London worked with The Enheduanna Society to tell *The Epic of Gilgamesh*. We visited the tablet room of the British Museum with them and saw a clay tablet from the burned ruins of King Ashurbanipal's palace. The fire had been so hot that a tiny corner of the tablet had turned to glass. One young storyteller held it in her hand, whispering, "This is something from my ancestors."

These ancient stories continue to touch people today.

Do not look at this book as a scholarly tome, but as a book of stories. In creating it, we have been introduced to a wealth of stories beyond the epic tales we already knew – to letters, comic anecdotes, spells, rhymes and folk tales. We have tried to give a flavour of this wide range in our choices for this collection. You will find different styles in the retellings. We have made intuitive decisions about how we tell the stories. Sometimes we have used our spoken word versions, at others we have stuck more closely to the original translations, our sources.

To distinguish the two, you would have to go to those original translations. And that would be our delight! If you want to go deeper, there is plenty of information out there. The number of untranslated cuneiform tablets in the British Museum alone is huge, and the number of people worldwide who can read cuneiform is, as yet, very small. There is still so much to discover. To really know Mesopotamian stories, you may have to learn cuneiform. But in the meantime, enjoy these glorious stories.

Acknowledgements

Versions of 'The Descent of the Goddess Inana to the Underworld', 'Enkidu in the Underworld' and 'Siduri' were first written for our book *Folk Tales of the Ever After*, The History Press, 2023, and appear here by kind permission of The History Press.

We owe thanks to the many storytellers, scholars and 'tablet-loving scribes' whose work has increased our understanding of these stories.

Among contemporary scholars, we are especially grateful to Jana Matuszak, Selena Wisnom and Martin Worthington, with extra thanks to Martin Worthington for writing the introduction to this book.

We would like to thank Catherine Taylor and Claire Gault, our editors at Flame Tree Publishing.

Most of all, we are very grateful to our friend Fran Hazelton for introducing us to the world of Mesopotamian stories. We dedicate this book to her.

Fiona Collins is a storyteller and author. She lives in Wales and has published books of Welsh folktales in English and Welsh. She has a long-standing interest in the stories of Ancient Sumer, and was a founder member of Zipang, the storytelling company specializing in Mesopotamian stories, told in English for modern audiences. Zipang worked closely with Professor Jeremy Black's Electronic Text Corpus of Sumerian Literature.

June Peters is a storyteller and author. She was chair of the Society for Storytelling in the UK. She is a member of the Enheduanna Society and Zipang, promoting the history, culture and literature of ancient Iraq. Her performances of Mesopotamian stories can be heard in the Zipang Recording Project online. She has published three books of folk tales.

Martin Worthington is Professor in Middle Eastern Studies at Trinity College Dublin. He directed the world's first Babylonian-language film and is currently, with Mark Chetwood, writing *The Cambridge Introduction to Sumerian*. His book *Ea's Duplicity in the Gilgamesh Flood Story* and his paper 'Sargon's Riddle' attracted international media coverage.

FURTHER READING

Books and Articles

Al-Rashid, Moudhy, *Between Two Rivers: Ancient Mesopotamia and the Birth of History* (London: Hodder Press, 2025)

Black, Jeremy et al, *The Literature of Ancient Sumer* (Oxford: OUP, 2006 ed.)

Dickson, Keith, 'Enki and Ninhursag: The Trickster in Paradise', *Journal of Near Eastern Studies*, January 2007, 66(1):1-32: https://www.researchgate.net/publication/249102817_Enki_and_Ninhursag_The_Trickster_in_Paradise

George, Andrew, *The Epic of Gilgamesh* (London: Penguin, 2020 ed)

Hazelton, Fran, *Stories from Ancient Iraq* (London: The Enheduanna Society, 2006)

Hazelton, Fran, *Three Kings from Warka* (London: The Enheduanna Society, 2012)

Jacobsen, Thorkild, *The Harps that Once... Sumerian Poetry in Translation* (New Haven: Yale University Press, 1987)

Kramer, Samuel Noah, *History Begins at Sumer* (Philadelphia: Doubleday, 1959)

Kriwaczek, Paul, *Babylon: Mesopotamia and the Birth of Civilization* (London: Atlantic Books, 2012 ed.)

Matuszak, Jana, '"She was dumbstruck and took it to heart." Form and Function of Insults in Sumerian Literary Disputations between Women', *Disputation Literature in the Near East and*

Beyond, SOAS Research Repository, 2018: http://eprints.soas.ac.uk/26567

Wisnom, Selena, *The Library of Ancient Wisdom* (London: Penguin, 2025)

Wolkstein, Diane & Kramer, Samuel Noah, *Inanna: Queen of Heaven and Earth* (New York: Harper & Row, 1983)

Worthington, Martin, 'Orality, Voicing and Interruption in Babylonian and Assyrian Literature', CUP, 24 February 2025: https://www.cambridge.org/core/journals/iraq/article/abs/orality-voicing-and-interruption-in-babylonian-and-assyrian-literature/5ADEC7A5100366A29C420FE7381A46DD

Worthington, Martin, *Ea's Duplicity in the Gilgamesh Flood Story* (London: Routledge, Taylor & Francis, 2020)

Websites

Electronic Babylonian Library: www.ebl.lmu.de

The Electronic Text Corpus of Sumerian Literature: etcsl.orinst.ox.ac.uk

The Enheduanna Society: enheduannasociety.org

Gateways to Babylon: https: gatewaystobabylon.com

Films

Are You a Woman?: A Storytelling Performance in English & Arabic. Translation: Dr Jana Matuszak; Script Editing and Performance: Zipang Storytellers June Peters, Badia Obaid, Fran Hazelton; Arabic Translations: Adam Assi; Production & Direction: Richard Wilding.

English version:

Introduction: https://vimeo.com/947799181/12e2889e9e

Performance: https://vimeo.com/947788671/d3987f8474
Arabic version:
Introduction: https://vimeo.com/1044295241
Performance: https://vimeo.com/1028555900
An online edition and English translation of the Sumerian text by Jana Matuszak can be accessed here: https://oracc.museum.upenn.edu/dsst/Q000771

Gilgamesh21: The Gilgamesh Epic Project for Young People: A project for young people, May 2015–October 2016. Organized by the Enheduanna Society and sponsored by the Heritage Lottery Fund and the British Institute for the Study of Iraq. A nine-minute film describing the project can be seen here: gilgamesh21.com/documentary

The Poor Man of Nippur: A Theatrical Performance in Sumerian with English Subtitles. Production & Direction: Kathryn Stevens & Martin Worthington; Direction: Martin Worthington.
https://www.youtube.com/watch?v=pxYoFlnJLoE

A SPELL: I'VE PUT MY SHOES ON MY FEET

This spell is to be said three times over a person's shoes when they put them on, so that, wherever they go, people will be glad to see them.

I've put my shoes on my feet.
I've taken my place before you.
My laughter is the flowering of my features,
The winsome charm of my eyes.
I'm a treat. Whatever I say to you will be amusing.

'IN THE FIRST DAYS, IN THE VERY FIRST DAYS...'

We begin with creation myths from different eras and locations in the Sumerian, Babylonian and Akkadian cultures. Each city was affiliated to a different god or goddess from the pantheon, and each city adapted the stories to honour their particular patron. The two Ninurta stories retold here come from tablets found in the city of Nippur, where Ninurta was worshipped. Current archaeology has uncovered tablets telling versions of these stories from the more ancient city of Girsu, where the god Ninurta is named Ningirsu. These much older and more complete tablets are still to be translated.

THE BABYLONIAN MYTH OF CREATION

When, on high, nothing existed, and below, there was not yet anything, then it was that the deep salt waters and the even deeper sweet waters met and mingled together.

Tiamat, the salt sea, and Apsu, the fresh streams, let their waters mix.

This was before meadows or reedbeds had formed, before any gods had come into being, before any destinies had been decreed.

Tiamat and Apsu, coming together, created the first gods. They brought the first gods into being. And those gods, offspring of the primordial waters, they soon also had children. The firstborn of Tiamat and Apsu was Anshar. Anshar himself was the father of many, but the greatest of them was Ea, god of wisdom. Soon there were many gods.

But – oh! Those new gods were noisy. So noisy!

Their racket got on Tiamat's nerves. Their noise gave her an upset stomach. Their playing around annoyed her. They would not obey Apsu, their father. They would not listen to Tiamat, their mother. She was not pleased with their behaviour. But she loved them nonetheless.

Apsu was displeased too. He turned to his sukkal, his trusted advisor, to ask what should be done. And Mummu, his counsellor, said this to Apsu, "My lord, you need rest in the daytime and sleep at night. These noisy children are displeasing to you. Why not break up their way of life? Why not destroy them?"

Apsu was pleased by this advice. He beamed. He sat down with Tiamat and said to her, "Our children's behaviour has become displeasing to me. I cannot rest in the daytime or sleep at night. I will break up and destroy them, so that peace can prevail and we can sleep."

When Tiamat heard this, she cried out in distress. She raged at her husband. She said, "How can you think to destroy those I have given birth to? Although it is true that their behaviour is causing us distress, there is no need for cruelty towards them. Let us be gracious, let us tighten discipline in a firm but kind way."

But Apsu was more ready to listen to his counsellor, Mummu, than to his wife, Tiamat, mother of his children. His face lit up at the evil he plotted and planned. When the gods – Apsu's own offspring, Tiamat's children – found out what their father planned, at first they were frantic. Then they were overcome with fear and sat in silence.

But there was one god among them who had the power of incantation. Ea, god of wisdom, set a spell of slumber upon the sweet waters, and drenched his grandfather Apsu with sleep. Then he killed his grandfather Apsu, tore off his crown, carried away his aura and took them both for himself. Ea took Apsu's home for himself too. He called it the Apsu, the Place of Deep Sweet Water. He made a splendid home for himself there with his beloved, Damkina. There, in the Apsu, in the inmost chamber, the Chamber of Destinies, Damkina conceived their son.

Marduk was conceived in the Apsu.

Marduk, wisest of the wise, was born in the Apsu.

His father, Ea, god of wisdom, begat him. His mother, Damkina, goddess of the joyful heart, birthed him.

From the very beginning, Marduk was mighty.

He was perfect. He was wonderful. He was lofty, and superior in nature to all the lesser gods. His vision was fourfold, his hearing was fourfold. His fourfold perception was formidable.

Flames burst from his lips when he spoke. He was robed in the auras of ten gods. Above him glittered five fearsome rays. His father, Ea, gave him the four winds, saying, "My son, let them rage!"

Marduk took the hurricane, the tempest, the whirlwind and the storm wind.

He sent these winds howling and roaring, to bring trouble to Tiamat. He sent a flood wave to stir her waters. She was confused and made frantic by the clamour of the winds and the swirling of the waters.

By day and by night, Tiamat heaved. She had no rest. Then her noisy children sent messages to her. They laid blame on her. They said, "When our ancestor, your husband, was killed, you did not help him. When Ea took Apsu's house to be the birthplace of Marduk, you did not stop him. Now the four dreadful winds and the raging flood have been sent against you. You gave no thought to Apsu, and now you sit alone. And as for us, we cannot rest! You should see us: our hands are weak, our eyes are hollow, we cannot sleep. You do not love us. If you loved us, you would care for us. Avenge our father! Reduce these enemies to nothing! Do this, so that we can sleep!"

Tiamat heard her children's words. She listened to them. She said, "Very well, I shall do as you advise. I shall make demons." Those gods were reconciled to her then, and came to Tiamat's side, against Ea. They were lusting for battle, raging, storming, plotting by day and by night. They convened to create conflict.

Tiamat, who formed everything, now gave birth to giant serpents. She filled their bodies with poison instead of blood. She clothed them in auras of dread, and made them as powerful as the gods. She said, "May those who look upon my creatures perish. May they fall back in dismay before my creatures." In total, she made eleven deadly creatures, among them a scorpion-man, a horned serpent, a rabid dog and an aggressive demon. Then, from among the throng of gods who followed her, she chose Qingu to be her supreme commander, the leader of her army, her chief power of battle.

Tiamat said to Qingu, "I have made this incantation for you:

I have exalted you among the gods.
I have made you king among the gods.

You are applauded and renowned.
Let all the lesser gods obey you.
You shall decree their destinies and decide their fates."

She made him a Tablet of Destinies to clasp to his breast.

Tiamat gathered the eleven monsters she had created, and proclaimed war against Ea. When Ea heard what Tiamat was doing, he sat silently in the inner chamber of the Apsu and reflected, until his anger was under control. When his anger was under control, he went to find Anshar, his father. He entered the presence of his begetter, and related to him all of Tiamat's deeds: "My father, Tiamat hates us, because of the loss of her husband Apsu. She has raised an army, and her children have all taken her side. She is eager for conflict – plotting, lusting for battle, raging and storming. She has created eleven monsters with poison for blood. She has endowed them with auras and made them godlike. And she has made Qingu leader over all the other gods. She has given him the Tablet of Destinies and the power of leadership."

When Ea's father had heard all this, he was greatly disturbed. His heart was in a fury. His mind could not be calmed. He turned on Ea. "My son, you provoked this war. You set out and killed Apsu, you took his home. Take responsibility for all you have done! And as for Tiamat, whom you have infuriated, who can equal her? What is to be done?"

Ea is the god of wisdom.

He gently answered raging Anshar, with soothing tone and calming words, saying, "Dear father, you who decree destiny, I want to say something. What you decree I will try to bring about. I will try to make it come to pass."

"Very well," said his father. "Your words are fitting and godlike. Go to Tiamat and stand your ground. Soften her fury with your incantation."

Ea set out, but when he got a glimpse of what Tiamat had in store, he stopped, went very quiet and turned back. He returned to Anshar and said, "My father, I am sorry, Tiamat is too much for me. My incantation is not equal to hers. Her strength is mighty, she filled me with dread. She shouted out and her voice was too loud for me. I was afraid of her noise and I turned back. But please, do not lose hope. Send someone else. Although her strength is very great, it is not the greatest. Send someone stronger to stop her, before she lays her hands on us."

Ea's father was in a fury. He spoke to his son Anu, brother to Ea. He said, "My son, you are an honoured hero. Your strength is mighty, your attack is irresistible. Go to Tiamat, appease her rage. Relax her heart. Do all you can to soothe her."

Anu set out, but when he got a glimpse of what Tiamat had in store, he stopped, went very quiet and turned back. He returned to Anshar and said, "My father, I am sorry, Tiamat is too much for me. My incantation is not equal to hers. Her strength is mighty, she filled me with dread. She shouted out and her voice was too loud for me. I was afraid of her noise and I turned back. But please, do not lose hope. Send someone else. Although her strength is very great, it is not the greatest. Send someone stronger to stop her, before she lays her hands on us."

The father of the gods lapsed into silence. He stared at the ground. He shook his head glumly. The gods gathered round him. They stared anxiously at him, in tight-lipped silence. Not one of them would dare to face Tiamat. They knew that. So did he. He did not know what to do.

But Ea, god of wisdom, was thinking. His thoughts were about the younger generation. He was thinking of his son. He went to his private chamber, in the heart of the Apsu, and sent for Marduk. He said, "Marduk, my son, the sight of you fills my heart with pleasure. Go to Anshar and stand your ground. Soften his fury with your incantation, for the sake of all the gods. Drive your storm chariot without delay. Turn Tiamat away with an incantation that cannot be repelled. Set your foot upon her neck!"

Marduk was delighted by his father's faith in him. With a glad heart, he went to Anshar and said,

"Lord of the gods, I will become your avenger. I will bind Tiamat and save you. You shall soon set your foot upon her neck. And when you do, proclaim me as the greatest among you. Grant me the power to decree the destinies of you all."

Anshar turned to his sukkal, his wise adviser, and gave him orders: "My sukkal, invite all the gods to come here. Let them feast on our grain and our beer. Let them confer as they feast. Let them decree a great destiny for Marduk. Go, be gone! Stand before the gods and repeat to them all that I have told you. Say, 'My lord has sent me to you, and I am to explain his plans'. Say, 'Marduk, wisest of the gods, Ea's own son has come forward, where two generations of his family fear to go. He has determined to meet Tiamat. Quickly now, decree his destiny without delay, so that he can go and face this powerful enemy.'"

When they received Anshar's message, the gods moaned in distress, saying, "What has gone wrong, to make Tiamat turn against us in this way? We did not know this was going on."

The gods gathered and came to the Apsu. They kissed one another as they assembled. They ate grain, they drank ale. As they drank the beer and began to feel good, they became quite carefree. Their mood grew merry, and they decreed a wonderful destiny for Marduk.

This is how the ceremony went:

A throne was set up on a dais for Marduk, and he was seated on it to receive kingship. Great speeches were made and Marduk was given sovereignty over the whole universe.

The gods said, "Take your seat in the assembly; let your words be exalted."

To prove Marduk's powers, they set a constellation of stars in the middle of the chamber. They said to him, "Make this constellation disappear at your word. With another word, make it reappear."

With no effort he completed this, and the gods rejoiced. Then they invested him with a mace, a throne and a rod of power. They gave him irresistible weapons. They exhorted him, "Go, cut Tiamat's throat. Let the winds carry her blood away."

Marduk made himself a bow. He strung it and notched an arrow in place. He took up his club and slung his bow and quiver over his shoulder. Lightning went before him. His body was filled with flames. He made a net to enmesh Tiamat's entrails, and set the winds of the four directions around her to prevent her escape.

Then he sent out the Seven Deadly Winds to harass Tiamat's entrails: the Evil Wind, the Dust Storm, the Tempest, the Four-fold Wind, the Seven-fold Wind, the Chaos Wind and the Whirlwind. He raised a floodwave, his great weapon.

Marduk rode at Tiamat in the fearful chariot of the irresistible storm. His chariot horses were named Slayer, Pitiless, Racer and Flyer. Their lips were drawn back, their teeth dripped with poison. They were strangers to exhaustion.

At his right hand were Battle and Strife.

At his left, Overwhelming Conflict.

He wore a fearful coat of mail. About his head was an aura of terror. Between his lips there was a spell; in his hand was a protective herb.

But when Marduk saw Tiamat, when he heard her cast her spell, he lost his nerve. His determination faltered. She was a powerful foe.

Then he remembered that he had the support of the gods, and with an effort he lifted up his great weapon, the floodwave, and cast it at the raging Tiamat. He challenged her.

"Why are you aggressive and arrogant? Why do you want to provoke battle? You have stirred up trouble. Well, now I am here. Deploy your troops. Take up your weapons. Let us do battle!"

When Tiamat heard this, she shouted out fiercely. But her legs trembled beneath her. She kept reciting her incantation. Marduk joined battle. He spread out his net and encircled her. He hurled the Evil Wind in her face. Tiamat opened her mouth and swallowed the wind. But once inside her, it distended her belly and forced her jaws open. Marduk fired his arrow and it pierced her belly. He tore her open and slit her heart. He bound her and extinguished her life. He threw her down and placed his foot upon her corpse.

Her army dispersed, beating a fearful retreat. But they could not escape. Marduk bound the eleven creatures and broke the weapons of her throng of evil spirits. He captured Qingu, the commander, and tore the Tablet of Destinies from him, placing it on his own breast. Then he decreed a destiny for Qingu: "Soon you will join the dead gods."

When all his enemies were bound or slain, Marduk returned to the body of Tiamat.

He trampled her body, and with his merciless club he smashed her skull. He severed her arteries and the winds carried her blood away. Then he split her corpse in two, like a fish to be dried. He stretched half of her corpse, high above as the heavens. He went around the heavens and adjusted them to mirror the shape and size of the Apsu.

He put gates in Tiamat's ribs at left and right, fixing strong bolts on both sides. He put Tiamat's liver at the zenith.

Then he created heavenly shrines for the great gods, Anshar, Ea and Ellil, and set up patterns of the stars, shaping them into constellations. He put the year in order, allocating three stars to each month, fixing the intervals between the stars.

He created the moon, appointing it the jewel of the night. Month by month he elevated the moon to a crown, saying, "Shine over the land at the beginning of each month, resplendent with horns for six nights. By the seventh night, your crown will be half-size. From the fifteenth night, halfway through each month, when the sun sees you on the horizon, begin to diminish in your proper stages. Let your shine go, until by the thirtieth night, you stand once again in conjunction with the sun."

Marduk made the interchange of day and night. He made the year.

Then Marduk gathered Tiamat's spittle and made it into clouds. He took her head and poured out the water of her two eyes, making the Tigris and the Euphrates begin to flow. He heaped up radiant mountains on her breasts. With her thighs, he wedged the heaven in place. With half her skin, he roofed the earth. He made her entrails surge and extended his net over them, to fix the earth.

When he had finished this work with Tiamat's body, he turned to the gods. They were jubilant and happy. They embraced him and gave him gifts. They washed the dust of combat from his body, sprinkled him with cypress and dressed him in a princely garment, a regal aura and a noble crown. The gods gathered and kissed his feet. They shouted out, "Behold the king!"

Marduk spoke to the gods.

"I will build a house to be my luxurious abode. I will set it above the waters of the Apsu and in front of a great temple. Whenever the gods come up from the Apsu for an assembly, I shall receive them all there to pass the night. Whenever the gods come down from the sky for an assembly, I shall receive them all there to pass the night. I will name my house Babylon, Home of the Great Gods. I shall make it the centre of our world."

Then the gods bowed down before Marduk and raised him to be the highest of the high. They took a holy oath, making him king over them all. All this was greatly pleasing to Marduk. He made up his mind to perform a miracle.

He spoke to his father, Ea, saying, "I wish to change the ways of the gods and unite them. I want the gods to be at leisure. I will make a primeval creature to do all the work of the gods. Human will be its name. I will make blood and put bones together to create this creature."

Ea advised his glorious son. "The best way to do this is to mix the blood of a god with river clay. This will result in a suitable creature. Order the gods to surrender the one who was chosen by Tiamat to lead her army. Let that culprit be given up for punishment. His blood can be used to create the human."

Marduk assembled the gods and pleasantly gave them his instructions. "You have chosen me to declare the laws. Listen now to my decree. Let the one who accompanied Tiamat to war and led her army be given up, that he may bear the penalty for his crime, and you may live in peace."

The gods answered, "It was Qingu who accompanied Tiamat to war and led her army."

They bound Qingu and brought him to Ea and Marduk. The penalty was imposed and Qingu was killed. The destiny that Marduk had decreed for him was fulfilled. Qingu joined the dead gods. The great god took Qingu's blood and mixed it with river clay. He created humans to do the gods' work, so the gods could be at leisure. Once Marduk had performed this miracle, he divided the gods, some to guard the sky and some to guard the earth.

Then the lesser gods praised Marduk and said, "Lord, now that you have set us free from drudgery, what can we do for you? We would like to build you the luxurious house of which you spoke. We would like it to be a place where you can receive us when we travel up or down to our assemblies. May we make a magnificent shrine for you?"

Marduk was delighted by this. His face shone as bright as day.

"Oh, yes," he declared. "Create Babylon for me. Mould many mud bricks, build high my shrine!"

The gods began shovelling, and for a whole year they made baked bricks. By the second year they had built a high ziggurat, with dwelling places and shrines for all the greater and the lesser gods.

They made Marduk's magnificent shrine. And he invited them all to a banquet in his sanctuary.

"May Babylon be your home too!" he declared, while they made merry.

The gods fixed seven destinies for the cult of Marduk. Then they looked at the weapons he had used. Anshar lifted Marduk's war bow and kissed it, saying, "May it go far!"

He named the bow 'Bowstar' and set it to shine in the sky that Marduk had created from Tiamat's body.

Then all the gods paid homage to Marduk and confirmed his mastery over all things.

They gave him names and titles to honour his qualities.

"Let Marduk be the shepherd of the black-headed people, let them worship him.

"Let him be director of justice, uprooter of enemies, lord of the countryside, controller of canals and bringer of abundance."

The gods praised and glorified Marduk.

And may the people of Marduk, his creation, weave and reweave this tale, remembering him. May they call upon his name.

THE POEM OF ATRAHASIS

In the beginning, the great gods, the Anuna gods, were carving up creation and deciding how to share their authority over it. They did this by throwing lots. Enki got his lot in the Abzu, the region of fresh water beneath the land. He became the god of subtle wisdom and fresh water. An was allocated the region of the heavens and he became father god, with authority over all. Enlil took up residence in the Ekur and became the god of earth. These great gods were the managers and the planners.

The actual physical work of shaping the land fell to the Igigi gods, the lesser gods. It was these lesser gods who had to do the hard digging. They were the ones who created canals, watercourses and channels and created the lifelines of the land. They dug out the bed of the Tigris. They dug out the bed of the Euphrates. They found the work very hard indeed. Though they were lesser gods, still they were gods, and they were not well equipped to deal, hands on, with the material world. But, at the command of the Anuna gods, they did this forced labour day in day out, seven days a week, for three thousand six hundred years. Then, one day, the misery became too much and all at once it was as if they snapped. They rebelled. They burned their spades and hoes in a great big bonfire and, carrying their flaming tools like torches, that night they surrounded the Ekur, the house of Enlil, the earth god. His servant, Kalkal, the gatekeeper, woke Nusku, the chamberlain. He, in turn, roused his master and got him out of bed. Nusku said, "Master, your house is surrounded. A rabble is running around your door." Enlil had the door barred and the weapons brought out.

Nusku said, "Master, your face is as pale as a tamarisk flower. Are you afraid of the lesser gods? Send for Enki. Send for An. Summon an assembly of the greater gods."

Enlil, furious, called an emergency meeting of the great gods, the Anuna gods. An, father god, came down from the heavens and Enki, god of wisdom and fresh water, came up from the Abzu. Enlil said, "The lesser gods have surrounded my house. They have risen up against me. What is to be done?"

An said, "Send to find out who is their leader."

Nusku, the chamberlain, went to find out. When he came back, he said, "They say they have no leader. No one is in charge. Every single one of them is in agreement. They say the work which has been given to them is too hard. The load is excessive. It is killing them, and they have come to complain."

When Enlil heard that, he became furious. He said, "I will show them my power. Someone must die!" But An said, "Wait a moment. Consider. They have been working day in day out for three thousand six hundred years." Enki, god of subtle wisdom, said, "It's true. They have worked hard, and, to be frank, they're not suited to the work of clay and earth. They're made of spirit and breath. Let's think about this. Rather than destroying something, shouldn't we, who have the power, create something which is better designed to do the job?"

The council agreed and they called on Mami, the goddess of birth and the womb. "Create something, please!" they implored. She agreed, but she said, "I will need the help of Enki. He will have to prepare absolutely the best clay from the Abzu."

The preparation began. Enki brought the best clay from the Abzu. But there was need for more than clay. The blood of a god was essential to the process. A god had to be slaughtered. They say that the one chosen was the god of inspiration and intelligence. His name meant 'ear' and 'wisdom'. Mami took the clay and mixed it with the god's blood. She spoke at the assembly of all the gods. She gave them a warning. She said, "Before I continue, you must know that in this action, I am undoing the fetters of the lesser gods and I am granting them freedom. But I am also granting freedom to another new spirit. Each one of you must add the spit of your mouths to this clay, and in the gift of your spit, you will be giving a voice to these new beings."

All the gods, lesser and greater, were undeterred and said, "Impeccable! You're doing a great job. We used to call you Mami. Henceforth you'll be called Belet-ili, Mother of All!" They all gave the gift of their spit and Mami mixed it into the clay. Then she called for fourteen womb goddesses. There were seven womb goddesses to the left and seven to the right. Mami broke the clay into fourteen pieces and distributed them. The whole process took nine months.

When the tenth month came, Mami covered her head, put on her belt, made a blessing, made a drawing in the flour and put down a mud brick. She was the midwife. She opened the wombs of the goddesses with her staff. And humankind was created. There were seven girls and seven boys, who grew fast. They liked each other, were delighted by the world, were happy and set to work. They flourished, married and produced their own children. Soon there were dozens, then hundreds and thousands of them, and they called themselves the black-headed people. Each of their bodies was made of the clay of the Abzu. Each of their hearts sounded with the intelligent inspirational drumbeat of a god. They had an intuitive understanding and a feel for the work of earth, and they did it gladly. They never felt better than when they were working in the natural world and their work was really good. Their demeanour was cheerful and thankful, and they gave gifts and feasts to the gods in gratitude for the good things they enjoyed in the world. The gods found these feasts surprisingly tasty and nourishing, and soon got used to receiving them.

But as well as the inspiration and intelligence of a god, humankind was also gifted with the spit of the gods. The black-headed people had strong views, strong feelings and strong opinions, and they expressed all of these with their good, strong, god-given voices. They talked, they argued, they spoke poetry, they told stories, they fought, they laughed and they sang. They could be quite loud. The earth became a noisy place. As the population increased, it became noisier.

Enlil, the angry earth god, did not like it. He called an assembly of the gods. He said, "I've had enough of them. You all have your own given domains, An in the sky, Enki in the Abzu. But I'm stuck here with them on earth. They are driving me mad. They are too noisy. I am losing sleep. I say, wipe them out." All the other gods protested. All the evidence proved that, on balance, humankind was a really good thing. But Enlil was adamant.

"No. I'm in charge of earth. It's decided. I'm going to send Namtar, the plague god, to wipe them out." So the plague began. The black-headed people began to suffer and to die. Nothing like this had ever been known before and none of them knew what to do.

At that time, there was one human who was extra wise. His name was Atrahasis. His ear had always been open to his god, Enki. Regularly he would speak with Enki and Enki would always reply. They would chat. When the plague came, Atrahasis prayed to Enki. He said, "What's happening? We've never known anything like it. How can my people be freed from this terrible plague?"

Enki, subtle god of wisdom, answered. "I'm extremely sorry about this. It's not my will and it's beyond my influence. But this is my advice. Pray to the plague god, Namtar, and offer him nourishment. Tell all your people to go to the House of the Plague God and offer up prayers, gifts, sacrifices. The plague god will not be able to resist. He will be pleased at the gifts and ashamed of what he has been doing. Then the plague will abate."

Atrahasis did exactly as Enki had advised. He prayed. He instructed all the black-headed people, and they all prayed. All of humankind offered prayers and sacrifices and nourishment to

Namtar. Namtar was delighted by the prayers and sacrifices. The plague abated and humankind was saved.

And for a long time, humanity was really quiet. But hardly six hundred years had passed before people perked up. World production, yield and output and the nourishing sacrifices to the gods increased, but so did the arguing, singing and storytelling. Once again, the noise of humankind tormented Enlil, the angry earth god. He called an assembly. He said, "This is intolerable. The plague wasn't effective. I've thought of another solution. This time I'm going to cut off the food supply. Adad the storm god must withhold the rain. And in case anyone was thinking of passing on this information" – and he gave a sideways glance at Enki – "the rule is, no one is to tell this plan to any of humankind."

No reasoned argument from the other gods could change his mind. When the drought began, Atrahasis spoke and prayed repeatedly to his god Enki, but there was no answer. After a year, the people had exhausted all their stores. After three years, their features were distorted. They were shrivelled and hunched. Atrahasis still had no word from Enki. In desperation, he went to the nearly empty river and asked for a dream. As he slept, Atrahasis dreamed. In his dream, Enki was saying, "Take your people to the temple of the rain god, Adad. Give gifts, offerings and sacrifices. Pray."

Atrahasis followed his dream. He did as Enki said. All the people did as Enki said. Adad received the prayers, gifts and nourishment. He was pleased and ashamed of what he had done. The drought broke, the rains fell and crops grew.

All the people tried hard after that to be quiet, for a really long time. They tiptoed about. But how could they be quiet? They had the blood of the gods and the spit of the gods within them. They had strong hearts and strong spirits, and they were always thinking about the work and planning the world they wanted for their children. They really needed to talk about it. They were wordy!

Hardly six hundred years had gone by and yet again it became too noisy for the earth god. Enlil called an assembly of the gods. He said, "I will destroy humankind through a flood. There are to be no arguments. I know there has been a leak from this assembly in the past. No information will pass from our assembly. I demand a promise that no word of this decision will pass from our assembly. There will be no message, either by word or dream, to humankind. There will be no leak from this assembly."

By now Enlil had become a terrible bully and there was no arguing with him.

Late that night, Atrahasis was meditating in his reed house, when he heard a strange whispering at his reed wall. A voice seemed to be saying, "Oh reed wall! I have a tale to tell to you, reed wall. Enlil the angry earth god will destroy the black-headed people. He has commanded a flood, and no human is to be told of this. I'm telling no one, oh wall. I'm merely telling it to you, oh wall, not to a human at all. Oh, if only Atrahasis knew, he would build a big boat – a great big spherical coracle of a boat – and bring into it all the seeds and plants and insects and birds and beasts that are necessary to the maintenance of this marvellous earth and to humankind, whom the gods love, whom we have all worked so hard to create, and whom we hope will survive this inevitable flood."

Atrahasis heard the words spoken, by Enki, to the reed wall. Then he spoke quietly. He said, "What should I do? What should I say to my people?"

Enki said, "Let them know that your god, Enki, has argued with Enlil, the angry earth god, so you must leave for the Abzu. Don't say anything else, oh reed wall."

Atrahasis' conversation with the reed wall went on far into the night. At the end he understood about the boat: that the roof must be strong fore and aft; that the boat must be caulked with firm pitch; and that it must accommodate his wife, his kith, his kin and skilled craftsmen, as well as all the necessary wildlife, seeds and plants. The instructions even included a design which manifested itself in the dust on the ground.

Next day, Atrahasis told the elders of the city, "My god is out of favour with your god. Enki and Enlil have become angry with each other. I have to leave my house. I must leave for the Abzu. Please help me. I must go down to the Abzu to be with my god."

All his friends and neighbours were happy to help. The carpenter brought his axe. The reed worker brought his stone. A child brought bitumen. The poor fetched what was needed. The heart of Atrahasis was heavy as he asked all his neighbours to help him create the boat. Everyone who came was paid well. Atrahasis paid over the odds for all the necessary materials, and over the odds for the wages of the craftsmen. More and more people flooded to help in the work of the great ark. Every night there were marvellous parties. They ate the best of food, and they drank the best of beer. But each night, as the people were eating and drinking, Atrahasis, who was the host, was unable to stay still or to rest with his friends. His heart was breaking and while his friends were feasting, he was outside vomiting bile.

Then the face of the weather changed. As the storm started, Atrahasis ordered the packing of the ark. He filled the boat with the animals and seeds of all things.

Adad was bellowing from the clouds. Atrahasis called his family. The winds were raging even as he went up and cut through the rope to release the boat. While they were closing up the door, Adad kept bellowing. Bitumen was brought and they sealed the door.

Anzu was tearing at the sky with his talons. No one could see anyone else. No one could be recognized in the catastrophe. The flood roared like a bull. The darkness was total. There was no sun.

Then when the wild storm was raised, and the servants of the storm god were striding across the skies, then Mami and Enki saw the devastation, then they cried out and wished they had not submitted to the bully, to Enlil, in the assembly. Wise Mami was crying out, "Let daylight return. How could I have allowed this destruction? What happened at the gods' assembly? How did we give Enlil such strength to make such a wicked order? Why did An not make a better decision?" Mami wept. All the gods wept. Some god was heard to say, "I'm dying for a glass of beer, but with the black-headed people gone, who is going to serve it?"

After seven nights, the storm stilled. Atrahasis opened up the shutters and saw the grey sky and the grey water. On the grey water, he saw all the remains of his neighbours and companions. They were just grey clay. There was silence. All the god-given drumbeat of intelligent hearts and all the voices were gone. Only the grey clay remained, floating, then sinking. On the seventh day, Atrahasis released a dove. It found no branch to perch on and returned.

He released a swallow. It found no branch to perch on and returned.

He released a raven. It did not return. It had found a branch to perch on and was nibbling a berry, lifting its tail and preening itself.

Then Atrahasis knew they were not far from land. When at last they reached land, Atrahasis and his family lit a fire and sent up blessings and gratitude for their own survival. He burned a sacrifice and held a thanksgiving feast. Then the sky lit up with the joy of the gods. They were like a great circle of flies in the sky, delighted at the sacrifice. They all descended like guests to a party. All the gods came.

Mami greeted Atrahasis and his family, "I'm so glad to see you all. Here is my lapis lazuli necklace. I'm placing it in the sky for you to remember that when it rains, there's going to be no more flood."

But then Enlil, the angry earth god, turned up at the party too. He was furious. He said, "How did these people survive? It's treachery." He turned to Enki. He said, "I know it was you. You betrayed the secrets of the gods." Enki shrugged. He said, "I might have whispered something to a wall. But you are the one in the wrong."

And at this, all the rest of the gods faced the bully at last. They faced Enlil, the angry earth god. They told him in no uncertain terms: "What you did was wrong. This must not happen again. This must never happen again. If you're angry, you may send a lion, send a wolf, send illness, send impotence. But do not send a wholesale massacre and wipe out our beloved humankind."

Enlil saw he was vanquished. He gave a wry look. He said, "What has Mami to say about this?"

Mami said, "I say some humans will be parents and some will not. I say that not all babies will live, and not all children will be viable and some will die."

Enlil bowed to the decision of the gods and of Mami, and he turned to Atrahasis. He granted to Atrahasis, and to his family, eternal life.

NINURTA AND THE ASAG

I sing of the superb son of the king of the populated lands,
Beloved of Mami, the powerful god, Enlil's son.
I praise superb Ninurta, beloved of Mami,
The powerful god, Enlil's son,
Who waters cattle pens and gardens in country and town.
Flood-wave of battles, who darkens the sash warrior.
The fiercest gallu-demons, though tireless, fear his attack.
Listen to the praise of the strength of the powerful one,
He who subdued and bound the Mountains of Stones in his fury.
He who conquered soaring Anzu with his weapon.
He who slew the bull-man inside the Sea.
Strong warrior who slays with his weapon,
Powerful one who is quick to form a battle array.

This is a story of the mountains, but it comes from a time before mountains existed. It is a story of stone, from a time before there was stone.

In the very beginning, the mountain lands were not as we know them today. There were no mountain forests, no verdant perfumed mountain meadows, nor the gleam of tin, copper or gold. There were no tinkling streams or rivers flowing down in channels to irrigate the valley, make the barley grow or feed the Tigris and Euphrates. There were no waters. It was as if the waters were encased, frozen or imprisoned.

How was it that these waters and these wonders of the mountains were released from their prison? That was the work of Ninurta.

He is the god of the thunder, flood and plough. Ninurta is the shadow which covers the land like the southern storm. He is the deluge which engulfs the banks. Ninurta rides on a chariot that is made of the eight winds. The Hurricane pulls his chariot. He ties the Sirocco, the Evil Wind, to a pole. He has the lance of lightning in his left hand, but in his right hand he holds his weapon, the mace, his Sharur. The Sharur is his faithful servant, his minister. This is the advisor who loves him. The Sharur is lion-headed and sharp-toothed. It flies out on little wings all around the horizon. It has the capacity to spin out across the unformed world to bring him back news; intelligence of all he needs to know to make good decisions.

One day Ninurta was sitting on his royal throne, the carved boxwood throne of the land. He was sitting at the feast given in his honour beside his father, the great god, Enlil. Ninurta was drinking and eating his fill: eating and drinking and rivalling his father. All around them were the lesser gods. Ninurta was listening to their disputes and giving good decisions and wise judgements, when suddenly a cry went out and all eyes turned to the far horizon. There they all saw a being hurtling towards them. The company parted, and into Ninurta's presence there flew the Sharur, its little wings flapping like the southern storm. It approached Ninurta. It hovered before him. It was bringing important news. "Oh great master Ninurta! Warrior! Great god! Great king and lord of lofty station. The heavens have copulated with the verdant earth and she has borne to him a child." Now this was news indeed, and the Sharur had everybody's undivided attention. The Sharur carried on, "This child, this son, is a warrior, who knows no fear and no shame. He is impudent of eye. He is an arrogant male. He's the murderer in the mountains. His name is the Asag." Everybody gasped and they all looked at Ninurta to see what his response would be, but Ninurta merely narrowed his eyes. He showed focused attention and nothing else. He knew the Sharur had not yet completed its message. So the Sharur carried on:

"In the mountains, the plants have unanimously named the Asag their king. His roots spread out. His branches spread out. He drops his seeds everywhere. His seeds are his children. His children are the stones, and the stones are his warriors, his great army: the Hematite, the Dolerite, the Lapis Lazuli and the Flint. All these young warriors march down the hills; they roll down the hills and destroy the mountain cities winning more and more territories for their lord Asag. Master Ninurta, the Asag has set up a throne in the mountain lands. There he sits as king. There he hands out judgements and decides the lawsuits of the land, just as you do. There he gives decisions. Lord Ninurta, day by day, the Asag adds lands to its domains. Now the mountains take their offerings to him. He plans to take away your kingdom."

Everybody looked at Ninurta. Clearly, the Sharur had completed its message. Ninurta took action. He stood. He clenched his fists. With his fists he beat his thighs. He opened his mouth and the cry that came was the roll of the thunder. He roared, "Alas," and heaven trembled. Then he roared out, "We fight," and earth huddled at his feet and was terrified at his strength. Even Enlil became confused and left the Ekur. The mountains were devastated. That day, the earth became dark, the Anuna gods all trembled. The hero beat his thighs with his fists. The gods dispersed; they disappeared over the horizon like a flock of sheep. The lord arose, touching the sky. He took his lance of lightning in his left hand. He reached out with his right, and the Sharur, his mace, his faithful servant that loved him, spun to his hand. Ninurta went to battle. With one step, he covered a league. He was an alarming storm. Then Ninurta rode on the chariot of eight winds towards the rebel lands. He tied the evil wind, the Sirocco, to the pole. He placed a quiver and arrows on its hook. The Sharur, snarling at the mountains, began to devour all the enemy. Wherever the eight-wind chariot went, the enormous hurricane, irresistible, went before the hero, Ninurta. It tore up trees, raised mounds, filled in hollows. It caused a rain of coals and flaming fires. The fire consumed men. It overturned the trunks of tall trees. It reduced the forests to heaps. Earth put her hands on her heart and cried harrowingly. The Tigris was muddied, disturbed, cloudy, stirred up. The people did not know where to turn. They bumped into walls. The birds tried to lift their heads and fly away, but their wings trailed on the ground. The storm flooded out the fish from the subterranean waters and their mouths snapped at the air. It reduced the animals of the open country to firewood, roasting them like locusts. It was a deluge rising and disastrously ruining the mountains. The hero Ninurta led the march through the rebel lands. He killed their messengers in the mountains. He crushed their cities. He smote their cowherds over the head with debris that was like fluttering butterflies. He entangled their hands and feet with long grass so that they dashed their heads against walls. The lights of the mountains did not gleam in the distance any longer. People gasped for breath and were ill. They hugged themselves. They cursed the earth. They considered the day of the Asag's birth a day of disaster. The lord caused bilious poison to run over the rebel lands. When at last they came to the mountain lands, he restrained the hurricane. There he spoke to his Mace, the Sharur. "See what is to be seen. Hear what is to be heard."

It flew out, but at last returned, on little wings flapping like the southern storm. It flung its arms around its master and cried out, "Master Ninurta, change your mind. Don't fight this fight. Run away. I have seen the Asag and it is terrifying. It is hard: hard of eye, hard of heart and hard of flesh. No weapon will overturn it. No axe or spear will penetrate that flesh. He's beyond all control. His weight is too heavy. His strength is too massive, and he is clever. Remember the battles that you have fought. You killed the dragon. You killed the seven-headed snake. You killed the Anzu bird. Let these successes be enough. Lord, do not venture again to a battle that is more terrible than those. Do not lift your arm to the smiting of weapons, to the festival of the young men, to Inana's dance with this creature! Lord, do not go to such a great battle as this! Do not hurry. Fix your feet on the ground. Ninurta! The Asag is waiting for you in the mountains. Hero who is so handsome in your crown; firstborn son whom Ninlil has decorated with numberless charms; good lord, hero who wears horns like the moon, who is long life for the king of the land, who opens the sky by great sublime strength, Ninurta, lord, full of fearsomeness, hurrying towards the mountains, proud hero without fellow: this time you will not equal your opponent, the Asag! Ninurta, do not make your young men enter the mountains. Run away!"

Ninurta frowned. He called for the eight-wind chariot. He tied the sirocco to a pole, he took his lance of lightning in one hand, and with the Sharur in the other, in his wind-drawn chariot, he hurtled off into the mountain lands.

They came to the place where the Asag towered over them. It was immense. It shut out all the sunlight. The Asag looked down on Ninurta. The ground began to shake. There was a crack, and the sound of the groan of stone. A great arm, craggy and huge, reached up into the sky. The Asag thrust its arm deep into the sky, turned the sky inside out, gave it a twist and made the sky into a club for its hip. Then he raised it up and beat the earth.

That was the beginning of the battle between Ninurta and the Asag.

Alongside the Asag fought his children, who were the stones: the Hematite, the Dolerite, the Lapis Lazuli, the Flint. The Asag was like a wall collapsing, thundering down and crushing Ninurta. Great fires engulfed the land. The land was black as pitch. Animals roasted like locusts. Birds tried to fly away, but their wings trailed on the ground. The waters threw up their fish, which gasped on dry land in air. The air was filled with dust. Ninurta's eyes were filled with dust. His mouth was filled with dust, and then he realized that the hand that had held his faithful mace, the Sharur, was empty. Where was his faithful companion? Where was his weapon, his advisor and servant?

Where was he? The Sharur was flying, hurtling away from the mountain lands and returning to father Enlil. There it was, telling great Enlil the whole story. When father Enlil heard the words of the Sharur, he smiled. He said, "Say this to my son Ninurta: 'Why did I set you on the throne of the land? Why did I raise you up above myself? Because you, and you alone, will destroy the Asag'. Say to my son Ninurta this: 'Why did I give you the deluge? Why did I give you the lightning?' Tell my son Ninurta: 'Bring down your deluge and wash the dust from the air. Bring down your flood and wash the dust from your eyes, and when you can see clearly, raise up your lance of lightning and pierce the Asag. Pierce its liver.'"

The Sharur returned, spinning across the plains. It returned through the dust-filled air to the hand of its master. Blinded by dust, Ninurta felt the Sharur return to his right hand. He heard its words in his ear. "I bring you the words of your father Enlil. Your father Enlil says, 'Why did I set you on the throne of the land? Why did I raise you up above myself? Because you, and you alone, will destroy the Asag'. He says, 'Why did I give you the deluge? Why did I give you the lightning?' He says, 'Bring down your deluge and wash the dust from the air. Bring down your flood and wash the dust from your eyes, and when you can see clearly, raise up your lance of lightning and pierce the Asag. Pierce its liver.'"

Ninurta heard the words of his father Enlil. He reached up. He brought down the deluge and the flood. He washed the dust from the air. The flood washed the dust from his eyes, and he saw clearly and saw the Asag towering above him. He took his lance of lightning, and he let it fly and his aim was true. There was a crack and splinter of rock. Sparks flew. His lance of lightning struck the Asag. He pierced its liver and the power of the Asag was contained. It began to fade. It looked wonderingly upwards. It began to fade. Ninurta put out his hand into the heart of the Asag. It felt as if he was putting his hand into liquid. Ripples spread out. Like water, he agitated it. He scattered it and then like weeds he ripped it up, like reeds he pulled it up, and then he ground it like barley and piled it up, as if he was piling heaps of broken brick. He heaped it up as the miller heaps up flour, heaped it up as the potter heaps up coals. He piled it up like stamped earth.

The sun bade the mountain lands goodbye. It was the end of the day. And as the sun sank over the horizon, it stained the sky red. It was sunlight mixed with dust and blood. The sky was red that day for the very first time, as it has been ever since at evening time.

Ninurta took his faithful bloodstained servant, his weapon: the Sharur. He took it to the waters and washed the blood from himself and from the Sharur. Then he returned to the body of the Asag and, standing in the fading light, he sang a victory chant over the body of the Asag. His voice was the sweet voice of the southern wind, and it brought the gods flocking over the landscape. Like a flock of sheep, they came running to their master and their king, to surround him and congratulate him.

But it was his faithful servant, the Sharur, who sang his praises:

"Oh Ninurta, my lord, my master, darting dragon, snarling lion, swaying serpent, roaring hurricane, it is Ninurta who has defeated the monster of the mountain lands. He has laid waste the rebel lands, cast his net over the foe, defeated all around him, reclaimed the mountain lands. The Asag is dead. Henceforth let no one call it Asag. Let its name be stone. Let its body be the mountain. Let its entrails be the underworld and its body be the region of the lord."

These were the words of the Sharur, and all that remained now was for Ninurta to deal with the prisoners.

So he sat on the seat of the land, the royal carved boxwood throne, and one by one the prisoners came to stand before him. All the children of the Asag came before him. All those young warriors, who are the stones, came before him. And to each on that day, he gave a fate and gave a destiny, according to its loyalty. To the Dolerite, he said, "You called out, 'This battle is wrong. The lord alone is warrior'. So I say: Let you be set in copper to decorate the warrior's arm. Let the king make his statue from you."

But to the Limestone, as he walked forward, Ninurta said, "You called out, 'I will be the Asag's great advisor'. Let you lie like a pig on the ground broken into bits, humbled by the builder."

And to the Granite and the Basalt he said, "As you two refused to stand against me, may the silver smith and the foundry man love you and praise you and use you for their craft work, and for their small work." But to the Shugara stone he said, "You tramped the highland to pinion me, so may the reed worker make you leap from the reeds. May no man live in need of you. May no man mention the loss of you." To the Emery stone he said, "You moved against me, so let you be torn to pieces and crushed into black sand and heaped up like flour, to be used as an abrasive."

And so on till, at last, when all the destinies of the stones had been set down and all the stones had been dealt with, Ninurta turned to the body of the Asag. He began to shape and sculpt. He dug channels and ditches so that the trapped waters within could be freed and the streams sprang, rushing and singing, flowing down to feed the Tigris and the Euphrates. That day, the mountain lands became the fertile verdant mountain lands we know: thick with forests; teeming with animals and birds; abundant with honey and vine; ripe with fruit; and ringing with copper and tin and silver and gold.

Now you know how it was that the mountain lands came into being.

It was all created by Ninurta.
All praise to Ninurta.

THE ANZU BIRD

In those first days, the great land masses had already been created. The flowing waters, which had previously been locked up in the mountains, had already been released by the heroic work of Lord Ninurta. The Tigris and the Euphrates had already been established. But the organization of the world had not yet been completed. A god had been appointed responsible for canals, but there were, as yet, no canals. Similarly, clouds, rainfall and irrigation were still concepts, and not yet operational. However, the greater gods, the Anuna gods, were planning and laying out the land. They had planned the forests in the mountains, the metals in the rock and the waters sitting in the valleys. They had already selected their own holy centres and cities. Indeed, they had all stepped into their appointed and comfortable homes. On the other hand, no meeting places had yet been created for the lesser gods, the Igigi. In those days, these worker gods might be called to assemble for instructions from Ellil, the earth god, at any moment and to any place. They never knew, until the last moment, when or where the meeting place would be.

The greater gods had all their power through the Tablet of Destinies. These Destinies were the shining and powerful plans of creation. This Tablet of Destinies, this potent key to power, had first been given by Tiamat into the hands of Qingu. When he died, they had been given, by the Anuna gods, into the guardianship of Ellil, the god of the earth. He was making sure the rules were kept. All was going smoothly and according to plan.

But then terrible news came to the Anuna gods.

"Oh great gods, terrible news! There is an unknown and alien power in the mountains. No one knows whence it comes. It lives in a tree in the north. It is dressed in eleven coats of protective feathers. It has a beak like a saw. It has a cry which has the power of the south wind and the whirlwind."

There was great consternation among the lesser gods, the Igigi. "Where has this creature come from? What is its intention? How shall it be dealt with?" Ea, god of wisdom and fresh water, spoke first. "You ask where this creature has come from. Surely the waters of the spate, the flood of the new waters has fathered this monstrous force. This has combined with the holy water of the Abzu and together these great beings have begotten this monstrous child. The broad earth herself has conceived him and he has been born from the mountain rock. He is a creature of our newly created wilderness. He has great power and intelligence, and his name is Anzu." There was even more consternation and distress among the Igigi. So Ea, the clever and subtle one, spoke again. "I have a suggestion. Let his incredible power be channelled. Let his sharp intelligence be trained. Ellil, our leader, why don't you take all the glory of your power, take the Tablet of Destinies that we have given you, dress yourself in your radiance and then approach Anzu in his tree. Impress him with your radiance. Then offer him a job."

Great Anzu, who is child of the floods, the holy waters of the Abzu and of earth and rock, was in his tree on his northern mountain. He was looking to the four directions. He was enjoying the grandeur of the mountains, feeling the warmth of the sunlight, watching the glitter of light on the distant waters and thrilling as the winds ruffled his feathers. Then from the south he saw that something new was approaching. It was a wonder. It seemed not to be of earth, air, fire or water, but a mixture of all four. It was a being all bedecked in another glorious radiance. Anzu was uplifted, delighted and aghast. He did not bow down, but he was attentive. The radiant being spoke: "I am Ellil, lord of the earth and of all the Anuna and Igigi gods. I am lord of all. Bow down to me, my beloved servant. I have a very special and highly important position for you in my governance." Anzu marvelled at the radiance and the beauty of the lord Ellil. He was impressed by the authority and command of the words of the god. He bowed down, and when radiant Ellil turned and walked down the mountain, Anzu took wing and circled overhead, following him. Ellil returned to his newly established hall and stood at the entrance. Anzu alighted on a nearby rock. Ellil said, "Greetings, Anzu. I appoint you as my honoured guard."

It was Anzu's job to stand at the entrance to the hall. He barred the way to the innermost chamber. He served Ellil and he never ceased. He was proud and pleased to do it. The radiance of Ellil delighted him and filled his heart.

But as time passed, great Anzu started to notice some inconsistencies about radiant Ellil. He noticed that when Ellil got into his bath, his radiance was diminished. In fact, in the bath, he hardly shone at all. He noticed that when Ellil prepared for his bath, he would place the Tablet of Destinies in an alcove outside the bathroom, and that, even before he got undressed, Ellil had lost his brilliant shimmer, and by the time he got into the water he was just plain dim. It was the tablet within the alcove which still shone with the radiant light. Now Anzu's eyes looked narrowly at the trappings of Ellil-power. He saw the lordly crown, the robe of divinity, the shining Tablet of Destinies in his hands. Anzu gazed and gazed and came to a decision. His purpose was to usurp the Ellil-power. "I shall take the gods' plans, the Tablet of Destinies for myself. I will control the plans of all the gods. And I shall possess the throne and be master of rites. I shall be the one to direct every one of the lesser gods, and the greater gods too." He plotted opposition in his heart. And at the chamber entrance, from which he had often gazed, he waited for the start of day. When he saw Ellil remove his crown, lay aside his clothing, place the Tablet of Destinies within the alcove and get into the bath, Anzu reached a claw out into the alcove and took the beautiful tablet. He tucked it into his finger feathers, his pinion feathers. He spread his wings in full freedom and took the Tablet of Destinies back to his home in the tree at the top of his northern mountain.

When Ellil got out of the bath, Anzu was gone, and so was the Tablet of Destinies.

There was consternation among the gods. All rites were abandoned. Radiance faded in the land of the gods. Now, it was the far northern mountains which shone with radiance.

Silence reigned. Father Ellil, the god of the land, was dumbstruck. Anzu had stripped his chamber of its radiance. Ellil searched high and low for a solution. But he had none. Something had to be done.

Anu the decision maker, Sky Father, called on Adad, whom the gods had recently appointed in anticipation of the role 'Canal Controller'. Anu said, "You are powerful and ferocious, Adad, Canal Controller. Now we will give you other powers. You will also have the power to whip up the waters. In this role, your attack will not be deflected. You can also be storm god. Send your storm against him. Strike Anzu with your lightning, your weapon. Your name will be great in the great gods' assembly. You shall have no rival among the gods your brothers. Then you can establish your own cult centres and shrines all over the four quarters. Show your prowess to the gods and your name shall be powerful."

Adad said, "Wait a moment. Lightning? Attack? I was appointed 'Canal Controller', not 'Storm Controller'. Have you seen Anzu? Now *he* has the authority to appoint. Not you. We need to think about this. Father Anu, who can rush off to the inaccessible mountain? Which of the gods, your sons, can be Anzu's conqueror now that he has gained the Tablet of Destinies for himself? He has taken away the Ellil-power. All rites are abandoned! His utterance has replaced the utterance of the gods. He has only to command and whomever he curses turns to clay. At his utterance the gods must now tremble."

So the Anuna gods called on Gerra, fire god. Anu, the decision maker, spoke to him. He said, "Powerful Gerra, ferocious Gerra, your attack cannot be deflected. We have allocated you fire. Burn. Send your weapon of fire. Burn Anzu with your fire." Gerra answered in the same way as Adad had: "Who can rush off to the mountains with the little power you have given us? Now he has all the power. At his utterance, we are clay."

They called Shara, Inana's son. He too said, "He has gained the Tablet of Destinies for himself. He has only to command, and we are all clay. At his utterance the gods must now tremble." And Shara, the last of their hopeful saviours, left the assembly.

The Igigi grew despondent and shivered where they sat, troubled. All the gods fell silent and despaired.

Ea, lord of intelligence, the wise one who dwells in the Abzu, was considering. He formed an idea in the depths of his watery being. He shared his thoughts loudly with Anu. "Let me give orders and search among the gods. We will find from the assembly Anzu's conqueror. I myself shall search among the gods and will pick Anzu's conqueror." While all the Igigi breathed a sigh of relief, Ea was whispering in Anu's ear: "I am afraid we're going to have to ask for the help of Mami. We are going to have to ask Ninurta's mother. We are going to have to ask her to wake Ninurta up." Anu shuddered. Everyone was a little uncertain of Ninurta's power. The hero was weary after the defeat of the mountain demon, the Asag, and he was taking a well-earned rest. But Anu agreed that there was nothing else to be done.

So Ea cried out, "Have them call for Mami, sister of the gods. She is the wise counsellor of the gods. Have them announce her supremacy in the assembly. Have all the gods honour her in their assembly. I shall then tell her the idea which is in my heart." They called Mami to the assembly. When she arrived, she was welcomed warmly. The gods honoured her in their assembly. Ea told her the idea he had had in the depths of his inmost being: "Previously we called you Mami. But now your name shall be Belet-ili, Mistress of All Gods." Everyone cheered. Mami acknowledged the cheering. She knew her own worth. She already knew she was mistress and mother of gods, but until now it had rarely been acknowledged. Her demeanour was reserved. There was a pause and Ea continued: "Offer us the powerful one, your superb beloved, broad of chest, who forms the battle array! Give us Ninurta, then shall his name be Lord in the great gods' assembly. Let him show his power to the gods. Let his name be made great in all the populated lands."

Mami listened to this speech. She observed the gathering. She said, "He is sleeping." They said, "Please, Belet-ili. Please, Mistress of All Gods. Wake him." Then she uttered a word. "Yes."

She was Belet-ili the Supreme, and the gods of the land were glad at her utterance. The Igigi were freed from anxiety, and they kissed her feet.

She called her son, Ninurta. She said, "My son Ninurta, awake!" She called his presence into the gods' assembly and gave instruction, saying, "In the presence of Anu, I gave birth to all the Igigi; I created all the Anuna, and I created the gods' assembly. I, Mami, assigned power to my brother. I, Mami, designated the kingship of heaven for Anu. Now it seems I have become Belet-ili, Mistress of All Gods. Now at last I am acknowledged to be the mother of you all.

"Now I release your power, my son. I release your power to set all to rights for the Anuna gods. I say this to you my son, Ninurta, wake! Anzu has disrupted the kingship that only I have the power to designate. He has obtained for himself the Tablet of Destinies. He has robbed and ejected Ellil, your father. He has stolen the Tablet of Destinies and turned them to his own use. My son, make a path! Fix the hour. Let light dawn again for the gods whom I have created. Muster your devastating battle force against him. Make your evil winds flash and march over him. Capture soaring Anzu and inundate the earth which I have created. Wreck his dwelling and let terror thunder above him. Make the devastating whirlwind rise up against him. Coat your arrow with poison and set it to the bow. Your form must keep changing like a galla-demon. Send out a fog, so that he cannot recognize your features. May your rays proceed above him. Make a high, attacking leap. Give a glare more powerful than that which Shamash generates. May broad daylight turn to darkness for him. Seize him by the throat and then slit the throat of wicked Anzu. Conquer Anzu and let the winds bring his feathers as good news to Ekur, to your father Ellil's house, and inundate the mountain pastures. Then shall kingship enter the Ekur again. Then shall rites return for the father who begot you. Then surely shall shrines be created for you. Establish your cult centres all over the four quarters. Your cult centre shall enter Ekur. Show prowess to the gods and your name shall be powerful!"

In his sleep, the warrior heard his mother's words. The warrior woke.

At first, when he heard the task, he hunched in trepidation. He went into hiding. But he had his good old faithful servant, the Sharur, at his side.

So Lord Ninurta took the Sharur in his hand and he marshalled the Seven Evil Winds of Battle. He did as his mother told him. He hung his quiver and arrows on their hook. He danced in the dust of the Seven Whirlwinds. He mustered a battle cry. His gales created a terrifying battle formation. Then, when the moment was right, his gales fell silent at his side poised for conflict.

On the mountainside Anzu and Ninurta met. Anzu looked at Ninurta and shook with rage at him. He bared his teeth like an umu-demon. His mantle of radiance covered the mountain. He roared like a lion in a rage. In utter fury Anzu shouted to the warrior, "I have taken away every single rite. I am in charge of all the gods' orders. Who are you to come and do battle against me? Give your reasons."

The warrior Ninurta answered Anzu:

"I am the avenger of the gods who established the god of the earth-road, who established Ellil, king of destinies. I have come to do battle against you, to trample on you."

Anzu listened to his speech, then hurled his wordless shout furiously amid the mountains.

It was chaos. Darkness fell over the mountain. The faces of the earth were overcast. Shamash, the light of the gods, was overcast by darkness. Adad roared like a lion and his noise joined that of Anzu. A battle clash was imminent, the flood weapon was waiting.

Then the armour-plated breast was bathed in blood. Clouds of death were raining down, an arrow flashed lightning, the battle force roared between them. Ninurta, the powerful one, the superb one, the trusted one of Anu, beloved of Ea, Mami's son Ninurta, with his winds cleared a view to Anzu. He set his shaft to his bow, pulled the bow string taut and aimed his arrow straight at Anzu. At the top of his tree, Anzu stood open and vulnerable. Ninurta let loose his deadly arrow. But in his claws Anzu held the Tablet of Destinies. He had creation at his command. As the arrow flew, Anzu gave a great cry. Suddenly the arrow disappeared and did not reach its target. Ninurta let loose another arrow. Anzu gave another cry. The arrow disappeared. A third time Ninurta let an arrow fly, but this time he heard the words of Anzu: "You, arrowhead that comes, return to your stone. You, shaft that comes, return to your reed thicket. You, fletch that comes, return to the bird." And Ninurta's carefully shaped arrowhead had become once more a stone in the mountains. Ninurta's carefully shaped arrow shaft had become once more a reed in the marshes. And the feathers of the arrows were once more in their place, neatly on the wing of the small bird, flying free. Ninurta's arrow had disintegrated and returned to its component parts, and the component parts had returned to their natural origins, at the command of the possessor of the Tablet of Destinies.

Undeterred, Ninurta engaged his bow again. He sent out his arrows towards Anzu at the top of his tree in the mountains. But Anzu, radiant with the Tablet of Destinies in his claws, was calling out. "Arrowheads, return to your stones. Arrow shafts, return to your reed thickets. Arrow fletches, return to the flight feather of the birds." This time he was also calling out, "Bow frame, go back to your copse, and bow string, return to the gut of the sheep." Obediently the flint returned to the mountain, the reed returned to the marsh, the feather returned to the bird and the carefully crafted bow frame was once more a tree growing in the forest. The bow string was in the gut of a sheep happily grazing in the field. All had disintegrated and returned to their component parts, and the component parts had returned to their natural origins.

Deadly silence came over the battle. Conflict ceased. Weapons were disabled and could not capture Anzu in the mountains.

Ninurta did not know what to do, so he shouted. He instructed his Sharur.

"Repeat to far-sighted Ea the action you have seen. Say, 'While wrapped in devastation's dust, Ninurta set the shaft to the bow, drew it taut and aimed from the bow's curve, but Anzu called, "Shaft return to your reed thicket. Bow frame, go back to your copse. Bow string, go back to the ram's gut. Feather return to the bird."' Tell my father that Anzu has in his hand the Tablet of Destinies. He has all creation at his command, and he has the capacity to turn all of us gods to clay."

The Sharur bowed and took the message to far-sighted Ea.

Everything Ninurta had told him, he repeated to Ea.

Ea, the far-sighted one, listened to words of his son. He instructed the Sharur: "Say this to my son:

"'Do not let the battle slacken. Press home your victory. Send your storm and tire him out so that he opens his flight wings in the clash of tempests. Direct your throwstick, your faithful Sharur, to be your arrow. Strike the flight wing of Anzu with your winds. Strike the pinions of Anzu and detach them. Detach them both left and right. Let the Sharur seize them. Sharpen them before he sees that they are gone. When he sees his pinions are missing, he will cry out. He will use the Tablet of Destinies. He will call "wing to wing". Do not panic. Draw taut the curve of your bow. Let shafts fly like lightning. Let the wing feathers dance like butterflies.'"

Sharur memorized the message, bowed and took the message with him.

Everything Ea had told to the Sharur, the Sharur repeated to Ninurta.

"Tire him out so he opens his flight wings. Send me. Let him shed the flight wings. Use his own flight wings as weapons."

Ninurta listened to the words of far-sighted Ea. He hunched in trepidation and went into hiding. The lord marshalled the seven of battle, the Seven Evil Winds, who dance in the dust: the Seven Whirlwinds. He mustered them as a battle army and prepared to make war with a terrifying formation. All the gales were silent at his side, poised for conflict.

Then he released devastation, blazing heat, confusion, all the winds and even frost. All was uncertain and bathed in battle. There was mayhem in the mountain meadows. Ninurta folded the vast earth in his fury. Anzu grew weary, and in the clash of tempests, he shed a few pinions, just a few flight wings. The Sharur was hovering in the gale and saw the feathers fly, so it grabbed them – instantly the Sharur delivered them into the hand of Ninurta. Anzu saw his wings fly out and he cried, "My wings, return to me." But by the time he clutched the Tablet and cried out, "Wing, return to wing," and his feathers returned to him, it was too late. Ninurta had already armed those feathers as his arrows. When the arrows returned to Anzu, they struck him hard. His own feathers shot straight through his wing and into his heart and his liver. The Anzu bird was destroyed, and he fell from his mountain home. Ninurta had killed Anzu. He took control of the Tablet of Destinies. Then he threw Anzu's wing feathers into the wind, and the wind bore the feathers to the gods, as a sign of the glad tidings from the Lord Ninurta.

The Anuna and the Igigi celebrated wildly while they waited for Ninurta's return. They were saying, "Let him rejoice. Let him dance. Let him celebrate."

And this should be the joyous end of a glorious story.

But it is not.

NINURTA AND THE TURTLE

The gods waited for Ninurta to return to them the Tablet of Destinies. They waited patiently, but when at last, several aeons later, Ninurta had still not returned, Ea sent his servant to ask politely when Ninurta would be coming back with the Tablet of Destinies. The reply came: "Why should I surrender the trappings of kingship? My words are the words of the king of gods. Why would I return the Tablet of Destinies?"

Ninurta had become the usurper!

So Ea decided the only thing to do was to make a death turtle.

The turtle that Ea made was a terrible thing indeed, created from the earth beneath his fingernails. It was full of claws. It oozed up through the depths of the Abzu. Ea also created a place of thought for Ninurta and the turtle. It was a sort of pit, or maybe a dream place.

Ninurta found himself cast into the dark pit with the turtle. He was confounded by the horror of the turtle and its claws. Then, while trapped in the claws of the turtle, Ninurta experienced a dream. It was as if he had escaped the turtle and was sitting talking in a friendly way with the Anzu bird. But, in his dream, he was puzzled because he knew he had destroyed the Anzu bird. In his dream, he saw that the Anzu bird had become a little chick. The Anzu chick was speaking. It said, "At his command your weapon struck me evilly. As I let the Me, the symbols of power, go out of my hand, the divine plan returned to the Abzu. The Tablet of Destinies returned to the Abzu and I was stripped of the Me." Ninurta was stunned at these words of the Anzu chick. Then Ninurta heard a woman's wail: "And what about me? I am queenship. I am the crown. I am as I am. I am the birth of the world. When will the Me fall again into my hand? I shall not exercise their lordship. I shall not live for ever under the kingship of the Abzu." The voice sounded very much like the voice of his mother, Mami, but Ninurta could not make any sense of it. Then the Anzu chick took Ninurta by his hand and drew near with him to Ea's Abzu. Together Ninurta and the chick proclaimed their names in the seat of honour. They heard these words: "I am the lady of the crown."

That is all we have of Ninurta's dream. Until the gaps in this tablet have been found and translated, we do not know what happened to Ninurta and the turtle and the Tablet of Destinies. But from later stories, it seems that Ea must have regained the Tablet of Destinies, the Me. As you will read, when the young goddess Inana comes to visit Ea in the Abzu, he gives them to her.

ENKI AND NINMAH

At the very beginning of everything, when earth and the heavens had been created and the destinies decided, the greater gods watched over all things, while the lesser gods did all the work. They had to dig the irrigation canals and dredge out silt and clay to keep the water flowing. It was hard work, and the lesser gods began to complain that their life was one of drudgery.

Nammu, the mother goddess who created all things, decided to appeal on behalf of the lesser gods to Enki. Enki was dozing lazily in the Abzu, his home and temple in the deep sweet water. When Nammu saw this, she called out, "Are you really lying there, napping at your ease, while the lesser gods are slaving away? Wake up, my son! Use your ingenuity and wisdom to find a way to relieve the lesser gods from their labours."

Enki, of course, took notice of Nammu, the mother of all things. He went to his place of pondering and set himself to sort things out. He said to Nammu, "I will make creatures to take over the work, to free the lesser gods from their duties. You, Nammu, and the birth goddesses must follow these instructions: Nammu, knead clay from the Abzu to soften it. You, birth goddesses, you must nip off pieces of the softened clay and shape my new creatures. Then Ninmah, goddess of the womb, shall birth them. Then they will take over the work from the lesser gods, who can rest from their labours."

And so it was.

Nammu kneaded the clay from the Abzu until it was soft. The birth goddesses, Ladies of the Ovaries, nipped off pieces of the softened clay and shaped the new creatures. Ninmah, lady of the womb, gave birth to them. The goddesses named the new creatures 'human beings' and set them to work.

The lesser gods were, of course, delighted to be freed from their labours. The gods held a fabulous feast to celebrate.

Enki and Ninmah were sitting together at the feast. They were sharing beer: plenty of it!

With their bellies full of beer, they began to pontificate.

Ninmah said, "It's my work with the clay, growing in the womb, which determines the destiny of every human that is born."

Enki took offence at this. He said, "I am the leader of the gods. You are just the birth goddess. Whatever kind of person you give birth to, I determine their destiny. I challenge you to a test!"

It was a challenge Ninmah would not refuse.

She picked up some clay. First of all, she made a man who could not close his outstretched hand.

"No problem," said Enki. "He will be a courtier, his hands always open to give praise to the king."

Secondly, Ninmah made a man whose feet were twisted, so he could not easily stand.

"No problem," said Enki again. "He will be a silversmith, seated always at his work table."

Thirdly, Ninmah made a woman who was blind.

"That woman," said Enki, "will be a royal musician."

The fourth one Ninmah made was a man who could only think very slowly, and found it hard to work things out for himself.

"He will be a servant to the king," said Enki. "There is no reward for initiative at court. The king will welcome one who willingly takes instruction."

Her fifth was a man who could not hold in his urine. Enki simply bathed him in magical water and drove out the demon that caused this problem.

Next, Ninmah made a woman who could not give birth.

Enki said, "She will be a weaver, honoured in the queen's own household for her fine fabrics."

For her seventh attempt, Ninmah made a person with neither penis nor vagina.

Enki said, "This one will be a eunuch at the king's court, leading the celebrations there."

There was no way Ninmah could outsmart Enki. In frustration, she threw down the pinched clay that was left. A long silence fell between them.

Enki broke the silence. "I have decreed a destiny for every one of your creatures, and made sure that they can all earn their daily bread. Now, let me make a being for you, and you shall decree its destiny."

Enki shaped the clay into a little being with a big head and a wide mouth.

He said to Ninmah, "I will pour semen into a woman's womb, and the woman will give birth to my little being."

Ninmah stood by for the birthing, and the little creature was born. She held it carefully. Its limbs were floppy, its head was heavy, its face was wrinkled. It had no control over its bladder or bowels. It started to cry.

Enki said to Ninmah, as she sat holding the newborn, "I found a destiny for every one of your creatures and made sure they could earn their daily bread. Can you do the same for my creature?"

Ninmah looked at the little being.

She asked it a question, but it could not speak, so it did not answer. She offered it bread to eat, but it could not reach out, so it did not take it. She held the food to its mouth, but then she saw that it had no teeth to gnaw the bread. It could not stand up, or even sit up, without her support. She did not think it could understand her. She was at a loss.

She said to Enki, "This one you have made is not properly finished. It cannot look after itself. It cannot work or earn its daily bread. In fact, it cannot even eat its daily bread – it has no teeth!"

Enki looked smugly at Ninmah. "I found a destiny for all the creatures you made: the one with weak hands, the one with bad feet, the blind woman, the barren woman, the slow man, the man with the leaky bladder, the one who was neither man nor woman. My dear, are you telling me that you cannot decree a destiny for this one poor little creature?"

Ninmah wept with frustration. She said, "You have silenced me. How can I continue to be the goddess of birth? You are taking my powers and stripping me of my purpose!"

But Enki said, "No, indeed, no. Who could change your work, who could take your role? This helpless little creature I have made is called a baby. It needs you to watch over it in the womb and help it to grow. In time it will learn how to eat and speak, to walk and talk, to work and pray, to find and fulfil its destiny. For the penis is powerful, Ninmah, ejaculating the fertile seed in the semen. But only in the womb, under your care, can a human being develop."

Ninmah replied, "And only after being born, with my care and its mother's love, can a human being grow to fulfil its destiny."

With these words, the two who had challenged each other reached an understanding. To celebrate, they toasted each other in more beer.

LOVE, LUST & THEIR CONSEQUENCES

These stories deal with raw sexuality and its relationship to fertility, abundance, nature and the taming of nature. Lovemaking is celebrated. The story of Ninhursag and Enki, which introduces Enki when he is plunging his penis into the earth, makes explicit the role of the gods and goddesses in bringing fertility to both earth and womb.

NINHURSAG AND ENKI

The Land of Dilmun

Dilmun, lying in the east, a sacred land, was pure, clean and bright. Birds of prey, partridges and carrion crows were silent there. Lions, wolves and wild dogs did not kill there. If a widow spread malt on her roof, no birds flew down to eat it. Disease, death, old age and ill health were all unknown there. No one crossed the river of death there, no one mourned, no laments were heard and no sacred rites of death were needed.

Dilmun was pristine. It was virginal. That place was pristine and virginal.

Yet this fair land was dry: no sparkling water ran through its cities, no canals irrigated its fields. Lady Ninhursag brought this news to Enki, and she told him her complaint. "You have given me a city that has no river quay. What good is it to me? The canals of Dilmun are empty, the fair place has no fields, furrows or water meadows. It lacks water."

Enki heard the words of Ninhursag. He listened to the great mother. He said, "When the sun god Utu steps up into the heavens, fresh water shall run for you. May your city drink water a-plenty. May your city become great. May it become a great market place on the quay."

From the Abzu, the deep sweet waters, he drew water, making it come welling up. Enki's waters filled the wells and watered the furrows, so that the fields produced grain.

And Dilmun, bright place, began to prosper. Its buildings were beautiful, its grain and dates plentiful, its triple harvests were celebrated. Barges laden with barley and oil sailed its canals. Into its new cities, bright cities, were brought riches from all over the known world. From Tukric came Harali gold and lapis lazuli. From Meluba came cornelian and the best Magan wood. From Marhaci came precious stones and topaz; from Magan came copper, dolerite and stone; from the Sea-Land came ebony fit for a king; from the Nomads came fine, multicoloured wools; from Elam came tribute of choice fleeces. The wide sea yielded its wealth to Dilmun. The markets of Dilmun displayed precious wood and gemstones, wool, spices and woven cloth.

In the Marshlands

Under that sun, on that day, this is what happened. Ninhursag went out to the riverbank. She walked on the border of the marshlands. Out in the marshlands, far from the cities, Enki was digging channels in the marsh mud with his penis. He plunged his penis again and again into the mud, fertilizing the reedbeds with his seed. His penis swelled and burst through his clothing. Out in the middle of the marshes, Enki looked about. He saw Ninhursag. He said to his sukkal, "Isimud, shall I not kiss the fair one? Shall I not kiss Ninhursag?" Isimud answered, "Kiss the fair one, Lord Enki. Kiss Ninhursag. Let me raise up a wind to take you to her."

Ninhursag pushed his phallus away from her and spoke. "Let no man take me in the marsh!" But Enki cried out, "By the life's breath of heaven, I beg you, lie down for me in the marsh. Lie down for me in the marsh: that would be joyous!"

Ninhursag accepted that it could be joyous, and she lay down with him the marsh. Enki ejaculated his semen, he poured out his seed into Ninhursag's womb, and she conceived from Enki's semen.

Ninhursag's pregnancy passed in a flash, easily and swiftly. Her one month was as one day; her two months were as two days; her three months were as three days; her four months were as four days; her five months were as five days; her six months were as six days; her seven months were as seven days; her eight months were as eight days; her nine months were as nine days. In the month of womanhood, like juniper oil, like oil of abundance, Ninhursag, mother of the land, gave birth to Ninsar.

In time Ninsar, Ninhursag's daughter, went out to the riverbank. Enki was able to see up there from the marsh. He said to his sukkal, Isimud, "Is this nice youngster not one to be kissed? Is this nice Ninsar not one to be kissed?" Isimud's reply was encouraging. "Is this nice youngster not one to be kissed? My master will sail. Let me navigate. He will sail, I will navigate."

First Enki put his feet in the boat, the next minute he was on dry land. He did not think to speak with Ninsar. Instead, not waiting to know her wishes, he clasped Ninsar and kissed her. He poured his seed into her womb and she conceived from his seed, from Enki's semen. Ninsar's pregnancy passed in a flash, easily and swiftly. Her one month was as one day; her two months were as two days; her three months were as three days; her four months were as four days; her five months were as five days; her six months were as six days; her seven months were as seven days; her eight months were as eight days; her nine months were as nine days. In the month of womanhood, like juniper oil, like oil of abundance, Ninsar, daughter of the land, gave birth to Ninkura.

In turn Ninkura, Ninsar's daughter, went out to the riverbank. In turn Enki said to his sukkal, Isimud, "Is this nice youngster not one to be kissed? Is this nice Ninkura not one to be kissed?" Again, Isimud's answer was encouraging. "Is this nice youngster not one to be kissed? My master will sail. Let me navigate. He will sail, I will navigate."

First Enki put his feet in the boat, the next minute he was on dry land. He did not think to speak with Ninkura. Instead, he clasped Ninkura and, lying between her thighs, kissed and penetrated the young woman. He poured his seed into her womb and she conceived from his seed, from Enki's semen. Ninkura's pregnancy also passed easily and swiftly. Each month was as one day to her: her nine months were as nine days. In the month of womanhood, like juniper oil, like oil of abundance, Ninkura, granddaughter of the land, gave birth to Uttu.

Ninkura raised the child Uttu and made her flourish. Her great grandmother, Ninhursag, spoke to Uttu, saying, "Let me advise you: listen to my advice. In the marshlands, there is a man who can see up here. Enki is able to see up here, from deep in the marsh. He will be able to see you, and he will set his eyes on you from down in the marsh. Be careful. Be cunning. Things cannot go on as they have done. He is too free with his semen. He asks no permission, gains no consent. This cannot go on."

When Enki saw Uttu from deep in the marsh, yet again he called to Isimud. Isimud set the boat ready, and in one stride Enki crossed from it to the river bank. But before he could speak, Uttu said, "Enki, if you would kiss me, if you would make love to me, you must woo me first. Bring gifts to my house. Do not grab for me here on the river bank. That is not the way. Bring me cucumbers and apples, with their stems sticking out. Bring grapes in their clusters. Then, in the house, you may 'take hold of my halter'. Only then, Enki, may you indeed 'take hold of my halter'."

Enki inundated the marshlands with sweet water, filling the canals and the dykes and the furrows. A gardener joyfully rose from the dust and welcomed Enki, embracing him. The grateful gardener brought Enki just the gifts he needed: sweet cucumbers, apples with their stems sticking out, grapes in their clusters. He filled Enki's lap with the gifts.

The New Plants

Enki made himself look attractive and took his staff in his hand. He walked until he came to Uttu's house. He knocked on the door, calling, "Open up." She asked, "Who are you?" He answered, "I am a gardener. Let me give you cucumbers, apples and grapes in exchange for your 'yes'."

Full of joy, Uttu opened the house to Enki. He gave her the gifts, and he poured out beer for her in large measures. Uttu smiled and waved her hands for him. He clasped her to his chest, and he lay between her legs, fondling her thighs and touching her with his hand. He kissed Uttu and made love to her. He poured his seed into her womb.

But for Uttu there was to be no pregnancy that passed in a flash, no smooth labour, like juniper oil, like oil of abundance. She cried out in pain, "Woe, my thighs! Woe, my liver! Woe, my heart!"

Her great grandmother, Ninhursag, came to her aid. She wiped Enki's semen from Uttu's thighs. She flung it into the wetlands. There it fertilized the land, and new plants grew. Because of Ninhursag's actions, eight new plants appeared, that had never been known before. They were to become known as the tree plant, the honey plant, the vegetable plant, the esparto grass plant, the atutu plant, the actaltal plant, the unknown plant and the amharu plant.

Enki was able to see up there from the marsh. He was able to see these new plants. He said to his sukkal, Isimud, "I did not determine the destinies of those plants. What is this one? What is that one?" Isimud had all the answers. "Master," he said, "this is the tree plant." He cut it for Enki, and Enki ate it. It was delicious. "Master, this is the honey plant," he said, as he cut it and gave it to Enki. Enki ate it. It too was delicious. "Master, this is the vegetable plant," he said, as he cut it and gave it to Enki. Each of those eight new plants was named in turn by Isimud, and eaten in turn by Enki. Each of them, Enki found delicious. He ate them all up. He determined their destinies.

When Ninhursag learnt what Enki had done to her plants, she cursed him. "Until my dying day," she vowed, "I will never look on Enki with the life-giving eye."

Enki's Ailments

Enki was struck down. The all-seeing, all-knowing one, lord of wisdom and the deep sweet waters, was struck down. Every part of his body ached, every part was painful to him. He could find no relief. The Anuna, the great gods, grieved for Enki, but they could not help him. They sank down in the dust. Even Enlil could not help him. But a fox came to Enlil. It was able to speak to him. It said, "If I persuade Ninhursag to help Enki, what will be my reward?" Enlil answered immediately, "If you persuade Ninhursag to help Enki, I shall erect two standards to you in the city. You will be renowned."

The fox was pleased with this answer. He prepared to go to Ninhursag. He anointed his body with sweet-smelling oil; he shook out his fur and put kohl on his eyes. The fox found Ninhursag and spoke with her.

What he said has not yet been translated, but the effect was that her heart softened towards Enki.

She hastened to the temple where he lay. The Anuna were relieved and determined her destiny. They begged her to slip off her garments and help Enki. Ninhursag sat down naked on the ground, and made Enki lie with his head at her vagina, as if he were in her birth canal.

Then she asked, "My brother, what part of you hurts you?'" Enki answered, "The top of my head hurts me." Ninhursag gave birth to Abu, Lord of the Grasses, out of the top of Enki's head.

She asked again, "My brother, what part of you hurts you?" Enki answered, "The locks of my hair hurt me." Ninhursag gave birth to Ninsikila, ruler of Magan – where the best wood flourishes – out of the flowing tresses of Enki's hair.

She asked again, "My brother, what part of you hurts you?" Enki answered, "My mouth hurts me." From Enki's mouth, Ninhursag gave birth to Ninkasi, Goddess of Beer, the beer which satisfies the heart.

Again and again she asked, "My brother, what part of you hurts you?" Enki answered, "My nose, my throat, my arm…" Ninhursag birthed the children of each place.

When she asked again, "My brother, what part of you hurts you?" Enki answered, "My ribs hurt me." From his ribs, Ninhursag gave birth to Ninti, named Lady of the Month because of her connection to life, to birth.

Ninhursag asked for the last time, "My brother, what part of you hurts you?" Enki answered for the last time, "My side hurts me." Ninhursag gave birth to Ensag, Lord of Dilmun, the sacred land: pure, clean and bright.

Then Ninhursag decreed the destinies of these new children. "For these little ones to whom I have given birth, rewards shall not be lacking."

All their destinies were decreed by Ninhursag. And so it became.

An Incantation

Let all who visit Dilmun, the pure place, the bright place, land of prosperity, the market place known all over the world, give praise to Ensag, Lord of Dilmun.

Let all, wheresoever they be, give praise to Ninhursag, the fierce great grandmother who shared wise words with Uttu, teaching her how to cool Enki's unbridled ardour.

But let all remember also what happened to Ninsar and Ninkura, who did not receive protection or wise words, but were taken in the marshes by Enki. May Ninhursag be always alert, to take care of all her daughters.

ERESHKIGAL AND NERGAL

The gods were holding a great feast. What a marvellous feast! There was plenty on offer: bread, beer, meat, cresses, vegetables – all that could be desired. There was a place for every god, and every god was in their place. Only one god had no place.

For the Queen of the Underworld there was no place. She, Ereshkigal, could not come up from her domain, could not leave the Great Below. Equally, the other gods had no dominion over her realm. They could not go down there to meet her.

So Anu, greatest of the gods, called to his sukkal, his favoured servant, to take a message to the gates of the underworld.

He said, "Take my words to the underworld, give the queen my message. Say this to Ereshkigal: 'The greater gods and the lesser gods are feasting. There is plenty on offer, all that could be desired. There is a place for everyone and everyone is in their place, saving only you, Ereshkigal, who cannot leave your domain. Not once in a year can you come up. Nor can other gods descend to feast with you there. Not once in a month may we go down. Nonetheless, you are honoured here for your power and majesty.' Ask her to send a messenger up the long stairway to heaven to collect her portion, that she too may feast. Take my message to the gatekeeper of the underworld. These are my words and my command to you."

Anu's messenger accepted the god's word and took the message into his heart. He descended the long stairway from heaven. When he reached Ganzer, the outer gate of the underworld, he called out to the gatekeeper, "Gatekeeper, open the gate for me!"

The gatekeeper replied, "May the seven gates of the underworld bless you."

He brought Anu's messenger through the first gate.

He brought him through the second gate.

He brought him through the third gate.

He brought him through all seven gates to the hall of the Queen of the Underworld.

The messenger bowed down, and, given permission to speak, repeated the words of Anu.

"Lady, the greater and lesser gods are feasting. There is plenty on offer, all that could be desired. There is a place for everyone and everyone is in their place, saving only you, Lady, who cannot leave your domain. Not once in a year can you come up. Nor can other gods descend to feast with you in the Great Below. Not once in a month may they come down. Nonetheless, you are honoured there for your power and majesty. Will you therefore send a messenger of your choice up the long stairway to heaven to collect your portion, that you too may feast?"

Ereshkigal's reply was courteous and majestic. "Messenger of Anu, who is father of all things, I hope all is well with Anu, Enlil and Ea, the greater gods. I hope all is well with the husband of the Mistress of Heaven and with Ninurta the Mighty."

The messenger replied, "Lady, all is well with the gods and goddesses in heaven. May all be well with you here, in your domain."

Ereshkigal turned to her sukkal and wise companion, Namtar, and made ready to speak to him.

"Namtar, I will send you to heaven, to Anu the Great. Go up the long stairway to heaven. Receive my portion from the table of the gods. Whatever Anu gives you, bring it safely to me."

When Namtar arrived in the presence of the gods, the gods knelt before him, greeting him respectfully, for he bore the authority of the Queen of the Underworld. Only one god, Nergal, showed no respect. He did not bend the knee. He behaved as though he were not aware that a visitor was there. He looked at the ground, not at Namtar.

Namtar received the portion of Ereshkigal. He returned the gods' courtesies, then he left to go back to the underworld. But the behaviour of Nergal had not been hidden from him. He was well aware of that discourtesy.

After Namtar left the home of the gods, Ea himself upbraided Nergal. "What was wrong with you, Nergal, to show such discourtesy to a holy messenger? I kept winking at you, to signal you to change your behaviour, but you affected not to notice me, looking at the ground, so that I could not catch your eye. You should atone for that behaviour."

Nergal pretended to be abashed. He said, "Let me make a work, a mighty throne. Let me make it as a gift for Ereshkigal. I will take it to her, down the long stairway of heaven, to the underworld."

Ea agreed this would be fitting, and gave Nergal permission to cut down cedar trees and sisoo trees, mesu trees and juniper trees, to make the throne.

Nergal took his axe and his sword. He went to the forest and cut down many trees, easily enough to make a fine throne. But he did not decorate it with silver and gold, or deep blue lapis. Rather, he used cheap gypsum instead of silver; yellow and red paste instead of gold; blue glaze instead of precious lapis lazuli.

When the chair was complete, Ea called Nergal to him. He gave him instructions on how to behave in the underworld.

"My son, this journey that you intend to make is a perilous one. Who, having once gone down to the underworld, has ever returned from that place? Let me instruct you in the protocols you must follow to keep yourself safe. After you arrive in the underworld, when they bring you a chair, do not sit on it. When the baker brings you bread, do not eat it. When the butcher brings you meat, do not eat it either. When the brewer brings you beer, do not drink it. When they bring you a footbath, do not wash your feet. When Ereshkigal has bathed and dressed herself in a fine robe, allowing you to glimpse her body, do not become aroused or do what men and women can do together."

Nergal heard the words of Ea. He listened to the protocols. Then he turned his face towards the dark house of Ereshkigal, the house where those who enter are bereft of light; where dust is their food, clay is their bread. They are clothed like birds, in feathers, with wings for garments. They see no light; they dwell in darkness, moaning like doves.

Nergal set his foot on the path to the place from which no one has ever returned. Somewhere on the way, the second-rate chair that he had made was left behind. Whether he realized it was not a fitting gift, or whether he was constrained by the laws of the underworld, which forbid the traveller to bring anything into that kingdom, Nergal no longer had it with him when he reached Ganzer, the outer gate of the underworld.

There, the gatekeeper stopped him and said, "Wait here, Lord. I must let my lady know that a traveller is standing at her gate."

The gatekeeper was soon in the presence of Ereshkigal. He said to her, "Lady, a traveller is standing at your gate. He is not dead. I do not know who he is, but he is one of the gods."

Ereshkigal looked around at her servants. "Who will go there to identify him?"

Namtar said, "Let me identify him. I will look at him from inside the gate, while he is standing outside, and bring back my report to you."

Namtar went to the gate and looked through the crack. When he recognized Nergal, his face turned as livid as a cut tamarisk tree. His lips turned as dark as the rim of a drinking vessel. He went back to his mistress and said, "Lady, when you sent me to the gods to collect your portion of the feast, the gods knelt and greeted me respectfully, acknowledging the authority that I bore as your representative. Only one god showed no respect. He stayed on his feet. He did not look at me. He is the one who has come to your land, the land from which no one has ever returned."

Ereshkigal listened. She said, "My dear Namtar, do not let your feelings show. Go and bring that god here to me. We will deal with him."

Namtar returned to Ganzer, the outer gate.

He let Nergal in through the first gate of the underworld.

He let Nergal in through the second gate of the underworld.

He let Nergal in through the third gate of the underworld.

He brought Nergal through all seven gates of the underworld, into Ereshkigal's spacious court.

Nergal knelt and kissed the ground before Ereshkigal. He said, "The father of the gods has sent me here."

They brought him a throne to sit on. He reminded himself, "Do not go to it," and did not sit on it.

The baker brought him bread. He reminded himself, "Do not go to it," and did not eat the bread.

The butcher brought him meat. He reminded himself, "Do not go to it," and did not eat the meat.

The cupbearer brought him beer. He reminded himself, "Do not go to it," and did not drink the beer. They brought him a footbath. He reminded himself, "Do not go to it," and did not wash his feet. Finally, Ereshkigal went to the bath. She dressed herself in a fine robe, allowing him to glimpse her body. He reminded himself to resist his desire to do what men and women can do together.

However, after a little time had passed, Ereshkigal went again to the bath chamber, letting her robe fall open, that he might glimpse her body. This was too much for Nergal. This time he did not resist his desire to do what men and women can do together. Ereshkigal and Nergal embraced each other and went passionately to bed.

For one day and a second day, Queen Ereshkigal and Nergal lay together.

For a third day and a fourth day, Queen Ereshkigal and Nergal lay together.

For a fifth day and a sixth day, Queen Ereshkigal and Nergal lay together.

But when the seventh day arrived, Nergal said to Ereshkigal, "I ought to return to the gods in the heavens. I will come back to you another time."

Ereshkigal's lips turned dark with rage. She forebade him to leave her, in no uncertain terms.

But when she went to the bathhouse, he slipped out to the gate. He told the gatekeeper, "Ereshkigal, your lady, sent me. She said, 'I am sending you to speak to An our father.' So, let me out to deliver her message."

The gatekeeper, suspecting nothing, opened the gate for Nergal. Nergal went back up the long stairway to heaven. When the gods saw him, they said, "Nergal has come back from the place from which no one has ever returned. Ereshkigal will certainly send out her servants to search for him. We had better disguise him."

Ea sprinkled him with holy water so that his hair fell out and he became bald. He cringed and blinked, blinked and cringed. No one would have known him for Nergal the warrior.

Down in the underworld, Ereshkigal came back from the bathhouse. She gave orders that a chair be brought for Nergal, and a nice breakfast prepared for him. When Namtar told her, "He made off before daybreak," she was both furious and bereft. Angry tears ran down the sides of her nose.

She cried out, "I have not yet had my fill of him!"

Namtar offered, "Lady, send me up to heaven to arrest that god. Let me bring him back, so that he can kiss you some more."

Ereshkigal said to Namtar, "Go, Namtar, yes. You must speak to the assembly of the gods. Tell them this, 'Since I was a young girl, I have not had the company of other girls. I was lonely then as a child, and I am lonely now, here in my domain. That god you sent to me – let me sleep with him again. Send me that god to be my consort and to spend the nights with me again. If you do not send that god back to me, I will raise up the dead, and they will eat the living. I will make the dead outnumber the living.'"

Namtar accepted his lady's words and took the message into his heart. He ascended the long stairway to heaven.

Ea listened to Ereshkigal's message and responded by saying, "Enter, Namtar, the court of the gods. Search out your wrongdoer and take him back with you."

Namtar went right up to first one god, then another, then a third. He did not recognize Nergal, disguised as he was: bald, blinking and cringing.

When Namtar returned alone to the underworld, he described to Ereshkigal everything he had seen and done. As soon as he mentioned the blinking and cringing god, Ereshkigal interrupted him.

"Go and seize that blinking and cringing god, and bring him to me. Ea has sprinkled him with water to make him seem bald and feeble. He is there, disguised, hiding in plain sight among the gods."

Namtar went back up the long stairway to heaven. When he reached the gates of heaven, the gods asked, "Why are you back here again?"

"My lady sent me back. She gave me an order: 'Seize that blinking and cringing god, and bring him to me.'"

"Then enter once again, Namtar. Search out your wrongdoer and take him."

And so he did. Then Namtar led Nergal back down the long stairway from heaven.

At the first of the seven gates of the underworld, the gatekeeper stopped Nergal, saying, "It is forbidden to take anything with you to the underworld." At each of the gates, the gatekeeper stopped him. Nonetheless, Nergal at last reached the courtyard of the underworld. As he entered, he burst into laughter. He caressed Ereshkigal's hair, once again aroused by her allure.

They embraced each other and went passionately to bed.

For one day and a second day, Queen Ereshkigal and Nergal lay together.

For a third day and a fourth day, Queen Ereshkigal and Nergal lay together.

For a fifth day and a sixth day, Queen Ereshkigal and Nergal lay together.

After seven full days, a messenger came from the great gods in heaven, saying, "That god who came down to you, let him dwell with you for ever."

Ereshkigal said to Nergal, "You can be my husband and I can be your wife."

Nergal listened to her words. He seized and kissed her.

"What have you said to me?" he asked. "After so many days and nights together, it shall certainly be so!"

And so it was. From that time, Nergal became the husband of Ereshkigal. She was lonely no more.

THE MARRIAGE OF MARTU

When the city of Inab already existed, but
the city of Kiritab did not yet exist,
When the holy crown existed, but
the holy tiara did not yet exist,
When the holy herb already existed, but
the holy cedar did not yet exist,
When the holy salt already existed, but
the holy alkali did not,
When sex and kissing already existed,
When giving birth in the fields already existed,
I was the grandfather of the holy cedar,
I was the ancestor of the mes tree,
I was the mother and father of the white cedar,
I was the relative of the hacur cedar.

At that time, there was a prince among cities which sat in the fertile valley. Inab was this prince of cities. The people who lived within the city of Inab were settled and sheltered. They farmed. They sowed seed and reaped barley.

They grew dates. They built with clay bricks. The lives of the people of the city of Inab were organized and orderly. They dressed in clean linen. They bathed in perfumed water and oiled their hair with scented oils. They were civilized, sophisticated, cultured and elegant. The city was governed by rules, laws and customs and the people knew the rules and kept the laws. They knew when to stand up straight and when to bend the knee. Within the city walls, they had a king, whom they honoured. At the king's side sat his lovely wife and his beautiful daughter.

But beyond the walls, beyond the fertile valley, in the wild and mountainous wastelands, there lived another people.

These people were not like the city people. They were wild. They had no settled home. They lived in tents of animal skin. They roamed where they wanted. They were exposed to wind, rain and sun. They dug up roots, caught birds in nets, hunted gazelle. They ate what they could find, dressed in skins. Their eyes were bright, their hair flew in the wind, their skin was rough and weatherworn. They observed their own customs, but they did not bend the knee. Sometimes they raided and carried away the produce of the fertile valley. These were the nomads of the steppe. They were Martu's people.

It was the custom among Martu's people that when the gathering was sufficient and the time came, they would select an assembly place and distribute fairly to all, that which had been gathered. They would distribute rations in the presence of their god. It was accepted that the ration of a single man was one portion, the ration of a married man was two portions and of a married man with a child was three portions. Martu, the young man, and all his friends gathered at the assembly.

Now, since the last gathering, all Martu's friends had become married men. So for the first time they were receiving a double ration. Martu alone remained single, and so he alone received a single ration. His friends looked at his portion and then at their own. One said, "What is this? We are brothers and have always been together." Another said, "Yes, this does not feel right." A third said, "We have always done everything together. We were children together, playing. We were boys together, fighting. Martu is our friend. We have always done the same and been treated the same."

Each one shared a little of their portion with him. He ended up with more of a share than any of them and he was ashamed. But he said nothing.

When, some time later, the next assembly gathered for the giving out of rations, the same thing happened. Martu's friends got double and Martu got single. They each gave him a little of theirs. Again he ended up with more than any of them, and he was ashamed. But this time he went home and spoke to his mother. He said, "Mother, there is a problem. At the gathering, my friends insist on giving me a part of their rations. They are married and I am still single. I get a single ration, and rightly so. Yet I end up with more than anyone. Mother, I am ashamed. I think it is time I got married. Mother, find me a wife."

His mother smiled. She said, "I will give you advice. May my advice be heeded. I shall speak a word. May my word be heard. Find a nice girl that you like. Find a girl of your heart's desire. Marry a wife of your own choosing and bring her home to be a companion to me."

Meanwhile, in the fertile valley, in the city of Inab, a big festival was announced. News travelled to the wastelands, and Martu and his friends came to hear of it. Martu said to his friends, "Let us go.

Let us all go to the festival in the valley. Let us visit the ale houses of Inab."

They left their community, their tents and their families and travelled through the hills. Long before they could see the city, they could hear it. They heard the sounds of the coming festival. The bronze sem drums were rumbling. All seven of the ala drums were resounding like the voices of strong men. As they approached the city below, they saw the irrigated fields, green and verdant; they saw the river flowing past and the boats tied at the quay. They saw the city walls of baked brick and the great wooden city gates open wide. They saw the crowds of the black-headed people streaming into the city. They ran down the hill and let themselves be swallowed by the crowds, swept along in the current of people, through the streets and alleyways of Inab. They found themselves in the crush in the great courtyard of the temple.

Horns were blowing to announce a competition. Martu pushed his way to the front of the crowd. In the open space in the temple courtyards, strong men, the girdled champions, were strutting up and down. It was to be a wrestling match. The wrestlers were demonstrating the curve of their bronzed muscles and the expanse of their oiled chests. Some were tossing clubs and catching them. Some were doing push-ups. Some were adjusting their wrestling girdles and belts. Beyond them Martu saw, on the other side of the courtyard, a dais. On the dais sat the king of Inab and his queen. Between them sat their beautiful daughter.

The horns were still sounding. The wrestling match of the girdled champions had not yet begun. Martu had his eye on the beautiful daughter of the king. He tore off his shirt and wrapped it round his waist as a wrestling belt. All his friends further back in the crowd gasped at the sight of Martu. He was strutting up and down like the competitors, demonstrating the curve of his muscles and the expanse of his chest. The horns fell silent; the call went out for the competitors to make themselves ready and Martu was there in line. He was watching the technique of the city wrestlers. He watched as the girdled champions seized each other by their shoulders, their arms, their legs, their heads. They seized each other by their belts and delivered takedowns, hip throws, leg locks. He watched their stance, their motion, the way they changed levels, their styles of lifting, their backstops, their back arches, their head locks and their arm drags. He watched them fall and he watched them pin each other down.

Then Martu threw himself into the contest. He gouged and twisted and squeezed with compelling strength. He hit out and pummelled and thumped with irresistible force. The courtyard echoed with the slap of oiled flesh hitting stone, the crack of broken bone, the cry of the felled champions. Champion after champion was carried out of the temple courtyard, some groaning, some screaming, some pale and silent. Martu stood alone, panting and sweating. His eyes sparkled and his skin shone. He was impressive. The crowds went wild.

The king was impressed too. He stood and all fell silent. The king rejoiced over Martu. "Impressive. Unorthodox, but without doubt impressive and a clear winner."

The king called for silver. The servants brought the silver and the god offered it to Martu. But Martu politely refused. The king called for jewels, but Martu politely refused. The king offered silver and jewels, but Martu would not accept it. Again the king offered the gifts and this time, Martu spoke. He said, "What is silver? What is its worth? Where does it lead? What are jewels? What is their worth? Where do they lead?"

The king was impressed. "Though you do not want them, even so, these are yours," he said. "You are the victor and I must also give you a prize that you value and desire. It is the rule. What do you desire?"

Martu said, "What do I desire? I desire your beautiful daughter. Rather than silver or jewels, I would rather marry your beautiful daughter. Let the prize be your consent."

The king of Inab sat down heavily. He looked at his feet. Then he looked at his daughter. She was looking wide-eyed at Martu. The king tapped his chin and narrowed his eyes. Then he nodded. "Very well," he said. "I give my consent. But there is a condition. You may marry my beautiful daughter, if she wishes. But you must give for her a wedding gift. It is this: You must give for my daughter calves, and cows to feed the calves. You must create a byre to house the cows and the calves, and the cows and the calves must lie down in the byre. Thus and only thus will I give my consent. You must give for my daughter lambs, and ewes to feed the lambs. You must create a fold to house the ewes and lambs. The ewes and lambs must lie down in the fold. Thus and only thus will I give my consent. You must give for my daughter kids, and goats to feed the kids. Create a pen to house the goats and the kids, and the goats and kids must lie down in the pen. Thus and only thus will I give my consent. Do you agree to my condition?"

Martu said, "I give my word to all this." He cried, "I swear it." He laughed and threw back his head. His black hair whipped in coils and waves around his shoulders, and the king's daughter saw it. He bowed to the king. The king turned to speak to his beautiful daughter. "Daughter, consider." Martu bowed to the beautiful daughter. She caught his dark glance and she watched him as he strode out of the courtyard with the crowd parting before him. She said, "Father, I will consider."

Martu was running through the streets of Inab shouting for joy. He ran down to the quay and shouted his joy across the water. Wherever he went, he gave away the gifts he had been given. He gave gifts to the elders: gold bracelets to the old men and gold shawls to the old women. He gave gold coins to the men and the women. He gave silver jugs and coloured cloths to the slaves.

Then Martu sent his friends home with the rest of the gifts from the king, to find out about how to look after cattle, sheep and goats. He himself took lodgings in the city of Inab to wait for a word from his beloved princess.

But the days passed and he heard nothing from the daughter of the king. The days were multiplying and she did not make her decision. She was sitting in her chamber. It seemed she did not know what to do. She sat with her friend. She lowered her eyes. She said, "I just do not know what to do." Her girlfriend spoke.

She said, "Listen, I will speak a word. Let my word be heard. I will give advice. Let my advice be heeded. Are you mad? How can you even think of marrying Martu? Who is this Martu? What are his customs? What are his people? Who are you? What are your customs? Our people are settled, sheltered. We sow, we reap, we bake bread, we brew beer, we dress in clean linen, we bathe in scented water, we dress our hair elegantly with perfumed oils. We know the rules, we keep the laws, we know when to bend the knee. Martu's people do not live like that. They live a wild life, their faces are rough and worn by wind and rain and sun, they dress in leather, they do not obey the rules, they do as they like."

"Thank you," said the daughter of the king, "I hear your words. I'll marry Martu."

Man of my heart, my beloved man, your allure
is a sweet thing, as sweet as honey.
Lad of my heart, my beloved man, your allure
is a sweet thing, as sweet as honey.
You have captivated me.
Of my own free will, I will come to you.
Man, let me flee with you into the bedroom.
You have captivated me.
Of my own free will, I shall come to you.
Lad, let me flee with you into the bedroom.

THE MOON GOD SIN AND HIS COW

There was once a moon cow. Such a beautiful cow: her form was perfect, her limbs were lithe.

Her name was Geme-Sin. When the moon god Sin saw her, he lost his heart to her, he fell in love with her. He set the glory of moonlight to shine on her. He made her the leader of the herd. He gave her precedence over the whole herd. All the cattle followed her. He found her the best moist grass for her pasture. He led her to fresh meadows with clear pools, where she could drink.

Then, one day, out of sight of the cowherd, when the herdsman was not looking, a fierce young bull mounted this moon cow. She gladly raised her tail for him.

Her months passed, her days were counted, until she went into labour. She knelt down to give birth. But the labour was not easy. She was a young heifer, too young perhaps for such toil. The cowherd was dismayed for her. The herdboys tried to comfort her. Hearing her bellows of pain, her moans in labour, the radiant moon was distressed. The bright moon in heaven, hearing her cries, was desperate. He raised his hand. At this signal, two protective spirits came down from the heavens. One brought a jar of oil. The other brought the water of labour.

The first spirit rubbed oil from the jar on the moon cow's brow.

The second sprinkled the water of labour across her whole body.

Again, the first spirit rubbed oil from the jar on the moon cow's brow.

Again, the second sprinkled the water of labour across her whole body.

A third time, oil was rubbed on the moon cow's brow. A third time, her body was sprinkled.

Like a gazelle in flight, her calf was born and fell to the ground. The calf was named Suckling Calf.

Just as Geme-Sin, the moon cow gave birth successfully, may it be so for any young woman having a difficult labour.

May every woman with child give birth successfully. Let her midwife's work go well.

The midwife says these words to the baby about to be born:

"Run here to me like a gazelle.

"Slip out like a little snake into my hands.

"I am here.

"I am your midwife, ready to receive you!"

NISABA, GODDESS OF WRITING

The initial need for a writing system came from trade. Merchants needed a record of how much they had sold; buyers an account of how much they had spent; the king's officers to know how much tax they could charge. Nisaba, goddess of grain, extended her patronage to the capacity for counting, thence to accounting, and then to recording those accounts. Only after the first simple writing systems had grown more complex was writing used for literary purposes.

In retelling stories which would have been forgotten, had they not been written down, we acknowledge Nisaba, the goddess of writing. By King Ashurbanipal's time, the divinity of writing was considered to be male, the god Nabu. But on one tablet from Ashurbanipal's library, Nisaba is thanked for the gift of writing, showing that she was remembered, from a much earlier time, as goddess of writing and scribes.

A PRAISE HYMN TO NISABA, GODDESS OF SCRIBES (AND ACCOUNTANTS)

Nisaba, you are the lady of the stars of heaven.
You hold the lapis lazuli tablet in your hand.
You are the great wild cow,

The wild sheep nourished on good milk.
You are endowed with fifty divine powers,
Our most powerful lady.

You are a glorious dragon at the festival,
You are a birth goddess of the land.
You set words onto clay.
Your wisdom comes from the Great Mountain,
Enlil's own temple.
You are An's chief scribe, Enlil's record keeper,
The wise one for the gods.

When you have cleaned your body,
When you are adorned in your holy garment,
You oversee the great festival of Enlil,
Making barley and flax grow, making grain flourish,
Providing food in plenty for the harvest.
You have built up abundance for the people.

You appoint the priest of the land,
The one who establishes grain offerings,
Where none were made before,
The one who pours libations to honour Enlil and Ezina.

Enki himself comes close when you, Nisaba, are at prayer.
He brings the pure food offerings.
Then he opens Nisaba's house of learning,
The house of scribes.
He places the lapis lazuli tablet on your lap,
So that you may consult it.

When Enki has completed the purification rites,
He opens your house of learning.
He stands in the street of your house of learning.
He praises your name, Nisaba,
He cherishes you, saying:

"O, Nisaba, good woman, fair woman,
Woman from the mountains!
"You are the butter in the cattle pen,
"The cream in the sheepfold,
"The keeper of the seal of the treasury,
"The steward of the palace
"The heaper-up of grain in the grain stores!"

Because Enki cherishes you, Nisaba,
And because of all that you are,
It is sweet and meet for us to praise you.
Nisaba, goddess of scribes, great is your name!

A SUPERVISOR'S ADVICE TO A YOUNGER SCRIBE

The supervisor speaks: "One-time student at the school, come here to me, and let me explain to you what I learnt from my teacher. Like you, I was young once and had a mentor, who assigned tasks to me. It was man's work. I was like a springing reed; I would leap up and set to work, following my teacher's instructions to the letter. I did not start doing things on my own initiative. He was delighted with my work on the assignment. He was pleased that I was humble before him, and he spoke in my favour. I just did whatever he outlined for me; everything was in place. Only a fool would have deviated from his instructions. He guided my hand on the clay and kept me on the right path. He made me eloquent. He gave me advice. He kept me focused on the rules that guide a man with a task. Zeal is appropriate to a task; time-wasting is not. Anyone who wastes time while at work is neglecting his task.

"He did not boast about his knowledge. He was modest. If he had boasted, people would have frowned on him. Do not waste time, do not rest by night – get on with the work! And do not reject the pleasant company of a mentor or his assistant: contact with such great brains will make your own words more worthy.

"And another thing: you will never go back to your blinkered ways – that would demean due deference, the decency of humankind. When the heart is calm, sins are absolved. Even an empty-handed man's gifts are respected. Even a poor man offers a kid goat, held to his chest, as he kneels. You should defer to the powers that be. This will calm you.

"There, I have recited to you all that my teacher revealed, and you will not neglect it. You should pay attention – taking it to your heart will benefit you!"

The scribe humbly answered his supervisor: "Let me now reply to what you have just recited like some sort of incantation, together with a rebuttal to your charming song and dance, delivered at full volume. Do not make me out to be an ignoramus – I will answer you once and for all! You have done so much for me: you opened my eyes like a puppy's, and made me into a human being. But why do you go on laying down the law to me, as if I were a shirker? Anyone would feel insulted by your words. All that you have taught me about the scribal arts, I have repaid to you. You put me in charge of your household and I have always worked hard for you. I assign the duties of the slaves and servants of your household. I have kept them happy with their allotted rations of food, clothing and oil. I set out their duties to them, so that there is no need for you to follow them around checking up on them. I work on this from the moment I wake, and I drive them like sheep. When you have ordered offerings to be prepared, I have made those offerings for you, on the due days. I have prepared the sheep and the banquets attractively, so that the gods are pleased. When the boat of your god arrives, I ensure that it is greeted with respect.

"When you have ordered me to the fields, I have kept the men working there. It is challenging work, which permits no sleep either by night or in the heat of the day, if the labourers are to do their best in the fields. I have restored quality to your fields, so that they are admired. Whatever task you have set for the oxen, I have exceeded it. Their loads have been fully completed. You have watched over me since my childhood and kept an eye on my behaviour, checking it like fine silver. Without emulating your shortcoming of speaking grandly, I serve you. But know that I want to make something clear to you: you habitually ignore those who undervalue themselves."

The supervisor speaks again: "Raise your head now, you who were formerly a youth. Now you can match any man, so act as is befitting."

The scribe responds: "You offered prayers and blessed me, you filled me with instruction. As if I were consuming milk and butter, you showed the meaning of unceasing service. Through you I have experienced only success, never evil."

The supervisor answers: "Teachers and learned men should value you highly. Your name will be hailed as honourable. For your sweet songs, even the cowherds will strive gloriously. For your sweet songs I too shall strive. You, who as a youth sat at my feet, have pleased my heart.

"Nisaba has placed in your hand the honour of being a teacher. For her, your fate will be changed and you will be generously blessed. You were created by Nisaba! May she bless you with a joyous heart and free you from all despondency in the school, the place of learning. For your sweet songs, even the cowherds will strive gloriously. For your sweet songs I too shall strive. You should be recognized as one who practises wisdom. The little fellows in the school should enjoy, like beer, the sweetness of your words: experts bring light to dark places, to alleyways and to avenues."

Praise Nisaba: the lady whose divine powers are divine powers that have no rival!

ENMERKAR AND THE LORD OF ARATTA

There were two great cities.

The first was a city beside the river on the fertile plains between the River Tigris and the River Euphrates. What a city it was! Two temples were built there. One was in the district of brick-built Kulaba. There the great god An sat down to eat his evening meal. The other was for glorious Inana. That was in the area of Eanna, and there the great goddess, Inana herself, lifted her head up high. This city was like a majestic vigorous bull. It was a city of plenty. It was blessed with all the riches provided by the rains and the river: carp from the waters, bread and beer from the dappled barley in the fields, vegetables, dates and flowers from the gardens, milk and cheese from the sheep pens and baked brick from the red clay. The city of the plains was called Unug. It was built by its young king, Enmerkar. He was wise, successful and strong and he ruled there, they say, for four hundred and twenty years.

The second city was high up in the Zubi Mountains. It was protected and surrounded all about by a strong wall of the mountain ranges. It was a city of great riches and resources. The mountain people would break open the rocks and mine for precious metals: gold, silver, copper and tin. They would uncover precious stone: granite, lapis lazuli, carnelian and obsidian. This city of the mountains was called Aratta. It was also ruled by a fine lord and his name was Ensouggirana.

Both these fine leaders, King Enmerkar and the Lord of Aratta, were empowered by their consort and queen. They both had the same consort and queen, and that was the lady of life herself, the great immortal goddess Inana. Both lords had created for the Lady Inana a magnificent dwelling place with a fantastic bedroom.

In Aratta, Inana's holy place was decorated with the resources of the mountain. Gold, silver and flawless lapis lazuli were formed into the beautiful image of a white mes tree bearing fruit. Inana was pleased with it, and the Lord of Aratta placed on his own head the golden crown for Inana. But it was to become clear, in time, that the gifts of Aratta did not please Inana nearly as much as the gifts of Unug.

In Unug, her holy place was decorated daily with the produce of the river and the plain. There were always scented flowers, dates, beer, cheese and milk, all fresh and beautifully and tastefully arranged. It seems that these pleased Inana very well indeed.

One day, after feasting on the plenty of the fertile plains, King Enmerkar, lord of Unug, went to visit his Lady Inana in her bedroom. He knelt down and prayed. "Oh lady of life! Sister! Wife! Am I not your favourite husband? I'd like to give you something special. I'd like to add to the wonders of your bedroom here in Unug, something even more wonderful: the treasures of Aratta. Let Aratta fashion gold and silver on my behalf for Unug. Let them cut flawless lapis lazuli from the blocks. Let them carry the translucence of the lapis and transport the treasures of Aratta to Unug and build a holy mountain here. Let them bring a temple down from the heavens to your place of worship here. Then may I, the radiant youth, be embraced by you in that new and glorious dwelling. Then, when I am adorned with my holy crown, may the people marvel admiringly and the sun god witness it in joy."

His prayer was answered.

The lady said, "Yes! Good idea. Do it. I shall offer you advice. Let my counsel be heeded. I shall speak words. Let my words be heard. Choose a good messenger from your troops. He must be intelligent, eloquent and have good strong legs and endurance. Send him to Aratta with the message of Inana. Let them know they must send you all the riches of the mountains."

So Enmerkar summoned a fleet-footed messenger. When the messenger came and bowed before the king, Enmerkar said, "Be my envoy. You must run to the Zubi Mountains. You must climb and descend with the message I will give you. It is the message of Inana. When you come at last to Aratta, you must stand before the Lord of Aratta and say this: 'Lest I make you and your people fly like wild doves, lest I make you fly like birds from their nests, lest I sell you like slaves at a market, lest I destroy your city and cover it with dust, lest I do all this, you shall pack nuggets of gold in leather sacks, package up precious metals, bring stone from all stores, load the packs on the donkeys of the mountains and have them come to Unug, and then fashion the gold and silver and copper and tin, cut the translucent lapis lazuli from the flawless blocks. I ask this of you with the blessing of Inana.'"

"Then," said Enmerkar, "You must sing to the Lord of Aratta the Enki song – you know, the one that goes, 'In the fullness of time, when there is no snake, when there is no scorpion, when there is no hyena, when there is no lion, neither dog nor wolf, neither fear nor trembling, when man has no rival, then the whole universe will address the gods together in a single language.' Then you could say, 'But that time has not yet come.' Say it in a sad but subtly threatening way. Have you got that?"

And the messenger said, "Yes." So the king said, "Good! Now go. By night, drive on like the south wind. By day, be up like the dew."

The messenger heard the words of his king. He journeyed by starry night and by day, by the light of Utu, the sun god. He climbed mountain after mountain. He drove on like the south wind. By day he was up like the dew. He was like a sand fly flying through the mountains.

He crossed five, six, seven mountains. He lifted his eyes and saw Aratta. He stepped joyfully into the courtyard of Aratta and before the Lord of Aratta, he made known the authority of Enmerkar, his king.

The messenger said, "Your father, my master, has spoken. The Lord of Unug, the Lord of Kulaba, has sent me to you."

Ensouggirana, Lord of Aratta, asked, "What message has your master sent to me?"

"My king, who from his birth has been fitted for lordship, Lord of Unug, snake in the mountains, stag of the tall mountains, princely antlers, wild cow, kid pawing soapwort with his hoof, King Enmerkar, Lord of Unug, has sent me to you with a message."

Ensouggirana, Lord of Aratta, was affronted. He felt that, from a strange messenger, it was he who should be getting praise in his own city. But he said, "What is it to me what your master has spoken? What is it to me what he has to say?"

"This is the message my master has sent: 'Lest I make you and your people fly like wild doves, lest I make you fly like birds from their nests, lest I sell you like slaves at a market, lest I destroy your city and cover it with dust, lest I do all this, you shall pack nuggets of gold in leather sacks, package up precious metals, bring stone from all stores, load the packs on the donkeys of the mountains and have them come to Unug, and then fashion gold and silver and copper and tin, cut translucent lapis lazuli from flawless blocks. I ask this with the blessing of Inana.'"

And then the messenger sang the Enki song and finished with, "But that time has not yet come." He said it in a sad but subtly threatening way. Then the messenger said, "Say whatever you will say to me, and I shall announce that message as glad tidings to my great lord, husband of Inana in the shrine E-ana."

The Lord of Aratta rose. He said, "These are the 'glad tidings' I send to your king: It is I, Ensouggirana, who is the great lord. I am the husband of Inana. I dwell on the bright mountains. I am the crown of the mountains. I bow to her. She has barred the mountains to others, and I am her lord. How shall I submit to

Unug? Aratta's submission to Unug is out of the question. Say this to him."

The messenger began to improvise. He replied, "But it is the great queen of heaven herself who has told him to send this message. It is clear she does not love you any more. Look! The sky is too blue. There is no rain and the wild barley is not growing."

And it was true. This was the problem in Aratta. There was no rain, there was no food and the people were thin.

The Lord of Aratta was deeply troubled. He became depressed. He had no answer for the messenger. He searched his heart for an answer, but there was none. He stared at his own feet, trying to find an answer. Then an answer came and he gave a cry. He raised his head and bellowed like a bull.

"Speak to your king and say, 'This great mountain is like a tree grown high to the sky. Its roots are a net. Its branches are a snare. It may look like a sparrow to those down there on the plains, but this mountain has the talons of an eagle. My consort Inana has made the mountain ranges into a barrier for us. It is impenetrable.' It is true we are weeping. It is true we suffer. But Inana lacks for nothing. Still we offer water libations for her. Still we sprinkle flour for her. If your king comes, he is heading against a hard foe. He is like the bull who ignores the strong bull at his side. He should acknowledge the bull at his side. That is me. He must acknowledge me as his equal! He should be sending me gifts, not the other way around. Yes! He must send me barley. He must pile it up in my court, but the barley must not be in sacks. It must be barley brought in nets! If he can accomplish this task, then I will submit to him."

Then the Lord of Aratta made the messenger repeat the message, just as he himself had said it. That was no problem for the messenger. He learned the message and turned on his thigh like a wild cow. Like a sandfly he went on his way in the calm of the morning. At last, he stepped joyfully into brick-built Unug and rushed to the great courtyard of the throne room. He repeated the message word for word to his master, the king. He even bellowed at him like a bull. Enmerkar the king listened, received the bellowing and thought. Then he invited the messenger to sit at his own right side. He turned towards him and said, "Does Aratta really understand the implications of his own strategy? Does he think this will confound me? Does he not realize how easy it is for us of the fertile valley to accomplish his request? Carry the grain in nets? Of course we can do this. The brewers do it all the time in preparation for the beer."

After day had broken and Utu the sun god had raised his head, Enmerkar sent for vessels of the waters of the two rivers. He laid out large vessels and small vessels and golden vessels. They looked like lambs lying in the grass. He combined the waters of the Tigris and the Euphrates in the vessels. Then he approached Nisaba the scribe, Nisaba the goddess who measures out the grain. She opened for him her holy house of wisdom. He entered with respect and full attention. She opened to him his mighty storehouse. He removed the old barley from the other. He soaked the barley till it sprouted and became green malt. He narrowed the meshes of the carrying nets so the green malt would not fall through, and he measured the green malt into the nets, adding a generous measure for the teeth of the locusts. It stayed in the nets. It did not fall through the holes. Then he loaded the nets onto the packasses, at whose sides reserve donkeys were placed. He despatched them directly to Aratta. He watched them till they were very far off and they looked like ants climbing through crevices. After an appropriate amount of time, he called the messenger.

"Messenger, go to Aratta and speak to the Lord of Aratta. Say to him, 'The base of my sceptre is the divine power of magnificence. Its crown provides protective shade over Kulaba. Under its spreading branches, holy Inana refreshes herself in the shrine Eanna. I have accomplished what you asked. Now you must submit as you promised, and to show that you submit, you must hold in your hand a mace, but the mace that you hold must be a splinter of mine, to show I am the overlord and you are subservient.' Have you got that?"

"Yes!"

And the messenger went on his way to Aratta. His feet raised the dust of the road and made the little pebbles of the hills thud. Like a dragon prowling the desert, he was unopposed. When he caught up with the packasses, he broke into a trot, fell into step with them and entered Aratta alongside them. The people of Aratta stepped forward to admire the packasses. In the courtyard of Aratta, the messenger measured out the barley for the granary. As if from the rains of heaven and the sunshine, Aratta was filled with abundance. Aratta's hunger was sated. The people were fed. In hope, they planted the sprouting barley.

Then the people of Aratta called for their lord to submit to Unug. The elders of Aratta were wringing their hands in despair. The messenger stood before the lord and spoke. He recited the message about the mace, "Your mace of power must be a splinter of mine to show you are subservient. What is your answer?"

Aratta listened to the message and then went inside to his sanctuary. He lay down and he fasted. Day broke. The sky was blue and the sun was unrelenting. The Lord of Aratta called the elders and advisors. They discussed the matter at length. He spoke words his advisors had thought unspeakable. He talked the matter round and round, as if it were being eaten by a donkey. What did one speak to another? What did one say to another? The matter was thoroughly discussed, and at last a decision was made. What one said to another, so indeed it was.

Aratta called the messenger. He said, "Messenger, speak to your king. Say, 'I will submit, but there is a condition. Let Enmerkar put in his hand a mace that is not of any sort of metal, nor any sort of stone, nor any sort of wood, nor any sort of thing that grows. Let him bring me a little mace like that and I will take it and submit and show I am subservient.'"

The messenger ran like a young donkey, trotted like an onager, then walked a bit. Then he filled his mouth with wind and ran on one track. He set foot, dusty and exhausted, but joyful, into brick-built Kulaba. He transmitted the message word for word and the Lord Enmerkar listened and was thoughtful. Enmerkar entered the shrine of Enki, god of wisdom and fresh water, and great god Enki gave wisdom. Enmerkar listened to the words of the god and he gave instructions to the people. The people searched for the largest reeds from the riverbank. They pulled them up by the roots and brought them back, and they planted them in soil they had prepared. From the sunlight, they passed into the shade and from the shade they emerged into the sunlight. There grew a huge strong reed. He ordered the people to pound animal hides into a paste, and the resin that ran from the paste they poured into the big hollowed reed. After time had passed, the king split the reed with an axe. The king took out the hardened resin wand from within the reed. It was a strong sceptre made not from metal, stone or wood. He oiled it and put it in the hands of the messenger.

The messenger was like a pelican on the hills, like a fly over the ground. He darted like the swimming fish and reached Aratta. He set foot joyfully into the courtyard of Aratta, got out the sceptre, polished it and put it into the hand of the Lord of Aratta.

The Lord of Aratta eyed the sceptre but said nothing. He called his elders. They said, "What is it made of? Aratta is indeed like a slaughtered sheep. Holy Inana has given the primacy of Aratta to the Lord of Kulaba. Now it seems that she is looking with favour on the one who has sent the message. Where can we go in this crisis? Are we to prostrate ourselves before the Lord of Kulaba?" But the Lord of Aratta was resourceful. He called the messenger. He said, "Very well. I will submit. But we do of course have to have the formality of the champion fight. Once we've had the champion fight, I will submit. And if your champion can defeat my champion, I will submit. And by the way, our tradition is that a champion must dress in a garment that is not black-coloured, a garment that is not white-coloured, a garment that is not brown or red or yellow-coloured or any mixture of colours! If your king does this, then I will hold the little sceptre and I will submit. Tell your master this."

The messenger dragged his feet home. In brick-built Kulaba, in front of King Enmerkar, he gave the message. King Enmerkar heard the message. At first, he was speechless. Then he rolled his eyes. He gazed like a goat on the mountain slopes. Then he lifted his head and addressed the messenger like a raging torrent. He said, "For goodness' sake! He is just prevaricating. Tell him this: 'A garment that is not black-coloured, a garment that is not white-coloured, a garment that is not brown or red or yellow-coloured or any mixture of colours?' I shall give you such a garment! My champion is embraced by Enlil, the earth god. I shall send you my champion. Say that to him. Then secondly, tell him immediately to pass from subterfuge. Then repeat my original message: 'Lest I make you and your people fly like the wild doves, lest I make you fly like birds from the nests, lest I sell you like slaves at a market, lest I destroy your city…' and all the rest of that. And the bit about fashioning the gold and the lapis and bringing it to Unug. What is more, say, 'You must lead your people in procession when they bring these treasures to Unug. We will process into the temple of Inana and I will go first and hold the big sceptre, and you will go last and hold the little sceptre, to show you are subservient. All this with the blessing of Inana.' Then sing him the Enki song – you know, the one that goes 'In the fullness of time all creatures will be at peace and speak the same language', and then you say, 'But that time has not yet come,' in a really threatening way. Have you got that?"

His speech was substantial and its contents extensive. The messenger was not able to repeat it. The messenger said, "No! It is too much and I am too tired. Even my mouth is tired. My mouth is heavy."

And the Lord of Unug looked at the messenger and saw it was true. The messenger was completely worn out.

So the king took clay and he folded and rounded and slapped it into a tablet. He took a stylus and he pressed it into the clay. He pressed shapes into the clay: shapes, symbols, letters, words, language into the clay. Before this moment, the writing of messages on clay was not established. Now, under that sun and on that day, King Enmerkar inscribed his message on a clay tablet. He wrote the first diplomatic letter. He baked the clay tablet. He gave it to the messenger.

The messenger gave it to the Lord of Aratta.

The Lord of Aratta looked at the tablet. All the little dark shadows in straight lines on the clay looked like pictures of nails. It looked to him for all the world like an army of soldiers marching over a plain. He said, "What can I do? All these soldiers! I must submit."

Then there was a rumble of thunder in the distance, clouds rolled across the sky and it started to rain. The gods were thundering in heaven and earth. There was a raging storm making the mountains quake. The mountain range raised its voice in joy. On Aratta's parched flanks, in the midst of the mountains, wheat grew of its own accord and chickpeas grew of their own accord. The people brought the wheat into the granary for the Lord of Aratta and heaped it up before him in the courtyard of Aratta.

All the people of Aratta were cheering. And just at that moment the great gates of the city of Aratta creaked open and there was a host from Unug. There was King Enmerkar. There was his champion. The champion was dressed neither in black nor white nor any colour. He was dressed in untreated animal skin. King Enmerkar looked sternly at the Lord of Aratta and said, "Submit."

But the Lord of Aratta held out his hand to indicate the rain and raised an eyebrow at the king. It was an impasse. Everyone knew that the next step might be war.

Then a woman walked down from the mountains and in through the gates of the city of Aratta. She was old and beautiful. She walked into the city and the crowds parted before her. She raised her arm and it was like a beam of moonlight. She spoke. "It is the will of Enlil that this contest ends. It is not the will of

Enlil that there will be war. Instead there will be a sharing. The people of Aratta will dig in the mountains. They will mine gold, silver, tin, copper, carnelian and lapis and they will send it to Unug. The people of Unug will dig. They will sow and grow and harvest. They will harvest figs, grapes, barley, cheese. They will send it to Aratta. Let this exchange be called trade. Let there be trade, not war."

King Enmerkar looked at the Lord of Aratta, and the Lord of Aratta looked at Enmerkar. Enmerkar pursed his lips and Aratta raised an eyebrow. Enmerkar held out his hand and Aratta took it. They both smiled and everyone cheered. King Enmerkar said to Aratta, "Your wife is a clever woman." The Lord of Aratta said, "I thought she was your wife." Everyone looked round, but the beautiful old woman was gone.

A DUEL BETWEEN WIZARDS

Look at the fine city of Unug: like a rainbow arching across the sky, like the shining new moon!

Look at Kulaba, the god's temple in Unug, reaching from earth up to the heavens!

Founded on an auspicious day, made of magnificent brickwork, built with all the great powers, bright as moonlight and sunshine, abundant as a herd of good cattle: all this is Unug. Its radiance is like fine silver scattered over Aratta, its beauty like a linen garment spread over Aratta. Is this not a fine setting for Lord Enmerkar, lord of this story?

At that time, the day was lord, the night was lady, and Utu the sun was king over all.

The Lord of Unug, Enmerkar, had a minister. The Lord of Aratta had a minister too.

In consultation with his minister, the Lord of Aratta sent a disrespectful message to Enmerkar.

He told his messenger, "Say this: 'Let Unug submit to me, let it bear my yoke. Enmerkar may share his walled house with Inana, but here in Aratta I share the lapis lazuli house with Inana. Enmerkar may lie with Inana on a splendid bed, as he considers it, but I sleep sweetly with her on our decorated bed. He may dream of Inana by night, but I talk freely with her by day. He may feed his geese with barley, but I definitely do no such thing. Into my basket go the eggs and the goslings. The small ones go in the pot, the large ones go in the kettle. Those who submit to me may share what remains of the geese.' Give him this message!"

Aratta's messenger left in the early morning: by dusk he had already returned. He raced like a wild ram, he flew like a falcon. He disappeared in the mountainous lands, like a small bird at midnight; he re-emerged in the open country, like a small bird at dawn. Like a thoroughbred donkey, large and powerful, he ran across the mountains. He rushed forward like a slim donkey. He roared like a lion in a field. He ran like a wolf that has seized a lamb.

In no time he was in Lord Enmerkar's presence in his holy shrine.

"My king has sent me to you. The Lord of Aratta has sent me to you. This is what my king says..." The messenger repeated his lord's message, word for word.

Enmerkar heard the message of Aratta. He listened to it but he did not submit to it. Instead he weighed it up as if it were a lump of clay, he read it as if it were a clay tablet.

Then he replied, "Aratta may share a lapis lazuli house with Inana, but I dwell with her as her earthly consort. Aratta may lie with Inana on a splendid bed, but I rest in sweet slumber with her on our bed strewn with perfumed plants. At the head and foot of our bed, lions are carved. As the lions chase each other from head to foot, the night does not progress, the dawn does not come. When Inana makes a journey, I accompany her. Utu the sun god watches out for me. Enlil, father of the gods, has given me the true crown and sceptre. Ninurta, Enlil's son, the warrior god, held me on his knees. Aruru, Enlil's sister, goddess of childbirth, suckled me from her right breast, from her left breast. When I go up to the great shrine, the goddess cries out like an Anzud chick. No city is as well built as Unug. It is in Unug that Inana dwells: what does Aratta have to do with that? Her temple is brick-built Kulaba: what can Aratta do about that?

"For at least five, maybe ten years, the great lady will not go to Aratta. Because the holy lady of the temple took counsel with me about whether to go to Aratta, and because she consulted me about this matter, I know that she will not go to Aratta.

"How might one who has no barley feed the geese with barley? I am the one who will feed the geese with barley. Into my basket go the eggs and the goslings. The small ones go in the pot, the large ones go in the kettle. Those who submit to me may share what remains of the geese."

When Enmerkar's response was brought back to him, the Lord of Aratta searched for an answer, asked for instructions. He summoned all his priests and took counsel with them.

"What shall I say to him?" he asked in frustration. "What shall I say to him? What shall I say to the Lord of Unug, the Lord of Kulaba? Look at what is going on! His bull stood up to fight my bull, and his bull won! His man wrestled with my man, and his man won! His warrior struggled with my warrior, and his warrior won!"

Those he had assembled answered him plainly. "It was you who started it! You sent a boastful message to Unug for Enmerkar. You cannot stop Enmerkar. You have to stop yourself! You must calm things down."

"Even if my city becomes a ruined mound," declared the Lord of Aratta, "I will be a broken tablet there. I will never submit to the Lord of Unug!"

Now there was, at that time, a sorcerer in the service of the Lord of Aratta. When his home city, Hamazu, had been destroyed, he had come from there to Aratta. He had brought his skills of sorcery from Hamazu and now practised in the inner chamber of Aratta's shrine.

He said to the Lord of Aratta's minister, "My Lord, why is it that the great fathers of the city do not give advice? I can make Unug submit to the shrine of Aratta. I can make the whole land, from below to above, from the sea to the Cedar Mountains, from the aromatic mountains to the skies, submit to my forces. I will make the people of Unug dig canals, I will make them bring us their goods by boat, I will make them bring a whole flotilla of offerings to the lapis lazuli temple of Aratta."

The minister spoke with his lord. "My Lord, why is it that the great fathers of the city do not give advice? The sorcerer says he can make Unug submit to the shrine of Aratta. He can make the whole land, from below to above, from the sea to the Cedar Mountains, from the aromatic mountains to the skies, submit to his forces. He will make the people of Unug dig canals, he will make them bring us their goods by boat, he will make them bring a whole flotilla of offerings to the lapis lazuli temple of Aratta."

This made the lord extremely happy. He gave the sorcerer five minas of silver. He promised him allocations of fine food and fine drink.

The sorcerer set off for Enmerkar's lands, the lands under the care of the goddess of writing and grain, Nisaba. He went straight to the cattle pen. The cow trembled with fear before him. The sorcerer used his powers to make the cow talk with him as if it were human. Its voice was soft as butter and sweet as milk, and almost too low to be heard.

"Cow, who will eat your butter? Who will drink your milk?"

"My butter will be eaten by Nisaba. My milk will be drunk by Nisaba. The bright crown of my cheese is destined for the great dining hall of Nisaba herself. Until my milk and butter are sent from the cattle pen, Nisaba, first lady of the land, will impose no duties on the people."

"Cow, I send your butter to your shining horns. I send your milk to your back!"

So the cow's butter was wasted on its horns, its milk wasted on its back. Poor cow!

The sorcerer went further, to Nisaba's holy sheepfold. The goat trembled with fear before him. The sorcerer used his powers to make the goat talk with him as if it were human. Its voice was shrill and whiny, though it did its best to speak clearly.

"Goat, who will eat your butter? Who will drink your milk?"

"My butter will be eaten by Nisaba. My milk will be drunk by Nisaba. The bright crown of my cheese is destined for the great dining hall of Nisaba herself. Until my milk and butter are sent from the sheepfold, Nisaba, first lady of the land, will impose no duties on the people."

"Goat, I send your butter to your shining horns. I send your milk to your back!"

So the goat's butter was wasted on its horns, its milk wasted on its back. Poor goat!

That was a dark day for Enmerkar's people. The cattle pen became a silent house, the sheepfold was dealt a disaster. There was no milk in the cow's udder: its calf went hungry and wept bitterly. There was no milk in the goat's udder: its kid went hungry and both goat and kid lay starving. The cow spoke bitterly to its calf. The goat spoke bitterly to its kid.

It was indeed a dark day. The cattle pen became a silent house, the sheepfold was dealt a disaster. The cowherd dropped his staff: he was shocked. The shepherd put down his crook: he wept. The shepherd's boy did not go into the sheepfold: he went another way. The milk carrier did not sing loudly, but walked away, sobbing quietly. Nisaba's cowherd and shepherd were brothers who had grown up in the cattle pen and the sheepfold. They knelt down at sunrise before the great gate of the city and appealed to Utu for help. They told him everything. "The sorcerer of Aratta entered the cattle pen and the sheepfold. He dried up all the milk, so that the little calves had no nourishment, so that the young kids could get no milk. He caused great distress and made both milk and butter scarce. It is a disaster."

These were the holy lands of Nisaba, they were in her care. She was not about to allow them to be overwhelmed by disaster. She called for her Wise Woman, Sagburu, to challenge the wizard of Aratta. She knew well that Sagburu was more than a match for any Hamazu-trained wizard.

And so Wise Woman Sagburu challenged the sorcerer. At Nisaba's command, she made her way towards the Euphrates, the river of the gods. There she met Aratta's sorcerer.

Both of them threw fish spawn into the river. The sorcerer used this to create a giant carp, which he brought out of the river. What was he thinking of? What use could it be? Wise Woman Sagburu used the spawn to create an eagle, which rose from the waters. Her eagle seized his giant carp and flew away with it to the mountains.

A second time they threw fish spawn into the river. The sorcerer made a ewe and a lamb, which came out of the river. Why did he choose such puny creatures? Wise Woman Sagburu made a wolf come from the waters. Her wolf seized his ewe and lamb and dragged them into the wide desert.

A third time they threw fish spawn into the river. The sorcerer made a cow and its calf, which came out of the river. These were not animals to inspire fear or awe! Wise Woman Sagburu, however, made a lion. Of course, her lion seized his cow and its calf and dragged them off to the reedbeds.

A fourth time they threw fish spawn into the river. The sorcerer made an ibex and a wild sheep come out of the river. But Wise Woman Sagburu made a mountain leopard, which seized his ibex and sheep and took them to the mountains.

A fifth time they threw fish spawn into the river. The sorcerer made a young gazelle come out of the river. What kind of defences does a young gazelle possess? It was easy prey to the tiger and lion created by Wise Woman Sagburu. Her tiger and lion seized his gazelle and took it to the forest.

What happened darkened the face of the sorcerer and his mind became confused.

Wise Woman Sagburu spoke to him, "Sorcerer, you have plenty of magic, but not much sense! What on earth made you think you could do sorcery in the city of Nisaba, the city beloved of An and Enlil, the primaeval city?"

The sorcerer answered humbly, "I went there without knowing all this. I acknowledge that you are greater than me. Please do not resent me."

He pleaded for his life, he prayed to her, "Set me free, my sister, set me free. Let me go home in peace to my city. Let me return safely to Aratta. There I will tell everyone of your greatness. I will sing praise to you in Aratta, on the lustrous divine mountain."

But Wise Woman Sagburu answered him severely, "You brought distress to the cattle pen and the sheepfold, to the cows and goats and to their herdsmen. You made butter and milk scarce. You cut off food from the lunch table, the morning table and the evening meal in the great dining hall, causing great hardship. Long ago, Nanna the king established this would be a capital offence, and I am not pardoning your life. Your deeds cannot be forgiven."

Wise Woman Sagburu brought her decision to Nisaba's assembly. They had no objections. So she threw her prisoner from the bank of the Euphrates. The river carried him away. Wise Woman Sagburu took his life force and then returned to her home.

When the Lord of Aratta heard all that had happened, he sent a messenger to Enmerkar to speak words of penitence.

"Enmerkar, you alone are the beloved of Inana, you are the exalted one. Inana has truly chosen you alone: you are her beloved. From the west to the east, you are the great lord, and I am only second to you. From the moment of my conception, I was never your equal. You are the older brother. I can never match you."

In this contest between Enmerkar and the Lord of Aratta, Enmerkar was proved superior.

Praise be to Nisaba, mighty goddess, whose wise sorceress easily outmatched Aratta's best hope.

NISABA, GODDESS OF WRITING

INANA

This grouping of Inana's stories is modern. We have no evidence that these stories were intended as a cycle, though they are interlinked and connected, making the story arc thus created very pleasing.

Inana grows from a young woman to a queen by winning the Me, symbols of power, and thence to a bride and mature woman. The story in which she abandons everything and descends to the underworld is frequently cited today in feminist circles and studies of grief and loss. Whether or not it is possible to explore such an ancient story from a modern mindset, it remains undeniable that this myth is one of the best-known of the Sumerian stories translated to date.

THE HULUPPU TREE

In those days, those distant days,
In those nights, those distant nights,
In those ancient days, when everything that
was needed was brought into being,
In those ancient days, when everything that
was needed was properly nourished,
When bread was first baked in the shrines of the land,

When bread was first eaten in the homes of the land,
When the sky separated from the earth,
And the earth moved away from the sky,
When the names of all things had been fixed.
It was when An took the heavens as his domain.
And Enlil took control of the earth.
When Ereshkigal, great queen, was given the underworld to rule;
When destinies were established.
This was when he set sail.
The god of wisdom set sail.
Enki set sail for the underworld. He sailed into a great storm.
It was a storm of small hailstones, a storm of large hailstones.
The small ones struck like hammer blows,
The large ones like missiles hurled by a catapult.
Small waves butted Enki's little boat like turtles.
Large waves at his bow rose like wolves;
Fierce waves at his stern attacked like lions.
The force of that storm threw the whole world into confusion.

At that time, a tree, a single tree, a Huluppu tree, grew on the bank of the pure Euphrates. Its roots were watered by the pure Euphrates. Its crown of leaves was stirred by the great river's breezes. But the force of this storm tore out its roots, stripped off its branches and the flood waters carried it away. A woman who walked respecting the words of the sky god An; a woman who walked respecting the words of the earth god Enlil; the woman Inana was walking along the river bank. She saw the tree in the river. She caught it, pulled it out of the river and took it to her garden, her lovely garden, her own garden, in her own city of Unug. She planted that tree in her garden with her own hands. She pressed down the earth around its roots with her own feet. She looked at the tree. She wondered, "When will this become a glorious throne, for me to sit on? When will it become a luxuriant bed, for me to lie on?" She knew those times had not yet come. So she waited. Five years went by. Ten years went by. The tree grew massive, yet its bark still had not split.

But then a snake that could not be charmed coiled in the roots of her tree.

An Anzu bird made its nest in the branches of her tree.

And the phantom maiden, the laughing maiden, made her home in the trunk of her tree. She laughed. Oh, how the phantom maiden laughed. Inana wept. Oh, how she wept. Yet they would not leave her tree.

When dawn was breaking, when the horizon grew bright and the little birds began to sing, the sister came to her brother's house. The Lady Inana came to the sun god, Utu.

She said to him, "Brother, a tree, a single tree, a Huluppu tree, grew on the bank of the pure Euphrates. Its roots were watered by the pure Euphrates. Its crown of leaves was stirred by the great river's breezes. But a mighty storm tore out its roots, stripped off its branches and the flood waters carried it away. I was walking along the river bank, and I saw the tree in the river. I caught it, pulled it out of the river and took it to my garden, my lovely garden, my own garden, in my own city, Unug. I planted that tree in my garden with my own hands. I pressed down the earth around its roots with my own feet. I looked at the tree, wondering, 'When will this become a glorious throne, for me to sit on? When will it be a luxuriant bed, for me to lie on?' I have waited for five years, for ten years. The tree has grown massive, yet its bark still has not split. But now a snake that cannot be charmed has coiled in the roots of my tree. An Anzu bird has made its nest in the branches of my tree. And the phantom maiden, the laughing maiden, has made her home in the trunk of my tree. I wept. Oh, how I wept. Yet they will not leave my tree."

Utu, the sun god, heard the words of the Lady Inana. But the brother did not listen to the sister. He would not help her.

When a second dawn was breaking, when the horizon grew bright and the little birds began to sing, the sister came to her other brother's house. The Lady Inana came to the Hero King, Gilgamesh.

She said to him, "Brother, a tree, a single tree, a Huluppu tree, grew on the bank of the pure Euphrates. Its roots were watered by the pure Euphrates. Its crown of leaves was stirred by the great river's breezes. But a mighty storm tore out its roots, stripped off its branches and the flood waters carried it away. I was walking along the river bank and I saw the tree in the river. I caught it, pulled it out of the river and took it to my garden, my lovely garden, my own garden, in my own city, Unug. I planted that tree in my garden with my own hands. I pressed down the earth around its roots with my own feet. I looked at the tree, wondering, 'When will this become a glorious throne, for me to sit on? When will it be a luxuriant bed, for me to lie on?' I have waited for five years, for ten years. The tree has grown massive, yet its bark still has not split. But now a snake that cannot be charmed has coiled in the roots of my tree. An Anzu bird has made its nest in the branches of my tree. And the phantom maiden, the laughing maiden, has made her home in the trunk of my tree. I wept. Oh, how I wept. Yet they will not leave my tree." Gilgamesh, the Hero King, heard the words of the Lady Inana. The brother listened to his sister. He stood by her.

Gilgamesh strapped on his heavy belt – to him it was light as a feather. He took up his bronze axe – this also was, to him, as light as a feather. He went to Inana's garden, her holy garden in Unug. He raised his axe and struck a mighty blow against the tree. With this first blow, he killed the snake that could not be charmed. He raised the axe and struck again. At this second blow, the Anzu bird spread its wings and flew away into the mountains with its young. He raised the axe a third time. At this, the phantom maiden abandoned the tree and fled into the wilderness. As for the tree, Gilgamesh uprooted it and stripped off its branches. His men cut up the branches and bundled them up.

From the trunk of the tree Gilgamesh made a glorious throne for his sister Inana to sit on.

From the trunk of the tree Gilgamesh made a luxuriant bed for the Lady Inana to lie on.

Inana looked at her glorious throne, her luxuriant bed.

"Ah," she said, "Long have I waited to sit upon my glorious throne and rule my people. Long have I waited to lie upon my luxuriant bed and love my consort."

And she knew those times had not yet come, but that come, in time, they would.

INANA WINS THE ME

Inana placed on her head the shugurra, the crown of the steppe. She said, "I will go walking in my holy garden, in my city of Unug." In her garden, Inana leaned back against an apple tree to admire her genitals. Rejoicing at her own remarkable genitals, the Lady Inana applauded herself.

She said, "I will go to visit Enki, the god of wisdom. I will go to his temple, the Abzu, at the place of deep sweet waters. I will visit Enki there, in his own temple."

Inana set out.

While she was still far off from the Abzu, Father Enki, the all-seeing, all-knowing one, became aware that she was on her way.

He called to his sukkal, his faithful servant, "Isimud, come here!"

"My lord, I stand to serve you."

"Isimud, the young woman is on her way to the Abzu. When she reaches my temple, make her welcome. Pour out cool water, that she may refresh herself. Offer her butter cake and beer. Make her welcome here, in my house. Greet her as my equal. Make her as welcome as if she were in her best friend's house."

Isimud heard the words of Enki. He listened to them. When Inana arrived at the Lions Gate, Isimud was waiting for her. He poured out cool water for her to refresh herself. He offered her butter cake and beer. He made her welcome. He greeted her from Enki as an equal.

Inana went through the Lions Gate. She entered the Abzu.

Enki and Inana drank beer together.

They drank more beer together.

They drank more and more beer together.

Enki drank deep, but Inana was circumspect in her drinking.

They raised the bronze vessels, they filled them to overflowing, they clashed them together. They toasted each other. They challenged each other.

Enki rose, swaying with drink. He said, "In the name of my power, in the name of my holy shrine, to my daughter Inana, to holy Inana, I give heroism and power; wickedness and righteousness; the plundering of cities; both lamenting and rejoicing."

Inana said, "I take them!"

A second time, swaying with drink, Enki arose. He said, "In the name of my power, in the name of my holy shrine, to my daughter Inana, to holy Inana, I give deceit and kindness: the rebel lands; both movement and stillness."

Inana said, "I take them!"

A third time, swaying with drink, Enki arose. He said, "In the name of my power, in the name of my holy shrine, to my daughter Inana, to holy Inana, I give the craft of the carpenter, the craft of the coppersmith, the craft of the scribe, the craft of the leather worker, the craft of the fuller, the craft of the builder, the craft of the reed worker."

Inana said, "I take them!"

Enki continued to give to Inana, time after time, the Me, the symbols of power, always in the name of his power, the name of his holy shrine. Inana accepted them all.

She accepted wisdom, attentiveness and holy rites. She accepted the shepherd's hut, the glowing charcoal, the sheepfold. She accepted awe, reverent silence and respect. She accepted the kindling and extinguishing of fire. She accepted ancestors and descendants. She accepted the family. She accepted strife, triumph, counselling, comforting, passing judgement and making decisions.

Each time, Enki offered the Me. "In the name of my power, in the name of my holy shrine." Each time, Inana said, "I take them!"

When Enki had exhausted his generosity, Inana rose to her feet. She was not swaying with drink. Her mind was unclouded.

She related all the Me, symbols of power, which Enki had given to her, naming each one according to its quality, reciting them in the right order. She thanked Enki. Then she gathered up the divine powers and had them loaded into the Boat of Heaven. The Boat of Heaven was pushed off from the quay. Inana left the Abzu.

When the beer had gone out of the one who had drunk beer, when the beer had gone out of Father Enki, he lifted his aching head, prized open his bleary eyes and squinted around the Abzu. He noticed the dusty shelves, the dark corners, the empty niches.

Enki called to his sukkal, Isimud. Isimud came at once. "My lord, I stand to serve you." Enki, his expression pained, motioned to Isimud to speak more quietly. Enki found even his own voice harsh and troubling. He beckoned to Isimud to come closer, and whispered to him, "Isimud, where is the passing of judgement? I do not see it."

Isimud replied, "My lord, you have given it to the Lady Inana."

"Oh," said Enki. "Where is the making of decisions?"

Isimud replied, "My lord, you have given it to the Lady Inana."

"Ah," said Enki. "And where are the ancestors and descendants?"

Isimud replied, "My lord, you have given them to the Lady Inana."

"Hmmm," said Enki. "And what about the craft of the carpenter, the craft of the coppersmith, the craft of the scribe, the leather worker, the fuller, the builder, the reed worker?"

Enki was not altogether surprised, though less than pleased, when Isimud replied, "My lord, you have given them to the Lady Inana."

Fourteen more times, Father Enki enquired about three, four, five Me: holy symbols of power.

Fourteen more times, Isimud replied, "My lord, you have given them to the Lady Inana. You have given them all to the Lady Inana."

Enki gave this some thought. Then he asked, "Isimud, where is Inana now?"

"My lord, she is upon the waters, in the Boat of Heaven. She is one quay away from Eridu, from the Abzu."

Then Enki said, "Go, Isimud, and take the enkum creatures with you! Let Inana continue on her journey, but bring back the Boat of Heaven with the Me."

When Isimud reached the Boat of Heaven, he called out, "My lady, a word, if you please, a word from Lord Enki."

Inana turned to Isimud. "What more has Father Enki said?" she asked. "He has been generosity itself. What other words has he spoken?"

"My lady, Father Enki's words are serious. Very serious. His words may not be countermanded. He bids you continue on your journey. He bids me bring back the Boat of Heaven with the holy Me to Eridu."

Then Inana spoke up angrily, "Deceitfully did my father speak to me! Deceitfully he offered me the Me!"

The enkum creatures surrounded the boat. Inana stood. She called out. "Ninshubur, my sukkal, come to me now. Once you were queen of the East. Now you are my faithful companion. Water has not touched your hand, water has not touched your foot. Defend the gifts that were freely given to me!"

Ninshubur struck the air with her hand. She uttered an earth-shattering cry. The enkum creatures fled from her in terror. They raced back to Eridu.

When Enki saw Isimud returning empty-handed, he asked, "Isimud, where is Inana now?"

"My lord, she is upon the waters, two quays away from Eridu, from the Abzu."

Then Enki said, "Go, Isimud, and take the fifty uru giants with you! Let Inana continue on her journey, but bring back the Boat of Heaven with the Me."

When Isimud reached the Boat of Heaven, the uru giants surrounded the boat. Inana stood. Once again she called for Ninshubur. Ninshubur struck the air with her hand. She uttered an earth-shattering cry. The uru giants flew away in terror at the sound. They fled back to Eridu.

When Enki saw Isimud returning empty-handed, he asked, "Isimud, where is Inana now?"

"My lord, she is upon the waters, three quays away from Eridu, from the Abzu."

Then Enki said, "Go, Isimud, and take the fifty lahama monsters with you! Bring back the Boat of Heaven with the Me."

The lahama monsters of the deep sweet waters surrounded the Boat of Heaven. But Ninshubur drove them away, and Inana kept possession of the divine powers, the Me that had been presented to her.

However, Enki spoke to Isimud a fourth time, saying, "Where is Inana now?"

"My lord, she has just reached the Field Hill."

"Go, Isimud, take all the great fish together. They are to remove the Boat of Heaven from her!"

While Inana's words of complaint were still in her mouth, the great fish went to seize the Boat of Heaven. So Inana called out to Ninshubur. She routed them.

A fifth time, Enki sent the guardians of Unug.

A sixth time, he sent the watchmen of the Surungal Canal.

Each time, Ninshubur kept the Boat of Heaven and the holy Me safe for Inana.

As Enki went to speak to Isimud a seventh time, the Boat of Heaven reached the gate of Inana's city Unug, the gate called the Gate of Joy. Ninshubur spoke to Inana, "My lady, today you have brought the Boat of Heaven to the Gate of Joy. Now there will be rejoicing in your city, the people will throng the streets, full of awe."

Inana replied, "Yes, the Boat of Heaven shall pass in magnificence through the city. The people shall stand in the streets full of awe."

As the Boat of Heaven passed through the city streets, the people lined the streets in awe. Old men offered comfort, old women offered counsel. Young men offered strength of arms, young women offered strength of purpose. The children were full of joy; they danced and sang.

When the Boat of Heaven reached the White Quay, Inana disembarked. On her orders the Me were unloaded and presented to the people. Inana named each of the Me as it was presented.

Meawhile, back in the Abzu, Enki spoke again to his sukkal Isimud, asking, "Isimud, where is Inana now?"

"My lord, Inana has reached the White Quay. She has disembarked and is presenting the Me to the people of Unug."

"Very well," said Enki. "Go, Isimud! Go to the White Quay. Do honour to Inana in her holy city. Listen as the Me are presented, and give more Me to Inana. Take her the art of women. Take allure to her, and the placing of the garment upon the ground. Take her the tigi drums and lili drums. Take her the perfect execution of the Me. Let Inana's name be praised in her own city."

And so it was that there were more Me, more than Inana had been given.

When all the Me had been presented, Inana said, "Where the Boat of Heaven docked, that place shall be known as the White Quay. Where the Me have been presented, that shall be known as the Lapis Lazuli Quay."

The citizens of Unug rejoiced, and Enki spoke once more.

"In the name of my power, in the name of my holy shrine, let the Me remain in your shrine, Inana, in the holy temple of your city. Let your citizens prosper, let their children rejoice. Let the city of Unug, Inana's holy city, be restored to its great place."

May Unug indeed be restored.

DUMUZI AND ENKIMDU

Lady Inana met the sun god Utu. The sister met her brother.

He said to her, "Lady, the fields are lovely in their fullness. The flax is glistening in the furrows. Let me harvest it for you, let me bring it to you. A piece of linen, large or small, is always needed. Let me bring the flax to you."

She answered him, "Brother, if you bring flax to me, who will comb it for me?"

He replied, "Sister, I will bring it to you combed."

Inana said, "But, Lord, if you bring combed flax to me, who will spin it for me?"

Utu replied, "Lady, I will bring it to you spun."

Inana said, "But, Lord, if you bring spun flax to me, who will braid it for me?"

He replied, "Lady, I will bring it to you braided."

She said, "Then, brother, if you bring braided flax to me, who will warp it to the loom for me?"

He replied, "Sister, I will bring it already warped."

His sister said, "So, brother, if you bring it warped, who will weave it for me?"

Her brother replied, "Sister, I will bring it to you woven."

Inana said, "And if you bring it woven, who will bleach it for me?"

"Don't worry, sister, I will bring it to you bleached."

"So, brother, if you bring me the whitened sheet, the sheet for the bridal bed, who will lie with me? Who will lie with me upon my bridal sheet and be my consort?"

And Utu answered, "Sister, take the shepherd as your husband; take Dumuzi to your bridal bed!"

Inana did not look pleased. "No, brother! The man of my heart is Enkimdu, the farmer. He gathers grain into great heaps, he piles up the grain in my storehouses."

Utu said, "But why are you unwilling? Marry the shepherd: his milk is good, his cream is good, whatever he touches shines brightly. Marry Dumuzi, sister! He will share his good cream with you. Why are you unwilling?"

Inana answered, "I do not want the shepherd. I will not accept his coarse wool. I will not wear his coarse garments. The farmer is the man of my heart. He grows many plants, he grows flax for my clothes. He grows many grains, he grows barley for my table. Enkimdu is the one I would marry."

Then Dumuzi spoke for himself, saying, "Why do you speak about the farmer? Why do you speak about him? If he brings you black flour, I will bring you black wool. If he brings you white flour, I will bring you white wool. If he pours out dark beer, I will pour out thick milk. If he pours out light beer, I will pour out skimmed milk. If he brings bread, I will bring sweet honey-cheese. If he brings small beans, I will bring small cheeses. If he brings large beans, I will bring large cheeses. When I have eaten and drunk, I will leave him the surplus: I have enough and more. What does Enkimdu have, more than me?"

Inana said, "Shepherd, if it wasn't for my mother, Ningal, I would drive you away. If it wasn't for my father, Nanna, you would have no roof over your head. Without my brother, Utu, you would have no one to speak for you."

Dumuzi looked at her. He said, "Inana, do not start a quarrel. My mother, Sirtur, is as good as your mother, Ningal. My father, Enki, is as good as your father, Nanna. My sister, Gestinana, is as good as your brother, Utu. Queen of the palace, let us talk things over. Inana, why don't we sit and talk together?"

As they talked, Enkimdu came towards them from the fields. Dumuzi, fired by his passion for Inana, was ready to begin a quarrel with Enkimdu, but the farmer was in an amenable frame of mind. He had no wish to argue, or to bid for Inana's hand. He said to Dumuzi, "Shepherd, why would I want strife with you? May your sheep safely graze on the river bank. May they pasture in my fields. Let them eat my grain from the stalk, let them eat from my storehouses when the fields dry out. Let your flocks drink from my canals."

Dumuzi was mollified by these words. He offered the hand of friendship to Enkimdu. He said, "Enkimdu, from now on, you will be counted as my friend. At our wedding, you will be honoured as a friend." Enkimdu smiled and offered to bring gifts to the marriage feast. "I will bring you wheat and beans, I will bring you lentils and grain. Lady Inana, I will bring you gifts that are fitting." Then he bowed, and left them together.

Dumuzi put his arm around Inana's shoulder. "Let us dally in the moonlight," he whispered. "Let me spread out a couch for you here, let me loosen your combs. Let me pass a sweet time with you in joy and plenty."

"Listen, you wild bull," chided Inana. "Let go of me, that I may go home. What would I say to my mother?"

"Let me tell you, let me teach you," smiled Dumuzi. "Let me suggest to you the sort of story young women tell. Say to your mother, 'My best friend and I were strolling in the square. We were dancing to the sound of recorder and tambourine. We were enjoying ourselves, and time went by.' Tell Ningal that story. It is a good story. As for us, let us dally in the moonlight, let us pass a sweet time in joy and plenty."

Inana looked him full in the face. "What do you take me for? I am not one of those girls you can meet in alleyways. If you want to be with me, you must be honourable. Do not tell me stories with which to deceive my mother. Come to see her yourself and ask for me in marriage. Then we will talk about dallying and loosening combs." With those words, Inana left him and went home to her mother, Ningal.

There she dithered between hope and despair, wondering whether he would come or not.

Suddenly, there came a knock on the door. It was Dumuzi, carrying pails of milk on a yoke across his shoulders, with gifts of butter and small cheeses hung over his arm. He called, "Open the house, my lady. Make haste to open the house!"

Now Inana was thrown into confusion. She did not know what she wanted. She did not know what to do. She went to her mother, Ningal, asking for advice. Ningal was quite certain. She said, "Open the house, my daughter. This man will be like a father to you. He will be like a mother to you. The marriage rite will bring you together. Adorn yourself, my daughter. It is time for you to leave this house. Make yourself ready for your bridegroom."

Inana did as her mother advised. She bathed and scrubbed herself with soap. She rubbed her body with sweet oil. She combed her tresses and let them fall about her shoulders. She painted her lips with amber and outlined her eyes with kohl. She dressed herself in a royal robe, put on gold rings, sacred amulets and lapis lazuli necklaces. She held her cylinder seal in her hand. She was ready, she was waiting. She opened the door, and her radiance shone out like the beams of the moon. Dumuzi rejoiced to see her. He put his hand in her hand. He put his hand on her heart. Sweet is the sleep of the hand to hand, sweeter still the sleep of hand to heart.

Then Inana called for it, she called for the bed. She called for the bed that refreshes the heart, she called for the bed that refreshes the loins. She called for the bridal bed. She said, "Bring in the bridegroom. May our hearts rejoice. Spread the bridal sheet upon our bed, that I may lie there and love my consort."

And so the sacred marriage rite was celebrated, between the goddess and the king. The farmer, Enkimdu, brought honey and wine. The fisherman brought precious carp, the fowler brought bright birds. Inana's friends sang a song of desire: "Now our breasts stand up, now our loins have grown hair. Inana is going to the bridegroom's loins. Let us be happy for them! Dance, dance! Inana, rejoice in our sexual nature. She will please him! He will please her! Let him come, let him come! By any means, let him come!"

Dumuzi took Inana into the shrine of his god. He said to her, "You will sleep in the presence of my god, you will sit upon the seat of honour in this shrine. Your table will be a splendid table, and you will eat at the splendid table. O, my bride, you will not have to weave for me, you will not have to spin, or braid, or warp. You will knead no bread!"

Inana and Dumuzi lay down together on the marriage bed. She put her hand in his hand, she put her hand on his heart. Sweet is the sleep of the hand to hand, sweeter still the sleep of hand to heart. Skin to skin, sweat to sweat, they lay together until the morning came.

The people sang praises to Inana: "Inana, you who are the morning and the evening star, whose pure splendour glows on heaven's horizon, great is our praise. Mighty, majestic, radiant and ever youthful; to you, Inana, we sing!"

THE DESCENT OF THE GODDESS INANA TO THE UNDERWORLD

Inana was Queen of Earth and Heaven. But she was not Queen of the Underworld. That honour belonged to the goddess Erishkigal. Her realm was the Kingdom of the Dead. No one went there out of choice, for no one who went there ever returned.

Yet Inana decided to go. Was it to challenge Ereshkigal's authority? Or was it, as she would tell the gatekeeper of the underworld, to attend the funeral rites for Erishkigal's husband?

She made her preparations with care. She dressed herself in the seven symbols of her power. She did not intend to go there naked, like a corpse, but adorned, like a queen.

On her head she set her crown, the shugurra. About her neck she wore her beads of lapis lazuli. Across her shoulder she draped a long string of lapis beads. She strapped her golden breastplate about her chest. She slipped circles of gold around her wrists. She took her measuring rod and line in her hands. She wrapped her body in her royal robe, the pala garment.

When she was ready, she called her dear companion Ninshubur. "My friend, I am about to set out on the path to the place from which no one has ever returned. Walk with me. Walk with me until we come to the place from which each one must go on alone. Wait for me there, until I return."

Ninshubur agreed. Why would she not? She was a good friend.

Inana had more to say, more to ask. "Wait there for three days and three nights. If, after three days and nights, I have not returned, you will know that I need your help. You must be my voice when I cannot speak. You must ask the gods to help me. Will you do this for me, Ninshubur?" Ninshubur agreed. Why would she not? She was Inana's heart-companion.

They set their feet on the path from which no one has ever returned. They walked together until they came to the place from which each one must go on alone. There Inana stopped.

She said, "Wait for me here, Ninshubur. Do not forget what you have promised."

Ninshubur pressed Inana's hands, and sat down at the roadside. Without a backward glance, Inana went on alone. She walked until she came to the great gate of the underworld. She knocked loudly on the gate, crying out, "Gatekeeper, open the gate! I am Inana, and I would enter."

Neti, the gatekeeper of the underworld, answered from behind the great gates. "If you are truly Inana, Queen of Earth and Heaven, why has your heart brought you on the path from which no one has ever returned?"

Inana replied, "Because of my sister, Ereshkigal. Her husband has died. I have come to witness the funeral rites. Open the gate. Let it be done."

Neti did not know what to do. No one had ever come to these gates of their own free will. He called out, "Wait there, Inana, I will tell my queen what you have said."

Down he went: down to the great hall of Ereshkigal's dark palace. His queen sat on her great stone throne. He bowed low before her. "My Lady," he said, "a woman waits at your gates. She is as tall as the sky, as broad as the horizon, as strong as the city walls. She is wearing the symbols of power. On her head she wears a crown. Around her neck are chains of lapis beads, both short and long. Across her shoulder is a long string of lapis beads She wears a golden breastplate and golden bracelets. She carries a measuring rod and line. She is dressed in a royal robe, a pala garment."

When she had heard all this, Erishkigal chewed her lip. She considered the facts. She planned her response. She said, "Let her enter, Neti. But make sure she enters naked and bowed low, as do all who enter here. Lock the seven gates of the underworld against her. Bolt the seven doors of the underworld against her. As she comes to each gate, take one of her symbols of power from her. Let her enter my realm naked and humbled, as do all who enter here."

Neti, the gatekeeper, heard the words of his queen. He listened to her commands. He obeyed them. He locked the seven gates of the underworld. He bolted the seven doors of the underworld. He opened the first gate of the underworld a crack, saying, "Come, Inana, enter."

As Inana went through the gate, the crown was snatched from her head. She said, "What is this?"

Many voices replied, saying, "Be silent, Inana. The ways of the underworld are perfect. They may not be questioned." She was shaken, but she went on.

Neti opened the second gate of the underworld a crack, saying, "Come, Inana, enter."

As Inana went through the gate, the lapis necklaces were pulled from her neck. She said, "What is this?" They said, "Be silent, Inana. The ways of the underworld are perfect. They may not be questioned." She was troubled, but she went on.

She came to the third gate of the underworld. Neti opened it a little, saying, "Come, Inana, enter."

As Inana went through the gate, the long chain of lapis was dragged from her shoulder. She said, "What is this?" They said, "Be silent, Inana. The ways of the underworld are perfect. They may not be questioned."

And so it went on.

At the fourth gate they took her golden breastplate.

At the fifth, her golden bracelets.

At the sixth, they took her measuring rod and line.

At the seventh, her royal robe was torn from her body. She cried out, "What is this?"

They said, "Be silent, Inana. The ways of the underworld are perfect. They may not be questioned."

When she entered the great hall of the underworld, she was naked and bowed low, as were all who entered there. Ereshkigal was sitting on her great stone throne. She watched Inana enter. Ereshkigal fixed upon Inana the eye of wrath. Ereshkigal fixed upon her the eye of guilt. Ereshkigal stretched out her hand and spoke a word of power. Inana was struck down. She was changed to a corpse, a piece of rotting meat, which they hung from a hook on the wall.

For three days and three nights, it hung there.

For three days and three nights, Ninshubur waited at the appointed place.

When, after three days and nights, Inana had not returned, Ninshubur tore at her face, at her arms and at her thighs. She rubbed ash into her hair and dressed herself in a mourning garment. She cried out for Inana in the market place. She beat the drum for Inana in the gathering place. She went to the temples of the gods to ask for their help.

When she entered the temple of the god Enlil, she bowed before the altar. She lifted her hands in prayer. She cried out, "O, Father Enlil, do not let the Lady Inana be lost in the underworld."

Father Enlil heard the words of Ninshubur, but he did not listen to them. He simply said, "The ways of the underworld are perfect. They may not be questioned. Who, having once gone down to that place, would expect to come back again?"

He would not help her.

Ninshubur went on. She came to the temple of the god An. When she entered An's temple, she bowed before the altar. She lifted her hands in prayer. Once again she prayed: "O, Father An, do not let the Lady Inana be lost in the underworld."

Father An heard the words of Ninshubur, but he did not listen to them. He too said, "The ways of the underworld are perfect. They may not be questioned. Who, having once gone down to that place, would expect to come back again?"

He would not help her.

Ninshubur went on. She came to the temple of the god of wisdom, Enki, the all-seeing, all-knowing one. She entered Enki's temple, the Abzu, beside the deep sweet water. A third time, she bowed before an altar. A third time she prayed: "O, Father Enki, do not let the Lady Inana be lost in the underworld. Do not let your bright silver be covered by the dust of the underworld. Do not let your fragrant boxwood be chopped into pieces for the woodworker. Do not let your precious lapis be broken into fragments for the stone worker. Do not let the Lady Inana be lost in the underworld."

Enki, all-seeing, all-knowing, heard Ninshubur's words. He listened to her.

He said, "What has happened to the Lady Inana? I am troubled. I am grieved. I will help her."

Father Enki stretched out his left arm. From the nail of the middle finger of his left hand, he scraped out dust. From it, he made a creature neither male nor female: a kurgarra.

Then he stretched out his right arm. From the nail of the middle finger of his right hand, he scraped out more dust. From it, he made a creature neither female nor male: a galatur.

To the kurgarra he gave the water of life. To the galatur he gave the food of life. He spoke to these creatures. He said: "Make yourselves as small as flies. Slip through the cracks in the seven gates of the underworld. Slide through the bolts of the seven gates of the underworld, until you reach the great hall. There you will see Ereshkigal moaning and groaning, as if with the cries of a woman about to give birth.

"When she sighs, 'Oh, oh, my heart,' you must sigh, 'Oh, oh, your heart.'

"When she cries, 'Oh, oh, my liver,' you must cry, 'Oh, oh, your liver.'

"When she hears you crying and sighing, moaning and groaning, for her, she will be moved by your empathy. She will offer you a gift. She will offer you the grain gift, the fields ready for harvest. Do not accept it. She will offer you the water gift, the river in spate. Do not accept it.

"Ask her only for the corpse that hangs from a hook on the wall. When it is taken down and given to you, sprinkle it with the water of life. Sprinkle it with the food of life. Inana will arise. Send Inana back from the underworld."

The kurgarra and the galatur obeyed Enki. They made themselves as small as flies. They slipped through the gates, and slid through the bolts, until they reached Ereshkigal's great hall. There they found Ereshkigal. She was sighing and crying, moaning and groaning. No clothes covered her body. Her breasts were bare.

She sighed, "Oh, oh, my heart." They sighed, "Oh, oh, your heart."

She cried, "Oh, oh, my liver." They cried, "Oh, oh, your liver."

She moaned, "Oh, oh, my inside." They moaned, "Oh, oh, your inside."

She groaned, "Oh, oh, my outside." They groaned, " Oh, oh, your outside."

She stopped sighing and crying, moaning and groaning. She looked at them. She said, "Who are you? If you are gods, I will worship you. If you are mortal, I will give you a gift. I will give you the grain gift, the fields ready for harvest."

They said, "We do not want it."

She said, "I will give you the water gift, the river in spate."

They said, "We do not want it."

She said, "What do you want?"

They said, "We ask only for the corpse that hangs from a hook on the wall."

She said, "That is the corpse of Inana."

They said, "We know."

The corpse was taken down and given to them. The kurgarra sprinkled the corpse with the water of life. The galatur added the food of life. Inana was restored.

She turned to leave the underworld, but the galla, the demons of the underworld, surrounded her. They cried out, "The ways of the underworld are perfect. They may not be questioned. Who, having once come down to this place, can expect to go back again?"

Inana answered, "I do, and I will."

The galla spoke again, "If Inana would return from the underworld, she must send another in her place. The bargain with death cannot be broken."

Inana looked around her: at the galla, at the great hall, at its queen. Then, without another word, she left.

As she climbed the long stairway, through the seven gates and the seven doors, the galla surrounded Inana. They could not stop her, but they would not leave her. They walked with Inana until she came to the place where she had parted from Ninshubur. Ninshubur, ash in her hair, her face gashed and torn, her body wrapped in a mourning garment, was waiting at the appointed place. When she saw Inana coming, she flung herself into the dust at Inana's feet.

The galla said, "Walk on, Inana. We will take Ninshubur in your place."

But Inana said, "No! Ninshubur is my heart's companion. She is my friend. She waited here for me. She cried out my name in the houses of the gods. Because of her I am restored. I will never give Ninshubur to you!"

"Very well," said the galla. "Walk on, Inana. We will go further with you."

Ianna walked on until she came to the city of her son Shara. Shara, ash in his hair, his face gashed and torn, was dressed in a mourning garment. When he saw Inana coming, he flung himself into the dust at her feet. The galla said, "Walk on, Inana. We will take Shara in your place."

But Inana said, "No! Shara cuts my nails and combs my hair. He is my son. I will never give Shara to you!"

"Very well," said the galla. "Walk on, Inana. We will go further with you."

Inana went on until she came to the city of her second son, Lulal. Lulal, ash in his hair, his face gashed and torn, was dressed in a mourning garment. When he saw Inana coming, he flung himself into the dust at her feet.

The galla said, "Walk on, Inana. We will take Lulal in your place."

But Inana said, "No! Lulal is a leader. He is my right arm. He is my son. I will never give Lulal to you!"

"Very well," said the galla. "Walk on, Inana. We will go further with you."

Inana went on until she came to the city of her husband Dumuzi. Dumuzi was dressed in gleaming garments. He wore the shugarra crown on his head. He was seated on a shining throne. When he saw Inana coming, he did not move.

Inana looked long at Dumuzi. She fixed upon him the eye of wrath. She fixed upon him the eye of guilt. She stretched out her hand and shouted: "Take him! Take Dumuzi in my place!"

The galla surrounded Dumuzi. They dragged him away.

Inana said, "The ways of the underworld are perfect. They may not be questioned." She turned away and went into her city.

DUMUZI'S DREAM

Dumuzi's heart was filled with tears. The shepherd's heart was filled with tears. The young man's heart was filled with tears.

He stumbled about, calling out, "Weep for me, flat lands! Mourn for me, crabs in the river! Wail for me, frogs in the river! My mother will call to me, she will call out to me. She will call me five times. She will call me ten times. If she does not know the date of my death, you, my land, you must tell her! Here, on my land, my mother will weep for me. Here, on my land, my little sister will weep for me!"

Exhausted, Dumuzi lay down to rest. He lay down and fell asleep. And in his sleep he dreamed a dream. When he woke he remembered everything about the dream, and he was troubled by it. He asked for his sister, so she could interpret his dream. "Bring me my sister! Bring me Gestinana, my tablet-knowing scribe, my music-loving singer of songs! Bring me my wise sister, who knows the meaning of dreams!"

When Gestinana sat down beside Dumuzi, he related his dream to her.

"My sister, listen to my dream. In my dream, rushes were growing thickly around me. A single reed was trembling, a double reed was split. Tall trees grew up all around me. My holy fire was doused, my holy churn was broken, my shepherd's cup fell from the peg, my shepherd's crook disappeared. A lamb was snatched from the sheepfold, a falcon took a sparrow from the reed fence. My goats dragged their black beards in the dust. My rams scratched the earth with their thick legs. The churns were tumbled about, no milk was poured, the drinking cups were shattered. I no longer existed. The wind howled through the sheepfold."

Gestinana shuddered when she heard these words. "Oh, my brother, this is an ill-starred dream! Do not tell me any more! The rushes growing thickly around you are your demons, ambushing and attacking you. That trembling single reed is our mother, mourning for you. Those twin reeds are you and I, my brother – we are going to be torn apart. The tall trees are evildoers surrounding and trapping you. When your holy fire is put out, the sheepfold will be abandoned. When your holy churn is smashed, you will be in the evildoers' hands. When the cup falls, you will be tumbled from your mother's lap. When your crook is gone, you will be lost. As the lamb is snatched, so will demons seize you, my brother. As the sparrow is caught, so will you be taken. That your goats drag their beards in the dust means that my hair will swirl about my head in my grief. That your rams scratch the earth means that I will tear at my cheeks in my loss. The churns are silent; no milk is poured; the cups are all broken: these all mean that you, my brother, are dead. The sheepfold will shelter nothing but the howling wind."

She had hardly finished speaking when Dumuzi cried out, "Sister, go up onto the mound to be my lookout! Go up onto the mound. Run! Take your friend with you and look for the evil ones whom all fear. They are coming in their boats. They are bringing wood to bind my neck, and wood to bind my hands. Run!"

With her friend Gestindudu, Dumuzi's sister Gestinana went up to the top of the mound.

Dumuzi called out, "Can you see them?"

Gestindudu answered, "Yes! They are coming. Carrying the wood to bind your neck, they are coming!"

Dumuzi called again, "Gestinana, my sister, are they really coming?"

"Yes, brother, they are! Quickly, crouch down in the grass!"

"Yes, sister, yes, I will crouch down and hide in the grass. Do not tell them where I am! I will crouch down in the ditches of Arali. Do not tell them where I am hiding!"

The two women answered together, "If we give you away, may your dog devour us! May your black dog, your sheepdog, your noble, lordly dog, devour us!"

The ones who were coming for Dumuzi were a frightening crowd, a strange crowd. They knew no food, they knew no drink, they received no gifts. They had no parents, no sisters or brothers. They had no lovers to embrace, no sweet children to kiss. They were thistles in dried-up mud, thorns in stinking water. Two men from Adab came for Dumuzi, carrying weapons on their shoulders. Two men from Unug came for the king, with head-smashing clubs tied to their belts. Two men from Urim came, and two from Nibru, all wearing gleaming garments.

They came for Dumuzi. They came to the sheepfold and the cattle pen. They caught Gestinana there. They offered her the water gift. She would not accept it. They offered her the grain gift. She would not accept it. So they said to each other, "Who, since the most ancient times, has ever known a sister to betray her brother? Let us go instead to Dumuzi's friend."

They offered Dumuzi's friend the water gift. He accepted it. They offered him the grain gift. He accepted it. He told them, "Dumuzi crouched down in the grass, but I do not know the exact place." They searched for Dumuzi in the grass, but they could not find him there.

"He crouched down in the short grass, but I do not know the exact place." They searched for Dumuzi in the short grass, but they could not find him there.

"He crouched down in the long grass, but I do not know the exact place." They searched for Dumuzi in the long grass, but they could not find him there.

"He crouched down in the ditches of Arali, but I do not know the exact place." They caught Dumuzi in the ditches of Arali. Dumuzi began to weep and turned very pale. "My sister has been true to me. My friend has betrayed me." He was surrounded and dragged from the ditch. They twisted a cord and knotted a net to hold him. They cut sticks and hurled missiles at him. His hands and arms were bound.

Dumuzi raised his bound hands to the heavens, calling on the sun god, Utu. "Utu, you are my brother-in-law. I am the husband of your sister Inana. I am the one who carries offerings of food to the holy shrine. I am the one who brought the wedding gifts to Unug. I am the one who kisses the holy lips and dances on the holy knees of Inana. Change my hands to the hands of a gazelle! Change my feet to the feet of a gazelle! Let me escape from my captors! Let me escape with my life to Kubires!"

The sun god Utu granted the prayers of Dumuzi. The brother-in-law heard his sister's husband's pleas. He changed Dumuzi's hands to gazelle hands. He changed his feet to gazelle feet. With the swiftness of the gazelle, Dumuzi fled to Kubires. He escaped his captors.

They searched for him. "Come, let us go to Kubires!"

They caught Dumuzi in Kubires. He was surrounded again. They twisted a cord and knotted a net to hold him. They cut sticks and hurled missiles at him. His hands and arms were bound.

Dumuzi raised his bound hands to the heavens, calling on the sun god, Utu. "Utu, you are my brother-in-law. I am the husband of your sister Inana. I am the one who carries offerings of food to the holy shrine. I am the one who brought the wedding gifts to Unug. I am the one who kisses the holy lips and dances on the holy knees of Inana. Change my hands to the hands of a gazelle! Change my feet to the feet of a gazelle! Let me escape from my captors! Let me escape with my life to the house of Belili!"

Utu accepted Dumuzi's tears. He changed his hands to gazelle hands. He changed his feet to gazelle feet. With the swiftness of the gazelle, Dumuzi fled, escaping his captors. He came to the house of Belili, calling to her, "Old woman, I am not an ordinary man. I am the husband of a goddess. Please, please, pour some water that I may drink. Sprinkle some flour that I may eat."

She poured water and sprinkled flour, and he came into her house to eat and drink. Belili went out of the house. Dumuzi's pursuers saw her. They said to each other, "That old woman looks frightened. She is screaming in fright. Let us see whether he is in her house."

Once again they caught Dumuzi, inside Belili's house. They twisted a cord and knotted a net to hold him. They cut sticks and hurled missiles at him. His hands and arms were bound.

Dumuzi raised his bound hands to the heavens, calling on the sun god, Utu. "Utu, you are my brother-in-law. I am the husband of your sister Inana. I am the one who carries offerings of food to the holy shrine. I am the one who brought the wedding gifts to Unug. I am the one who kisses the holy lips and dances on the holy knees of Inana. Change my hands to the hands of a gazelle! Change my feet to the feet of a gazelle! Let me escape from my captors! Let me escape with my life to the holy sheepfold, to my sister's holy sheepfold!"

Once again, Utu accepted Dumuzi's tears. He changed his hands to gazelle hands. He changed his feet to gazelle feet. With the swiftness of the gazelle, Dumuzi escaped with his life to his sister's holy sheepfold.

Gestinana was there, mourning and keening, crying out to the heavens, crying out to the earth. Her grief covered the earth like a garment. She had torn at her eyes and face. In public she lacerated her ears, in private she lacerated her thighs.

Dumuzi's pursuers were closing in. They saw Gestinana and said to each other, "Gestinana looks frightened. She is mourning and wailing. Let us look for Dumuzi in her sheepfold."

When the first of the demons entered the sheepfold, he set fire to the bolt. When the second demon entered the sheepfold, he burnt the shepherd's crook. When the third entered, he destroyed the holy churn. When the fourth entered, he doused the holy fire. The fifth snatched the drinking cup from its peg. The sixth silenced the churns, so that no milk was poured. The seventh cried out, "Rise Dumuzi! Rise from your false sleep! Your sheep are seized, your goats are seized. Now you come with us!"

Dumuzi was taken. His sheepfold sheltered nothing but the howling wind.

The people of the city wept for Dumuzi. Dumuzi's mother wept for her son. His sister Gestinana wept for her brother. She cried out, "Who is my brother? You are he. Who is your sister? I am she. This world held both you and me. This is the same world we both did see. I would find my brother. I would share his fate."

She came weeping to Inana. Her tears moved Inana. Inana spoke. "Your brother's house is no more. Dumuzi has been taken by the galla. I would take you to him, but I do not know the place."

Then a fly appeared. The fly buzzed about around Inana's head, and spoke. "If I told you where Dumuzi was, what would you give me?"

Inana said, "If you told me where Dumuzi was, I would give you the gift of frequenting the beerhouses and taverns. I would let you dwell among the words of the wise, the gossip of the garrulous."

This pleased the fly, and it said, "Lift up your eyes to the steppe. Lift up your eyes to the ditches of Arali. There you will find Gestinana's brother. There you will find Dumuzi."

Inana and Gestinana went to the edges of the steppe. There they found Dumuzi. Gestinana wept for her brother. Her tears moved Inana. Inana spoke. "He shall go to the underworld, but for half the year only. Because you have asked it, you will share his fate. On the day that Dumuzi comes up from the underworld, on that day you will go down, Gestinana. On the day that you come up, on that day he will go down."

And so it began.
The turning of the seasons.
Turning then, turning still,
Even today.

QUEEN OF EARTH & HEAVEN

This group of stories explores the more volatile aspects of the goddess Inana. The story 'Inana and Ebih' is attributed to Enheduanna, the first named author in history. Enheduanna was the daughter of Sargon the Great, king of Akkad from 2334–2279 BCE. She received her education in one of the Edubba, the Sumerian schools called the Houses of Tablets, training in reading, writing, the interpretation of texts and general knowledge. Her education would have begun with the set compositions of the Tetrad and Decad, moving on to more complex works, through copying and recitation. During the twenty-third century BCE, Enheduanna became High Priestess of the moon god Nanna in the city of Ur, ruled by her nephew, Naram-Sin.

To date we have forty poems known to have been written by Enheduanna. 'Inana and Ebih' begins with Enheduanna's invocation to Inana.

ENHEDUANNA'S INVOCATION TO INANA

Goddess of fearsome divine powers, you are a warrior, clad in terror, riding on the great divine powers.

Inana, made complete by the strength of the holy Ankara weapon, drenched in blood, rushing around in great battles, covered in storm and flood, great Lady Inana, great in war strategy, you destroy mighty lands with arrow and strength. You overpower lands. You are a force of nature. In heaven and on earth you roar like a lion and pacify the insubordinate. Like a huge wild bull you triumph over the hostile lands with your gall.

My lady, you have acquired the stature of heaven.

Maiden Inana, you have become magnificent. Your arms are held wide as you walk in the heavens. You are like Utu the king of the heavens. So you stretch your arms wide. You are clothed in brilliant daylight, you are walking the heavens and, walking in brilliance on the earth and onto the mountain ranges, you bring forth brilliant beams onto your mountain plants, brilliant beams giving birth to these bright mountains. You are the mother of the mountains. You are like a joyful young lord of the mountains, with your mace in hand.

All the mountains ring with song.

All lands sing sweet songs to her.

The black-headed people sing songs to her.

I, Enheduanna, I too sing songs to praise the lady of battle, the great child of Suen, Maiden Inana.

INANA AND EBIH

One day Inana was walking around the whole heavens and around the whole earth, as was her habit. She was exhibiting her radiance, as usual, shining her light over creation and allowing life to thrive wherever she went. Wherever she went, she was receiving adulation and gratitude.

But when at last Inana reached the regions of Elam and Subir, she sensed there was a strange and subtle change in the atmosphere. Inana noted that there was a change in the enthusiasm of the respect that was paid to her. It seemed to her that she was not receiving the required honour and admiration. In the Lulubi Mountains she paid particular attention. This was an area that she herself had permitted to exist. She was among the very mountains to which she had given birth. She approached the mountain range of Ebih. Here was the source of the problem. Ebih was showing no respect at all. Ebih had acquired a radiance of its own. It was fruiting in glorious abundance perpetually and, in spite of her presence, it did not bow down, it did not submit to the pulse of life, as it should. Inana was furious. She was outraged. She had created this being. She had allowed and commanded the particular pattern and the rules of its fruiting and its dying, out of the seed of her own radiance.

"I, the goddess, walking around heaven and earth, came to the Lulubi Mountains and got respect. But when I came to the mountain range of Ebih, it showed me no respect. The beings showed me no respect. They did not put their noses to the ground for me. They did not rub their lips in the dust for me. Everything just kept blossoming and growing and fruiting and lambing as if I was not there! As if I had not set down the rule! Since they showed me no respect, since they did not put their noses to the ground for me, since they did not rub their lips in the dust for me, I shall take action. I shall personally fill the soaring mountain range with my terror.

"This is what I will do. Against its magnificent sides, I shall place magnificent battering rams. Against its small sides, I shall place small battering rams. I shall storm it. I shall begin the

Game of Inana. That is, I shall prepare for conflicts and prepare to start battles in the mountain range. What is more, I shall prepare arrows in the quiver. I shall collect slingstones from the rope. I shall begin the polishing of my lance. I shall prepare the throw stick and the shield. And another thing – I shall set fire to the thick forests. I shall take an axe to the evildoing of the forests and the mountain. I shall call Gibil, the purifier, the god of fire. I shall make him bare his holy teeth at the watercourses of the mountain. I shall spread this terror throughout the inaccessible mountain range of Aratta. Like a city which An has cursed, may it never be restored. Like a city at which Enlil has frowned, may it never again lift up its neck. May the mountain tremble when I approach. So Ebih must give me honour and praise me."

Inana, the child of the moon god Suen, began to get ready for action. She began to dress for action. She put on the garment of royalty and girded herself with joy. She bedecked her forehead with terror and fearsome radiance. She arranged her cornelian rosettes around her throat and placed straps of lapis lazuli on her feet. Then she brandished her seven-headed weapon. Then she stood regally, and, at dusk, came forth, following the path to the Gate of Wonder, to Inana's gate of lapis lazuli, and there she made an offering to the sky god, An. She addressed a prayer to him. An was delighted when he heard the prayer of Inana. He was delighted at Inana herself. He stepped forward and he took his place before her. He filled the seat of heaven.

Inana spoke. "An, my father, I greet you. Lend your ear to my words. You have made me terrifying among the gods in heaven. Thanks to you, my word has no rival in heaven or on earth. You have given me the great weapons and emblems: the Cilia weapon, the Anibal and the Mansium. You have given me the ability to make the foundations of the throne firm. You have given me the might of the seven-headed Cita weapon which bends like a tree in the wind. You have given me the ability to hold the ground with the sixfold yoke, to extend the thighs with the fourfold yoke, to pursue murderous raids and widespread military campaigns. Thanks to you, I appear to earthly kings like moonlight. I can shoot the arrow from the arm so the arrows fall on fields, orchards and forests like the teeth of the locust. I can take the harrow to the rebel lands. I can remove the locks from the city gates so the doors stand open. King An, you have given me all these powers. I am at the right hand of my favoured king, so that he destroys the rebel lands. He, with my aid, smashes heads like a falcon in the foothills of the mountain. May my earthly king destroy the lands as one destroys a snake in a crevice. May my king make them slither around like a snake coming down from a mountain. May he establish control over the mountain, examine it, survey it and know its length and know its depth. The king must do all this because the mountain does not fear me and does not do as I say. How can it be that the mountain range of Ebih did not fear me in heaven and on earth? How can it be that it shows me no respect? Because it showed me no respect, because it did not put its nose to the ground, rub its lips in the dust, may I fill my hand with the soaring mountain range and hand it over to my terror. Let me place magnificent battering rams against its magnificent sides. Let me place small battering rams against its small sides. Let me storm it and start conflicts and battles. Let me start the Game of Inana. Let me prepare arrows in the quiver, slingstones with ropes, throw stick and shield. Let me set fire to the forests, take axe to its evildoing, call Gibil the fire to bare his holy teeth. Let me spread all this terror through the inaccessible mountain range of Aratta. May it never be restored. May it never again lift its neck up. May it tremble. So Ebih may give me honour and praise me."

An, the king of the deities, raised his forefinger to his upper lip. He gave a quiet cough. He said, "My little one." He looked at the ground and took a deep breath. He said, "My little one demands the destruction of this mountain. What is she taking on? Inana demands the destruction of this mountain. Has she thought it through? The mountain has poured fearsome terror on the abodes of the gods. It has spread fear among the holy dwellings of the Anuna gods. It has poured its terror and ferocity over this land. It has poured the mountain range's radiance and fear over all the lands. Its arrogance extends grandly to the centre of heaven. But dearest Inana, sweet child, it is beautiful. Fruit hangs in its flourishing gardens and luxuriance spreads forth. Its magnificent trees are themselves a source of wonder to the roots of heaven. In Ebih the lions are abundant under the canopy of trees and bright branches. It makes wild rams and stags freely abundant. Wild bulls stand in flourishing grass. Deer couple among the cypress trees of the mountain range. True, the mountain range is powerful and fearsome, but it is a radiant, verdant and luxuriant power. You cannot pass through its terror and fear without wondering at it. Maiden Inana, perhaps you have birthed it, but it has a wonderful life and a wonderful power of its own now and you surely cannot want to possess or oppose it."

The mistress, in her rage and anger, paid no attention to the words of An. Though she had asked for permission, she needed none. In her rage and anger, she opened the arsenal and pushed on the lapis lazuli gate. She brought out magnificent battle and called up a great storm. Holy Inana reached for the quiver. She raised a towering flood with evil silt. She stirred up an evil raging wind dense with potsherds. My lady confronted the mountain range. She advanced step by step. She sharpened both edges of her dagger. She grabbed Ebih's neck as if ripping up esparto grass. She pressed the dagger's teeth into its interior. She roared like thunder. The rocks forming the body of Ebih clattered down its flanks. From its sides and crevices, great serpents spat venom. She damned its forests and cursed its trees. She killed its oak trees with drought. She poured fire on its flanks and made its smoke dense. She, the goddess, destroyed all nature and natural resources and established authority over the mountain. Holy Inana did as she wished. Then she explained her actions. She went to the mountain range of Ebih and addressed it. "Mountain range, because of your elevation, because of your height, because of your attractiveness, because of your beauty, because of your wearing a holy garment, because of your reaching up to heaven, because you did not put your nose to the ground, because you did not rub your lips in the dust, I have killed you and brought you low. As with the elephant, I have seized your tusks. As with a great wild bull, I have brought you to the ground by your thick horns. As with a bull, I have forced your great strength to the ground and pursued you savagely. I have made it so that tears are always flowing from your eyes. I have placed laments always in your heart. The birds of sorrow are building nests on your flanks."

She went on and on, rejoicing in her fearsome terror. She spoke out confident in her own righteousness. "My father Enlil has secured my great terror over the centre of the mountains. On my right side he has placed a weapon. On my left side more power is placed. My anger, a harrow with great teeth, has torn the mountain apart. In my victory, I rushed towards the mountain.

In my victory, I rushed towards Ebih, the mountain range. I went forward like a surging flood and the rising water overflowed the dam. I imposed my victory on the mountain. I imposed my victory on Ebih. Now I have built a palace. I have put a throne in place. I have made its foundation firm."

"For destroying Ebih," says Enheduanna, "let the great child of the moon god Suen, Maiden Inana, be praised."

Enheduanna tells how, for Inana, they have established a great festival of performance in commemoration, and that Inana now cries, "The Kurjara cult performers have a dagger and a prod. My Gala cult performers have ub and lilis drums. I have established the headgear of the Pilipi cult performers. All to commemorate the time when in my victory I rushed towards the mountain, like a surging flood and like rising water I overflowed the dam. I imposed my victory on Ebih."

SUKALETUDA

This story is about gardening, about what it is to be an apprentice gardener, and about what happens if you do not water your garden properly with a very good shaduf.

A shaduf is a cleverly counterweighted watering mechanism designed in Ancient Sumer, to lift water easily from the well.

How do we know about this and about this story? Through what was reported and through what was pulling up and settling down and said, from one person telling the story to another. And through what was added by the other in the detail. The only reason we know this story is through gossip and the telling of tales time upon time. And now I am telling it to you. Listen to the thump, the sound of the shaduf. Hear it behind this story. The story of the very first date palm.

At the beginning of time, Enki, the teacher, the god of subtle wisdom and fresh water, gave his teachings to a raven. Enki spoke to the raven. He said, "Raven! I give you instructions. Pay attention to my instructions. Raven! Go to the shrine. First chop and chew the black kohl which the incantation priests mix with the oil and the water. You will find it in the back room of the shrine in a lapis lazuli bowl. Then you must plant the pieces in the vegetable plot, in the trench that was dug for the leeks."

How do we know this story? We know it through what was said in one person telling this story to another. And through what was added by the other in the detail. Through gossip and the telling of tales time upon time. And now I am telling it to you.

The raven paid exact attention to the instructions of his master. He chopped and chewed the kohl. He planted the pieces in the vegetable plot. Then the raven performed the work of a man. He made the counterweight blocks of the shaduf bump up and settle down.

That a bird like a raven should perform the work of a man; that he should make the counterweight blocks of the shaduf bump up and settle down; that he should make the shaduf bump down and rise up: who had ever seen such a thing before?

How do we know this story? We know it through what was said in one person telling the story to another. And through what was added by the other in the detail. Through gossip and the telling of tales time upon time. And now I am telling it to you.

Then a plant grew up. It was like a leek. But it was an oddity – it was much bigger – standing straight up. It was sticking up like a leek stalk, but who had ever seen such an enormous thing before?

The raven stood up. He climbed up the length of this oddity with a harness. With his beak, he rubbed the kohl paste into the pistils of the plant.

And now it was a date palm. The very first one.

Who had ever seen such a thing before?

It had scaly leaves surrounding its palm heart. Its dried palm fronds could serve as weaving material. Its shoots were like the surveyor's gleaming line, fit for the king's fields. Its branches were good for the king's palace for cleaning. Its fruit were fit food for the great gods.

That a bird like the raven, performing the work of man, could make the counterweight blocks of the shaduf bump up and settle down, that it could make the counterweight blocks of the shaduf bump down and rise up again and could cause the first date palm to grow: who had ever seen such a thing before?

This is what one person said to another. And the other added detail.

Then, at his master's command, the raven stepped into the region of wisdom and fresh water – into the Abzu.

* * *

Now what else did one person say to another? What further did one add to the other in detail?

This!

The story of Sukaletuda, the spotty youth:

What did one say? What did the other say?

Once, when the goddess Inana had spent an aeon going around the heavens; after she had gone around the earth; after Inana had gone around the heavens, gone around the earth, gone around Elam and Subir; gone around the intertwined horizon of the heavens and the earth, after all of that, she felt so tired, she just had to lie down.

There beside the Euphrates was a garden. In the garden was a poplar tree so immense, and its shade so large, that it was not diminished even at noon. So Inana lay down and slept in the shade of the poplar tree in the garden beside the Euphrates. She slept the deep sleep of the goddess.

Now, the garden was tended by a gardener. Sukaletuda was his name. Sukaletuda was the son of Igisigsig. Sukaletuda was to water the garden plots, to build the shaduf for the irrigation by the well among the plants and to do the weeding. But really, he was just the apprentice gardener. He was just Sukaletuda: 'spotty youth'. He wasn't this and he wasn't that. He was an inbetweener. He wasn't a child. He wasn't an adult. He wasn't a man and he wasn't a boy. And he wasn't much of a gardener. He hadn't done the watering and he hadn't built the shaduf, and as for the weeding, he had got mixed up and pulled all the plants out by their roots and destroyed them. Not a single plant remained there. Not even one. Then what did the storm wind bring?

It blew the dust of the mountains into his eyes. Of course it did. There were no plants to protect him. He tried to wipe the corner of his eyes with his hand and he got some of the dust out, but not all. Some was left. And when he raised his clouded eyes to the lowlands, he saw, where the sun rises, the exalted gods of the land themselves. When he raised his eyes to the highlands where the sun sets, he saw the exalted gods of the land themselves. And when he looked into his own garden, there beneath his poplar tree, he saw a solitary sleeping spirit – someone fully in possession of all the divine powers – someone whose destiny was decided by the gods. In his own garden plot beneath the poplar tree – had he not looked there five, six, ten times before, beneath the broad shade of that Euphrates poplar and seen nothing? Now he saw a sleeping goddess.

She was so beautiful. A girdle of seven divine powers covered her genitals.

What is it that one person says to the other? What further does the other add in detail?

If only he had been a year younger, a little boy, he would have backed away – afraid, scared because she was a girl.

If he had been a year older, a man, he would have bowed down – awed and overwhelmed because she was a goddess.

But he was Sukaletuda, the spotty youth: the teenager, the inbetweener. He could not help himself. He lay down beside her in her resting place, he undid the girdle of seven divine powers and touched what should never have been touched. And he entered her inner sanctum without invitation.

And then he kissed her and covered her up again and went back to his garden plot.

And all the time Inana slept the deep sleep of the goddess.

But when the day had broken and the great sun god Utu had risen, then she awoke and then she knew. Then she knew the disrespect and the violation that had been committed by that child-man.

Then the woman in her was furious. Inana was considering what should be destroyed because of that violation.

In her fury she filled the watercourses of the land with blood. There was no more water. Water no longer irrigated the land. It was blood that seeped into the land. The slaves no longer drew water from wells. They drew blood. The black-headed people no longer drank water. Blood was their only drink.

In her fury Inana searched for the one who had committed the violation, the disrespect – the one who had entered her inner sanctum without invitation. Where was he?

What is it that one person says to the other? What further does the other add in detail?

He had returned to the mountains, to his father. He was telling his father the tale:

"My father! I was to water the garden plot, to build the shaduf by the well among the plants and to do the weeding. But I didn't do the watering and I didn't build the shaduf and as for the weeding, I pulled all the plants out by their roots and destroyed them and not a single plant remained there. Not even one. Then what did the storm wind bring? It blew the dust of the mountains into my eyes. When I tried to wipe the corner of my eyes with my hand, I got some of it out, but not all and some was left in.

"When I raised my eyes to the lowlands, I saw, where the sun rises, the exalted gods of the land themselves. When I raised my eyes to the highlands where the sun sets, I saw the exalted gods of the land themselves.

"And then I looked into my own garden and I saw a solitary sleeping spirit – someone fully in possession of all the divine powers – someone whose destiny was decided by the gods. In my own garden plot beneath the poplar tree – had I not looked there five times – ten times – before, beneath the broad shade of that Euphrates poplar and seen nothing? Now I saw a sleeping goddess.

"She was so beautiful. A girdle of seven divine powers covered her genitals. Why did I do it? I could not help myself. I lay down beside her in her resting place. I undid the girdle of seven divine powers and touched what should never have been touched. I entered her. Then I kissed her and covered her up again and went back to my garden plot. And all the time she slept the deep sleep of the goddess. But when day had broken and sun god Utu had risen, then she awoke and she knew. Then she knew the disrespect and violation. In her fury she has filled the watercourses of the land with blood. In her fury Inana searches for the one who has committed the violation: me. What am I to do? She is searching for me!"

His father, Igisigsig, replied "My son! Run! Run to the city. Join the city dwellers. In the company of all your brothers, the multitude of the black-headed people, she will never find you."

But now Inana was mounted on a cloud. The south wind and a fearsome flood storm went before her and a dust storm followed her. She cried out, "I search everywhere for the one who had intercourse with me."

Where was the boy? At home with his father. "Father. She still searches. It is because of her genitals. Now she is on a cloud. There is a flood storm before her and a dust storm follows her." His father replied, "My son! Run! Run to the city. Join the city dwellers. In the company of all your brothers, the multitude of the black-headed people, she will never find you."

In her fury the woman was considering what should be done, because of the disrespect of her person; what should be destroyed because of the disrespect of her genitals. She took a single rock in her hand. She blocked the highways of the land with it. Because of her, the black-headed people had no transport and no escape. She said, "I will search everywhere for the man who had intercourse with me."

But nowhere could she find him.

Where was he? At home with his father.

"She has blocked the highways. Because of her, no one travels, no one escapes."

His father replied, "The city. Do not let her find you in the mountains."

He found a way. He joined the city-dwellers, his brothers all together, the black-headed people, his brothers. He was not to be found in the mountains.

The day had broken and Utu had risen. The woman inspected herself closely. Holy Inana inspected herself closely.

"Ah! Who will compensate me for the wrong done to me? Ah! Who will make amends for this violation? Should it not be the concern of my own father, Enki?"

She directed her steps to the Abzu of Eridug, the region of wisdom and fresh water. She prostrated herself on the ground before Enki and stretched out her hands towards him. "Father Enki, I should be compensated! Someone should pay for what's happened to me. I shall only re-enter my shrine and be quiet and still and leave peace, after you have handed that man over to me. You have all wisdom and knowledge here in the Abzu. Give him to me!"

Enki, god of wisdom and fresh water, said, "Well he's not really a man yet. But he has done the work of a man, so all right!"

Holy Inana rose, she brushed herself off. She left the Abzu of Eridug. She lifted up her arms. She stretched herself like a rainbow across the sky and reached as far as the earth. She let the south wind pass across. She let the north wind pass across.

What passes between the north wind and the south wind, who knows? But Sukaletuda was afraid. Afraid, Sukaletuda made himself as tiny as possible. When he peeped out, he was alone, and in the mountains where he belonged, and that is where the great woman found him. She spoke.

"Dog. Ass. Pig."

Sukaletuda replied to holy Inana, "My lady, I was to water the garden plot, to build the shaduf by the well among the plants and to do the weeding. But I did not do the watering and I did not build the shaduf and as for the weeding, I pulled all the plants out by their roots and destroyed them and not a single plant remained there. Not even one. Then what did the storm wind bring? It blew the dust of the mountains into my eyes. When I tried to wipe the corner of my eyes with my hand, I got some of the dust out, but not all. Some was left in. When I raised my eyes to the lowlands, I saw, where the sun rises, the exalted gods of the land themselves. When I raised my eyes to the highlands where the sun sets, I saw the exalted gods of the land themselves. And then I looked into my own garden, there beneath my poplar tree, I saw a solitary sleeping spirit – someone fully in possession of all the divine powers – someone whose destiny was decided by the gods. In my own garden plot beneath the poplar tree – had I not looked there five, six, ten times before, beneath the broad shade of that Euphrates poplar and seen nothing? Now I saw a sleeping goddess. I saw you. I had never seen anything so beautiful. A girdle of seven divine powers covered your genitals. Why did I do it? I could not help myself. I lay down beside you in your resting place. I undid the girdle of seven divine powers and touched what I should never have touched. I entered you. Then I kissed you and covered you up again and went back to my garden plot. And all the time you slept the deep sleep of the goddess. And then you woke and you were so angry."

"So! What is this to me? You did the work of a man without respect or responsibility. You knew right. You knew wrong. You chose. You will die."

She struck him. She hit him. She changed him there and determined his destiny. But as she did, Holy Inana spoke a word to Sukaletuda.

This was her word. It is a cry of outrage across the universe. It is the cry of Inana: "Hannahhannah. Nin. Nana. Irina. Agushaya." She is the daughter of Ningal's might and power. Let us extol her. This is the cry against the rape.

The goddess said to him, "No excuse. You chose so young. You chose so wrong. Even though you were young, you knew it was wrong. And you will die. But I decree your name will not be forgotten. Your name will exist in songs down the ages and make the songs sweet. The youngster will sing your name when he grazes the sheep. The goatherd will hum your name as she tumbles her butter-churn. The glamorous young singer will perform the song of your story to great acclaim in the king's palace."

What did one person say to the other? What did the other one add? This! This story I have told you. This song I have sung you. This is the song of Sukaletuda the adolescent, who broke the rule in the worst possible of ways.

How do we know it? Through what was said in one person telling the story to another. And through what was added by the other in detail. Through the singing of songs, the whispering of gossip and the telling of tales time upon time. And in the making of the marks, the cuneiform marks, on the tablets of clay.

And I have heard the story and I am telling it now to you.

What do you make of what I have said to you? What will you add? What detail will you add?

THE AGUSHAYA HYMN

Let loose the cry and let it echo!
HANNAH NIN NANA IRNINA INANA AGUSHAYA.
She is daughter of Queen Ningal's might and power.
Her mother and her father are the moon.
Her name is Inana. Her name is Ishtar.
Let me extol her!

I am praising the greatest of the gods. I am praising the warrior among the gods. She is the daughter of the might and power of the great queen. Let me extol her. She is Ishtar, the greatest one. Let me praise this warrior among the gods. Let me tell you of her might. She is young but she is powerful. She wears the crown of heaven. Her sign is the eight-pointed star. Her brother is Utu, the sun, and her father is Nanna, the moon. She is queen of heaven and earth, with the capacity to visit the Great Below as well. Her sign is the plaited reed that marks the storehouse door, and she holds the capacity of the snake. Because of her, the land is fertile and the harvests come. She is the benefactor. Be grateful and beware. Her feast is the mad dance of the grim reaping. Her song is the harvest song of the young men, hacked off as if for spear poles. Her harvest is the valorous boys. Her feast comes with the task which Ea gave her. He gave her frenzy in battle and passion in strife.

Ishtar, the young goddess, had wit, boundless drive, enthusiasm, energy and intelligence. She was assertive, strategic, well organized and brave.

Ea, father god of wisdom and fresh water, saw all her potential and so he gave to the young Ishtar his protection. He surrounded her with abundance, with flashing lightning bolts and, though it was by accident, he gave to her fertile energy all the blueprints of civilization, the Me. He gave her fame and he gave her might. She had in her possession all the traditions and skills that would structure and balance life and society and the nature of humanity.

She took them all gladly – the crown, the sceptre and the throne. Then she was all powerful. Then she became more fearsome than the bull. Her clamour and her might raging, she set forth. Then horror and destruction were unleashed. Adorned with awesomeness, her onslaught was terrible. She became bizarre in her actions. She behaved without reason. At her uproar the gods became afraid. None of them could stop her. They were afraid that she was spinning out of control. They said, "In her glory and her terror is the possibility of chaos." She was sovereign to her people, to their kings and even to the great gods. Neither the gods nor the assembly of the gods dared resist her. So the great gods called on Ea. They said, "This sovereignty is a problem. Nothing disastrous has happened yet, but she is unpredictable. The strength applied should be in proportion to the best desired result. She's out of balance. Anything could happen."

Ea, the wise god of wisdom, subtle intelligence, always good in a crisis, said, "Yes. You're right. She has no equal. Nothing can match her. We must create something to challenge her. We will create someone to challenge her and mirror her." At this all the gods nodded. Ea said, "Let the challenger be trusty. Let her have muscle. Let her raise riot. Let this challenger be always ready to fight. Let her be fierce." All the gods nodded again. "Let her hair be extraordinary." More nods, and some said, "Yes. Because that's a sign of primitive strength." But then Ea said, "Let the challenger be adorned with awesomeness. Let her awesomeness and her onslaught be terrible. And she should be bizarre in her actions. She should behave without reason. She should be mighty. Her cry should be the cry of battle, but murderous, bullying and vicious." This time there was more reserve. Most of the gods said, "Hm." A few said, "Isn't this going a bit far?" But Ea was determined. He said, "Yes. We must go too far, to show where too far leads. She needs to see it. She must see her future self in the mirror." Then all the gods said, "All right. Try that. You do it. Make it so. You who made humankind, you who made Enkidu, now make something that sorts out all this mayhem!"

Ea heard their words. Great god Ea, source of wisdom and fresh water, scooped out the earth of the Apsu that was always underneath his nails, and, as he had done in so many significant moments before, he spat on it and he shaped it and he baked it. As humanity had been created, as Enkidu had been created, so he created yet another new being – he created Saltu.

God Ea has straightaway set to his task! He is making Saltu that she fight with Ishtar! Powerful is her form, monstrous are her proportions! She is artful as none could rival, she is a fighter. Monstrous are her proportions, she is a fighter. Her flesh is battle, the melee is her hair. Discord is her form and her name means Discord. Father Ea made Discord so that she might fight with Ishtar. He said, "She is adorned with awesomeness and her onslaught is terrible. She is bizarre in her actions. She behaves without reason. She is mighty, her battle cry is not a battle cry, but a cry of the murderer, the bully, the vicious one. She is surpassing, she is fierce, she has extraordinary strength. My Saltu is girded with combat as her clothing. She is strange and terrifying to behold. Raging, she takes her stand in the midst of the depths. There are horrible words which come from her mouth and stream around her. Very good."

Ea, the lord of wisdom and fresh water, addressed his creation, Saltu. He said, "Saltu, Discord, know me. I created you. Keep quiet now. Listen. Pay heed to what I say. Hear my orders. Do what I tell you to do!" Amazingly, Saltu calmed down at the words of Ea and she listened. So Ea began to speak.

"Saltu, there is a certain goddess, whose greatness is surpassing beyond all gods. Her name is Ishtar, Inana. Well, she has many names. To you, she may be Irnina, the snake. She is dressed all in battle mail. But I have created you to humiliate her. Look at you! You have stature, valour and might in abundance. But she thinks you are weak and worthless. Off you go now, to her private quarters. When you get there, speak rudely. Say, 'Hey! You in there!' Something like that. She will rush out, furious. She may say, 'Now then, woman, explain your behaviour.' Something like that. But you, though she be beautiful and powerful and furious, you should show no respect to her. Whatever she says, answer her never a word submissively. Instead speak out proudly what is on your tongue. Speak proudly before her as an equal."

Then Ea, the wise, took to taunting Saltu, rousing her with insults in contempt. Ea, the wise, whose reasoning is extraordinary, knew just the way to choose the right words to spark the feelings of Saltu. "Ishtar the queen is brave. I think she is braver than you. Ishtar is grander. She is grander than you. Ishtar is proud and nothing can stop her. I think she is better than you. Listen, I've had second thoughts. Don't go. She'll definitely beat you. You had better not go."

Saltu flew into a rage. Her face altered horribly. She turned and she flew to her mission.

News travels fast in the world of the gods. Ishtar heard word and spoke to her servant Ninshubur, the true and trusted friend and servant, who had waited faithfully for Ishtar to return from the underworld. Ishtar said, "Find out all about her. Learn of her haunts, the signs of her strength. Bring me news. Recount to me her behaviour. Bring me signs and images of her."

Ninshubur was wise and strong. She went out alone to face what was to be faced. She was proud to be on her task, thinking there was no one greater or more terrible than Ishtar, the one she served. But she looked twice when she saw the exceedingly great one, Saltu. She heeded Saltu. She examined her form. In spite of her great love and respect for Ishtar, Ninshubur was shaken by the sight. Also, she saw the truth and understood this to be the worst manifestation of her mistress. Ninshubur returned to Ishtar. Shaking and stuttering, she described what she had seen.

"Saltu is adorned with awesomeness. She is like you, but her onslaught is terrible. She is like you, but she has no strategy and is bizarre in her actions. She is like you, but she behaves without reason. She is mighty. Her battle cry is not the battle cry of the rule of battle, but it is a cry of the murderer, the bully, the tyrant and the vicious."

So it was that Ishtar first heard the news from Ninshubur, her closest companion. She learned of Saltu. Angrily, she, all powerful, most capable, proud in her might and ferocity, she drew herself up. The warrior Ishtar, the most capable of all the gods, drew herself up. She had Ninshubur by her side.

In her greatness she grinds her enemies. She doesn't turn back. She is the greatest among gods. She is fearless like a young man, she has confrontational energy, the capacity to try anything regardless of risk to herself, regardless of life and the love of the living. She says the word that needs to be spoken. Proudly she speaks. These are the signs of her might. She is adorned with awesomeness, and her awesomeness and her onslaught are terrible.

But Saltu is bizarre in her actions, she behaves without reason. She is mighty, her cry is the cry of battle, but it is murderous and bullying and vicious. These qualities are terrible. Ishtar went to the fight and there was her shadow, Saltu, to confront her.

Let the cry echo: HANNAH NIN NANA INNINI IRNINA ENNINA NINNAR NINANNA INNINA ISHTAR NANNA INANA AGUSHAYA AAAA

Sadly, we do not know what happened next. We do not know what happened when Ishtar, the incomparable goddess, met Saltu, her shadow. We do not know what was said, how it all ended, what happened to Saltu. At this moment in time, there are many missing tablets.

When the tablet starts again, Ishtar is storming off to have it out with Ea. Of course she knew that he was at the bottom of it all.

She said, "Why? You gave me all the gifts I have. Why? After creating me, why did you set Saltu against me? You made a ghastly caricature of me. She was bizarre in her actions. She behaved without reason. She was a murderous bully and vicious. I still hear her clamour in my head! It was awful. Make it go away! Let her go back to the cave she came from."

Ea made ready to speak. He smiled and said to Ishtar, "I'm so happy to see you. I'm so happy to see that you see this. As soon as you said those words, 'Make it go away', then it was done. You had only to ask. You cheer me, daughter. You cause me delight that you, having had enough of your excess, you said it. As soon as you asked for Saltu to be dispelled, in that moment, she was gone. As soon as you had spoken, in that moment, I had let my Saltu go.

"But so that the future race of those who will live in future days, so that they might know about this moment and how to deal with this possibility of destruction, I say this: Let Saltu return yearly. Let her return in all her whirling power. Let the warning of your creative and destructive power return in her. Let you, Ishtar and Saltu, be the whirling dance of Agushaya and return every year, around kings and around gods."

They organized the first Ishtar festival in the time of King Hammurabi. It was an Agushaya festival. Look about at all the people! There is drinking. There is dancing in the street, singing, shouting, screaming. Hear the clamour. Are they all going mad? They are dancing the Whirling Dance to celebrate the whirling power of Agushaya. But then in the end, someone must say, "That's enough." And if that doesn't work, then someone must call out the name of a god, "Ea." Or call out, "Saltu." Or call, "Agushaya." Call on the gods to restore sanity to the world gone mad.

DEBATES

Dr Jana Matuszak described to us the genre of literary debates: 'They can be defined as a verbal contest between two antagonists, who are either quarrelling about who's more important (non-human rivals), or who's more competent (human rivals).

'The earliest indirect evidence comes from 2600 BCE, where contests between kings are mentioned in rhetoric collections of sayings that could be employed in such debates. I can well imagine that they were originally improvised and performed in life.'

Indeed, palace accounts record payments to performers. Debates remain a popular genre in Iraqi culture today.

We have much in common with these ancient people: the debates lay bare petty concerns and explore how quarrels and disputes escalate.

THE PICKAXE AND THE PLOUGH

O, the Pickaxe, the Pickaxe, the Pickaxe: made of poplar, with a tooth of ash; or made of tamarisk, with a tooth of sea-thorn: double-toothed or four-toothed: the Pickaxe started a quarrel with the Plough.

The Pickaxe spoke like this to the Plough:

"Plough, you draw furrows. What do your furrows matter to me? You break up clods. What does your clod-breaking matter to me? You cannot spread out clay to make bricks. You cannot lay foundations or build a house. You cannot strengthen an old wall's base. You cannot put a roof on a good man's house. You cannot straighten town squares. Plough, you draw furrows. What do your furrows matter to me? You break up clods. What does your clod-breaking matter to me?"

The Plough answered the Pickaxe:

"I am the Plough, servant of Father Enlil, assembled by a mighty hand. I am mankind's faithful farmer. The king celebrates my festival in the harvest month. He sacrifices cattle and sheep, he pours out libations. The drums are beaten. The king harnesses the oxen to the yoke, sets them between my shafts and takes up my handles. Nobles walk at my side. The people watch me with joy.

"The furrows I have tilled adorn the flat lands. The stalks rising up in the fields are there because of me. When the fields have been reaped and the grain has been gathered, the shepherd benefits. Dumuzi's sheep benefit. My threshing floors are yellow hillocks radiating beauty. I heap up the old emmer wheat and the new wheat for Enlil. I fill mankind's storehouses with barley. Orphans and widows glean my fields for scattered ears. People gather my straw for building. The herds thrive.

"Meanwhile, you, O Pickaxe, are burrowing in the mud, weeding miserably with your teeth, sticking your head into the mud in the fields. You spend your days with the brickmoulds in the mud: nobody cleans you. Digging wells, digging ditches, digging, digging, digging!

"Your wood is fit only for poor men, not for high-ranking people. All that adorns your head is a slave's hand. You dare hurl insults at me. You dare compare yourself with me. You insult me when you call me a 'Digger of furrows'."

Then the Pickaxe spoke to the Plough:

"Plough, do you think being small matters to me? Does being praised matter to me? Does being powerful matter to me? Here is what matters to me: in Enlil's temple I take precedence over you.

"I build embankments and dig ditches. I fill the meadows with water. When a canal is cut, or a ditch is cut, when water floods from a swelling river and creates lagoons on all sides, I, the Pickaxe, set up dams around it.

"The fowler collects eggs. The fisherman catches fish. The trapper nets birds. The abundance I have created spreads across the land.

"After the water has been diverted from the wetlands, and work begins on the meadows, I go to the fields long before you. I open the fields for you. I clear the embankments for you. I remove the weeds for you. It is true that when you eventually get to the field, you come in procession, but there are six oxen, four farmers: you are only the eleventh to turn up. And yet you want to compare yourself with me?

"When you come out to the field after me, your single furrow brings you pleasure. But when you get to work and become entangled in roots and thorns, your tooth breaks. Once your tooth breaks, you are useless, and even once your tooth is fixed, it is loose, and you cannot hold on to it. Your farmer says, 'This plough is done for!'

"He has to hire carpenters to work on you. Artisans scurry around you. The fullers scrape a skin for you. They stretch it over the frame for you. They toil at the straps for you: then they put the foul hide on your head.

"Your behaviour may be grand, but your work is slight. I work all year round, but you are only here for four months: for eight months you are not needed. You are gone for twice as long as you are present.

"I am the Pickaxe and I live in the city. No one is more honoured than I am. I am a servant who is loyal to his master. I am the one who builds a house for my master. I am the one who widens the cattle stalls and enlarges the sheepfolds. I spread out clay and make bricks. I strengthen an old wall's base. I put a roof on a good man's house. I straighten the town square. I am the Pickaxe!

"When I have finished building the sturdy walls of the city, I make the temples splendid and embellish them. Then I work in the city palace, where the high-ranking officials live.

"They rest and refresh themselves, when their work is done, in the cool and pleasant houses I have built. They employ labourers and pay their wages, providing them with food and drink. And so I have enabled workers of all classes to support their wives and children.

"I make a kiln for the boatman so he can heat pitch and caulk his boat. I enable him to support his wife and children.

"I mark out a garden for the householder. When the garden has been encircled by mud walls, he again takes up the pickaxe. When a well has been dug, a water lift constructed and a water hoist hung, I straighten the plots. I am the one who lets water irrigate the plots. I cause the apple tree to grow and bring forth its fruits. The apples adorn the temples of the great gods. Thus I enable the gardener to support his wife and children.

"After I have worked on the watercourse and the sluices, put the path in order and built a tower on the bank, the fieldworkers, whether on the day shift or the night shift, can go into that tower. They can rest and revive themselves there. I put life back in their hearts.

"Insultingly, you call me 'Digger of Ditches'. But I dig out watercourses to irrigate the plains and the dry lands where there is no water. I make it possible for those who thirst to refresh themselves.

"What do the common folk say? 'After the heavens had been turned upside down, after Sumer endured great trouble; as houses were overwhelmed by the floods and Enlil frowned in anger at us; though Enlil flooded the harvest, though he acted mightily, yet he did not abandon us: the single-toothed pickaxe was struck into drying earth for us. The pickaxe ties the sheaves for us. It binds bird traps and knots the reed baskets for us. It supports the solitary labourer and the destitute.'"

Then the Storm spoke:

"The mortar lies still while the pestle pounds. The sieve disputes with the strainer. People fight with grindstones. Why do you two argue over the ripening grain?"

Then Enlil addressed the Pickaxe:

"Pickaxe, do not start getting so mightily angry. Pickaxe, you are like a maidservant, always ready, always reliable, always completing every task. Remember, Nisaba is your inspector and your overseer."

In its dispute with the Plough, the Pickaxe had triumphed. Praise be to Nisaba!

THE BIRD AND THE FISH

In those ancient days, when the good destinies had been decreed, An and Enlil set up the divine rules of heaven and earth.

Then it was Enki who founded the dwelling places. He took in his hand the waters to encourage the good seed. He laid out the Tigris and the Euphrates side by side to bring the water from the mountains. He scoured out smaller streams and positioned watercourses. He made sheepfolds and cattle pens. He created shepherds and herdsmen. He founded cities and settlements throughout the earth and made the black-headed people multiply. He gave them a king to be their shepherd.

It was Enki who knitted together the marshlands, making young and old reeds grow together there. He created the pools and lagoons and reedbeds and marshes, so that birds and fish could live there. He filled these dwelling places with fish and birds and indicated to them their positions and instructed them in the divine rules of their existence.

Then Fish laid its eggs in the lagoons, and Bird built its nest in a gap in the reedbeds. All was well.

But one day Bird let out a sudden loud twitter and frightened Fish in his lagoon.

Fish took up a stand and cried out. The whole street was roused by Fish quarrelling. Grandiosely, Fish initiated hostilities. Fish addressed Bird murderously and in an overbearing manner.

"Bird! I have had enough. What is all this croaking? This squawking! This noise in the marshes? I have had enough. You make a big fuss – a big commotion. I have had enough. We've all had enough. The farmer has had enough of you. The farmer digs his field, he sows his grain, and there you are pecking away at his crop, before it has even grown. You are forever gobbling greedily, while your heart is dripping with evil. The farmer's son lays lines and nets in the furrows to try to catch you.

"The gardener has had enough of you. He works hard on his fruit trees and his vegetable patch, and there you are, pecking away, making holes in his harvest, damaging his fruit. He has to set up nets against you in gardens and orchards. He cannot rest his arms from firing his sling. You cause damage in the vegetable plots. You are even a nuisance in the damp parts of the fields. Look at the wet earth! There are your ugly footprints. Bird! You are shameless. You fill the courtyard with your droppings. Even the little temple sweeper boy has had enough of you. He sweeps the temple courtyard all day long. He turns his back for a moment, and the yard is full of bird droppings again. He cannot rest because of you. He cannot sit down because of you. He has to use his sling against you.

"Why are you always flapping about? With your ugly voice, you frighten the night. Get away! Get lost! Leave the marshes! Get this noise of yours off my back! Get a hole in the rubbish heap. That is where you belong."

This is how Fish insulted Bird on that day. Fish was furious and did not hold back. But Bird, with her multicoloured plumage and multicoloured face, was convinced of her own beauty, and did not take to heart the insults Fish had cast. As if she was a nursemaid singing, she paid no attention to the ugly words uttered.

Calmly Bird answered Fish.

"What's got into you? You who live in the depths and are so lowly? How has your heart become so arrogant? How can that flabby mouth of yours come out with so much rubbish? Take a look at yourself. Your mouth goes so far around your head, I'm surprised your head doesn't drop off altogether. You've got no hips or arms or legs or hands or feet. You have got a tail, it is true. But how would you know that? You've got no neck, so you can't turn round to look. And to be frank, you smell awful. People screw up their noses and bare their teeth at you. They throw up. If they touch you, they have to wash their hands.

"But I know the real problem. It is jealousy.

"You're jealous of me. You know that I am the wise, the clever, the beautiful, the multicoloured, the soft-feathered Bird. My voice irritates you because you know you cannot sing. My presence annoys you because you are confined and cannot travel and fly free as I do. Well, let your heart be at peace. The key to peace lies in acceptance. Accept that I am superior – that I am predominant and pre-eminent. Accept this and be at rest."

These words were fanning the flames of Fish's anger into fury.

"Ha! Pre-eminent? I'll have you know that I am very important. Where would the people be without me? I provide abundance in the storehouses. No feast is complete without me. At the festivals, when the table is laid, the place of honour is occupied by me. I am the centrepiece on the big platter; it is I who am superior. I am pre-eminent."

But Bird had already flown off with her beak in the air, leaving Fish with fury boiling in his belly.

Fish conceived a plot. Silently and furtively, he slithered alongside the banks of the lagoon. When Bird rose up from her nest to fetch food, Fish attacked. He destroyed her house and tore down her storeroom. He turned her well-built nest of brushwood into a haunted house. He smashed the eggs she had laid and threw them into the lagoon. Then, smirking, he swam into the depths of the lagoon.

When Bird flew back to her nest, she saw what had happened. She stopped in mid-flight. She shrieked to heaven and circled in the sky. Then she sought Fish. She searched the marshes, peering into the deep water. There, close to the surface, she saw Fish's tiny fish-spawn. Silently she gathered them all together, and lifting them, she piled them in a wiggling heap in the reeds. Then she called down, "You utter fool. Dumb. Muddle-head. Swine. Rascal. Stay there at the bottom gorging yourself on your own excrement, you freak."

This raised Fish to the surface. He saw what she had done. The quarrel broke out hotter than before. The insults flew like missiles.

"Chopped off beak." "Deformed feet." "Cleft mouth." "Thin tongue."

"Right," said Fish. "That's it. You still don't understand my true greatness, my true worth. Our judge shall take this up. I am taking our case to litigation. I will have arbitration at the highest level. I am going to our judge Enki in the Abzu of the Eridug."

They agreed that was what they would do. They would go to Enki in the Abzu of Eridug and find out once and for all who was pre-eminent and superior.

Jostling and pushing, the air full of insults, they carried their evil quarrel into the Abzu itself. There, Enki from his throne heard their clamour and called out, "How long will you persist in your quarrelling?"

Both Bird and Fish fell silent. Then they crept forwards. Humbly they requested a verdict. They registered their litigation and their request for arbitration in the Abzu of Eridug.

Bird spoke first. She put her case to establish her pre-eminence. "Lord of true speech, pay attention to my words. Fish has destroyed my house. He has turned my nest of brushwood into a haunted house. He has torn down my storeroom. He has smashed my eggs and thrown them into the lagoon. All this because he will not accept my superiority and my right and my pre-eminence."

She prostrated herself on the ground and withdrew.

Then Fish spoke. He put his case to establish his pre-eminence.

"Lord of true speech. Pay attention to my words. Bird has piled up my fish spawn, insulted me and disrespected me. All because she will not accept my superiority and my right and my pre-eminence."

Enki listened to both. He considered, and then spoke. "I shall instruct you both in the divine rules and just ordinances of the different dwelling places which I created at the very beginning. You, Bird, must acknowledge that Fish has strength and worth. He stocks the storehouses of the land. He has pride of place on the banqueting table. You, Fish, must acknowledge that Bird has strength and worth. Her song fills the air and delights the ear. Each of you has a place set down in the divine rules and just ordinances of the dwelling places.

"But the destiny of Bird is to add sweet song to the air, and the dwelling place of the Bird is the skies above the reeds, while the destiny of Fish is to provide abundance from his dwelling place in the depths of the lagoons below. So I say this: Fish must always and for ever look up from the depths to Bird above. And Bird must always and for ever look down from the reeds onto Fish in the lagoons below."

These are the words of Enki, spoken from the wisdom of the Tablet of Destinies.

Thus, in the verdict from the Abzu of Eridug, Bird was proclaimed pre-eminent over Fish. Thus, in the dispute between Bird and Fish, Bird was considered victorious.

THE DATE PALM AND THE TAMARISK

In the long-ago days, in the very first days, in the days when the gods established the land, when they shaped it and formed it, they raised up mountains to be its skeleton and scooped out rivers to be its lifeblood. Then the gods created their assembly: the gods of the land, with the greatest of the gods and goddesses gathered together. Because the gods love people, they shared the power of kingship and queenship with the black-headed people – gave them a city where they could gather, a king to rule over them. The king of the city of Kish protected his people, gathered them into his city. The heart and centre of the city was the palace, and the heart of the palace was its garden. In the heart of the garden the king planted a date palm: beside her he filled the space with a tamarisk tree. People gave praise, the palace enjoyed leisure: there was feasting and drumming, discussion and learning, in the shade of these trees.

The trees were different, they had different qualities: they became rivals, he and she, Tamarisk and Date palm. They argued and quarrelled, each aiming to lord it over the other.

Who will be the winner? Who will be judged the better tree? Wait and see; and see you shall.

The Tamarisk boasted: "I am much the greater tree: I am bigger than you, my branches are expansive, the crown of my branches is luxuriant and my trunk is tall and thick."

The Date palm replied: "Tamarisk, you are a large tree: what of that? Size doesn't matter – what good is it? Trees are for bearing fruit! That is our purpose. You are a useless tree – what fruit do you bear? None at all! My dates are eaten by all! They delight everyone, and everyone says they are delicious – from the king and queen; to the gardener who takes care of me; to the mother who raises her child through the gift of my strength – everyone delights in my fruit."

But at this the Tamarisk spoke out very proudly in reply:

"Fruit!...Dates!...Trees are for bearing wood – that is our purpose: wood for creating, for making the things that the black-headed people need. My supreme quality is my wood. Humans can make the things they need from me: the palace dishes are made from me, the queen drinks from my cups, the king eats from my table. You, you are like my slave girl, the one who fetches and carries, bringing your produce to decorate my table. I am the one who is useful here."

But the Date palm only answered: "The Tamarisk may be useful, but being useful is only sterile and dirty: you do not know divine pleasure, for fertility is divine pleasure. The king can make no sacrifice unless I am by his side: only with me can the rites of sprinkling to the four winds be performed. Because of me, the people can hold their festival parties: but you are only fit for the brewers' hands: dregs are piled up on you."

The Tamarisk said: "Let me show you the city quarter of the craftsmen, where the surroundings are filled with the sweet smell of my resin. Let me fill out the picture for you: my craftsmen are working in their booths in the woodworkers' quarter, they are making furniture and utensils, craftily carving and skilfully shaping my wood. They are making sturdy tools and brooms, confident that my wood will not fail. Delicate details are added to the statues of the gods by the temple craftsmen: the far-reaching fingers and flexible toes of both the greater and the lesser gods are made from my supple branches and strong trunk. My quarter of the city smells sweet – the air is filled with the perfume of my aromatic resin. The incense burners blossom full of my sweet-smelling smoke. The sacred temple prostitutes enjoy my sweet sap there. Everyone is busy and productive; everyone is energized by my presence there. Even the ploughman, outside the city, is motivated, and has his work eased by my help. He makes his spade from my lap and with it digs a canal. He opens up a ditch and waters the fields with the life-giving waters of the god Enki. Corn is planted, renewing the strength of the king and the vigour of the corn god."

The Date palm listened to his description of the workers. She laughed sweetly, saying only in reply, "Come, let me describe to you the festival parties in my quarter of the city, where there is always fun to be had. Rich and poor alike have sticky fingers and sweet lips from my syrup. Sweet cakes shaped like the sweetest and most hidden parts of the bodies of humans are shared at the goddess' feasts. Your worker, the carpenter, lies down at ease on my leaves, entertained by transvestites and musicians. He worships me at his ease, giving me praise every day."

This roused the Tamarisk to anger and he began to hurl insults at the Date palm: "Who do you think you are? I despise you. I glory in my greater strength: I can cut off your beautiful fronds. I'll make you sorry."

The Date palm replied, "I am six times better than you, seven times better – I take the place of the corn god for three months of the year: orphans, widows, poor men alike eat my food without restraint. My offspring are so sweet and so fertile – the date stones keep sprouting up everywhere."

But the Tamarisk said: "Children buy your fruit with the cheapest coins. Your seeds and stones drop into the graves of the dead. You are a whore – impregnated by the seed of many who are unknown to you. Your body, your timber, is never even used by musicians."

The Date palm replied to this abuse with dignity, saying: "I have no need to justify myself through lower function: I am divine of myself. It is useless for you to contend with me, since my worth is so much greater than yours. My deeds and my words show your worthlessness, and my word is Ishtar: I am the tree of Ishtar."

At this the Tamarisk could say no more. He bowed his head, he accepted defeat, recognizing the holy tree of the goddess Ishtar. He freely offered tribute to his sister, the Date palm. He praised Ishtar, goddess of the Date palm, tree at the heart of the garden.

And so ended the dispute between the trees: as we promised, you have seen who was the winner, who was judged the better tree. It was the holy tree of Ishtar, goddess of the city of Kish, the city with a Date palm at its heart, with the goddess at its heart, the city ruled by Ishtar's chosen king, in the land shaped and created, established by the gods, in the long-ago days.

Praise be to Ishtar, goddess of the Date palm!

SUMMER AND WINTER

The great god An lifted his head in pride and created a good day. He made plans for the future and sent out the black-headed people across the land. The great god Enlil set his foot upon the earth like a great bull. Enlil, lord of the earth, made plans to increase the good day of abundance, to make the dear night resplendent. He decided to make flax and barley grow; to ensure the spring floods at the quay, he lengthened the days. He decided to make sure that Summer closed the sluices of heaven; that Winter brought plentiful water to the quay.

Enlil copulated with the great hills, he shared his seed with the mountain. He filled its womb with Summer and Winter, those two which bring plentiful life to the land. As he made love with the earth, there was a roar like a bull's. That night, the hill opened her loins, and, as smoothly as the flow of fine oil, she gave birth to Summer and Winter.

Enlil nourished them in the pastures of the hills. Then, he set about determining the destinies of Summer and Winter. For Summer: founding towns and villages, bringing in abundant harvests, sending labourers out to the arable lands to work the fields with oxen. For Winter: abundance, the spring floods, planting good grain in the fields and fruitful earth, gathering in the harvests. Enlil determined the destinies of Summer and Winter.

Winter, Enlil's heroic son, guided the spring floods, life blood of the land, down from the ridges of the hills. He set his foot on the Tigris and Euphrates like a great bull, and released their sweet waters into the fields and fruitful acres. He shaped lagoons from the salt waters. He brought fish and birds, together, into existence by the sea. He surrounded all the reedbeds with reed shoots, young reeds and mature reeds. Summer, Enlil's heroic other son, drained the fields, sending the cool waters over the fruitful acres like a garment.

Holy Winter made the ewe give birth to the lamb, the goat give birth to the kid. He made the herds teem with cows and calves; he provided butter and milk. On the high plains he gladdened the hearts of the deer and gazelle. He set all the birds of heaven nesting in the broad spaces. The fish of the lagoons laid their eggs in the reedbeds. In the orchards, he made honey and fermenting juices ooze towards the ground. He made trees, wherever they grew, bear fruit. He founded gardens and provided plants. He filled the furrows with grain. He made the land as beautiful as the radiant maiden Ezina, personification of grain. His harvest, the great festival of Enlil, rose towards the heavens.

Summer founded homesteads and farms, he made wide cattle pens and sheepfolds. He increased the sheaves across the arable lands. He ripened flax, brought a plentiful harvest into the temples, heaped up golden piles of grain. He founded towns and villages, created temples for the gods. He established abundance for Enlil. Summer, Enlil's heroic son, decided to bring offerings to his father's temple. He brought animals: cattle and sheep from the hills; fully-grown wild rams, deer and gazelle; long-fleeced sheep, barley-fed sheep, thick-tailed sheep; fat pigs from the reedbeds; birds with their eggs; porcupine, tortoise, turtle. He brought harvest crops: flour and malt, butter and milk from both cattle and sheep, baskets piled high with small and large beans, onions, shallots, turnips, saffron. Summer, Enlil's heroic son, offered them all.

Winter released the water of life and opened the sluices. He gathered oxen and sheep. He brought tribute from the land: pouches of quartz, gold and silver; cedar, cypress and boxwood; figs and dried fruit; tribute from the hills: honey and beer; song birds, fattened ducks, carp; pomegranates from the orchards, bunches of grapes, winter cucumbers, large turnips, long leeks.

Summer and Winter set about organizing the offerings for Enlil's temple. Like huge butting bulls, they reared triumphantly. But Winter turned away, because his limbs had grown tired from the heavy grains, emmer and wheat, and from all the watering he had undertaken. He would not draw near. Consequently, his anger grew, and he started to quarrel with Summer.

"Summer, my brother," he said, "you should not praise yourself. The harvest you bring is not the product of your toil. You should not brag as if you were the one who did the hard work, as if you were the one who had worked the fields, controlled the irrigation during the spring floods, as if you had made the grain sprout with the morning dew…it is through *my* toil that you enter the palace! But after all the work that *you* do – wielding the destructive hoe, gathering vegetables, carrying straw to the byre, cutting briars and thorns, shovelling dung – you are like a hired man who has to go back in the fields, after finishing his paid work, to gather what he needs for himself."

In this way, Winter taunted Summer. Summer is a hero whom one does not challenge. He searched his head for insults with which to respond. He was as confident as a great bull eating rich grass when he raised his head and spoke. "Winter, even though you have to stay by the side of the oven, you should not launch such insults at one who leads a more active life. You do not look after the house, you do not till the land, with all the difficulties that entails. A young scribe is neglectful, and does not pluck rushes from the reedbeds. A singer does not embellish a banquet simply by turning up. Winter, do not launch such insults! My working term of duty is seven months of the year. My diligence does not speak softly. Tirelessly and constantly, I pour abundance into the fields. When water has been closed off from the arable lands, when bowls have been placed, when fish have been piled up, I am Father Enlil's great auditor. I harrow his fields. When you have given the signal for field work, concentrating your efforts on damp tracts of land, I do not work for you. If the grain bends and breaks in the spring furrows, no one builds a fence. Nothing you do will make the farmer's oxen angry with me."

In this way, Summer taunted Winter. And Winter replied, "Summer, this is as if I hear a grazing donkey braying noisily, or an ox chafing its neck on the pegs, or a bragging fieldworker who does not know the extent of the field he works. Summer, my brother, you are boasting about *my* toil! A man from the storehouse stands before you and instructs you. Pay attention. When tribute is brought in your boats, when the grass has been carried into the storehouse, what will the penned sheep eat? Your reeds are exhausted. As long as you go with my term of duty, great and small order you about. Although you are the one who gathered the harvest and filled the storehouses, I am their owner when your strength fails. And when the clouds pour down my life-giving rain, when the waters of the first greening sweep down from the hills, when the new grain is added to the stores, the good farmer sees to his fields, shouts for joy and sets out confidently for the city with his carrier donkeys. My brother, when you have put away the holy plough, you roar like fire, you sit down to plentiful food and drink and receive the choicest goods from the land. When you have made a perfect feast for the gods, when a great banquet is prepared in the holy shrine of An, the Anuna dress in their holy garments, and drums and heart-gladdening instruments play. But it was I who created the abundance of food and wine. I perfected the holy garments with fine oil. And when your oppressive heat bears down, and the black-headed people put away blankets and cloths in their bedrooms, moths destroy them – because of you! I am Ninkasi's helper, bringing cold water as tribute from the hills, to sweeten her beer. After plump grapes have been laid up in the cool, I make my king's great palace pleasant. How can you compare yourself to me, when all are seeking a roof under which to rest?"

In this way, for a second time, Winter taunted Summer. But Summer was convinced of his own strong power, and consequently was full of self-trust. He replied as if in a friendly way to Winter's insults.

He said, "Winter, you should not boast about your superior strength, when you have given away the grounds for your boasts. You seem like a man of office, but you are inept. Helpless people run from the oven to the kiln and back again, in the face of your inconstancy. In sunshine you reach decisions, but now people's teeth are chattering with cold because of you. When the winter day is half done, no one walks the streets. The servant, basking in the heat of the oven, stays indoors all day. The maid does not check the water container: she passes the day among the warm garments. As for the fields in winter, the furrows are not straight, the grain, ungathered, is carried off by huge flocks of rooks. The vegetable cutter does not make money in the market. The lame labourer brings old reeds. Do not open your mouth so wide to speak of your superior strength. I will make its true nature known."

This was the second time Summer had taunted Winter. It was a feast day, to celebrate the bounty of the land. But the two of them braced their legs and faced each other combatively. Summer and Winter, like great bulls about to tear at each other with their horns, bent forward like wild bulls and took up their positions.

Winter raised his head to speak. "Father Enlil, you gave me control of irrigation, you brought me plentiful water. I created meadows, and heaped high the granaries with grain thick from the furrows. Ezina, personification of grain, came forth in her splendour, like a beautiful maiden. But Summer is like a bragging administrator who does not know the extent of the field he oversees. My thighs have grown tired from the toil, from providing tribute for the king's palace. I, Winter, admire your heart, Enlil."

Summer took these words into his heart and pondered them. He calmed down. He spoke respectfully to Enlil. "Father Enlil, your judgement is highly valued, your holy word is exalted. The judgement you make cannot be altered: who could change it? We quarrelled, brother to brother, but now, let there be harmony. As long as you occupy the throne, the people will remain awestruck. I will not humiliate you in your season. In fact, let me praise you."

Enlil answered Summer and Winter. "Winter controls the life-giving waters of all the lands, he is the farmer of the gods, producing everything. Summer, dear son, how can you compare yourself to Winter?"

Enlil's exalted words were artfully wrought. Who could gainsay him? His judgement would not be altered: who could change it? Summer bowed to Winter and offered a prayer to him. In Summer's own house he prepared emmer beer and wine, and invited Winter to come to feast. They spent the day at a succulent banquet. Summer presented Winter with gold, silver and lapis lazuli. They poured out brotherhood and friendship like fine oil. By changing quarrelling to sweet words, they established harmony and balance between themselves.

In the dispute between Winter and Summer, Winter, Enlil's faithful farmer, was superior to Summer. Praise be to the great mountain, Father Enlil!

EZINA, GODDESS OF GRAIN

Although An created the Anuna gods, he did not create Ezina, goddess of grain, at the same time. The Anuna gods did not even know her name. Likewise, An had not yet created a god or goddess to take care of domesticated animals. So there were no sheep or lambs, no goats or kids and no looms or yarn. There was no grain, no bread, no cakes. There was no cloth to wear. There was nothing for Uttu, the goddess of weaving, to work with, so she had not yet been born.

The people of those days did not know anything about eating bread, or wearing clothes. They went about naked and tore at grass with their mouths, like sheep. This may have amused the gods, who had expressly created humans as servants. Yet, after a while, they saw that humans would be harder-working, more productive and generally more useful if they were better nourished, and if they had garments to keep them warm in cold weather, dry in wet weather and protected from the sun in hot weather.

So, at last, in their holy home on the Holy Mound, the gods created Duttur, god of sheep, and Ezina, goddess of grain. The gods gathered the bounty of Duttur and Ezina in their divine banqueting chamber, but they found that they themselves received no benefit from the grain or the sweet milk. So, for their own wellbeing, they decided to give these gifts to humankind, to ensure that humans flourished enough to make sacrifices to the gods, nourishing them with offerings of food, live animals and, of course, the hymns and prayers that accompanied the ceremonies.

Enki spoke to Enlil, "Father Enlil, now that sheep and grain have been created on the Holy Mound, let us send them down from the Holy Mound to humankind."

So the gods sent them down to nourish humankind. They provided generous grass and herbs in the sheepfolds for Duttur. They created fields where grain could grow and gave Ezina the plough and yoke, together with oxen to pull the plough. Duttur, standing in the sheepfold, manifested as a shepherd brimming with charm. Ezina, in the grain field, manifested as a beautiful, charming girl; she was suffused by the beauty of heaven. Both were radiant in appearance.

They brought sustenance to the land. They brought wealth to the assembly. They filled the storerooms and the barns. They brought their bounty to the poor who crouch in the dust. Wherever they went, they increased the riches of every household. Wherever they stood, they were satisfying. Where they settled, they were seemly. They gladdened the hearts of An and Enlil.

Ezina and Duttur drank sweet wine. They enjoyed sweet beer together. But when they had drunk the wine and enjoyed the beer, they became argumentative. They started a debate, but it became a quarrel.

Ezina said to Duttur, "Brother, I am your better and I take precedence over you. I am the glory of the land, the gift of the Anuna gods. I foster neighbourliness and friendliness. When I come upon a captive youth, I give him his destiny, release his shackles and gladden his despondent heart. I am Enlil's daughter. You, with your sheep shacks and milking pens, what do you have to compare with what is mine? Give me whatever answer you can!"

Duttur was quick to answer. "My sister, whatever are you talking about? All the yarns of Uttu, goddess of weaving, come from me. All the splendour of a king arrayed in his finery comes from me. I receive offerings of sweet oil, aromatic oil and cedar oil. The great gods themselves are dressed in my body. The king on his throne rejoices in his garment of my white wool. After the priests have arrayed themselves in me, ready for the holy lustration, I accompany them to the holy meal. But your implements: harrow, ploughshare, straps and ties, are all tools that can be utterly destroyed. What can you put forward to match me? Give me whatever answer you can!"

Ezina spoke again. "When the bippur, the beer dough, has been carefully prepared, and the beer mash properly tended, Ninkasi, goddess of beer, mixes them for me. Meanwhile, your billy goats and rams are despatched for my banquets. They are kept standing well away from my bounty, on their thick legs! Your lonely shepherds, up on the high plains, look down enviously at my produce. When my grain stands proud in the furrows, my farmer chases away your herds with his cudgel. You are full of fear of the desert creatures, snakes and bandits, up there where your flocks graze, on the high plain. Every night your count is made and your tally stick put into the ground, so your shepherd can number the flock: how many ewes and lambs, how many goats and kids. When gentle winds blow through the city and strong winds scatter far and wide, a milking pen is built to shelter you. But when gentle winds blow through the city and strong winds scatter far and wide, I stand up to the god of storms and face him as an equal. I am Ezina, born for the warrior. I do not give up. The churn, the vat, the shepherd's crook, his milking stool – these are your poor properties. What can you put forward to match me? Give me whatever answer you can!"

Again Duttur answered Ezina. "When you are on the threshing floor, the slave's cudgel pounds your face, your mouth and your ears. Your body is crushed into flour. When you have filled the trough, the baker's boy mixes you and throws you on the floor, where the baker's girl flattens you out. You are put in the oven and then taken out. When you are brought to the table, I am before you, you are behind me. Ezina, listen to yourself! Just like me, you are destined to be eaten. If essence is being compared, why should I be judged second? What can you put forward to match me? Give me whatever answer you can!"

Ezina's pride was hurt. She went in for the killing blow. She replied, "As for you, the storm god is your master and the dry land your bed. You are like fire beaten down and extinguished in houses and fields; like small flying birds chased from the door of the house; like the lame and weak of the land. Should I really bow to you? I don't think so! When your entrails are taken away by buyers in the market place, when your neck is wrapped in your very own loincloth, then what does one man say to another? 'Fill the measuring cup with grain for my sheep.' Neither of them has any care for you."

Enki, god of wisdom, felt things were going too far. He spoke to Enlil, "Father Enlil, Ezina and Duttur should be reconciled. They should stand together, and both should be respected. But let Ezina be the greater of the two. Let Duttur kneel before Ezina, let him kiss Ezina's feet. From sunrise to sunset, let Ezina's name be praised. People should value grain, the staff of life, above all things. Whoever has silver, whoever has jewels, whoever has cattle, whoever has sheep, let them take a seat at the gate of whoever has grain, for Ezina is exalted."

Duttur was left behind, and Ezina came forward to take precedence. So it was decided by Father Enki, the all-knowing, all-seeing one. May his name be praised.

DEBATES

TALES OF EVERYDAY FOLK

These stories explore how ordinary people cope with the trials and tribulations of their lives. It may be that some of these texts were written as plays, intended for performance. However, any evidence of how they might have been presented is, so far, lacking.

'And Are You a Woman?' is adapted from the translation of Dr Jana Matuszak. She told us: "Despite featuring female protagonists, this text was written by male schoolteachers for their predominantly male students in the early second millennium BCE, when Sumerian had to be taught at school as a dead language." Strictly speaking, it forms part of the genre of literary debates, but we've put it here because it gives a clear picture of everyday life.

THE POOR MAN OF NIPPUR

Gimil-Ninurta was a wretched man. He lived in the city of Nippur, but he lived there in misery. He had no silver, he had no gold. Even his larder was empty. So too was his belly. He longed for some bread. He craved for meat and good drink. Every day, for want of a good meal, he suffered. Every night, for want of a good meal, he went to sleep hungry. He had only one set of clothes. He considered his situation, debating with himself. He had an idea.

"I will strip off my coat, even though I have no other, and I will exchange it for a ram in the city market."

He took his garment to the market, but no one considered it worth the cost of a ram. He ended up with a three-year-old nanny goat. He considered his situation, debating with himself.

"What if I slaughter the goat in my yard? There will not be a feast – where would I get beer? My friends and neighbours would get to hear of it, and be angry. My family would be furious with me. I'd be better off taking the goat to the mayor's house, offering him something to feast on. That way, I can win his favour."

Gimil-Ninurta got hold of his goat and dragged it off to the gates of the mayor's house.

He addressed the gatekeeper with these words: "Tell the mayor that I wish to enter to see him."

The gatekeeper told his master: "My lord, a poor man of Nippur is waiting at your gates. He has a skinny little nanny goat with him."

The mayor heard 'little nanny goat'. He did not seem to hear 'skinny'. He grew excited at the thought of the goat, and angry with his gatekeeper for being tardy.

"Why is a citizen of the city kept waiting at my gate when he has a gift for me? Let him come in."

The gatekeeper brought in Gimil-Ninurta, who came happily into the presence of the mayor. He held tightly to his nanny goat with his left hand. He raised his right hand high in the air and greeted the mayor.

"May Enlil and Nippur bless the mayor. May Ninurta bless his children."

The mayor eyed the skinny goat with disappointment, and questioned Gimil-Ninurta, "What has happened to you, that you bring me a gift?"

Gimil-Ninurta told his sad tale to the mayor.

"Every day, for want of a good meal, I suffer. Every night, for want of a good meal, I go to sleep hungry. I have only one set of clothes, but I stripped off my coat and exchanged it for a three-year-old nanny goat in the city market. Then I said to my wretched self, 'What if I slaughter the goat in my yard? There will not be a feast – where would I get beer? My friends and neighbours would hear of it, and be angry. My family would be furious with me. So I would be better off taking the goat to the mayor.' That's what I said to myself. So here I am. And here it is."

The mayor was less than impressed with the goat. He was even less impressed with Gimil-Ninurta. He called the gatekeeper to him and said: "When we sit down to eat, serve that poor man of Nippur a bone and some gristle. Give him third-rate beer to drink – then chase him away and throw him out of the gates!"

So when Gimil-Ninurta sat down at the feast, they served him only a bone and some gristle. They filled his cup with third-rate beer. Then the gatekeeper chased him away and threw him out of the gates.

As Gimil-Ninurta went out through the gates, he turned back to the gatekeeper and said, "May the gods bless your master! But tell him this: 'For this one bad turn you did me, I will pay you back with three!'"

When the mayor heard that, he laughed all day.

But Gimil-Ninurta set out to the king's palace. He knew the king's will was that princes and governors should be fair to the common people. When he came before the king, Gimil-Ninurta prostrated himself and did homage. He held his hand high and greeted the king: "O noble one, pride of the people, glorious and fortunate king! I beg you to command that I have the use of a chariot, for just one day, so that I can accomplish whatever I wish. For my one day's loan, I will pay with a mina of red gold."

The king did not ask him why he wanted the chariot, or what he intended to do. He simply gave the order that a chariot be loaned to Gimil-Ninurta. It was a new one, a grand one! Furthermore, they dressed him in a fine garment, with a sash about his waist. He looked like a nobleman. He mounted the chariot and, looking magnificent, he set off back to Nippur. On the way, he caught two birds. He stuffed them into a fine casket and sealed it with clay. He drove up to the gates of the mayor of Nippur. The mayor himself came out of the gates to greet him. He did not recognize the poor man he had chased away.

"Who are you, my lord," he asked, "who have travelled so late in the day?"

"The king, your lord, has sent me. I have brought gold for the Ekur, Enlil's temple."

He gave the mayor the sealed casket.

The mayor welcomed in this apparently noble visitor, and ordered that a sumptuous feast be prepared in his honour. A fine fat sheep was slaughtered, to be the centrepiece of a meal of many courses.

After a while, the mayor said, "Ho-hum, I'm so tired." But Gimil-Ninurta ignored the hint, and kept him talking for a long watch of the night, until the mayor was at last overcome by sleep. Then Gimil-Ninurta got up stealthily. He opened the lid of the casket, breaking the clay seal, so that the birds flew off into the sky.

At daybreak, the mayor woke up and went to open the casket, only to find that the lid was open, the 'gold' was gone. At this, Gimil-Ninurta pretended to be overcome by anguish. He tore the fine clothes he wore. He set upon the mayor and beat him until the wretch begged for mercy. Gimil-Ninurta thrashed the mayor from head to toe, until he was black and blue. He made him suffer. The mayor fell at his feet and cried out in terror, "My lord, do not make an end to this wretched citizen of Nippur! Do not stain your hands with the blood of one dedicated to Enlil."

The mayor ordered that two minas of gold be given to Gimil-Ninurta, in recompense for the lost gift. He gave him fine new robes to replace the ones he had torn.

As Gimil-Ninurta went out of the gates in the fine chariot, he turned back to the gatekeeper and said, "May the gods bless your master! But tell him this, 'For the bad turn you did me, I have paid you back once. Two remain.'"

When the mayor heard that, he was uneasy all day.

Once Gimil-Ninurta had returned the chariot and paid the king the one mina of gold they had agreed, he took the other mina of gold to the barber's and spent some of it having his head shaved, in the style of the physicians of Isin. He bought himself a cauterizing tool. He set off to the gates of the mayor of Nippur.

He addressed the gatekeeper with these words: "Tell the mayor that I wish to enter to see him."

"Who are you?"

"I am a physician of Isin, renowned for my skill in healing bumps and bruises."

When the mayor heard this, he immediately ordered that the 'physician' be brought in. He showed the 'physician' the bruises where Gimil-Ninurta had thrashed him.

"Hmm, yes indeed, a serious case," intoned the 'physician'. "The treatment must take place in a darkened room if it is to be effective."

The mayor immediately brought him to an inner chamber. It was just what Gimil-Ninurta wanted, dark and private, and closed-off from any friend or companion who might take pity on the mayor.

Gimil-Ninurta drove five pegs into the hard-packed earth floor. He tied the mayor to them by his hands, his feet and his neck. Then he thrashed him from head to toe. With the cauterizing iron he made him suffer. He left the mayor groaning in pain.

As Gimil-Ninurta went out of the gates, he turned back to the gatekeeper and said, "May the gods bless your master! But tell him this, 'For the bad turn you did me, I have paid you back twice. One remains.'"

When the mayor heard that, he was greatly troubled.

Now Gimil-Ninurta went off around town, looking closely at all his fellow Babylonians, until he found the person he wanted: a young man who was a very fast runner. No one could outrun him! Gimil-Ninurta gave this speedy fellow a present, and enlisted him in his scheme.

He told him, "I want you to go to the mayor's gates and start shouting, 'I'm the man with the goat!' When they hear this, the mayor will send out all his servants to catch you. I know that you can easily outrun them all. I want you to lead the mayor's household a merry dance, so that they leave the mayor alone and undefended."

Gimil-Ninurta heard the young man approaching the mayor's gates, shouting loudly and gathering quite a crowd. He pricked up his ears to listen. He crouched under the bridge like a dog.

Out came the mayor when he heard the noise, and, determined to be revenged on the 'man with the goat', he sent his entire household out in pursuit.

The young runner easily evaded them, leading them off in a merry dance. Even the mayor himself came as far as the bridge, urging on his household. But as they disappeared into the distance, Gimil-Ninurta sprang out from under the bridge and seized the mayor. He set upon him, thrashing him again, until, yet again, the wretch begged for mercy.

Gimil-Ninurta shouted at him, "For the bad turn you did me, now I have paid you back threefold!"

Gimil-Ninurta left the mayor there and went off for a pleasant walk in the countryside.

And the mayor? Moaning and groaning, he could do nothing but crawl in through the city gates.

THE HOME OF THE FISH

A **spell or song** to be sung by a fisherman to entice a fish into his net:

My fish! I have built for you a home!
My fish! I have built for you a store.
The house that I have built for you is bigger than a house.
The house that I have built for you is like a large sheepfold.
But this is not a house bothered by cords dividing the plots.
The threshold and the door bolt; the ritual flour and the incense burner are all in place.

Inside, there is incense. Inside, coloured cloths decorate the walls. The scent and the fragrance are like an aromatic cedar forest.

In this happy place, the waters of joy flow for you. In this house that I have made for you, the beer is poured out for you.

In this happy house there is food for you – food of the best quality, food in the very best condition.

No flies buzz around your house.

In the house that I have made for you there is good, sweet beer and honeyed cakes, extending as far as the reed fence.

Come to the house I have made for you!

Let your acquaintances come. Let your dear ones come. Let your father and grandfather come. Let the sons of your elder brother and the sons of your younger brother come. Let your little ones come, and your big ones too. Let your wife and your children come. Let your friends and companions come. Let your brother-in-law and your father-in-law come. Let the crowd at your front door come.

Do not leave the children of your friends outside. Do not leave your neighbours outside. Whoever they might be, invite them in.

Enter, my fish, my beloved son. Enter, my fine son.

Do not let the day go by. Do not let the night come. Moonlight will not enter your house. But even if the day has gone by and the night comes, still you are welcome. Enter, and I will let you relax here.

I have made it comfortable for you. Inside I have made a seat just for you. No one who sleeps in the seat will be disturbed. No one who sleeps there will be involved in a quarrel.

Enter, my beloved son. Enter, my fine son.

As in a river with brackish water, you do not need to investigate any canal. As in silt settled on the riverbed, you do not need to get up. As in flowing water, you do not need to fix your bed.

The moonlight does not enter this house.

Face me, my fish. You do not need to get away.

Face me, my fish. You will not succeed in getting away.

Face me, my fish. I am like the delicious scent, and you are the dog who goes sniffing.

Face me, my fish. I am like the cattle pen and you are the bull.

I am like the sheepfold and you are the sheep.

Face me, my fish.

Now just like the bull to your cattle pen, enter for me, and as you enter, the moon god Suen will be delighted with you.

Now, just like the sheep to your sheepfold, enter for me, and if you do, Dumuzid the shepherd god will be delighted with you.

When you raise your head like the bull towards the cattle pen, Lord Suen will be delighted with you. When you raise your head like a sheep in the sheepfold, Dumuzid the shepherd will be delighted with you.

Oh, my fish, out in the marshes is the one who utters its sinister cry in the marshes and the rivers: the Agane bird. You will be dangling from its claws, my fish! The one who circles the nets looking for you in the waters, where the nets are stretched: the Ubure bird. You will be dangling from its claws, my fish. The one with long legs, that laughs, the alien from faraway waters, that writes in the mud: the Anse Bar bird. You will be dangling from its claw, my fish. The one who seizes the rats and the lizards that wander into the marshes: the crocodile. You will be dangling from its claws, my fish.

Do not give yourself up to the claws. Do not let yourself be snatched up by their jaws. Time is pressing, my fish. Just you come to me.

Time is pressing. Just you come to me.

And Nanse, the queen of the fishermen, is delighted with you.

Come home, my fish, to me.

THE DIALOGUE OF PESSIMISM

Master: Servant!

Servant: Yes sir, I am here.

Master: Listen to me, servant! Obey me!

Servant: I hear and obey.

Master: I want you to hitch me a chariot. I will ride to the palace and see the king.

Servant: The king?

Master: Yes, the king.

Servant: Ride, master, ride! Drive, master, drive! All your wishes will be realized for you. The king will be gracious to you. He will pay attention to you. You will get where you want to go. Others will be outclassed. Ride to meet the king.

Master: No. I have changed my mind. I will not ride.

Servant: Do not ride, master, do not ride. The king will send you off on a mission. He will send you on a journey to a land that you do not know. He will expose you to discomfort and to trouble day and night. He will let you be captured. Do not ride to meet the king.

Master: Servant!

Servant: Yes sir, I am here!

Master: Listen to me servant! Obey me!

Servant: I hear and obey.

Master: The king is not to be depended on. I will start a rebellion – a revolution!

Servant: A revolution?

Master: Yes, a revolution.

Servant: Do it, master, do it! Start a revolution! It is not fair the way the world runs! And the way things are going at the moment, who knows about the future – whether we will have the wherewithal to clothe ourselves? Whether there'll be any food in the larder? Anything to fill our stomachs? Start a revolution.

Master: No. I will not start a revolution.

Servant: Do not do it, master, do not do it! The revolutionary is executed or skinned alive or blinded or jailed! Do not start a revolution.

Master: Servant!

Servant: Yes sir, I am here!

Master: Listen to me servant! Obey me!

Servant: I hear and obey.

Master: Hitch the chariot so I can drive to the open country, into nature.

Servant: Nature?

Master: Yes, nature!

Servant: Drive, master, drive! The roaming man has a full stomach. The roving dog cracks open the bone. The roaming bird will find a nesting place. The wandering wild ass has all the grass he wants. Go and live in nature.

Master: No. I will not drive to the open country.

Servant: Do not drive, master, do not drive! The roaming man loses his reason. The roving dog breaks his teeth. The roaming bird puts his home on the corner of the wall. The wandering wild ass has to live in the open desert in sun and wind. Do not go and live in nature.

Master: Servant!

Servant: Yes sir, I am here!

Master: Listen to me servant! Obey me!

Servant: I hear and obey.

Master: Bring me water to wash my hands, so I can dine.

Servant: Dine?

Master: Yes, I will dine.

Servant: Dine, master, dine! To dine regularly is the opening of the heart. It brings joy! Regular dining expands the inner self. He who eats well is his own god! The sun god Shamash himself comes with washed hands to a dinner eaten in happiness. Shamash goes with him whose hands are washed. You should dine.

Master: I will not dine.

Servant: Do not dine, master, do not dine! To be hungry and then to eat. To be thirsty and then to drink. This comes upon every man. Hunger and thirst! A little fasting – *then* eating, *then* drinking. This is what agrees with a man. Do not dine now.

Master: Servant!

Servant: Yes sir, I am here!

Master: Listen to me servant! Obey me!

Servant: I hear and obey.

Master: Bring me the water. I will wash my hands and make an offering to my god.

Servant: Your god?

Master: Yes, my god.

Servant: Offer, master, offer! A man offering sacrifice to his god is happy and prospers. His business flourishes. He makes a satisfying transaction. He makes loan upon loan and is repaid. Make an offering to your god.

Master: I will not make an offering to my god after all.

Servant: Do not offer, master, do not offer! Your god will always be on at you, like a dog at the heel, pestering you! He'll be whining, 'Celebrate my ritual!', whinging, 'I will not tell you anything unless you make a sacrifice!', droning on, 'Give me a magic figurine!' Do not make an offering to your god.

Master: Servant!

Servant: Yes sir, I am here!

Master: Listen to me servant! Obey me!

Servant: I hear and obey.

Master: I will love a woman!

Servant: Love a woman?

Master: Yes, love a woman.

Servant: Yes! Love, master, love! Fall in love! The man who loves a woman is exhilarated, uplifted, sees the meaning of life, forgets all pain and trouble and sorrow and care. What could be better? Fall in love with a woman.

Master: I will not love a woman.

Servant: That is right. Do not love, master, do not love! The man who falls in love is at the mercy of the loved one. It is like falling into a pit, into the depths. It is as if the woman is a deep well, a ditch. To fall in love is to fall into the depths. It is like you have given her a sharp dagger to stab your heart, to slash your throat! Do not fall in love with a woman.

Master: Servant!

Servant: Yes sir, I am here!

Master: Listen to me servant! Obey me!

Servant: I hear and obey.

Master: I will build a house and create a household. I will make a family – have children!

Servant: Make a household?

Master: Yes, a household.

Servant: Do it, master, do it! The man who makes a household is respected and looked up to. He is mature; a fine upstanding citizen. He knows who he is. He is surrounded by the sounds of laughter and the patter of little feet and caresses. His life is lived encompassed by love. Oh master, make a household.

Master: I will not make a household.

Servant: Do not do it, master, do not do it! The one who makes his own household exerts all his energy and strength for the good of others. His wife and children and parents are hale and healthy and hearty and well fed and clothed, whilst he himself becomes an impoverished weakling, old before his time. The one who makes a household makes a trap for himself. Even his father resents him, because he's broken up his father's household. Do not make a household.

Master: Servant!

Servant: Yes sir, I am here!

Master: Listen to me servant! Obey me!

Servant: I hear and obey.

Master: I will make a loan of grain.

Servant: Make a loan of grain?

Master: Yes, a loan.

Servant: Make it, master, make it! The man who makes a loan is a businessman. He gets interest on the loan. He makes profit. The grain is still *his* grain, while what comes back in interest is *his* profit too! Go into business. Make a loan of grain.

Master: I will not make a loan.

Servant: Do not make them, master, do not make them! Making a loan is worse than falling in love and setting up a household all rolled together! It is full of promises and smiles and hopes that come to nothing. You give the loan, but getting it back is as painful as giving birth, having a baby. They will get your grain, keep your grain, consume your grain, then swindle you out of your interest and abuse you into the bargain! Do not make a loan of grain.

Master: Servant!

Servant: Yes sir, I am here!

Master: Listen to me servant! Obey me!

Servant: I hear and obey.

Master: I will do a good deed. I will do something helpful for the good of all – for the good of my country!

Servant: Do a good deed?

Master: Yes, a good deed.

Servant: So do it, master, do it! The man who volunteers does a good deed for his country. He will gain favour with the great gods. His good deed rests in the basket of the great god, Marduk himself. He will know of it. Whoever does a good deed, he helps and improves his society. Oh, yes, do a good deed.

Master: I will not do a good deed.

Servant: Do not do it, master, do not do it! Climb the mounds of any ancient ruin, walk about: what do you see? You will see the skulls of men. Who can tell who was lowly and who great, who kind, who cruel, who good, who evil? Now who can tell, among these skulls, who did a good deed and who did an evil one? No sign! They are all the same. What is the point of doing a good deed?

Master: Servant, then what is the answer? What is for the best? Does anything we do matter? Tell me?

Servant: Master, you are asking me what is right and what is wrong? What is best? How can I say? Who is tall enough to ascend to heaven? Who is broad enough to embrace the earth?

Master: Yes, but what? What? You prevaricate! What is right?

Servant: What is right? What is wrong? Does it matter? For goodness' sake, in the end we all die. Perhaps the answer is to break both our necks: break your neck, break my neck and throw us both in the river.

Master: Break our necks? Aha, yes! Isn't that the truth? Death! Let us not put off the inevitable, the afterlife. Yes, servant! Break our necks! That is what I will do! Servant, you have hit on it. I will break my neck and go to the afterlife. But first I must break your neck, so you can go first to prepare a place for me.

Servant: Break my neck? So I go first? Steady on, sir. No, sir. Don't do that, sir. Let's think about the practicalities. It can't be done. How would I have the time to prepare a place for you? It would take me months to prepare a place in the underworld for such as you. And who would look after you while I was gone? How would you survive without me? I'd send you a message, 'All's ready. Come along'. But who would tell you about it? Break my neck? You couldn't live a day without me, master!

Master: You think not?

Servant: No master, forget that. Now, what would you like? Tea or coffee?

AND ARE YOU A WOMAN?

Act One

Imagine that we are in a family courtyard somewhere in Ancient Sumer. We hear the sound of children playing. Here in the courtyard something smells tasty. A pot is simmering on the outside oven and the housewife, who has just finished supervising the cooking, is tidying up ready for mealtime. This is Mrs A. She is the competent wife, mother and housekeeper of this household. She is dignified, mature, attractive and well-dressed. She is a woman at the height of her powers. Mrs A turns to fetch a pot and finds herself facing her neighbour, who has just entered through the courtyard door. This is Ninkuzu. These two women do not get along. They have had words before.

Mrs A: You again? Why are you here again? What do you want this time?

Ninkuzu: Yes, it is me again. What of it? Do not start a quarrel with me. Your words will not beat my words. You cannot win in a quarrel with me.

Mrs A: Of course I am going to stand up for myself. Why shouldn't I speak out to protect my honour and my reputation? What have I ever done to you?

Ninkuzu: What have you done to me? Come on! You have given me hell. I gave you as good as I got, but I still cannot sleep because of you.

Mrs A: What? You are a liar. Your words are slanderous. How would you feel if I told lies about you too?

Ninkuzu: Ah, you are going to tell lies, are you? You call me a liar and say my words are slanderous, but you are the liar.

Mrs A: When you tell lies like this, all you do is that you prove to everybody that I am the better person.

Ninkuzu: The better person? You think that you are a better person than me? You want to be my rival? Do not go talking down to me. Looking down on me! With your background, it's you that's at the bottom of the pile. There is no one for you to look down on.

Mrs A: Pretty one! Why should I not be your rival? You come here all dolled up. You might try to look pretty but that will not help you. Even though you have dolled yourself up, it will be me who will triumph over you. In a proper verbal dispute in front of witnesses I would be the winner.

Ninkuzu: I have my own good looks and I know how to use them. You? You are the slave girl of the neighbourhood – of the entire city quarter! You are at everyone's service! You offer services to every man. And another thing: you are a terrible cook!

Now the trouble has begun. Mrs A *and* Ninkuzu *are equals in social class and social role – they are both full-time housewives and there is competition between them about who is the better housewife.* Mrs A *possesses all the qualities needed to be a competent and respectable housewife. Her rival,* Ninkuzu, *does not. And* Ninkuzu *seems jealous. For one thing,* Mrs A *has more children than she has. The antagonism between* Mrs A *and* Ninkuzu *has been simmering for a while and now is about to be taken into the public arena. In front of their peers in the public square, each woman will try to prove her superiority. This is her superiority not only in the skills of housekeeping, but also in the rules of a proper verbal dispute. Each woman will try to prove that she is the better woman, and also that she is the better speaker – more articulate and more eloquent.*

As we listen to the dispute, we are listening just as the apprentice scribes of Sumer *listened, four thousand years ago. Like those boy scribes, we are learning the rules of eloquent disputation, and also what it was to be a good woman in* Ancient Sumer.

Act Two

The scene is now the city square. The community has gathered to hear the dispute between Mrs A *and* Ninkuzu. *These two are getting ready to set out their arguments, worded as eloquent insults and attacks on each other. The audience will decide who is the winner.*

Mrs A: She is always roaming the city. She is always roaming the harbour. She is always going in and out of every house and wherever she goes, she causes trouble. She causes dissension wherever she goes. She has caused arguments between the husband and the wife. She has instigated quarrels between the mother-in-law and the daughter-in-law. And then, while they are distracted, she steals away the child of the family. Ninkuzu has actually stolen a child from his mother's arms. For these crimes alone she is guilty. Ninkuzu, everyone knows you are guilty of taking the child.

Admit it.

Ninkuzu: I am a thief? No. She is a thief. She is the criminal. Robber! Robber even in her own house. Dog in her own trough. Mongoose in her own basket. She says I am guilty of these crimes. But she is the thief. She puts the fisherman's catch into her own basket. She thinks she got away with it but look at her hands. They are covered with fish blood. She is a thieving mongoose. She is like a dog. She eats anything whatever it is and wherever she finds it. She does not care who it belongs to. She is always opening the storehouse. She is always stealing from the slaves. When she was a bride and she first came to her husband's house, she did not bring a spindle, to spin. Instead she brought a step ladder, to steal. She is not interested in the hard work of making clothes for her household. She is only interested in the good things she can find for herself.

That has upset you, hasn't it?

Mrs A: No, I am not upset. You all know for yourselves that she has a reputation for shaming others in public. Here, clearly, she reveals herself as a child of shame. If she carries on in this way, she will know what shame feels like. The law will catch up with her. Half her skull will be shorn. Her lips will be rubbed with salt. Her ribs and shoulders will be flogged. That will be the clear outcome. Stop scorning others in public now. Accept your shame now, child of the scorned! You are as good as convicted under the law. Respond to my accusation of the theft of the child.

Ninkuzu: Stolen pigs! She has been eating stolen pigs! She says I am convicted. Well, I caught her in the act. She was holding a piglet in her hand. She had stolen it and she was eating it. She had it in her hand! Always stealing from my side. Always eating something. She was caught in the act. She was creeping about! She was creeping about. She creeps about in the night. She even steals the bowl of grain straight out of the oven. She has a big mouth! She cannot stop herself. Her mouth is full but still she will not shut up.

There you are. With your mouth so full of stolen food, you cannot reply to me.

Mrs A: Very well! It seems that the topic of our debate is now eating. On this topic I have this to say. She is greedy and rude. She opens her mouth wide to devour all of the soup. She devours her very household because she is so wasteful and disorganized. Wasteful? She wastes oil and she wastes wood. She burns entire beams of wood in the fire instead of using twigs and brushwood. She has not even established the women's quarters for cooking. When she was a bride and she first came to her husband's house, she did not manage the household properly. She did not establish the women's quarters. She did not manage the household properly. And she is mean. She has always kept her husband short. She only supplies him with cloth of bad quality.

With all this to your discredit, then why are you so arrogant? Answer.

Ninkuzu: Am I always to be working, working, working, like a pauper and a slave? Well as to her way of housewifery, I say ha! She is endlessly toiling. Always pressing oil, permanently roasting barley, constantly baking ridiculously huge loaves of bread! Worker. Child of misery. Offspring of paupers. Everyone scorns you. No one can depend on you! What will you do next? Oh look! You are creeping in through the window to get at the men!

Your go.

Mrs A: Very well. You talk of men. I will introduce the topic of fertility. Let us talk about giving birth. Her usefulness as a woman is finished. Her ever-so-pure womb is finished. When was the last time she had a child? Her womb produces no babies. Nothing is produced by her, in her womb, or in her household. Her household produces no nourishment. She talks about plenty, but her barley pot is empty. Her household survives on beer and take-aways. Her husband has no clean clothes and neither does she. She is dressed in dirty rags and you can see her – excuse me but I cannot say it any other way – her bottom sticking out. Personally my view is that babies, a tight household and nice clothes define a woman. So you cannot call yourself a woman, can you?

Ninkuzu: She says I am not a woman. Well she does not even qualify as a person. She is forever turning her back on us women and making fun of our men. She slanders everyone. Wherever she goes she treads on our toes, beats our heads with both her fists and she causes trouble wherever she can. Always looking down your nose at me, Mrs A. Her house is not a nice home for her man. It is like a pub.

Am I a woman? Are you even a person? Are you even a human being, Mrs A?

Mrs A: When she tries to draw the water from the well, she cannot do it. She brings back muddy water. When she tries to grind the flour, she does not know when to stop. She pounds and grinds until it is shredded. When she bakes the bread, she burns it. Where shall I stop? Whatever she touches, she ruins completely.

Face it, Ninkuzu. You have to admit it.

Ninkuzu: She says there are things I cannot do. Well, she cannot do anything at all. She is not fit for women's work – not real women's work. She does not know when to stop. She has got slow hands. She cannot comb wool and she cannot work a spindle. Her hands are not quick enough. She makes hardly anything and what she does make is bad quality. And she is bad company. As soon as she walks in through the door she is going back home again. Outside in the street, she is insulting people. If she turns to the legal assembly, they will flog her for sure. Then she will be contesting the verdict. She is shameless. She will tell them, 'I will be the judge of that'. They will flog her for sure.

This is my insult to you, Mrs A.

Mrs A: She is a false witness. This is a person who will treat you as if she is going to be a helpful friend and colleague. But you cannot trust her. She will let you down. She is a person of broken promises. She has no case. She is denouncing me. I am the one who has a case. Listen to her. She is confused. Look at her. She is restless – constantly searching. Anyone who trusts her will soon find out the truth. Then she will be furious and deny it. She will say, 'It is a trap.' She will try to wriggle out of it, but they will still find out the truth. The only way she will get off is if she bribes them.

You? You belong to womanhood?

Ninkuzu: In her own house, she is a ladle and a jug, pouring soup and serving beer. She is the cook for everyone, the whole neighbourhood. She strides into other people's houses and bosses them about with her big mouth. She marches straight in, takes over, sweeps the house, sprinkles water, bosses everyone. She has got a big mouth. 'Everything belongs to me,' she says to me. She says, 'I know what to do.'

Mrs A: Well, of course I do. I do know what to do. Her house is a pigsty. The oven is her bedroom. Her husband and her child are both grindstones, created only for work. Her husband's no better. In fact she was born among slaves, nursed by slaves, comes from a house set up by slaves, which is no house at all. Ninkuzu, you do not belong to us womankind, do you? You do not belong here at all.

Ninkuzu: Lunatic! Mad! Imbecile! She is turning everything topsy turvy. She twists her mouth at me and cuts her eye at me! Evil! Evil! Person of evil! Insulter! I do not know what you call this, but I call it garbage and gossip and telltale. Murderer. Pig. Mad dog. The arrogance of her words. Bastard. I am telling it like it is.

Go on now. Create language that is as balanced, thoughtful and well-structured as mine.

Mrs A: Always standing about on street corners. Always hanging around other people's doorways. Always snooping into other people's business on the lookout for gossip. Her ears are pricked up. Her eyes are bulging. Does she engage in the network of her neighbours? No, she instigates quarrels. She accuses them of things they never said. The rest of us, when we hear a rumour, we hold our tongues and check our facts. We do not say anything until it's confirmed. But her – as soon as she hears it, she is already repeating it. Ninkuzu, we women and children of the city cannot sleep because of you. And you are not one of us.

Ninkuzu: She says I am not a worthy woman. Well she cannot compete with me for sure. She destroys homes. She destroys the city. She is not nice. She has got lice. Her tongue hangs out. She is skinny. She looks as if she has not eaten for months. Her beer is thin and her bed is low and she cheats in the market. She is a dishonest dealer. She spreads lies among the young men of the city and the young girls of the city cannot sleep because of her lies.

Mrs A: Listen to her. Listen for yourself. She cannot string a decent argument together. She spoils the dispute with too many words. She is a haughty woman with worthless lips. She is arrogant, argumentative, quarrelsome, a squaller, a croaker, a dimwit. Even in her own home she is known as evil. She is not fit for the women's quarters. All she does is eat and sleep and look for transgressions and gossip and scratch her bum. Ninkuzu how much longer do you want to carry on with this?

Ninkuzu: She asks how much longer can I carry on with this? Well she cannot compete with me. See how ugly she is. She has the face of an old woman and she dresses like a slave. She is so ugly with her big square bald head and her bulging blinking eyes and her skinny nose and her swollen mouth. Do you really want to compete with me, Mrs A? Look at me! Look at yourself. You cannot compete with me.

Mrs A: Wicked woman! Unworthiest of women! Liar who has never achieved anything worthwhile! She talks of ugliness. If she wants an example of ugliness, she should look at herself. She is pallid and oozes pus. Her hips are long and her neck is thick. Her breasts are sagging and her buttocks are distorted. Her vulva is tiny, but her pubic hair reaches her knees. Her womb is sick. It is blocked up and swollen. Ninkuzu! The woman who could beat me has not yet been created, and if she was, she would certainly not be you.

Ninkuzu: She says I cannot compete with her. Well, she is a poor whore who tells lies in the pubs and the taverns. She tells lies and she chases men. As soon as she gets married, she gets divorced. She is a liar forever chasing men. She is a dog for ever begging with raised paws. The young men of the city cannot sleep because of her. Her vulva is forever being mounted. She pops out a bastard every day. Mrs A! You are a whore and an adulteress.

Mrs A: Ninkuzu! You have called me a whore and an adulteress!

Mrs A rushes off in anger. Ninkuzu is smiling. Ninkuzu has had the last word in this verbal dispute and the rules of a Sumerian dispute are clear. If you get the last word, you are the winner. So you might think that Ninkuzu is the winner here.

But there are higher rules in Sumerian society. For women, adultery is a crime punishable by death. In a verbal dispute with a person who is your social equal, you can insult your adversary by saying pretty much anything. But you cannot say that they are an adulterer or a whore. And that is exactly what Ninkuzu has done.

So this dispute must now go to the legal level. It must go to court. There must be a trial. If Ninkuzu cannot substantiate her allegation that Mrs A is a whore, she will be in trouble. If Mrs A does not clear her name and establish her innocence, then she will be in trouble.

Act Three

The scene is now the king's courtroom. The king will preside. He will be the judge. You can hear the sound of chatter as advisers, servant and courtiers take their places to await the entrance of the king.

Four thousand years ago, this sort of dispute might well have been performed for the Sumerian king and his court, to amuse them and to spark discussion. In this performance, the king actually appears in the play. Here he is now:

King: Who is the complainant?

Mrs A: I am.

King: What is your complaint?

Mrs A: I am her equal. My house is as good as her house. My husband is as good as her husband. My children are as good as her children. We are equals. We were having a dispute in front of witnesses. But then she called me a whore and an adulteress. Because of that, my husband divorced me. This wrong must be put to right. I must have justice.

King: Who was your equal? Who called you a whore and an adulteress?

Mrs A: It was her. She did. It was Ninkuzu, the daughter of Lugalnirgal.

King: Are you Ninkuzu?

Ninkuzu: I am.

King: Did you call your equal, Mrs A, a whore and an adulteress, causing her husband to divorce her?

Ninkuzu: Your honour, Mrs A and I had a proper verbal dispute in front of witnesses. We competed in insulting each other. When she insulted me, I did not take it to heart. But when I insulted her, she was dumbstruck. Because she was speechless, she went to the extreme of bringing me to court and putting me on trial. Your honour, grant me a fair verdict.

King: If I grant you a fair verdict, Ninkuzu, you will pay the divorce fee, which is a third of a mina of silver. Yes! A third of a mina of silver. Your back and bottom will be flogged with six lashes. Half your hair will be shaved off. Your mouth and lips will be rubbed with salt. The herald will tell the whole city about your punishment. You will never again call a woman who is your equal a whore and an adulteress.

And you, Mrs A, must take an oath before the god of justice. You must swear that you are not a whore or an adulteress.

The king leaves. As soon as the king and his attendants are safely out of earshot, a loud discussion starts among the townsfolk. Some say this and others say that.

Mrs A should not have had to take such an oath.

Ninkuzu should not be flogged.

Ninkuzu should not have called Mrs A a whore and an adulteress.

It was Mrs A who started the quarrel.

In the end, it is Mrs A who has the last word. She speaks to the people, and these are her words:

Ninkuzu came to me in my courtyard. All I said was, 'You again? Why are you here again? What do you want this time?' Then we had a proper verbal dispute. In that dispute, she insulted me deeply. She insulted me with words which dishonoured me, and as a result, my husband divorced me. I am not a whore or an adulteress. My husband was the only man in my life. Ninkuzu accused me of things which she should be punished for saying in court. With the god of justice present, the evil woman will be punished.

THE TOOTHACHE WORM

After An created heaven,
Heaven created earth.
Earth created rivers,
Rivers created watercourses,
Watercourses created marshes,
Marshes created the toothache worm.

The worm came crying to the sun god Shamash,
His tears were flowing before Ea.

"Oh, please, what will you give me to eat?
"What will you give me to suck?"
"I will give you a ripe fig and an apple."
"What good are a ripe fig and an apple to me?
"Let me live between the tooth and the jaw,
"So that I can suck the blood in the jaw,
"So that I can chew on the morsels that get stuck in the teeth.
"Let them drive in the peg, Ea, and try to catch my foot!"

THE EPIC OF GILGAMESH

The tale of Gilgamesh, together with that of Inana, is perhaps the best-known story from the canon of Ancient Sumerian and Akkadian literature. The tablets that tell the different episodes of the story were first arranged into an epic by the Akkadian scribe Sin-leqi-unninni, between the thirteenth and tenth centuries BCE. It is an extraordinary literary work of art which explores human issues of friendship, power, love, grief, loss and mortality. The tale has been adapted in print many times and, more recently, used in film and television. New adaptations continue to be published. Here is ours, inspired by the translation of Andrew George (2020 ed).

PROLOGUE

Look! See Uruk.

See its walls like a strand of combed wool. View its parapet that no one could copy.

Take the stairway of a bygone age, draw near to Eanna, seat of Ishtar the goddess, that no later king could ever copy. Climb Uruk's wall and walk back and forth. Survey the foundations, examine the brickwork. Were its bricks not fired in an oven? Did the Seven Sages not lay its foundations?

A square mile is city. A square mile is date grove. A square mile is clay pit. Half a square mile is the temple of Ishtar. Three square miles and a half is Uruk's expanse.

Find the tablet box of cedar.
Release the clasps of bronze.
Lift the lid of its secrets.
Take out the tablets of lapis lazuli.
Hear the story of Gilgamesh, and all that he endured.

Gilgamesh saw the Deep. He knew the proper ways and was wise in all matters. He explored everywhere the seats of power. He knew of everything the sum of wisdom. He saw what was secret, discovered what was hidden. He brought back a tale of before the Deluge. He came a far road, was weary and found peace. All his labours were set on a tablet of stone. He built the rampart of Uruk-the-Sheepfold, of holy Eanna, the sacred storehouse.

Surpassing all other kings, heroic of stature, brave scion of Uruk, wild bull on the rampage! Going in front, he was the vanguard. Going at the rear, he was one his comrades could trust. He was a mighty bank protecting his warriors and a violent floodwave smashing a stone wall.

He was the wild bull of Lugalbanda. He was Gilgamesh, perfect in strength. He was the suckling of the august Wild Cow, the goddess Ninsun. It was Gilgamesh, so tall, so magnificent and terrible, who opened bases in the mountains, dug wells on the slopes of the uplands and crossed the ocean and the wide sea to the sunrise. He scoured the world, ever searching for life. He reached through sheer force to Utnapishtim the Distant.

He restored the cult centres destroyed by the Deluge. He set in place, for the people, the rites of the cosmos.

Who is there who can rival his kingly standing and say, like Gilgamesh, "I am the king"? Gilgamesh was his name from the day he was born. Two-thirds god, one-third human, he was magnificent and terrible. And he was tall. He was over thirteen feet tall. The curls at his cheek were more than a foot long. His beard gleamed and his hair was as thick as the barley growing in the field. He was beautiful and powerful. When he strode through the city, his stride measured nine feet. He was a young man whom no one could match. He had no equal in Uruk.

GILGAMESH THE TYRANT

No one could contain him, and a young man without constraint or equal is a danger to all. He constantly challenged his companions to contests that they could not win. He bullied and defeated all the young men of the city. He seduced all the young women of the city. If there was a wedding, Gilgamesh was there with the bride first. No one could stand against him. It was as if he was the herdsman and the people were the cows. They had no choices. He was tyrannical.

So the people of Uruk, the black-headed people, called out for the help of their gods.

Anu the sky god heard the pleas of the people of Uruk and considered their plight. He called on Aruru, who is the mother of all. Anu said, "Aruru, you created humankind. Now here is another job. You must fashion one to be a match for Gilgamesh, so that Uruk may rest."

Aruru knew just what was in Anu's mind. She washed her hands, took a pinch of Enki's clay, fashioned it as she had with humankind all those many years ago, and she threw it down into the wild uplands. In the wild, she created a wonder. It was Enkidu, the immense beast man. In future years they were to call him the offspring of silence. All his body was coated with hair. The hair of his head was as long as a woman's. He had no people, no country. He kept no company but the company of the gazelle, grazing on grasses and joining the herd at the waterhole. He delighted in the company of the beasts at the water. He was like a beast, but he had a man's intelligence. He was like the god of the animals. If ever one of his friends, the gazelle, were caught in the hunter's trap, he would release it. Then, to protect his friends, he started pulling up the hunter's snares and filling in the pits that the hunter had dug.

The hunter was puzzled when he found his snares triggered but no animal there. He was disturbed when he found his pits filled in. He investigated. He saw Enkidu's footprints by the waterhole and sat down to wait. He saw Enkidu approach and he saw him drink at the waterhole in company with the gazelle. The hunter told his father what he had seen. "He is mightiest of men in the land, his strength is as mighty as a rock from the sky. He roams over the hills with the herds and he sets free from my grasp all the beasts of the field and he meddles with my work in the wild. But he is huge and I am afraid. I dare not approach him."

The father of the hunter told him to go to Uruk and to tell Gilgamesh.

When Gilgamesh heard the story, he shrugged and instructed the hunter to go to the temple and to speak to Shamhat, who is the priestess, the daughter of divinity, the temple woman.

"She will know exactly what to do. She will do the work of a woman."

The hunter led Shamhat, the temple woman, into the wilds. It was a long way. On the third day of their journey, they came to the waterhole and sat down to wait. At last the gazelle came down to drink the water and Enkidu, the enormous wild man, came with them. Shamhat watched quietly. The hunter whispered in her ear:

"This is he, Shamhat. Unbridle your bosom. Bare your sex. Let him take in your charms. Do not recoil. Spread your clothing so he may lie on you. Treat the man to the work of a woman. Let his passion caress and embrace you."

She turned to the hunter and gave him a long look. She said, "I know what to do." Then she dismissed the hunter. After he had gone, Shamhat rose from her hiding place. All the gazelle were startled at the movement and ran from the waterhole. Enkidu was about to run too, but then he saw Shamhat. She was unfastening her cloak. He saw that she was dropping her clothing and she was stepping, naked and graceful as a gazelle, from the rocks. She was setting her cloak down like a blanket and was stooping, sitting and reclining on it. Enkidu did not run away. Shamhat was smiling at him. She sighed. Nonchalantly, she drank from her water skin. Enkidu approached and she offered him water from the water skin.

There, on the cloak on the ground, Shamhat the temple woman taught the wild man the lessons of the temple woman. His passion caressed and embraced her. They say that for six days and seven nights Enkidu was erect. He was delighted by her and she was delighted by him, and they coupled. At the end of that time, he was tired and he turned from Shamhat to look for his friends, the gazelle. But when he approached them, they smelled his strangeness, sensed the change in him and they ran from him. He no longer had the strength to run after them. He had no choice but to return to Shamhat. He had no other friend. She welcomed him and embraced him. She said, "Look at you, Enkidu. You are handsome, just like a god. You do not belong with the beasts. You belong to Uruk, where King Gilgamesh is unequalled in strength and is lording it over the people. You are destined to be his equal."

She took Enkidu to a nearby shepherds' camp. All the shepherds gathered round. They were impressed. "Look at him. He is enormous. His build is like that of Gilgamesh. Perhaps he is shorter, but he is bigger of bone, proud as a battlement."

They set bread and beer before him, but he did not know what to do with it. Shamhat taught him to eat bread and drink beer. He ate the bread and drank the beer. He drank seven jugs of beer and his mood became free. He started to sing, his heart grew merry and his face lit up.

Enkidu lived with Shamhat there in the shepherds' camp. She completed the job she had begun beside the waterhole. She combed his hair and beard, she anointed him with oil, she dressed him in a garment and gave him a weapon. She taught him the ways of the black-headed people. Shamhat made the wild creature she had found by the waterhole into a man and this man, Enkidu, loved her. He became very interested in this 'Gilgamesh' she was talking about. "I would like to see him and challenge him."

One day he encountered a stranger on the road and they fell into conversation.

"Where are you hurrying to, fellow?" Enkidu asked. The stranger replied, "Well, I have been invited to a wedding banquet in Uruk.

Actually, I am the caterer. It is my job to load the ceremonial table with tempting food for the feast." As they chatted, the stranger explained how it would be Gilgamesh who first 'parted the veil' of the young bride. Enkidu paled in anger at this. If the young groom loved the bride as he himself loved Shamhat, he would want no other man to be 'parting her veil'. "I will go to this wedding," he said.

And Shamhat took him to the city. In the evening, before they slept, Shamhat told Enkidu stories. She said, "Gilgamesh used to have terrible dreams. He would tell them to his mother. One night he had a dream that a star of heaven appeared and fell on him, like a rock from the sky. He tried to lift it up and stand, but it was too heavy. Everyone else was thronging around the star that fell. Everyone loved the star. In his dream, Gilgamesh said he loved it too. In his dream, his mother, Wild Cow Ninsun, made the star his equal. When Gilgamesh woke, his mother told him, 'This is a good dream. It means that you will meet someone who will be your equal.'"

Shamhat said, "Enkidu, that falling star is you. That equal is you. You will be the equal of Gilgamesh."

When Enkidu entered Uruk, a big crowd gathered.

"Look at him. He is huge. He is the image of Gilgamesh."

"Well, he is shorter of stature but he is bigger of bone."

"It must be the one they say who was born in the uplands and was suckled on animal milk."

The wedding was in full swing and Gilgamesh was approaching the threshold of the marriage house. But there, in the doorway, stood Enkidu. His foot was blocking the door. He would not allow Gilgamesh to enter. They seized each other at the door of the wedding house. In the street they joined combat, then in the square of the land. The door jambs shook and the walls shuddered. Enkidu forced his opponent down. Gilgamesh knelt, one foot on the ground. His anger subsided. He broke off from the fight. He had found for the first time one who was a match for him, someone who could challenge him, someone who could be his equal and friend. What had begun as a conflict became an embrace. They became the firmest of friends that day and remained the firmest of friends till the end.

GILGAMESH THE ADVENTURER

Gilgamesh was delighted and took his new friend on a tour of the city. They climbed the walls and walked along the battlements. "See these walls. Are they not like strands of combed wool? These bricks were baked in ovens. Seven Sages laid these foundations. One square mile is city. One square mile is date grove. One square mile is clay pit. Half a square mile is the temple of Inana. This is Uruk, and I, Gilgamesh, am the king."

They turned their faces outward to where the River Euphrates flowed. There, floating past in the water, was the corpse of a man.

"As he is, so shall we be." Gilgamesh raised his eyes to the far distance where mountains were lined with cedars. "Enkidu," he said, "they say no man is tall enough to reach the sky. No man is broad enough to encompass the horizon. But I am tall and you are broad. What could we two not do together? Together let us reach to the sky. Together let us encompass the horizon. Since at last we must lie down and become clay, let us first enter the mountain and set up our names. Let us travel to the Cedar Mountains and bring back the mighty Cedars of Lebanon."

Enkidu was horrified. The colour drained from his face. The strength drained from his limbs. "Gilgamesh, you are a man of the city. I am a man of the wild. Nobody knows the wild better than me. Even lions are afraid of me. But I am afraid of Humbaba. He is the forest guardian, set there by the gods to guard those great cedars. No one enters the forest without Humbaba knowing it. He hears the forest murmur. His voice is the roar of the river in flood and the storm in the trees. This is a journey that should not be made. This is a creature that must not be faced." But Gilgamesh paid no attention.

"Yes, Humbaba! The cedars! The mountains!" He seized his friend by the arm and hurried him down the stairway and through the city to the forge. At the forge, the smiths gave them axes and hatchets and knives. Then they went to the elders. Enkidu said to the elders, "Tell Gilgamesh this is a journey that must not be made. This is a creature that must not be faced." But the elders knew better than to tell Gilgamesh what to do. They merely commended him into Enkidu's care. The two went to the palace of Ninsun, mother of Gilgamesh. Enkidu said, "Tell your son this is a journey that must not be made. This is a creature that must not be faced."

Ninsun turned without a word. She cleansed herself in tamarisk water and soapwort. She dressed in her finest clothes: the diadem on her breast, the belt at her waist, the jewel on her brow. She climbed the spiral stairway to the roof. There she lit ritual fires and burned and scattered incense. She raised her arms and addressed the sun god. "Oh great Shamash, why did you give my son such a restless spirit? I know that it is you who have placed the Cedar Mountains in his heart. Well, as you would have him go, use your weapons, the winds, to protect him." She watched the smoke carry her words to heaven. She smothered the censer and came down from the roof.

When she came again to the two friends, she spoke only to Enkidu.

"Enkidu, you are the wild man. You have no place in the city, no kith or kin. As the temple woman took in the orphan, as the priestess cared for the foundling, so I now take you as my son. No one knows the wild better than you. Go with your brother. Keep him safe. Return him to me. May your days be long and your nights be short. Now walk out on long strides on your journey."

GILGAMESH HAS FIVE DREAMS

The great gates of the city of Uruk closed behind them. They looked out onto the wilderness and the wasteland. Once they were in the wild, Enkidu had no fear. He spoke to Gilgamesh. He said, "I have begged you not to take this path and you have paid no attention. I have asked you not to undertake this journey and you have ignored my advice. But your mother has blessed us and she and the elders have entrusted you into my care, and I will stand by you and your desire. Where you have set your mind, begin the journey. Let your heart have no fear. Keep your eyes on me. In the forest I know his lair and the ways that Humbaba wanders. Let our stride and our days be long." And Enkidu and Gilgamesh strode out.

At twenty leagues they broke bread. After another thirty, they pitched camp. Fifty leagues they had travelled in the course of a day. By the third day they had travelled the distance a normal man would march in a month and a half. There, facing the sun, they dug a well and put fresh water in their water skins. Gilgamesh climbed to the top of the mountain and made an offering of flour.

"Oh mountain, bring me a dream, so I see a good sign." Then Enkidu made a House of the Dream God. He drew a circle within and made Gilgamesh enter it. Enkidu himself lay like a net in the doorway. Gilgamesh rested his chin on his knees and sleep overcame him. In the middle of the night he woke, crying out, "My friend! Did you call? Why did I waken? Did you touch me? Why am I startled? My flesh is frozen. Did a god pass by? I have had a dream."

"Tell me your dream."

"We were standing on a mountain slope. The mountain fell between us. But we were like flies and flew clean over it."

The one born in the wild knew how to give counsel. Enkidu gave meaning to the dream. "This is a good dream. It means we shall overcome all obstacles."

The next day they travelled. After twenty leagues they broke bread. After another thirty, they pitched camp. Fifty leagues they had travelled in the course of the day. After the third day, a normal march of a month and a half, they were all the nearer to Mount Lebanon. They dug another well, climbed another mountain, made another House of the Dream God. Enkidu drew the dream circle, and Gilgamesh slept while Enkidu guarded the door. In the middle of the night Gilgamesh rose in distress and spoke. "My friend! Did you call? Why did I waken? Did you touch me? Why am I startled? My flesh is frozen. Did a god pass by? I have had a second dream. I was propping up a mountain with my shoulder but it fell on me. I was weak and overpowered. A man like a lion grasped me by the arm and pulled me out." Enkidu explained the dream.

"This is a good dream. Humbaba is the mountain. He will pour out his rage and fury over you. But the man you saw was Shamash, the sun god. In your time of peril, Shamash will grasp your hand."

They travelled twenty leagues before breaking bread, thirty leagues before they camped, fifty leagues in a day. After three days, they made a third House of the Dream God and Gilgamesh had a third dream. "The dream that I had was utter confusion: heaven cried aloud while earth did rumble. The day grew still, darkness came forth, there was a flash of lightning and fire broke out. Flames flared up; death rained down. The fire, so bright, dimmed and went out. The flames diminished and became cinders."

"My friend, your dream is good. Its message is lucky. You will turn all your enemy's weapons into ashes. All these dreams are good. A god is with you and you will soon achieve your goal."

After another three days, they made a fourth House of the Dream God and there was a fourth dream. "I saw a Lion Bird in the sky. It rose up like a cloud, soaring above us. Its visage was distorted, its mouth was fire, its breath was death. There was also a man. He was strange of form. He bound the wings of the Bird and took hold of my arm. He cast the Bird down before him."

"Another lucky dream! The Lion Bird is Humbaba. The man you saw was mighty Shamash. We shall bind the wings of the Bird. The next day we will see a good sign from the sun god."

After three days, a fifth dream. "I had taken hold of a bull from the wild. As it clove the ground with its bellows, the clouds of dust it raised thrust deep into the sky. A man enclosed my arms and gave me water to drink from his waterskin."

Enkidu said, "All these dreams are lucky. All these dreams are good. My friend, why are you afraid? Shamash will protect us. Your god and father Lugalbanda holds you dear and will refresh you. We will do something unique, a feat that has never been achieved in this land. Look how far we have come. We can already see where the cedars grow. Why do your tears flow? You are Gilgamesh the king and you have completed your journey to the Cedar Mountains."

HUMBABA IN THE CEDAR FOREST

As he spoke, the stars faded, dawn crept into the sky and they saw they had come to the forest.

They stood marvelling and gazing at the forest in the dawn light. There was the forest entrance. Where Humbaba came and went, there was a track. The paths were straight and the way well-trodden. They saw the Mountain of Cedar, seat of gods and goddesses. They stood marvelling at the lofty cedars. On the face of the land the cedar proffered its abundance. Its shade was sweet and full of delight. Thick tangled was the thorn, the forest a shrouding canopy. Cedars and gum trees were all entwined and left no way in. For a league on all sides the cedars sent forth saplings. Cypresses grew thick for two-thirds of a league. Cedars scabbed with resin grew sixty cubits high. The resin oozed forth, drizzling down like rain flowing freely for ravines to bear away.

Through all the forest a bird began to sing. Hen birds gave answer. A solitary tree-cricket set off a noisy chorus, all singing the song, all making the neighbours pipe loud. A wood pigeon moans and a turtle dove calls in answer. At the call of the stork, the forest exults. At the cry of the francolin, the forest exults amid plenty. Monkey mothers sing aloud, a youngster monkey shrieks. Like a band of musicians and drummers, daily they bash out a rhythm in the presence of Humbaba.

As the cedar cast its shadow, terror fell on Gilgamesh. Stiffness gripped his arms and tremors beset his legs. Enkidu spoke. "Let us go deep into the midst of the forest and raise a loud cry."

Gilgamesh said, "Why do we tremble like cowards, we who came across the mountains?" Enkidu was not the one trembling. He was perfectly calm. He said, "One who has been in battle has no fear of death. You have been splashed in blood, so you need not fear death. Go berserk. Like a dervish, fall into a frenzy. Let your shout boom out like a kettle drum, may the stiffness leave your arms, the tremors your legs."

Gilgamesh said, "Take my hand, friend, and we shall go on together. Let your thoughts dwell on combat. Forget death. Seek life. Let him who goes first be on guard for himself and bring his comrade to safety." So the two of them set off for the heart of the forest. They ceased their talking and they came to a halt. And stood still, marvelling at the forest.

And now there are spaces and gaps in the tablets that tell our tale. All the time Humbaba is approaching. The pieces of Humbaba's thoughts that are preserved are fractured. Humbaba's thoughts rumble in the forest. He is wondering, "Are there not...? Did not a...? Why are my own...? How...? In my very bed...?" But then he realizes with clarity:

"It must be Enkidu."

Enkidu turned to Gilgamesh. He said, "One is one alone, but two are two friends. Two will succeed, two pups of a strong dog will overcome. We will overcome, but, my friend, now we need the winds that your god has promised." Gilgamesh lifted his head weeping before Shamash, his tears flowing under the rays of the sun. "Now come to my aid!" Shamash heard the words Gilgamesh was speaking. From the sky, a voice cried out, "Fear not. Stand against him. Humbaba must not enter his forest. He must not wrap himself in his seven auras, his seven cloaks of protection. One protects him, but six he has shed."

But Humbaba was already towering over them. "Let fools take counsel, Gilgamesh, with the rude and brutish. Why have you come here into my presence? Come, Enkidu, you spawn of a fish, you hatchling of terrapin and turtle. You knew no father. You sucked no mother's milk. In your youth I watched you, but I never harmed you. Now in treachery you bring before me Gilgamesh and stand there like a warlike stranger. I will slit the throat and gullet of Gilgamesh. I will feed his flesh to the birds of the forest, to the ravening eagle and vulture."

Gilgamesh turned to Enkidu. "His features have changed. We came here boldly but I had no idea! His face is the knotted gut. His voice is the storm in the forest. The heart that takes fright does not grow calm in a moment." Enkidu said, "My friend, why do you speak like a coward? Do not draw back. Make your blow mighty. Let the South Wind take him hostage. Be mindful of your god Lugalbanda and keep in your thoughts all the dreams that you had."

Then Gilgamesh went forward. He was like a lion launching a brutal attack. Enkidu was like a puma. They tried to seize hold of Humbaba in the midst of the forest. His terrible auras, insubstantial and indescribable powers, were filling the forest. They tried to grab the auras in their hands before Humbaba could wrap himself in the auras and become invincible. Then Shamash roused the mighty gale-winds: South Wind, North Wind, East Wind, West Wind, Blast, Counterblast, Typhoon, Hurricane, Tempest, Devil-Wind, Frost-Wind, Gale and Tornado. There arose the thirteen winds and the face of Humbaba darkened. He could not charge forward; he could not kick backwards. The weapons of Gilgamesh conquered Humbaba. Then Humbaba pleaded for his life.

"You are so young, Gilgamesh. I remember when your mother bore you. Indeed you are the offspring of Wild Cow Ninsun. By Shamash's command, you flattened ten mountains. In woe I am prostrated. Let me stay here in the forest at your beck and call. Trees I will keep for you. Myrtle, cedar and cypress, timber fine and straight grown, to be the pride of your palace. O, offshoot sprung from Uruk, Gilgamesh, king, never did a dead man please a master. Only a slave alive brings profit to his owner. Gilgamesh, be merciful."

But Enkidu said, "Do not listen. Do not trust him. If he returns to his home, he will put on his auras of power, he will bind us fast in the Forest of Cedar." Humbaba wept. "You know the ways of the forest and also the arts of speech. I could have fed you to the birds when you were young. But I spared you. Spare me. Tell Gilgamesh to spare my life." Enkidu said, "Slay him. Do away with his power." Humbaba heard how Enkidu abused him. He lifted his head under Shamash and cried, "May these two not grow old. Beside Gilgamesh his friend, none shall bury Enkidu."

Gilgamesh drew forth the sword at his side and stabbed Humbaba in the neck. Enkidu cut out his heart and pulled it forth with the lungs. Springing up, he took the tusks of Humbaba as booty. Blood fell in the mountain.

Gilgamesh went trampling through the forest raiding resin, wood, cedar, timber from the mountains.

They were cutting down the trees, seeking out the best timber.

Enkidu said, "I am going to make a door which is six rods in height, two rods in breadth, one cubit in thickness, and whose pole and pivots top and bottom are all of a piece. To the house of Enlil, in Nippur, the Euphrates shall bear it!"

They fashioned a raft of logs. They lashed the raft tight; they pushed all the rest of the great trees into the river. They were riding on the raft, bearing the head of Humbaba. In triumph they travelled, pushing the floating logs.

As they drifted downstream, a calm settled on them. Enkidu said, "But Gilgamesh, how will we answer to the gods for what we have done?"

ISHTAR AND THE BULL OF HEAVEN

When they returned to the city, they went straight to the river to wash away the grime of their adventure. Gilgamesh cleaned his equipment, cast aside his dirty garments, washed his matted hair. On the beauty of Gilgamesh, the Lady Ishtar looked with longing. She watched as he wrung the water from his glossy hair, saw how he flicked it back over his shoulder, how he wrapped clean cloaks around his glistening muscles and tied the cloaks up with a sash. Finally he put on his crown. Then she called to him from the battlements. "Come Gilgamesh, you are desirable. Be my bridegroom. Be my husband and I will be your wife. Such gifts I will give to you. I will give you a chariot of lapis lazuli and gold. As you enter our house, the doorway and footstool will kiss your feet. All shall kneel before you. All will bring you tribute. Your livestock will bear triplets. No ox shall match yours at the yoke."

This was not an invitation to refuse. Ishtar was the great goddess. Gilgamesh was the king. In times past, King Enmerkar and King Lugalbanda had accepted the invitation. This was the invitation to kingship.

But Gilgamesh answered like this: "What need have I of you? Why would I want you? You are like a slatted door that will not keep out the draught. You are like the enemy's battering ram destroying my wall. You are a shoe that bites the foot. Come, let me tell you the tales I have heard of your past lovers. You loved Dumuzi, but now he laments every year that you doomed him. You loved the speckled hoopoe but you struck him down and broke his wing. Now he stands in the woods crying, 'My wing! My wing!' You loved the lion, but you dug seven pits for him. You loved the horse, but you made his destiny the whip, the spur and the lash and the seven-league gallop. You loved the shepherd, but you turned him into a wolf and his own dogs bite at him. You loved the gardener, but you turned him into a gnome. Must you love me also – and what will you do to me? Perhaps past kings may have felt they should love you, but I will not."

The goddess Ishtar was furious. She went to her father Anu and her mother Antu and wept copious tears. "Father! Mother! Give me the Bull of Heaven. If you do not, I will smash the gates of the Netherworld and bring up the dead to consume the living." Anu was shocked. He said, "If I am to give you the Bull of Heaven, at least give the people seven years in which to build up resources. You well know that the Bull of Heaven will destroy everything. It will eat up everything if it has access to the earth." Ishtar spoke firmly, "I have already grown barley and stocked and filled the storehouses." Anu placed the nose rope of the Bull of Heaven into her hands and down came Ishtar, leading it onwards.

In Uruk, the Bull wreaked havoc. It dried up the woods, the reedbeds and marshes. It lowered the river by nine feet. It snorted and a pit opened up. A hundred men fell in. A second time it snorted and two hundred men fell in. A third time it snorted and Enkidu fell in as far as his waist, but he sprang out and grabbed the Bull by the horns. He shouted out, "Gilgamesh, I have tested the might of the Bull. I will seize it by the tail and set my foot on the back of its leg. Then you must thrust your knife into the spot between the horns. That is the slaughter spot." Enkidu rushed round to the rear of the Bull, seized it by its tail and set his foot on the back of its leg. Then Gilgamesh, like a skilful butcher, thrust his knife into the slaughter spot of the Bull. Then they bore its heart aloft and, falling prostrate, they set the heart of the Bull before the sun god, Shamash.

Ishtar wailed from the walls of Uruk. She stamped and hopped. "Alas! Gilgamesh, who mocked me, has killed the Bull of Heaven." Enkidu heard this cry. He tore off the Bull's shoulder and hurled it at the goddess where she stood, high on the battlements. "If I could reach you, I would drape your arms with its guts!"

Ishtar took the remains of the Bull of Heaven, assembled her priestesses, her temple women and her temple courtesans. Gilgamesh summoned smiths and craftsmen. They decorated the

Bull's horns with lapis lazuli and made them into receptacles for ointment in the chamber of his father Lugalbanda.

Then Gilgamesh and Enkidu washed once more in the River Euphrates, took each other by the hand, and made their way through the streets of Uruk to the palace. Everywhere they went, the people gathered to gaze at them. In the palace, Gilgamesh cried out, "Who is the finest of men, the most glorious of fellows?" And all the serving girls called back, "Gilgamesh is the finest. Gilgamesh is the most glorious." Then Gilgamesh made merry in his palace. They had a big party that went on late into the night.

Meanwhile, the priestesses were beginning the rites of mourning over the Bull.

THE DEATH OF ENKIDU

When Gilgamesh woke, it was dawn. He heard the voice of his friend Enkidu. "Why are the great gods in council?" Enkidu was standing in the chamber staring at the door. Gilgamesh rose and touched his friend's arm. "Enkidu, you are dreaming." "Yes. This night I have dreamed. I dreamed the gods held an assembly. The greatest, Anu, said, 'Since they slew the Bull of Heaven, since they slew Humbaba the forest guardian and cut down the cedars of the mountain, someone must die.' Then Enlil spoke. 'Very well. For the killing of the Bull of Heaven, for the killing of Humbaba, for the felling of the trees and for the insult to the goddess Inana, there must be a death as punishment. But let not Gilgamesh die. Let Enkidu die.' Gilgamesh, I must die. I shall cross the threshold of the dead. I shall sit among the dead."

He raised his eyes again to the door of the chamber. "Oh door of the woodland, listen. I built you. For twenty leagues I sought you. Your tree had no rival. I fashioned you. I lifted you. I hung you. Had I but known what I now know, I would have lifted my axe and cut you down and floated you down the river to the temple of Shamash. I, who made you, will break you." He staggered towards the door, but Gilgamesh caught him in his arms. His friend was wet with sweat. His eyes were glassy.

"Do not worry," said Gilgamesh. "Together we did those deeds. We will face this together. I will pray to the gods. They will intercede." But Enkidu shook his head. "My brother! Dear to me is my brother. But we will be parted. I shall cross the threshold of death and sit with the dead. Shamash! My life is precious to me, but I shall sit with the dead. I who was pristine. I who was defiled. A curse on the hunter who first saw me by the waterhole when I lived in the wild. May his profit dwindle. When he enters by the door, let his gods leave by the window. And a curse on Shamhat, the temple woman who lured me from the wild, a doom to endure for all eternity. Shamhat – never will you acquire those things you delight in. No household, no family, no chamber, no garment, no oil from the flask, no banqueting table, no thing of beauty shall you ever acquire. Your bed shall be a garret and your sleeping place a ruin. Your seat shall be the crossroads. Thorn and briar shall skin your feet. Drunk and sober strike your cheek. Because, in the wild, you degraded me. I who was undefiled, you degraded me."

Now the sun was rising. Sunlight bathed the walls of the room and the cedar door. And the sunlight carried the voice of Shamash, the sun god. "Enkidu, why do you curse the hunter? Why do you curse the temple woman? She loved you. And you loved her. She fed you bread fit for a god and poured ale for you that was fit for a king. She clothed you and taught you language. She taught you to sing and dance. She gave to you your beloved Gilgamesh to be your companion. Do not curse her. Rather you should bless her. Bless the one who made, of the animal that you were, the man that you are. Bless her who gave you your beloved Gilgamesh." Enkidu's eyes cleared and a calm descended on him. "Come Shamhat, I will fix your destiny. I who cursed you, I bless you now. It is true I loved you. May good and beautiful gifts rain down on you. Gold, lapis lazuli and sweet perfumes be yours. Let all the good things that life can give be yours. May all that you desire be yours. And let the hunter profit."

Quietly he spoke to Gilgamesh. "I had a dream. I dreamed the heavens thundered and the earth gave echo. I stood between them. There was a creature like the Thunder Bird, the Lion Bird, with lion's paws and eagle's talons. It seized me by the hair. It bound my arms like the wings of a bird and led me to the house of darkness. There was no light. Yet within the darkness, I saw a throng. There were all the kings and queens of the past. Those who had worn crowns were dressed in the feathers of birds. Those who ruled the land and served the roast, baked bread and poured cool water from skins – now soil is their only sustenance. And towering over them was Ereshkigal, Queen of the Underworld. She raised her head and saw me. She looked straight at me and she spoke. 'What is this? Who brought this thing here? It is nothing!'"

The day he saw the dream, Enkidu's strength was exhausted. For three days, he lay like that. Then his sickness worsened. For twelve days his sickness worsened, and he lay on his bed. He called for Gilgamesh. "My god has taken against me. I do not die like one who falls in the midst of battle. I do not make my name. I die in shame."

At the very first glimmer of brightening dawn, Gilgamesh called out, "Now what is this sleep that has seized you? You do not speak. You do not hear me." He did not lift his head. His heart beat no longer.

At the very first glimmer of brightening dawn, Gilgamesh spoke to his friend. "Enkidu! Son of the gazelle and the wild donkey. May the paths of the forests of cedar mourn you. May the high hills mourn you. May the pastures mourn you. May the forests mourn you. May the beasts of the wild mourn you. May the sacred rivers mourn you. The ploughman and the shepherd and the herd boy and the brewer – may they mourn you.

"And as for me – hear me elders, hear me craftsmen, hear me men, hear me women, hear me rivers, creatures, trees, pastures, paths, high hills: hear me. Hear me, gods. I shall weep for Enkidu my friend. Like the hired mourner woman, I bitterly weep. I wail for him who was the axe at my side, the trust of my arm, the sword of my belt, the shield of my face, my festive garment, my girdle of delight. He was all of these things, and a wicked wind has risen up and robbed me.

"My friend! My friend! Swift wild ass, donkey of the uplands, panther of the wilds. We met and we climbed the uplands. We seized and we slew the Bull of Heaven. We destroyed Humbaba and the forest of cedar. Now what is this sleep that has seized you?"

He covers the face of his friend as one covers the face of a bride. Like a lioness deprived of her cubs, he paces to and fro, this way and that. His curly black hair he tears out in clumps and his finery he rips to shreds. He casts it away in disgust.

Six days and seven nights Gilgamesh wept for his friend. He did not surrender the body for burial until, at last, a maggot dropped from his nostril.

Then, at the very first glimmer of brightening dawn, Gilgamesh sent forth a call to the land. He called the forge master, the coppersmith, the goldsmith and the jeweller. "Fashion for my friend a statue. Let the body be of obsidian, carnelian and alabaster. Let the chest be of gold, his eyebrows of lapis lazuli."

At the first glimmer of the brightening dawn, he opened up his gate and the ceremony began.

"A staff of gleaming wood for Inana queen of heaven and earth.

"May she welcome my friend and walk at his side.

"A flask of lapis lazuli for Ereshkigal the sun of the underworld.

"May she welcome my friend and walk at his side.

"A flute of carnelian for Dumuzi the shepherd god.

"May he welcome my friend and walk at his side.

"A chair of lapis lazuli for Nammur the vizier of the underworld.

"May he welcome my friend and walk at his side.

"A clasp of silver for Qasutabat the sweeper of the underworld.

"May he welcome my friend and walk at his side.

"A bowl of alabaster for Ninshiliha the cleaner of the underworld.

"May she welcome my friend and walk at his side.

"A double-edged dagger for Bibbu the butcher of the underworld.

"May he welcome my friend and walk at his side."

He laid out for his friend a magnificent bed of honour, a table of elammaki wood, dishes of carnelian filled with honey and ghee. He laid out gifts for the gods on this bed of honour.

SEARCHING IN THE WILDERNESS FOR UTNAPISHTIM

After Enkidu died, Gilgamesh lost all interest in the joys and the governance of Uruk. He took to wandering in the wild outside the city walls. Then, in his grief, he became preoccupied by the fear of his own death. One night, while wandering in the wild by moonlight, he saw lions in the valley and he was, at first, afraid. Then he was filled with fury at his own fear, and he fell on the lions and destroyed them. He threw back his head and called out to the moon god above. "Great Suen, I will not lie down and die." All night he sat in the valley. Then he stood. "I recall my ancestor. Once his name was Ziusudra, then his name was Atrahasis. Now we call him Utnapishtim. He attended the gods' assembly and he found life eternal. He of all men is immortal. I will find him. I will find out the secret of immortality. I will not lie down and die."

He dressed himself in the skins of the lions that he had killed and he began a journey in search of his ancestor, Utnapishtim.

He came to the Mashu Mountains, the twin mountains which are the mountains of the sun, guarded by monstrous Scorpion People. When he saw them, he was afraid. He shielded his face, but still he placed himself in their sight. The Scorpion Man cried across the divide to his mate, "What is this one who stands before us? I smell the flesh of the gods in his body." The Scorpion Woman called down, "Who are you?"

He said, "I am Gilgamesh, the King of Uruk."

She replied, "I see the flesh of a god is in your body, yet sorrow resides in your heart. How did you come here? It is such a far road. How did you get here into our presence? Tell us your story. We are listening."

"Enkidu, my friend, whom I loved, he who went through every danger with me, he who defeated Humbaba of the forest with me, he who defeated the Bull of Heaven with me, he who defied Inana with me: the doom of mortals came upon him. My friend, whom I have loved, has become like clay. Six days and seven nights, I wept for him. I did not surrender his body for burial until, at last, a maggot dropped out of his nose. Then I grew afraid that I too would die. I took to wandering the wild. What became of my friend was too much to bear. So on a far road, I am wandering in the wild. I am seeking the road of my forefather, Utnapishtim, who attended the gods' assembly and found life eternal. Where is the road to Utnapishtim? Tell me, oh, tell me. If it can be done, I will cross the ocean. If it cannot be done, I will wander the wild. Of death and life he shall tell me the secret."

The Scorpion People were sorry for him and called out, "Gilgamesh, Utnapishtim lives beyond the place where the river flows out to the sea. But to reach that place, you must travel the sun's path of the mountain. The darkness is dense and dangerous, but more dangerous still is the rising and the setting of the sun. You have twelve double hours to travel this path or the sun will overtake you, overwhelm you and consume you. Be quick." The Scorpion Woman raised her arm. Gilgamesh saw the gates of the mountain open. He stepped in and was engulfed in darkness. He set his foot on rough cold stone and he began to run into the darkness.

At one double hour, the darkness was dense and he was scrambling. On he scrambled for two, three, four, five double hours. After seven, eight double hours, the stone began to get warm. At nine double hours, he was covered in sweat. At ten double hours a hot wind roared. At eleven double hours he was battling over bright and burning rocks. At twelve double hours his beard and his eyebrows and his lion skin were singed and sparking, but he leaped out of the tunnel just as the bright sun roared past him and off, into the sky and away on its path.

He found he was standing in the otherworldly light of the garden of the gods. It was an orchard of fruit trees. But the fruits that hung on the branches were precious stones. The dates and walnuts were of carnelian. The clusters of grapes were jet. Quince and fig were lapis lazuli, gorgeous to gaze on. Cypress and cedar had leaf stems of emerald and the thorns of the fruit bushes were coral. Between the trees, he could see beyond the garden of the gods, and far below there was the sea, a star on every wave. On the seashore, there stood a little inn.

He set off out of the garden, over the hill and down towards the tavern beside the sea.

Siduri

By the water, she sits. She is Siduri, the wise one, the healer, the brewer of beer.

Her house stands between the garden of the gods on the mountain of the sun, and the ocean, which is the water of death.

Siduri raised her eyes to the garden of the gods, high on the hill where the sun emerges from the mountains, and she saw a creature clambering down the hillside towards her. It was like a man. But he was huge. He was thirteen feet tall. His hair was wild. He was covered in dirt and dust. He was dressed in filthy, uncured lion skins. He was coming on at a great speed towards her open doorway.

Quickly, she rose and pulled the big doors shut with a thud. She locked them and she bolted them and climbed the staircase to the roof terrace. The creature arrived at the big gates below. He howled and hammered with powerful fists. The whole house shook.

From the roof terrace, she called down, "Who are you?"

He looked up at her. "I am Gilgamesh, the King of Uruk."

She frowned and shook her head. "If you are Gilgamesh, the King of Uruk, where is your crown, your robe, your retinue? If you are Gilgamesh, the King of Uruk, why are your eyes and your cheeks so hollow? Why are your lips cracked? Why is your skin grimy and your hair and beard matted with dirt? Why are you wearing uncured lion skins?"

He replied, "My friend Enkidu whom I loved: the doom of mortals came upon him and he died. Now I am afraid of my own death. I seek my ancestor Utnapishtim. He alone of all humankind knows the secret of immortality."

She no longer saw the matted hair and dirt. She saw his suffering and felt sorry for him.

Siduri, the wise woman, climbed down the steps to the courtyard. She walked past the drying herbs and the rows of pots and urns and bottles. She unbolted and unlocked the great doors and pulled them open.

She took the wild man by the arm and led him to a seat in the shade. She brought him a bowl of water and a cloth to wipe his face and she gave him a cup of cool spring water, with a few drops of something calming from a nearby cask.

She sat down at his side and said, "Tell me all about it."

He bowed his head.

"I was the King of Uruk and the most powerful of all men. I had no equal. I was alone without a friend. One night I dreamed.

In my dream a meteor shot across the sky and fell at my feet. I saw it was an axe. I asked my mother the meaning of my dream. She said, 'It is a good dream. The gods are sending you a true friend at last.' And she was right. The gods sent me Enkidu the wild man. At first, we fought. But he was my equal. We became best friends. We were inseparable. We did everything together. We had adventures together. So many adventures. Together we destroyed Humbaba, the forest guardian of the gods. Together we killed the Bull of Heaven, sent to earth by Inana, queen of heaven and earth. So many adventures. Too many adventures. Together we stained the white gown of the goddess with the blood of the Bull of Heaven. The gods were offended. They said someone should be punished. Someone should die. We killed the guardian and the bull together. But it was my friend alone who received the punishment. My friend Enkidu, whom I loved, the doom of mortals came upon him and he died. He was punished. I was not punished."

Siduri said, "He does not suffer any more. It is you who suffers."

Gilgamesh paid no heed to her words.

"For six days and seven nights I would not leave his side. I would not give him up for burial until a worm crawled out of his nose. Then I gave his body to the priestesses. I called the craftsmen to make a statue of him – gold, carnelian, lapis and jade. After that, I lost all delight in city life. Then I became afraid that I too would die. I took to roaming alone in the wilderness outside the walls of brick-built Uruk.

"One night, roaming under the full moon, I saw lions in the valley below. I was struck by terror and fury at one and the same time. I called on the moon god, 'Oh great god Nanna Suen! I will not lie down and die.' Then I fell on the lions. I killed them all. I took their skins and clothed myself. Then I spoke an oath in the light of the moon god. 'I will find my ancestor, Utnapishtim. I will learn from him the secret of immortality. I will not die.' Since then I have searched. I have wandered in the wild land. I have stood at the gates of the mountains of the sun; I have told my tale to the Scorpion People who guard the entrance. They were sorry for me and they let me in. I have followed the path of the sun through the mountains. It took me twelve double hours and the sun did not overtake me till I stepped out into the garden of the gods. I have walked in the garden of the gods where the apples are rubies and the grapes are amethysts. From the garden of the gods I have seen your house by the sea. You sit here by the water. You are the wise healer! Heal me. Cure my pain. Relieve me of my suffering. Tell me where I will find my ancestor Utnapishtim. Tell me where he is. Tell me the way."

She said, "Gilgamesh, why are you ceaselessly roaming? Why do you seek the life you never will find? Don't you know that when the great gods first created humankind, they kept the gift of immortality for themselves? The gift they granted to humankind was death. But with that gift, they gave other gifts as well. The taste of this water you're drinking right now is their gift. These healing herbs within it, this beer, are gifts. They gave this brilliant sunlight, the sparkle on those waves and the cry of the seabirds. The breeze that is cooling your face right now. Gilgamesh! You are human and alive. Play your part. Be a king. Use the gifts of this earth that you have been given for the benefit of your people. Irrigate the land. Grow dates. Build homes. Paint pictures. Organize wonderful projects. Then dance and sing with your friends. Enjoy a refreshing bath. Comb scented oil into your hair. Put on nice clean clothes. Taste good food. Delight your wife with your repeated embrace. Hold the soft hand of your little child in yours. Because these too are the gifts of the gods, and you are missing them all in your useless search for the one thing you never can have."

Gilgamesh looked at Siduri. He narrowed his eyes. He said, "What are you talking about? Can you tell me where to find my ancestor, Utnapishtim, or can't you? Tavern Keeper, tell me. Where is the road to Utnapishtim? Where is its landmark? Tell me! If it may be done, I will cross the ocean. If it may not be done, I will wander in the wild."

For a moment the only sound was the waves washing on the shore. Then from far off in the trees by the sea, there was the sound of axe on wood. Siduri sighed.

She said, "Not since olden days can anyone cross the ocean. Only Shamash, the hero, crosses the ocean. Apart from the sun god, who crosses the ocean? The crossing is perilous, its way full of hazard, and midway lie the Waters of Death. When you reach the Waters of Death, what then will you do?"

"Where is he?"

"Listen. What can you hear?"

"I hear the sound of axe on wood."

"Follow the sound. It is the sound of Ur-shanabi, the ferryman. He is fixing his boat. His stone ones are with him. Follow the sound and find him. He alone knows the way. Let him see your face. He may carry you over the dark waters to the land of your ancestor Utnapishtim."

"Well, why didn't you say so before?! I will go to my ancestor Utnapishtim! He will teach me the secret of eternal life. Goodbye."

And he was up and out of the gates rushing along the shore. But when he came to the ferryman by the shore, he did not show his face. When Ur-shanabi saw the enormous figure approaching, he was startled and clad himself in his aura. He took up his axe, all a-tremble before him. Gilgamesh struck his head and grabbed his hair. He pinned his arm along his chest. As Gilgamesh seized the ferryman, the stone ones, who do not fear the water of death, sealed the boat and began to sail, but Gilgamesh halted the boat and the stone ones. He smashed the stone ones and tipped them into the water. And he tied up the boat with a rope and sat on the bank, and said to the ferryman, "You took up an axe all a-tremble before me. You sought to fight me, but I am Gilgamesh the king and I will not wage war against you."

The ferryman asked, "Why are your cheeks so hollow? Why do you wander in the wild?" Gilgamesh told him the whole story. "I seek my ancestor. Take me to him."

The ferryman shook his head. He said, "In your impetuous anger, you have destroyed the means of our propulsion across the ocean and across the Waters of Death to the land of Utnapishtim. If you still want to go, you must take up your axe and cut three hundred punting-poles. Each must be five rods in length. Then trim them. Then you must be the one who wields the poles."

He took his axe in hand and cut three hundred punting poles, trimmed them and furnished each of them with a boss. They loaded them onto the ferry and Gilgamesh pushed off from the shore.

"When we come to the Waters of Death, do not splash." Gilgamesh did as he was told.

Long before they reached the far shore, they ran out of punting poles. So he took off his lion skin, stretched it tight between his outspread arms and made that the sail, while he himself was the mast.

At last they reached the land of the ancestor, Utnapishtim.

Utnapishtim and his wife saw them coming from a long way off.

IN THE LAND OF UTNAPISHTIM

Utnapishtim asked, "If you are Gilgamesh the King of Uruk, where is your crown, your robe, your retinue? If you are Gilgamesh the King of Uruk, why are your eyes and your cheeks so hollow; why are your lips cracked; why is your skin grimy and your hair and beard matted with dirt? Why are you wearing uncured lion skins?" Gilgamesh replied, "My friend Enkidu, whom I loved, we went through everything together. We climbed the Cedar Mountains together, we slew Humbaba together, we slew the Bull of Heaven together. Then the doom of mortals came upon him and he died. For six days and seven nights I wept for him. I did not surrender his body for burial until a maggot dropped from his nose. Now I am afraid of my own death. I have come a long way seeking you. What became of my friend Enkidu was too much to bear. So on a far path I have wandered in the wild, looking for you. How can I keep silent? How can I stay quiet? My friend, whom I love, has turned to clay. My friend Enkidu, whom I love, has turned to clay. Shall I not be like him and also lie down, never to rise again, through all eternity? I thought, 'I will find Utnapishtim the Distant, of whom men tell.' And I have wandered journeying through every land. Of slumber I have had little. I scourged myself by going sleepless. I have filled my sinews with sorrow and toil. Now let the gate of sorrow be barred, let its door be sealed with tar and pitch. For my sake they shall interrupt the dancing no more. You of all mankind will live for ever. Tell me the secret."

They sat together and Utnapishtim spoke. He said, "Why are you chasing sorrow? Your parents gave you a seat between god and human, but you take the seat of fool! You toil away ceaselessly. There is no need! It brings closer the end of your days."

Gilgamesh did not listen. He said, "Look at you, Utnapishtim. Your form is not different; you are just like me. I was fully intent on making you fight, but now, in your presence, my hand is stayed. How was it that you stood with the gods in assembly and found life eternal?"

Utnapishtim said, "Let me disclose, O Gilgamesh, a matter most secret. To you I will tell a mystery of the gods. I used to live in the town of Suruppak, on the banks of the Euphrates. One night I heard a voice from the wall of my reed hut: "Oh fence of reed! Hear this: the man of Suruppak should demolish the house and build a boat. Abandon wealth and seek survival. Spurn property and save life. Put on board the boat all the seed that is living. The boat you will build, her dimensions all shall be equal: her length and breadth shall be the same. Cover her with a roof.

"I understood that it was the voice of Ea, my master: 'Great god Ea, I understand, but how shall I explain to my friends and my elders?' Ea said, 'Say this: I have fallen out with Enlil and he hates me, so I have to go away to the ocean below and to Ea my master, and if I can do that, Ea will send you a rain of plenty.'"

"So my friends helped me build an ark. The carpenter carried his hatchet; the reed worker, his stone; the shipwright, his heavyweight axe. The young men were doing the hard work. The old men were bearing rope of palm fibre. The rich man brought the pitch and the poor man brought the tackle. By the fifth day I had set her hull in position. One acre was her area, ten rods the height of her sides. At ten rods also, the sides of her roof. I set in place her body. I had drawn up her design. She had six decks, divided into seven. There were nine compartments in her interior. There were bilge plugs in her belly and a punting pole and tackle. Three myriad measures of pitch I poured into the furnace, three myriad of tar as well. The workforce fetched three myriad of oil and there was another myriad of oil consumed in libations. Two myriad of oil was stowed away by the shipwright.

"Daily I butchered oxen and lambs to feed the workers. There was beer and ale, oil and wine like water from a river for them. It was like New Year all the time. At the end it was hard work. At sunrise, I set my hand to the oiling, and before the sun set the boat was complete. We had to do quite a lot of last-minute adjustment. Everything I owned I loaded aboard. All silver, gold, living creatures, kith and kin. Beasts of the field, creatures of the wild, experts of every skill and craft.

"There was a strange message from the sun god. 'In the morning he will send you a shower of bread cakes, and in the evening, a torrent of wheat.' I did not understand. But then he said, 'Go into the boat and seal your hatch. The time has come,' and his meaning was clear. I examined the look of the weather. It was full of foreboding. I went into the boat and I sealed my hatch. To the one who sealed the boat, the shipwright, I gave my palace with all its goods.

"At the very first glimmer of brightening dawn, there rose on the horizon a dark cloud of black, and bellowing within it was Adad the storm god. Gods were uprooting the mooring-poles and making the weir overflow. The Anuna gods carried torches of fire, scorching the country with brilliant flashes. The stillness of the storm god passed over the sky and all that was bright then turned into darkness.

"For a day, the gale winds flattened the country. Then came the Deluge. Like a battle, the cataclysm passed over the people. One man could not discern another nor could people be recognized amid the destruction. Even the gods took fright at the Deluge. They left and went up to the heaven of Anu. They were like dogs curled up in the oven. The goddess Belet-ili wailed. She was sweet of voice. 'The olden times have turned to clay. I spoke evil in the gods' assembly. I agreed on the war to destroy my people. I gave birth to them; these people are mine. Now, like dead fish, they fill the ocean.' The Anuna gods were weeping with her. The downpour lasted for six days and seven nights.

"But then the gale relented and the Deluge ended. I opened up the roof and looked at the weather. It was quiet and still, but all the people had turned to clay. The floodplain was flat like the roof of a house. Through the opening, I felt the sunlight on my cheek. I fell to my knees and sat there weeping. Down my cheeks, the tears were coursing. I scanned the horizons of the ocean. In fourteen places arose islands. On the mountain of Ninmush, the boat ran aground. We waited for six days and after that time, when the boat allowed no motion, then we let out a dove. There was no place for it to land, so it came back to me. Then I brought out a swallow and let it loose. Off went the swallow, but it returned. There was no place for it to land, so it came back to me. Then I brought out a raven. I let it loose. Off went the raven. It saw the waters receding. It was finding food, bowing and bobbing. It did not come back to me.

"I brought out an offering and to the four winds made sacrifice. Incense I placed on the peak of the mountain. Seven flasks and seven more I set in position. Reed, cedar and myrtle I piled beneath them. The gods smelled it and they gathered like flies around the family making sacrifice.

"Then Mami, the great mother Belet-ili, arrived. She had lapis lazuli around her neck. She said, 'Oh gods, look at the great beads in this necklace of mine. Remember these days and never forget them. All we gods have come to the delicious incense of the people. But Enlil has not come because he did not listen to our counsel and he brought the Deluge.' But then Enlil did come anyway, all in a rage. 'What is this?' At last the other gods stood up to him, and there was a row. Ea said, 'You are supposed to be the sage of the gods, the hero. How could you so lack counsel that you brought on the Deluge? On him who transgresses, inflict his crime! On him who does wrong, inflict his wrongdoing. If you are angry, do not create a deluge, do not create a plague, do not create a drought.'

"We left them arguing and we went back to the boat. Then I realized that Enlil was with us, within the boat. He took hold of our arms. We knelt together. He touched our foreheads and blessed us. He said, 'In the past, Utnapishtim was a mortal man, but now he and his woman shall become like gods! Utnapishtim shall dwell far away, where the rivers flow forth.' So, far away they took us, and settled us here, where the rivers flow forth! It all came from one night when I was awake and heard the words of the gods. Can you stay awake to hear the words of your god? Can you do without slumber?"

Gilgamesh said, "Yes! Of course! Here I am. I will. I will stay awake." As soon as he squatted down on his haunches, sleep like a fog already breathed over him. Instantly he was sleeping. Utnapishtim said, "See the fellow who so desires life! Sleep like a fog already breathes over him."

His wife said, "Wake him." She went to waken him. But Utnapishtim the Distant said, "Let him sleep. He has travelled too far. But while he sleeps, mark on the wall the days he sleeps, and bake bread for him. So he knows."

Gilgamesh awoke to the smell of freshly baked bread. He said, "I was not sleeping. I was just resting my eyes." But Mrs Utnapishtim was smiling at him and shaking her head. She said, "Oh Gilgamesh! While you slept, I baked for you. Each day that you slept, I baked for you."

Beside the hearth, Gilgamesh saw there were six loaves of bread. The first was hot off the coals. The second was cold, the third was hard, the fourth was dry, the fifth was spotted with white mould, the sixth was covered with green mould. He had slept for six days.

Gilgamesh cried, "Utnapishtim, where will I go? Where will I lay my head? Wherever I go, Death stands there! Death stands in my bedchamber. Death stands always at my side."

Utnapishtim turned to the ferryman. He said, "You who brought him, and should not have brought him, you no longer have a place here. Clean him. Dress him properly. Take him home."

Mrs Utnapishtim gave a nudge to her husband. "He has come so far. Do not send him home empty-handed."

Utnapishtim said, "Oh, all right. Listen. You must enter the sweet place in the poisoned water and there, below, you will find the herb of youth. It will not ward off death, but it will restore to you your youth. If you eat it, you will become once more the youth you were."

THE RETURN

The ferryman took Gilgamesh, the wild man, helped him to wash and oil his hair and his skin, and then dressed him in a marvellous suit of nice new clothing provided by Utnapishtim. They conversed, then together they set out to find the sweet place in the water. There, Gilgamesh made a heroic dive deep down and brought back the herb of youth. Triumphantly he said, "I will take this back to Uruk and find someone really old and see if it works on him! Then I will eat it and become once more the man I was in my youth." The ferryman laughed.

Together Gilgamesh and his new companion travelled the long journey home. Within sight of the walls of Uruk, they camped and they prepared to wash at a waterhole. Gilgamesh folded up his nice new clothes and placed the precious herb of youth on top, while he went to the pool to bathe. The warm evening breeze carried the scent of the herb to the nose of a little snake that was snoozing under a stone. She slithered out and followed the scent to the pile of clean clothes. She tasted the herb of youth. Then she swallowed it down. She gave a little burp, wriggled and sloughed off her old skin. She became once more the snake she had been in her youth. As he emerged from the pool, Gilgamesh saw the whole thing. And he understood his loss. He turned to the ferryman. He said, "What's your name?" And the ferryman smiled. He said, "My name is Ur-shanabi." Gilgamesh took his new friend Ur-shanabi by the hand. They walked to the city and in through the great gates. Gilgamesh led Ur-shanabi up onto the walls and together they looked down on Uruk.

"Look! These walls are like strands of combed wool. View the parapet that none could copy.

"Take the stairway of a bygone age, draw near to Eanna, seat of Ishtar the goddess, that no later king could ever copy. Climb Uruk's wall and walk back and forth.

"Survey the foundations, examine the brickwork.

"Were its bricks not fired in an oven?

"Did the Seven Sages not lay its foundations?

"A square mile is city. A square mile is date grove. A square mile is clay pit. Half a square mile is the temple of Ishtar. Three square miles and a half is Uruk's expanse. And I am its king."

See the tablet box of cedar.
Release the clasps of bronze.
Lift the lid of its secrets.
Replace the tablets of lapis lazuli.
This was the story of Gilgamesh, and all that he endured.

A lament for the death of Gilgameš is found in older tablets:

And now the great wild bull is lying down, never to rise again.
Now great Gilgameš is lying down, never to rise again.
He who was perfect in combat is lying down, never to rise again.
He who learned to speak wisdom is lying down, never to rise again.
He who climbed the mountains is lying down, never to rise again.

Gilgameš, see what you are due! You have travelled each and every road.
You have fetched Anzu down from your heights.
You have slain Huwawa from his forest.
You have set up monuments and temples of the gods and remembered the rites of Sumer.

They have dammed up the Euphrates to make a grave for him.
They have dug a grave for him and buried him there.
Then they have let the Euphrates flow over his grave.
When you see the Euphrates, know it flows over the grave of that greatest of kings, Gilgameš.

MORE GILGAMESH STORIES

There are two stories in this section that you have encountered elsewhere in this book. We include them here as comparisons of the same story from different places and a different time.

To appreciate Enkidu in the Netherworld, we need to see how it relates to 'The Huluppu Tree', which appears in the section called 'Inana'.

The death of Humbaba is told in 'The Epic of Gilgamesh'. 'Gilgameš and Huwawa' is an older, Sumerian version of this story.

These lesser-known stories of Gilgamesh show us other facets of the hero-king of Uruk. They are light, direct and fresh. Gilgamesh is not a giant in these stories. He is more human, less 'epic'. We see diplomacy in action in 'Gilgamesh and Aga'. Also, there is an intriguing reference to an unknown story. When was Gilgamesh in such trouble that he needed the help of King Aga of Kish? We wait for the discovery of the tablet telling this story.

ENKIDU IN THE UNDERWORLD

In the first days, in the very first days, in the first nights, in the very first nights, in those ancient days, a little Huluppu tree was growing by the side of the River Euphrates.

One night a terrible storm ripped the little Huluppu tree up by the roots and washed it downriver. The next morning the young girl, Inana, was walking by the swollen river. She saw the little tree caught in the reeds by the river, waded in and pulled it out. She took it back to her garden, planted it, stamped down the earth with her foot and spoke. "As I grow to my full strength, so shall this little tree grow. In time it will give me the wood I need for my shining throne and my shining bed."

Time passed and she tended it. She watered and she weeded it. As she grew, so did the tree. At last it was strong and tall and Inana spoke. "Now I shall have my shining throne and my shining bed!"

But when she approached the tree, she saw that a snake had made its home in the roots of the tree, the Anzu bird had made its nest in the branches of the tree, and when she looked within its trunk, she saw there inside was the dark maid, Lilith, grinning and winking and laughing at her.

In distress, she called on the help of her brother, Utu, the sun god.

"Oh Utu! I pulled the little tree from the waters of the River Euphrates. I have cared for it so that in time it will provide me with the wood I need for my shining bed and my shining throne! Now it is big enough, but in its roots there is a snake, in its branches the Anzu bird has made a nest, and within its trunk, I see the dark maid Lilith sneering at me."

Her brother Utu was no help. He paid her no attention.

Then the young King Gilgamesh came striding by and, taking pity, said brightly, "Sister! Why so sad?" His tone was familiar but she did not take offence.

She told him everything. "The tree! The snake! The Anzu bird! The dark maid! My bed! My throne!"

Young King Gilgamesh strapped on his belt and took his axe. He struck at the tree once and the snake hissed and slithered away. He struck a second time and the Anzu bird flew. He struck a third time and, with a screech, Lilith was gone to the desert lands. Gilgamesh felled the tree, stripped the branches and the trunk and laid them before the young Inana. Gladly she took them for her shining bed and her shining throne. Out of gratitude, she left for him a gift. She left him a little of the wood – some of the roots and branches of the Huluppu tree.

Delighted, Gilgamesh took the roots and branches to the woodworker's shop in Uruk. When he returned next day, the woodworker showed him what he had made from the holy tree. He had made for his king an elag and an ekidmar.

(An elag and an ekidmar: what could these be? We don't know. But from what happened next in the story, it sounds as though they are rather like a big bat and ball.)

Gilgamesh called all his friends. Enkidu and all the lads of Uruk had to come to the city square, to play at the game with the elag and the ekidmar, made from the roots of the tree which had provided the shining throne and bed of the goddess Inana.

All the mothers and sisters and aunts and cousins were required to come too, to watch the young men prove their skill and to provide the refreshments. All day long Gilgamesh and his friends played with the elag and the ekidmar – throwing and hitting, throwing and hitting. It was endlessly entertaining for young King Gilgamesh. When the day was ending and the evening light was fading, very carefully Gilgamesh marked the spot where the ball last fell.

And, not long after first light the next morning, he was up again in the city square and calling for his teammates and their supporters. The young men were tired and the women were less than enthusiastic. However, Gilgamesh was refreshed and keen to get started. But hardly had the game started, when in his enthusiasm Gilgamesh hit the elag so hard that it flew right over the walls of Uruk and into the unknown regions beyond – down through the gates of Ganzer and into the underworld itself. That is the region of the dead.

Gilgamesh was dismayed. "My ball! I loved it. I was enjoying the game! I was nowhere near tired of it! Oh, if only it was yesterday! If only the wood was still in the woodwork shop! I would reward the woodworker. I would give gifts to his wife and daughter…now what will I do? Oh great is my grief! Who will enter the gates of death and bring me back my ball?"

Everyone was very quiet. Most were already slipping off home quietly. Then his friend Enkidu spoke. "I'll go. I will fetch your ball from the region of death."

"You'll go?"

"Yes."

"You, my best friend Enkidu, would risk going into the underworld, from which no one returns, to fetch back my ball?"

"Yes. I'll go."

It seems that Gilgamesh was more than happy for his friend to go into the realm of death to get his ball back.

"Very good," he said. "Hooray." He led his friend out of Uruk to the gates of Ganzer, entrance to the underworld. As they stood together, Gilgamesh gave his friend instructions. "Now you must know that there are certain rules to be obeyed in the realm below. If you keep the rules, you may go undetected, but if you break the rules, the dwellers in the world below will detect you and detain you. Then you and I will be parted. So listen to the rules."

"I'll listen," said Enkidu.

"Do not bathe and rub scented oils into your body."

"'I will not bathe and rub scented oils into my body," said Enkidu.

"Do not wear nice new clean clothes."

"I will not wear new clothes," said Enkidu.

"Do not wear nice new sandals."

"I will not wear new sandals," said Enkidu.

"Under no circumstances make eye contact."

"I won't make eye contact," said Enkidu.

"No hugging or kissing."

"I won't hug or kiss."

"And finally, don't drop anything and make a noise."

"I won't drop anything or make a noise."

"Keep to the rules and all may be well. But if you break them, they will detect you and detain you and we will never see each other again. I will wait for you right here."

But when Enkidu entered the underworld, he broke all the rules and he was recognized, detected and detained.

At the gates of Ganzer, Gilgamesh waited and waited, but his friend did not return. Then he knew that Enkidu had broken the rules and been detected and detained. Weeping, he went to Enlil, the stern earth god.

"My friend Enkidu, whom I love, entered the underworld and has been detained. I am Gilgamesh the king.

"Help my friend."

Enlil was the stern judge and he was implacable.

"Enkidu knew the rules. He broke the rules. The rules of the underworld are perfect and may not be broken."

Weeping, Gilgamesh went to Enki, god of wisdom and fresh water, in the Abzu.

"My friend Enkidu, whom I love, entered the underworld and has been detained. I am Gilgamesh the king.

"Help my friend."

"Oh no! Your friend? We can't have that. What are rules, if not to be bent a little, now and then? Each case is different and should be judged on its own merit."

Enki called on Utu the sun god. "Utu! Shine a beam of uplifting sunlight! Make a hopeful opening! Send in a warm loving breeze."

At the command of Enki, Utu, the sun god, shone a beam of sunlight and made an opening into the underworld. He sent in a warm breeze. Gilgamesh watched as a sunbeam shone down through the gates of death. Enkidu rose up on the warm breeze and the sunbeam, out of the gates of death.

When Enkidu and Gilgamesh were reunited, there was plenty of hugging and kissing and a good few tears. The story says nothing more of the elag and the ekidmar. Perhaps Gilgamesh realized then what was of importance and what was not.

But as they walked arm in arm back to Uruk, Gilgamesh started wondering. He said, "Enkidu, I find myself wondering. You are the only person who has ever gone into the land of the dead and returned. I'm wondering what it was like. Was it very terrible?"

"Very terrible indeed. There I saw the one who was eaten by a lion. He searches perpetually for his hands and feet. The one who fell from the roof tries to match bone with bone. The one who dived and hit his head on the shipboard calls out, 'Help me get this plank off my head.' I saw no sign of the one who was burned in the fire. He no longer exists in any realm. His smoke has dissipated in the skies."

"And did you see any of our old friends who have entered the underworld?"

"Yes. I saw them."

"Did you see the man who had seven sons?"

"Yes. I saw the man who had seven sons."

"How does he fare?"

"He fares very well. He is like a king on a throne in the palace. He sits and gives out judgements to lesser folk."

"Did you see the man who had six sons?"

"Yes. I saw the man who had six sons."

"How does he fare?"

"He fares well. He is as cheerful as the ploughman who drives his great ox through his own fields."

"Did you see the man who had five sons?"

"Yes. I saw the man who had five sons."

"How does he fare?"

"He fares well. He is like the good scribe. He goes in and out of the palace as he pleases."

"Did you see the man who had four sons?"

"Yes. I saw the man who had four sons."

"How does he fare?"

"He is as happy as the merchant who has four asses to carry his goods."

"Did you see the man who had three sons? How does he fare?"

"He drinks fresh water from water skins."

"Did you see the man who had two sons? How does he fare?"

"Not so well. He sits on a couple of bricks to eat his bread."

"Did you see the man who had one son?"

"Yes. I saw the man who had one son."

"How does he fare?"

"How does he fare? Badly. He hammers a nail into the wall and he weeps."

"Did you see the man who had no sons?"

"Yes. I saw the man with no sons."

"How does he fare?"

"He has nothing: no bed to lie on, no roof over his head, no food to eat, no water to drink. All he has is dust."

"But Enkidu, what of the little children, my little ones who died at birth and never saw life at all. How do they fare?"

Enkidu said, "I saw them. I saw all our little ones. I saw the children who never saw life, every one. They sit on seats of silver. They sit at tables of gold. They eat honey and butter and they play all day and the underworld echoes with the sound of their laughter."

Then hand in hand, Enkidu and Gilgamesh walked together. They were young men walking together, laughing, delighting in each other's company, optimistic. Walking towards their lives on the roads of endless sunlit days, away from the gates of Ganzer.

GILGAMESH AND AGA

There came a time when Aga, Lord of Kish, sent envoys to Unug, the city of Gilgamesh. Aga's message was a warlike one, threatening the city and its people. Gilgamesh presented the matter to the city elders, choosing his words carefully:

"There are wells to be finished, many wells in the land. There are shallow wells to deepen, and hoisting gear to be completed. We have much to do. We should not submit to the house of Kish. Let us smite it with weapons!"

The elders of his city met in assembly and answered Gilgamesh: "There are indeed wells to be finished, many wells in the land. There are shallow wells to deepen, and hoisting gear to be completed. We do have much to do. So we should submit to the house of Kish. We should not smite it with weapons!"

Gilgamesh put no trust in these words of his city elders. He put his trust in the Lady Inana. He presented the matter again, choosing his words carefully, but this time he addressed the able-bodied young men of his city: "There are wells to be finished, many wells in the land. There are shallow wells to deepen, and hoisting gear to be completed. We have much to do. Never before have we submitted to the house of Kish. We should not submit to them now! Let us smite them with weapons!"

In the assembly, the able-bodied young men of the city answered Gilgamesh: "Standing in attendance, serving on escort duty, grasping the reins of the donkey – we do have much to do. But you old men should not submit to the house of Kish. Let us, the able-bodied young ones, smite them with weapons! The gods themselves built our city of Unug, and the temple of Eanna was lowered from the heavens. You, our king, Gilgamesh, are its guardian, the watchman over its rampart, which is like a cloudbank resting on the earth, the residence of An himself. You are its king and warrior, an exuberant man, a prince beloved of An. When Aga comes, such terror will he face! His army is small, and out of his sight there is poor discipline. His men will not dare to face us."

Gilgamesh was glad to hear the words of the the able-bodied young men, and his heart was light. He spoke to his faithful servant Enkidu: "On account of these words, prepare the weapons of war. Let the battle mace be set at your side. We shall create a great terror and a great radiance. When Aga comes, my awesomeness will overwhelm him. His mind will become clouded and his judgement faulty."

Five days had not passed, ten days had not passed, when Aga, Lord of Kish, arrived at Unug with his soldiers and besieged the city. But it was the minds of the people of Unug that became clouded, at the sight of the enemy surrounding their brick-built walls. Gilgamesh, Lord of Unug, spoke to his people: "My warriors, let someone with courage volunteer to go to Aga, and I will send that brave one to speak with him. My warriors, let the choice be yours!"

Immediately Birhur-tura, a royal guard, spoke up, full of admiration for his king: "My king, I shall go light-footed to speak with Aga, so that his mind will become clouded and his judgement faulty."

Birhur-tura went out through the great gate. As soon as he was outside the shelter of the city walls, though still upon the causeway of the gate itself, they seized him and beat him and dragged him before Aga. He spoke up boldly. But before he had finished speaking, one of Unug's officers climbed up onto the city ramparts and leaned over, looking out. Aga saw him and interrupted Birhur-tura, asking, "Slave, is that man your king?"

Birhur-tura replied without fear: "That man is not my king! If that was my king, if that was his angry brow, if those were his bison eyes, if that were his lapis lazuli beard, if those were his elegant fingers, wouldn't he be casting down multitudes;

wouldn't he be raising up multitudes; wouldn't those multitudes be smeared with dust? Wouldn't all the nations of the land be overwhelmed? Wouldn't all the canals of the land be silted up? Wouldn't all the barge prows be smashed? And wouldn't he make a captive of Aga, King of Kish, in the midst of his own army?"

These bold words enraged Aga, and Birhur-tura was beaten and bloodied.

Then Gilgamesh climbed up onto the city ramparts, following his officer. His radiance overwhelmed both the young and the old. He armed the able-bodied young men of the city with battle maces and ordered them onto the causeway leading to the city gate. Only Enkidu, his faithful servant, went out through the city gate. Gilgamesh leaned over the ramparts, looking out. Aga saw him and said: "Slave, is that man your king?"

"That man is indeed my king!" It was just as Birhur-tura had said: Gilgamesh cast down multitudes and raised them up. Those multitudes were smeared with dust, all the nations were overwhelmed, the canals of the land were silted up, the barge prows were smashed and Aga, King of Kish, was captured in the midst of his own army.

Then Gilgamesh, Lord of Unug, approached. He remembered how once he had been helped by Aga. He was magnanimous in victory. He said: "Aga, you were my overseer and my commander, my military commander. You gave me breath, you gave me life. When I was a fugitive you sheltered me, you provided this fleeing bird with grain."

The able-bodied young men of the city shouted out in praise of Gilgamesh: "You, our king, are the guardian of Unug, the watchman over its rampart, which is like a cloudbank resting on the earth, the residence of An himself. You are its king and warrior, an exuberant man, a prince beloved of An!"

Gilgamesh replied, "I am the guardian of Unug, the watchman over its rampart, which is like a cloudbank resting on the earth, the residence of An himself. The city will repay the kindness that was shown to me by Aga."

Then Gilgamesh, Lord of Unug, said to Aga, Lord of Kish, "I am the guardian of Unug, the watchman over its rampart, which is like a cloudbank resting on the earth, the residence of An himself. The city will repay the kindness you showed to me. Before Utu, let your kindness be repaid to you."

Lord Gilgamesh set Aga free to return to Kish.

O Gilgamesh, Lord of Unug, praising you is sweet!

GILGAMEŠ AND HUWAWA

There was a time when Lord Gilgameš decided to set off to where The One lived, in the mountains. He spoke to his slave, Enkidu.

"Enkidu, because no one can live beyond their allotted span of years, I want to go off into the mountains to secure my eternal fame there. If my fame can be secured there, I will do it. If my own fame cannot be secured, I will secure the fame of the gods."

Enkidu answered, "Lord, if you decide to go off to the mountains, Utu should know about it from us. We should definitely tell youthful Utu. Anything to do with the mountains is Utu's business. Anything to do with the Cedar Mountains is Utu's business. He should hear about it from us."

So Gilgameš prepared sacrifices, a white kid and a brown kid. He held the brown kid close to his chest, and his staff close to his nose, and spoke to Utu in heaven.

"Utu, I want to go to the mountains. May you give me your help. I want to go into the Cedar Mountains. May you give me your help."

From above, Utu replied, "Young man, you are already noble. What do you want with the mountains?"

"Utu, please pay attention, listen to what I have to say: a word in your ear! In my city, people are dying and hearts are distressed. Loved ones are lost: that makes me sad. When I looked over the city wall I saw corpses down there, floating in the river. This is what I see. And I know it will happen to me, too. That is the way of it. No one is tall enough to touch the sky. No one is broad enough to stretch across the mountains. Since no one can continue life beyond its allotted span, I want to go off into the mountains to secure immortal fame. If my fame can be secured there, I will do it. If my own fame cannot be secured, I will secure the fame of the gods."

Utu saw that Gilgameš's tears were a fitting gift. He turned to him, full of compassion. He said, "There are seven warriors. They are brothers. The eldest has the qualities of the lion and the eagle. The second is like a snake, while the third is like a dragon snake and the fourth blazes with fire. The fifth is like another snake, the sixth is like a flood and the seventh like fire from heaven. They shall be the ones to guide you to the mountains."

Utu gave these seven to Gilgameš, who was filled with joy. He ordered that the trumpets sound in the city. He proclaimed, "Let the one who is head of a household go home. Let the one who cares for his mother go to his mother. Let the unmarried men, free of responsibility like me, join me for this adventure!"

All the heads of households went home, and so did those who cared for elderly relatives. The unmarried men, with no responsibilities, joined Gilgameš for the adventure. There were fifty of them.

Gilgameš had the smiths cast weapons for them all, strong enough for warriors to wield. He ordered that trees be felled in the plantations. The weapons made from the iron and wood were distributed to his companions.

When all was ready, the eldest brother, he of the qualities of both the lion and the eagle, guided them through the mountains. He crossed the first mountain range, but he knew that the cedars were not there. Once he had crossed the seventh mountain range, he led them straight to the cedars. He did not need to ask, nor to search any further.

Gilgameš began to chop the cedars, while Enkidu lopped off the branches, and the fifty young men from the city piled up the wood.

The Forest Guardian was soon aware that his trees were in danger. From his lair, Huwawa, The One, Guardian of the Cedar Forest, began to radiate his auras of terror. They carried the power of sleep and, sure enough, Gilgameš and all his companions were overcome with lethargy and sank into deep sleep. The fifty citizens of the city rolled around like sleeping puppies. Gilgameš could not keep his eyes open, and even Enkidu was affected by a strong longing to rest. But, after a time, Enkidu dragged himself from his dream, shuddering with sleep. He rubbed his eyes and looked around. There was an eerie silence. He shook Gilgameš, but could not rouse him. He spoke to him, but there was no reply. He called out, "You who have gone to sleep, Gilgameš, young lord of Kulaba, how long will you sleep? The mountains are in shadow, twilight lies over them. Proud Utu is already on his way to rest on his mother's bosom. Gilgameš, how long will you sleep? You brought the sons of the city here – don't make them wait for you to rouse! Their mothers will not want to hear that you kept them hanging around, while you slept!"

He shouted into Gilgameš's ear. His aggressive words covered Gilgameš like a sheet, but they did not wake him. So Enkidu gathered a cloth, smothered it in oil, and rubbed it over Gilgameš's chest.

Then, at last, Gilgameš rose up like a bull. He bent his neck and yelled at Enkidu, "By the life of my mother, divine Ninsun, and my father, holy Lugalbanda, have I fallen back into sleeping in my mother's lap, like a baby? By my mother's life and my father's life, until I find out whether a human or a god put such an enchantment on me, I will not go back to the city or leave the mountains!"

His slave, Enkidu, wanting to make his words seem attractive, replied gently to Gilgameš, "My master, you haven't actually seen that being. He should not be allowed to vex you. But he does vex me, for I have seen him before. His pugnacious mouth is like a raging flood. His brow devours the reedbeds: no one dares approach! He is like a man-eating lion, with blood dripping from his teeth and tongue. Travel on, my master, if you must. But I shall go back to the city. If I tell your mother, 'He's alive,' she will be joyful. But later I will have to tell her, 'He's dead,' and she will weep for you. Lord, come back with me, away from these dangerous mountains."

But Gilgameš answered, "Look, Enkidu, two people together will not perish. A grappling pole will not sink. A woven cloth cannot easily be torn in half. Water cannot carry away someone who has a wall to hold on to. A reed house on fire cannot easily be put out. What can anyone do against us, when we are united? When the barge sank, at least the punting pole was rescued. Come on, let's be after him. I want to get a look at him!"

Enkidu tried again. "If we go after him, there will be terror, there will be terror! Turn back! Is this advisable? Does it make sense? No! Please, let's turn back."

But Gilgameš had the bit between his teeth. "Whatever you think, come on, let's get after him!"

So Gilgameš and Enkidu went on, deep into the Cedar Mountains.

Before a man can get anywhere near him, Huwawa will already have reached his house among the cedars. When he looks at someone, it is the look of death. When he shakes his head at someone, it is a gesture full of reproach. When he speaks to someone, he tells it like it is:

"You may still be young, but you will never now get back to the mother who bore you!"

Fear and terror spread through Gilgameš's body. He could not lift his feet from the path. His toenails felt stuck to the ground. Frozen with fear, he heard Huwawa's challenge.

"So come on then, you hero with a powerful sceptre. You're the noble glory of the gods, you're an angry bull ready for a fight, or so I'm told. Your mother knew how to give birth to sons. Your nurse knew how to nourish children. Don't be afraid of me. Let your hand touch the ground."

So Gilgameš let his hand rest on the ground, and he drew strength to speak to Huwawa.

"By the life of my mother, divine Ninsun, and my father, holy Lugalbanda! No one knows where in the mountains you live. Everyone would like to know where in the mountains you live. You must be lonely here. Come, let me present my big sister to be your wife, here in the mountains. Give me one of your auras of power in exchange, and we will be brothers."

Huwawa gave up one of his auras of power. Gilgameš's band of followers began to lop and bundle up branches, ready to be transported.

A second time, Gilgameš spoke.

"By the life of my mother, divine Ninsun, and my father, holy Lugalbanda, let me present my little sister to be your concubine, here in the mountains. Give me another of your auras, and we will be kinsmen."

Huwawa gave up his second aura of power. Gilgameš's band of followers carried on lopping and bundling branches, ready to be transported.

A third time, Gilgameš said, "By the life of my mother and father, let me be close to you and your family! I have brought flour, the very food of the gods, and cool water here for you in the mountains. Give up another aura, so that we can be one family."

Huwawa gave up his third aura. All this time, Gilgameš's band of followers continued to lop and bundle branches, piling them up ready for transportation.

For Huwawa's fourth aura, Gilgameš, invoking his divine mother and holy father, offered Huwawa big shoes for his big feet. He said, "Hand over your terrors to me. I want to be your brother."

In exchange for big shoes for his big feet, Huwawa handed over his fourth aura of power.

For Huwawa's fourth aura, Gilgameš offered Huwawa tiny shoes for his tiny feet and Huwawa handed over his fifth aura of power. Meanwhile, the young men from the city lopped and bundled, lopped and bundled the timber of the Cedar Forest.

A sixth time, Gilgameš addressed Huwawa in his warmest tones, "By the lives of Ninsun and Lugalbanda, no one knows where in the mountains you live. Everyone is eager to know where you live. I have brought you precious lapis and rock crystal. Give up your sixth aura, so we can be brothers!"

Then Huwawa handed over his sixth aura of power. All this time, the young men carried on with their lopping and bundling.

When Huwawa had handed over his seventh and last aura of power, Gilgameš found himself right next to Huwawa. There was no longer a protective veil about the Forest Guardian. Gilgameš went up to Huwawa as though to kiss him, but suddenly drew back his arm and punched Huwawa in the face. Huwawa fell back, furrowing his brow in confusion and baring his teeth in rage. "Are you here only to act falsely, to speak deceitfully of brotherhood?" he demanded. "Shame on you!"

Both Enkidu and Gilgameš leapt on him and ordered him roughly to sit down. Huwawa sat down and began to weep. He tugged at Gilgameš's hand and pleaded with him.

"Gilgameš, let me go. Let me talk to Utu."

Gilgameš threw a halter over Huwawa, trapping him as though he were a captured wild bull. He tied Huwawa's arms as if he were a prisoner of war. Huwawa protested again. His words had the bitter sting of truth. "Gilgameš, you lied to me.

You have tumbled and manhandled me, after swearing oaths of brotherhood, invoking your mother and your father, divine Ninsun and holy Lugalbanda. Now you have haltered me like an animal; you have bound my elbows like a prisoner of war."

Gilgameš felt shame when he heard these words. The nobility of his character stirred his heart. He turned to his slave, Enkidu.

"Come on, let us set Huwawa free. He could be our guide through the mountains, spying out the pitfalls on our way. He could be my servant, carrying all my things. We should let the captured bird fly home to his nest. We should let the prisoner return to his mother's arms."

But Enkidu's heart was harder. "Come on now, you sceptre-bearing hero, you angry bull ready for a fight! Dear Lord Gilgameš, your mother knew how to give birth to heroes, your nurse knew how to nourish warriors. You, who are so exalted, yet naïve to the core, Fate will devour you before you have a chance to understand what is happening to you! The very idea that a captive bird should fly free; that a prisoner should be released! If you do that, you will never get back to your own city. To let a captive priestess return to her temple, to give a captured cult-priest back his wig? Who has ever heard of such a thing?"

Huwawa looked at him in disbelief.

"Enkidu," he said. "Why do you speak such hateful words to him? Why do you speak so hatefully to Gilgameš?"

Hearing Huwawa speak to him like this, Enkidu was filled with rage and anger. With one stroke, he slit Huwawa's throat. The Forest Guardian was silenced in an instant. Enkidu cut off his head and slung it into a leather bag.

There was nothing more to say or do. If Gilgameš had been moved to show mercy, now it was too late.

Once their party had returned to the city, bringing the precious cedar wood and leaving the ravaged mountains without the protection of the Forest Guardian, Gilgameš and Enkidu went to great Enlil's temple.

After they had kissed the ground before Enlil, they threw down the leather bag, tipped out Huwawa's head, and placed it before Enlil. When Enlil saw the head, he spoke angrily to Gilgameš. "Why did you act this way? Was it commanded that his name should be wiped from the earth? No! He should have sat in honour before you. He should have been offered the very bread you yourself eat, the very water you yourself drink. He should have been honoured by you. This was a misdeed, a great mistake."

Then Enlil, seated on his throne, set about assigning Huwawa's auras of power, that he might not be forgotten.

He gave Huwawa's first aura of power to the fields.

He gave his second aura of power to the rivers.

He gave the third aura to the reedbeds, and the fourth to the lions.

He gave Huwawa's fifth aura of power to the palace, and the sixth to the forests.

He gave the last aura of power to Nungal, Ereshkigal's daughter, the goddess of prisoners.

So the auras of power of the Forest Guardian were shared in both the natural and the human worlds. In this way, Huwawa, the Forest Guardian, was honoured.

MORE GILGAMESH STORIES

THE QUALITIES OF A KING

In many of the world's mythologies, we find stories exploring the skills and attributes needed to rule a kingdom: the Hindu *Mahabharata*, the Welsh *Mabinogi*, the Persian *Bahram Gur*. All show the values a king should espouse. Sumerian literature, mingling mythological feats with the lives of historical kings from the King List, contains many examples of this genre. They are adventure stories full of action. We include some of our favourites here.

LUGALBANDA

Now, it seems that after all the negotiating and to-ing and fro-ing and successful diplomacy and fruitful trading established between the kings of Unug and Aratta, sadly, in the later years of Enmerkar's reign, this diplomatic relationship fell apart and Enmerkar, king of Unug, declared war on Aratta.

In his old age and maturity, King Enmerkar set his mace towards Aratta. He set off to destroy the rebel land. His troops covered the ground like heavy fog. They whirled up a dense dust to the heavens. The king went at the head of the army. They were marching for five days. On the sixth they stopped to bathe. On the seventh day they entered the mountains. As they climbed and crossed the mountain paths, they were like an enormous flood billowing upstream into a lagoon and their ruler, Enmerkar, was riding on the storm. Their barbed arrows were like flashes of lightning. His pointed bronze axe shone sharp like the teeth of a dog eating a corpse.

Among this throng there were seven fine youngsters. They were brothers born and bred in Kulaba. They say the earth goddess had borne these seven and the Wild Cow had nourished them with her milk. They were heroes of Sumer. They were princely and in their prime. There was an eighth son. He was Lugalbanda. He was the youngest and he marched with the troops in awed silence. But when they had covered only half the journey, a sickness befell this little brother of princely heroes. It was a sickness of the head. He jerked like the snake which is dragged by its head with a reed. His mouth bit dust, like a gazelle caught in a snare. His hands could not return the hand grip. He could not lift his feet. No one could help him, not his brothers, or even the king himself. Some said, "Let them take him back to Unug." But it was too far.

His teeth were chattering, so they took him to a warm place: a cave overlooking the valleys. There they made him an arbour like a bird's nest. They made him a storehouse with baskets of dates and figs. They put sweetmeats suitable for the sick to eat. They set out for him the various fats from the cow pen, fresh cheese from the sheepfold and oil with cold hard-boiled eggs. It was as if they were laying a table for the Holy Place, the Valued Place, the Funerary Offering. Directly in front of the table, they arranged for him beer for drinking, mixed with date syrup, and rolls with butter. They poured provisions into leather buckets and leather bags. His brothers and friends placed these stores by his head in the mountain cave. It was like a boat unloading from the harvest-place. There was water in leather waterskins. There was dark beer, light beer and wine which is pleasant to the taste. They prepared for him first-class aromatic resin in pots. They suspended the pots of resin by his head in the mountain cave. At his head they placed his axe, made from tin imported from the Zubi Mountains. They wrapped up his dagger, made of iron imported from the Black Mountains, and they placed it by his chest. For a while Lugalbanda watched them and he wept. His eyes were like irrigation ditches flooding with water. But by the time they had finished the task he was unconscious. They lifted his neck and they could sense no breath. His brothers took counsel.

"If the god who has smitten him steps aside, and our brother rises, he will eat this food and drink this beer and this will make his feet stable. Then may he return to Unug and brick-built Kulaba. But if Utu calls our brother to the Holy Place, the Valued Place, the hereafter, then it will be up to us, when we come back from Aratta, to bring our brother's body home." Then, shedding many tears, Lugalbanda's older brothers set off into the mountains for Aratta.

For two days, Lugalbanda lay close to death in the cave. Utu the sun god warmed the cave during the day, but when the sun set and the animals lifted their heads and moved towards their lairs, and the evening was cool, then his body was covered with sweat as if he had been anointed with oil. Another half day passed and sunlight shone again into the cave. Lugalbanda lifted his eyes to heaven, to Utu, and cried out to him. He raised his hands towards the sunlight shining in through the mouth of the cave. "Utu, I greet you. Let me be ill no longer. Utu, you have let me come into the mountains. Here in this most dreadful spot, in this mountain cave, let me be ill no longer. There is no mother or father here to say 'Alas, my child.' My brother is not here to say 'Alas, my brother.' I am lost. A lost dog is a bad thing. A lost man is a terrible thing. Utu, here on the unknown way at the edge of the mountains is a lost man: me. I am a lost man. Do not make my life flow away like water. Do not let me fall and be lost like a throwstick in the unknown desert. Let me not come to an end here in these mountains."

Sun god Utu heard and accepted the tears of Lugalbanda. Lugalbanda felt the influence of the divine encouragement sent down by Utu and as the sun was setting, he became calm. Then he saw in the deep blue of the darkening sky, through the opening of the cave, the stellar brightness of the evening star. It was Inana. Her brilliance illuminated the mountain cave. When he lifted his eyes upwards to Inana, he wept and raised his hands towards her. "Inana, if only this were my home. If only this were my city. May my limbs not perish in the mountains of the cypresses."

Inana heard and she accepted his tears. She enveloped him with the power of life and with heart's joy. He felt as if he was being wrapped in a woollen garment. He slept.

When he woke, the holy astral bull that eats up the black soup was shining in the heavens. That is Suen, the moon. Suen was spreading bright light in the night and illuminating the mountain cave. Lugalbanda raised his hands.

"Suen whom one cannot reach, Suen who loves justice, when you encounter evil, your heart becomes angry at evil, you are like a snake which drools poison at evil. You spit your venom and destroy evil."

Suen heard his words, accepted his tears and restored him to life. Suen restored to his feet the power to stand.

As the sun rose, the unknown god which had smitten Lugalbanda departed and was gone. Full of gratitude, he praised the sun god Utu and stepped out of the mountain cave. His good protective god hovered ahead of him. His good protective goddess walked behind him. He saw, as if for the first time, that he was surrounded by the beauty of the mountains. He saw, as if for the first time, that there were rolling rivers and verdant plants. He saw there were life-saving plants. All day he nibbled the plants and sipped from the water. And he was healed. His strength returned. He packed all his provisions into leather pails and leather bags and set off alone, hurrying, by moonlight, through the mountain wasteland. He sped away like a horse of the mountains. When he was hungry and tired, he stopped. He remembered that he had seen his brothers bake bread on the ground and that they had left him all the things he needed for bread baking in his leather bags, but he himself had never baked bread, or even lit a fire himself before. Nevertheless, he made a start. He split coals and wood on the open ground. He used a fine flintstone to cause a spark. Its fire shone out for him over the wasteland like the sun. With just seven coals, he baked dough. While the cakes were cooking, he pulled up reeds, roots and all, stripped them and used them to pack up all the cakes as a day's ration. He was pleased with himself and overjoyed. Never having done it before, he had done it. He garnished the cakes with date syrup.

At that moment, he heard low mooing. Over a ridge came a fine brown bull, tossing its horns, chewing the short mountain grass, sniffing at the foliage, drinking from the river and calling for its fellows. Lugalbanda uprooted a little juniper tree, stripped its branches and stuck it in the ground. He caught and tethered the bull to the stake. Then there was the sound of bleating and over the ridge came two flea-bitten goats. They too were grazing and drinking and sniffing and doing a lot of belching. Lugalbanda caught them too and tethered them to the stake. He scanned the slopes of the mountain and saw he was utterly alone. Not a single person could be seen. He drank some beer. He laid down pure herbs from the mountains as a couch and unfolded a white linen sheet. There was no room for bathing, so he had to make do. He lay down. Sleep overcame him.

Sleep is like a towering flood, like a hand demolishing a brick wall, covering like syrup all in its way. It knows no captain. It overpowers the hero. Lugalbanda lay, not to sleep, but to dream. A dream will talk in lies to the liar. It will speak truth to the truthful. It is the counsellor of Inana. It is the closed tablet-basket of the gods. It can make one man happy. It can make another man sing. Lugalbanda did not turn his back at the door of the dream. In his dream, Lugalbanda heard the god of dreams bellow. It was Zangara, the god of dreams, bellowing at him. Like the calf of a cow he bellowed. "Who will slaughter the brown bull for me? Who will make the fat melt for me? Let him take my tin axe. Let him wield my iron dagger. Let him offer it before the rising sun and heap up the heads of goats. Let him pour out their blood into a pit. Let the smell waft out so that the mountain snakes sniff it."

Lugalbanda woke with the dream clear in his mind. He shivered. He rubbed his eyes. He was overawed, but he followed the instructions of the dream without hesitation. He took his tin axe and his iron dagger. He slaughtered the wild bull and the goats. He offered them before the rising sun.

He poured the blood into the pit and the snakes of the mountain sniffed.

Then as the sun was rising, he invoked the names of the great gods. He invited the gods to a banquet at the pit in the mountains which he had prepared. He set out the banquet: all the good things that his brothers had given him and the flesh of the bull and the goats and the blood in the pit. He let the smoke rise like incense. The great gods smelled the sacrificial feast. They all attended the banquet that Lugalbanda had provided. The gods consumed the best part of the food prepared by Lugalbanda. He set out the cakes last of all. Then along the mountain paths came the demons to Lugalbanda's feast. The demons are the ones bringing gifts and terrors. They can be like a string of figs dripping with deliciousness. But they can be gales running in flight. They can be the fine smooth cloth of Ninlil. They pile up flax and barley. But they can also be the wild animals on the rampage. They descend by surprise like a storm. They lie up during all the long day, and during the short night they will enter your house. During the long day and the short night, they lie in your bed. They sing out, talking constantly, talking in your head, nestling at the bedside. They watch at the window and the pot stand.

All night long, while Lugalbanda lay on the mountains after the feast of the gods, the demons beset Lugalbanda. But he gave himself up to them and survived them, and when the morning came, they departed. Then he knew he truly had the blessing of the gods with him and he set off once more. He had no idea which way to go. There was no mother or father to talk to him or offer him advice, no one to talk to him or for him to talk to. He was lost and did not know his way through the mountains.

But he knew that he had done his duty by the gods and he had their blessing.

He came to the place where the splendid eagle tree of Enki stands on the summit of Inana's mountain of multicoloured cornelian. Its shade covers the mountains like a cloak. Its roots rest like huge snakes and reach down into Utu's river of seven mouths. There the great Anzu bird had set his nest. His bower was made from juniper and box wood and bright twigs. Inside the bower he settled his young. The Anzu bird has shark's teeth and eagle's claws. When at daybreak he stretches and cries out, the ground of the mountains quakes. When he flies from peak to peak, wild bulls and stags run to hide into the hidden places of the foothills.

Lugalbanda took time to watch and to reflect and had become wise. He spoke to himself. "I shall treat the bird as befits him. I shall give gifts and seat Anzu and his family at a banquet. I will give him my brothers' beer. When the bird has drunk the beer and is happy, he can help me find the troops of Unug. Anzu can put me on the track of my brothers."

When he arrived at the boxwood bower, Anzu was not at home. Only the Anzu chick, the nestling, was in the nest. It looked at him warily. Lugalbanda began preparing sweet celestial cakes. He was good at it now. He was careful. He added carefulness to carefulness. He kneaded the dough with honey. He added more honey. Now the chick was watching with interest. Lugalbanda set the cakes before the nestling. Then he picked fatty meat from his pack and offered it to the chick. It sniffed and opened its beak. He fed it the meat. He fed it sheep's fat too. When it had gobbled this down, it opened its beak again. He popped a cake into its beak. He tidied up the nest and made the chick comfortable. Then he painted its eyes with kohl, dabbed white cedar scent onto its head, put up a twisted roll of salt meat and popped more cakes into its beak.

Meanwhile, Anzu was herding together wild bulls of the mountains. He held a live bull in his talons. He carried a dead bull across his shoulders. He and his wife returned to their nest, and as they approached, they called out to their chick. Lugalbanda withdrew from the nest. Usually when the parents called, the chick would answer. But this time there was no answering call. The Anzu birds called again. Silence!

Anzu gave a cry of grief that reached up to heaven. His wife called out, "Woe!" Her cry reached right down to the Abzu. The cries of the two Anzu birds made even the lesser gods crawl into crevices like ants. Anzu shrieked this great cry: "Foreboding weighs upon my nest. Terror lies upon it. Who has taken my child from its nest?"

With great fear the birds approached. With foreboding they looked into their own nest. But what did they see?

There was their Anzu chick, safe and sound, fat and happy, with its beak full of cake. It sat in a nest that seemed to Anzu like a god's dwelling place, brilliantly festooned. The chick was all fluffy and comfortable and well fed, its eyes were made beautiful by kohl, sprigs of white cedar were about its head, a twist of salt meat was hung up high. Both the Anzu parents were delighted.

Anzu spoke. "I am the power who decides the destiny of the wild rolling rivers. I keep the mountain paths straight and narrow for the righteous. I am like the door which bars the entrance to the mountains. If I fix a fate, who shall alter it? If I say a word, none shall change it. If you are a god who has done this to my nest, I will speak with you and befriend you. If you are a man, I will fix your fate. You will have no opponents in the mountains. You will be the hero with Anzu's strength."

In his hiding place, Lugalbanda was both terrified and triumphant. He stepped into view. He flattered Anzu with eloquent words. He cried out, "Bird with sparkling eyes, bird born of the mountains, Anzu with sparkling eyes. You who bathe and play in the mountain pool, the gods have placed heaven in your hand and set earth at your feet. Your wingspan is like a net stretching across the sky. Your talons are a trap. Your spine is as straight as the scribe's. Your back is like a verdant palm garden. You are breathtaking to look upon. I am Lugalbanda. I have run from the city in search of you. I have been waiting for you in the mountains. Be my father. Let your wife be my mother. Let your little ones be my brothers. I offer my greeting and leave you to decide my destiny."

The Anzu bird was very pleased. He said, "Very well. I will set your fate. Go forth, my Lugalbanda. You will be valued as a vessel full of blessings to your people. You will be like a boat full of precious metals, like a grain barge, a boat delivering apples, a boat piled high with cucumbers. You will always hold your head up high." But Lugalbanda said he did not want this.

"Very well. I bestow on you the capability to shoot forth your barbed arrows like sunbeams, to shoot forth your reed arrows like moonlight. Your arrows will be the bite of the horned viper. You will be a great hunter and bundle up your catch like logs hewn with the axe." But Lugalbanda said he did not want this.

"Very well. May Ninurta set the helmet called Lion of Battle on your head and the breastplate of invincibility on your breast. You will wield the battle net against your enemies." Lugalbanda said he did not want this either.

"Very well. You shall receive material abundance. The plenty of Dumuzi's holy butter churn shall be granted to you. The best milk of all the world shall be granted to you." Lugalbanda would not accept this.

Anzu paused. He said, "Now look, my Lugalbanda, just think again. I warn you. Be careful. The wilful plough ox will be put back in the track. The baulking ass will be made to take the straight path. Nevertheless, I shall assign you your allotted destiny according to your wishes. I shall grant you whatever you ask."

Lugalbanda answered straightaway. "Let the power of running be in my thighs. Let me never grow tired. Let there be always strength in my arms. Let them never become weak. Let me leap like a flame. Let me blaze like lightning. Let me go wherever I please and set foot wherever I cast my glance. Let me reach whatever location my heart desires and loosen my shoes in whatever place my heart has named to me. If you do this for me, then I shall have the woodcarvers fashion statues of you. Your images will be breathtaking to look at. Your name will be made famous in Sumer and add credit to the temples of the great gods."

Anzu said, "The power of running be in your thighs. Never grow tired. Strength be in your arms. May they never grow weak. Leap like a flame. Blaze like lightning. Go wherever you please. Set foot wherever you cast your glance. Reach wherever your heart desires. Loosen your shoes in whatever place your heart has named. This is your destiny. Your destiny is set. And I look forward to hearing about the breathtaking images and carvings of me in the temples of the gods."

Anzu spread his great wings and took to the air. Lugalbanda picked up his weapons and the remains of his provisions. Anzu flew on high while Lugalbanda walked on the ground. Soon he heard Anzu's cry from high above.

"I spy the troops. Look." Lugalbanda looked and saw the dust that the troops had stirred into the air. The great bird landed beside him. He said, "Now, my Lugalbanda, I shall give you some advice. May my advice be heeded. I shall say words. May my words be heard and borne in mind. Do not tell your brothers and your comrades what I have told you, or about the fate that I have fixed for you, otherwise fair fortune may conceal foul. This is so. From this time on, leave me to my nest and you must keep to your troops." Lugalbanda felt the full force of the high wind as Anzu took off and returned to his nest and his family. Lugalbanda set out to find his brothers.

The brothers, the seven princely heroes and their companions were setting up camp and getting ready for the evening meal when Lugalbanda stepped into their midst. There was joy and celebration and loud chattering. They had so many questions.

"How is it that you have come back from the mountains?" "We abandoned you as one killed in battle. You could not eat or drink." "How did you cross the mountains? How did you cross the waters?" "How did you get well again? How did you catch up with us so quickly?"

"I stepped over the mountains with my legs. I stepped over the waters with my legs. I was like a wild animal. I snarled like a wolf. I grazed the meadows. I pecked at the ground. I ate mountain acorns." The brothers and friends listened, transfixed. Then they gathered round him. As if they were small birds flocking together, all evening long, they embraced him and kissed him. As if he were the chick sitting in its nest, they fed him and gave him drink. Any trace of sickness that might have remained, they drove away.

The next day they set off to join the armies of Unug where they besieged Aratta. When they arrived, they saw that the army of King Enmerkar was in a terrible situation. Aratta rained down javelins as if from the clouds. There were slingstones as numerous as a year of raindrops whizzing down from Aratta's walls.

Enmerkar was troubled and afraid. He and his troops were hemmed in between dragon-infested mountain thornbushes and the walls of Aratta. He needed someone to return to Unug with a message for Inana. He had asked the foreign hosts. He had asked the elite troops. But whenever he asked, everyone looked the other way. No one said, "I will go." But now, Lugalbanda was there. Lugalbanda alone arose from the people and said, "My king, I will go to the city, but I need no one to go with me. I will go alone." Enmerkar did not argue. He gave to Lugalbanda the great emblems of Kulaba. He gave him a message. It was a message for the Lady Inana. "Say this: 'Once upon a time, my princely sister, holy Inana, summoned me from the bright mountains and had me enter brick-built Kulaba. It was marshland then and full of reed thickets, and where there was dry land, there were forests of Euphrates poplar. For fifty years I built. For fifty years I ruled. Martu's people, the nomads, came down from the wastelands, but the wall of Unug was like a bird net across the desert, protecting the city. All this I did at the command of the Lady and for her delight. But now my attractiveness to her has dwindled. My troops are loyal to me. But my lady has run from me back to brick-built Kulaba. If she loves her city and hates me, why does she bind the city to me? If she hates the city and yet loves me, why does she bind me to the city? If the mistress must abandon me, then let her at least bring me home to brick-built Kulaba. On the day that I return, I shall lay aside my spear. On that day, she may shatter my shield.'" Heartbroken, Enmerkar put his hand on Lugalbanda's shoulder. He said, "Speak thus to my princely sister, holy Inana."

Lugalbanda stepped out ready for his journey. All his brothers and friends were like dogs barking at him as if he was a lone dog trying to join the pack. "Are you mad?" "Why will you go alone?" "Let someone else go." "No one goes to the great mountains alone." "You will not come back." The hearts of his brothers beat loudly. The hearts of his comrades sank. But Lugalbanda was firm. "No one shall go with me over the great earth." He knew he had his secret power of travelling and that he would reach his destination without tiring, but he said no word of it to his brothers. He took his provisions and his weapons and he began his journey. He began to run. From the foot of the mountains, through the high mountains into the flat land he crossed five, six, seven mountains. By midnight, even before they brought the offering-table to holy Inana, he set foot joyfully in brick-built Kulaba. His lady, holy Inana, sat there on her cushion. He bowed and prostrated himself on the ground. She looked at Lugalbanda as she would look at her husband, the shepherd Dumuzi. She spoke to him as she would to her son. "Come now, Lugalbanda, why do you bring news from the city in the mountains? How have you come here alone from Aratta?"

"I come with a message from Enmerkar. He says, 'Once upon a time, my princely sister, holy Inana, summoned me from the bright mountains and had me enter brick-built Kulaba. It was marshland then, full of reed thickets, and where there was dry land, there were forests of Euphrates poplar. For fifty years I built. For fifty years I ruled. Martu's people, the nomads, came down from the wastelands, but the wall of Unug was like a bird net across the desert, protecting the city. All this I did at her command and for her delight. But now my attractiveness to her has dwindled. My troops are loyal to me. But my lady has run from me, back to brick-built Kulaba. If she loves her city and hates me, why does she bind the city to me? If she hates the city and yet loves me, why does she bind me to the city? If the mistress must abandon me, then let her at least bring me home to brick-built Kulaba. On that day I shall lay aside my spear. On that day, she may shatter my shield.'"

Holy Inana nodded. She uttered this response: "Beside the banks of the clear river that they call Inana's water skin are the water meadows. In the water meadows there is a little pool where fish eat honey herb and toads eat the mountain acorns. There is one fish which is the god of the others. He plays happily there and darts about, brushing the old reeds of the holy pool with his scaly tail. That fish in the subterranean waters provides the life-strength of Aratta. There are tamarisk trees all around which drink the water of the pool. One tamarisk stands alone. Let Enmerkar cut that tamarisk and fashion it into a bucket. He must cut the reeds and catch the god of the fish in the bucket. When he has caught it and cooked it and garnished it, when he has brought the fish that holds Aratta's power as a sacrifice to Inana's battle strength, then his troops will have success for him. Then he may bring from the mountain city its worked metal and smiths, its worked stones and stonemasons. But he must be generous to those he defeats. He must renew Aratta and restore the battle damage done to Aratta. Only then will the treasures of Aratta be his."

Lugalbanda has returned across the mountains. He has repeated to King Enmerkar the message of Inana. Enmerkar has sought and caught the fish. His troops have prevailed. He has restored Aratta.

Now Aratta's battlements are of green lapis lazuli. Its walls and its towering brickwork are bright red. The brick clay is made of tinstone dug out in the mountains where the cypress grows. And Enmerkar has returned to Unug with treasures. He has laid aside his spear. He has laid down his shield. And who is to be the next king of Unug?

It is Lugalbanda.

SHULGI, KING OF UR

Lord Shulgi, son of Queen Ninsun and King Ur-Nammu, was born a warrior. He grew to be a mighty man, like a fierce-eyed lion. He was king of the four corners of the known universe, the shepherd of the black-headed people, god of all the lands. He was blessed by Enlil, beloved by Ninlil, cherished by Nintu, endowed with wisdom by Enki and called to the heart of An himself. He was the mighty king of Lord Nanna; the open-mouthed lion chosen as her lover by Lady Inana. He was lithe as a princely mule on the road; swift as a tail-swishing horse on the highway; eager as a noble donkey for the race. He was a wise scribe of Nisaba, accomplished in wisdom, heroism and might. He loved justice and abhorred evil. He was the mighty, supreme king.

Because he was a good king, he improved the footpaths by enlarging them, and he straightened the highways of the land, making travel safer for all. He built rest houses here and there along the way, set in refreshing gardens and staffed by kindly hosts, so that whether one came from above, whether one came from below, one could be refreshed in the cool of the day. Furthermore, travellers by night could stop to sleep safely, as if in a well-built city. All these things made Shulgi a good king.

Lord Shulgi made a proclamation. He announced his intention: "In order that my existence may be preserved in memory unto distant days; in order that my name shall not leave the mouths of men; to ensure that my acclaim is spread wide across the land; and that praise to me is sung in all the lands, I shall run! I, the runner, full of strength and resolve, shall set out on the course from Nippur to Ur, a distance of no less than fifteen double hours. I shall make the journey in only one double hour! I will rise like a lion in its potency, never tiring. I will gird my loins, swing my arms like a dove opening its wings to flee a snake, and spread my knees wide, like an Anzu bird lifting its eyes to the mountain."

Shulgi was as good as his word. He made the journey from Nippur to Ur, a distance greater than a hundred miles, in only one double hour. When he arrived in Ur, the inhabitants of the city swarmed about him. His people, the black-headed people, marvelled as he came into their city, like a mountain goat hurrying to its shelter. Under the bright rays of Utu, the sun god, he entered the temple of the moon god, Nanna-Sin. There he made abundant offerings of oxen and sheep, slaughtering them before the altar. At his command, the drums and tambourines resounded. At his signal, sweet tigi-music was played.

Shulgi took a rest after making his offerings. But it was only a short one. Then he bathed in fresh water, scrubbed his knees, ate some bread and did his warm-up exercises. Then he set off again, back to Nippur. He spread his wings like an owl, he soared like a falcon. He left Ur and started out triumphantly.

But the weather turned against him. The storm howled. The tempest swirled. The north and south winds roared violently. Lightning burst across the skies; thunder made the earth tremble; the rain god Ishkur sent rain rushing down from the skies. The torrents emptying from above met the water gushing below. The storm's little stones lashed at Shulgi's back. The storm's big stones lashed at Shulgi's back. But Shulgi was unafraid, uncowed. He stepped out like a young lion ready to spring. He rushed forward like a donkey of the steppe. His heart was full of joy as he sped along his road. He was like a donkey foal journeying alone, as it raced for home; like the sun god Utu, turning homewards at the end of the day. He completed the home journey of fifteen double hours in no time at all, arriving back in Nippur before dark. He went straight to the temple to make offerings. His acolytes there gazed at him in wonder, as he celebrated the holy rites in both Ur and Nippur in one day, a feat never before accomplished.

Once the temple rites were fulfilled, he went to his palace, founded by great An himself, and bathed once more, then dressed in fresh garments and adorned himself for a feast. With great Utu, the sun god, his brother and friend, he drank beer in his holy palace. Seating himself by the side of the Lady Inana, Queen of Earth and Heaven, his heart's companion, he spoke to her, saying, "Wherever I set my eyes, there shall you go with me. Wherever my heart takes me, there you will be welcome."

Then An himself, god of the heavens, manifested in their hall. He set the holy crown on Shulgi's head, placed the lapis lazuli sceptre in his hand, raised the throne onto a white dais and exalted Shulgi's power and his kingship.

Shulgi's people bowed their heads and chanted holy songs in his praise: "He that is the noble power of kingship, the cherished one, presented to us by the moon god Nanna, blessed with noble power by Enlil, and endowed with heroism, a good life and might – Shulgi who makes the land of Sumer secure, who in accordance with the holy Me, divine rules of the universe, is without a rival, Shulgi, cherished by the moon god Nanna, we praise you! Oh Lady Nisaba, goddess of writing and literature, ensure that Shulgi's existence may be preserved in memory unto distant days; that his name shall not leave the mouths of men. Ensure that acclaim for Shulgi is spread wide across the land, and that his praises are sung in all the lands, for he is mighty!"

Nisaba, goddess of writing and literature, has indeed ensured that Shulgi's name and his record-breaking run are remembered. I heard it from someone, who heard it from someone, who heard it…but behind all the speakers is the person who impressed the words into clay. Who they were, we do not know. But because it was written down, in honour of Nisaba as well as Shulgi, the story of this epic run has won the long-lasting fame that Shulgi sought. May Nisaba, goddess of writing and literature, be praised!

ETANA AND THE EAGLE

The great gods made a city. They named it Kish. The gods made Kish, a beautiful city with everything that was needed for its people to flourish. On the throne of their city the gods placed Etana, beloved of all. In Kish, in his city, his own city, Etana built a temple to honour the gods. The temple was wonderful, gleaming with precious stones and glittering with jewels. Around the temple Etana planted a garden. It was magnificent, with glorious flowers and fine fountains. In the centre of the garden he planted a tall poplar tree. Its branches reached upwards as though in praise of the sky god. Its roots penetrated deep into the earth, as if to draw nourishment from the Queen of the Underworld.

After some time, when the tree was well established, an eagle made its nest in the branches of the poplar tree. A serpent made its nest in the roots of the poplar tree.

Because they were neighbours, because they both had young to care for, because they both needed to provide for their young and ensure that they grew strong and healthy, they made a vow of friendship to each other. They swore before Shamash, the sun god, that they would be fast friends.

And what do friends do? They help each other, and they share. So the eagle and the serpent shared the spoils of their hunting, making sure that both lots of eggs, both lots of hatchlings, thrived and flourished.

Whatever one of them brought back to their shared home was allocated fairly between their two families: wild ox, wild sheep, panther, tiger, bush gazelle, auroch…it made no difference whether eagle or serpent had been the hunter, the catch was divided equally, for the benefit of all.

All was well while the chicks were yet to fledge, the snakelets were yet to shed their skins. All was well while the young in both nests were still helpless. But once the eagle's chicks had fledged, his thoughts turned to evil plans against his friend's offspring.

"Those snakelets would make a meal for me," he said. "They would feed me and my family. Why should I continue to travel far in search of prey, and then struggle to bring back my catch?

Here is an opportunity so convenient and so expedient, surely the gods themselves have decreed this fate. So shall it be: I shall eat the serpent's children."

This is how the eagle persuaded himself to do a terrible deed.

The littlest fledgling was horrified to hear his father speak such words. He advised against such a terrible deed.

"Father, do not speak thus, do not turn against our neighbour. To do so would be a dark deed. Surely, if you do such a thing, Shamash himself, the sun god, will turn against you. Shamash will take revenge upon you. Father, I implore you, do not do such a thing!"

The eagle heard the words of his chick. He did not listen to them. He was led astray by his base instincts. He determined to satisfy this unnatural craving.

He waited until the serpent had gone hunting. Then he flew down to the serpent's nest, snatched up the snakelets in his cruel curved claws, and devoured every single one.

Shamash, sun god, whose gleaming eye perceives everything that passes, saw what took place, yet he did not intervene. And so, when the serpent returned to his nest that night, bringing food to share between both families, as had been their custom, his nest was empty, his children had gone.

Quickly the serpent realized what had happened; he understood the treachery of his former friend in committing this barbaric act. He was filled with sorrow and rage. He raised a lament to Shamash, grieving for his loss. And then he sent a plea for vengeance to the great god.

"Lord Shamash, you bring light and life to all that exists. In your name the eagle and I made vows of friendship. We became comrades and worked together, for the good of our young. But now he has killed my young ones, all my pretty ones. He has devoured them in his greed. How could he betray my trust, and break his vows? May he be cursed and punished. May the path vanish before him, may he not find the way. Shamash, lord, turn your face from him! Let not your life-giving eye shine upon him! Grant me revenge for the loss of my sweet children. Make him suffer as I suffer now."

Shamash heard the words of the serpent. He listened to his plea. He granted his wish.

"The eagle does indeed deserve a powerful punishment for this dire deed. I will turn my face from him. But I decree that you yourself should be the one to punish him. You shall be my instrument. Let vengeance be yours, not mine. Listen to my words, do as I command. The eagle will be brought low, and great suffering will be his lot, if you obey my decree."

The serpent listened attentively. He burned with fervour, eager to punish the eagle.

"Go up into the mountains to the eagle's hunting ground," instructed Shamash. "There you will find the corpse of an ox, which I will put there for you. Nearby, dig a deep pit in which to trap the eagle. Tear open the flank of the ox and hide yourself within. Be patient: soon the eagle will fly down to eat the flesh of the ox. In his feeding frenzy, he will penetrate further and further into the belly of the ox, seeking to devour the entrails. When he is helpless, right inside the belly of the beast, make yourself known. Drag him out of the corpse. Say whatever bitter words come to your lips, or keep silent and teach him your feelings by your deeds. Cut off his tail feathers. Cut off his pinion feathers. Then throw him into the pit to suffer hunger and thirst. Leave him in the pit, to suffer and die. He will know I have turned my life-giving eye away from him. He will weaken and die. Let this be your revenge."

The serpent gladly accepted the judgement of Shamash. He was eager to carry out this punishment. He went up into the mountains to the eagle's hunting ground. He found the corpse of an ox, which Shamash had provided for him to use. Nearby, the serpent dug a deep pit in which to trap the eagle. Once it was deep enough, he turned his attention to the ox. He opened its flank and slithered deep inside. He hid himself within it. He waited inside it for a long and wearisome time, but his desire for revenge made him patient. He waited for the eagle.

High overhead, flying with his little ones, the eagle saw the body of the ox. "I will fly down to eat the tastiest morsels," he declared. His littlest fledgling advised against this. "Do not go down to eat that meat. The serpent may be waiting there for you." Once again, the eagle ignored the words of his wise little son. "I am not afraid," he said, and flew down to eat the flesh of the ox.

At last the serpent heard the rush of wings in the sky. He felt a jolt as the eagle landed on the corpse, digging his claws into the flesh and at once tearing and swallowing chunks of meat. Greedily the eagle fed, thrusting his head further and further into the torn cavity of the belly, searching for the tender entrails. Patiently the serpent waited, coiled in the bowels of the beast.

Only when the eagle was completely enclosed in the corpse, guzzling and gobbling, did the serpent make his move, winding himself about the eagle's wings and dragging him from the corpse. The eagle stared in terror at his former friend, the one whose family he had destroyed. No words came to his dumbstruck tongue, but his eyes begged for mercy. No words passed the serpent's lips, but his eyes were implacable: cold as jewels, dark as obsidian, his gaze told the eagle everything; it told the eagle that there would be no mercy for him, just as he had shown none for the snakelets.

The serpent cut off the eagle's tail feathers. He cut off his pinion feathers. He stripped the eagle of his power of flight. Then he hurled him, helpless, into the pit, leaving him to suffer and die there. Shamash turned his face from the eagle. He was a condemned prisoner, left to die.

The eagle languished in the pit in the burning heat of the sun, in the bitter cold of the night. He tried to climb out of the pit, time after time, until he was exhausted and despairing. He could not climb out of the pit. He could not fly out of the pit. His fine tail feathers were gone, his mighty pinions were gone. He was weakening towards death. He saw no future, no mercy, no absolution for his crime. He regretted his deeds. He wept for his wickedness. He trembled before his fate. Desperate, knowing there was nothing he could do to save himself, he appealed to Shamash. He raised his weak voice to the heavens, shaped a plea with his parched tongue.

He spoke aloud, saying, "Lord Shamash, show mercy to me! Forgive my cruel deed. Let me learn from my punishment. Let me serve you and worship you in recompense for my crime. Do not let me die here, alone and miserable."

Shamash heard the words of the eagle. He listened to his plea. The all-seeing lord showed mercy and granted the eagle's prayer.

"It shall be as you ask. You shall be spared, but I myself will not be the instrument of your salvation. Rather, I will send a man to save you. This man has prayed to me. I have listened to his prayer as I listen now to yours. As he will be the instrument to grant your prayer, so you will be the instrument to help him."

The eagle was eager to agree to any condition to win back his life. He readily consented to do all he could to help the man. But when he tried to learn more about who this might be, and when he would come to his rescue, Shamash would say no more. He left the eagle still languishing in the pit, scorched by the sun and chilled by the moon, waiting.

In the city of Kish, in the beautiful city of Kish, Lord Etana, beloved of all, made offerings to the gods in the temple he had built for them.

Lord Etana prayed for a child to inherit the kingdom, a successor to follow in his footsteps and rule the great city of Kish. Without a child to secure his line, he risked being forgotten. He knew it. He had prayed and prayed for a child, as indeed had his wife, but the gods had remained silent, the omens had been unfavourable. No child had come to them. Heartsore and brought low, Lord Etana fell into an exhausted sleep.

At last, in his dream, Shamash spoke to him. The sun god's message was one of hope.

"Etana, you are favoured in my sight. Your prayers and sacrifices have not gone unnoticed. But the time was not yet right. Now all is in place. Listen to my words. Take heed of my commands. Follow my instructions. You must go into the mountains. Go alone. Take no servant or soldier with you. I will protect you, you need fear no harm. In the far mountains you will find a deep pit. In it lies an eagle. Its wings are broken, its tail is cropped, its pinions plucked. It is close to death. Rescue the bird from the pit and tend it until its feathers have regrown and its strength has been restored. Once it can fly again, bid it carry you on its back to where the plant of birth can be found. Once the plant of birth is in your hand, you will father many children. Your name will not be forgotten."

Etana listened to Shamash. When he awoke, he recalled every word he had heard in his dream. He gave thanks to Shamash before the altar. He sacrificed kids, goats and a bull. Then he bade farewell to his wife and his advisors, and set out alone towards the mountains. He feared no harm. He knew that Shamash protected him. He went on the quest ordained by Shamash, to search for the eagle in the pit.

High in the mountain peaks, he saw a pit. When he looked into it, he realized that the emaciated form of a bird was crouched in the corner. The creature's head hung down, its naked wings dragged in the dust, its naked tail looked vulnerable. It did not move. Etana wondered if it were dead, but nonetheless he called to it. At the sound, the eagle lifted his head, just a little, and looked up.

"I have come to rescue you," said Etana. "Lord Shamash has sent me to rescue you, that my destiny may be fulfilled. Be of good heart. I will bring you out of this pit."

The eagle stirred at these words and tried to rise, but he was too weak. Etana stretched down his arms, but the pit was too deep to reach it. Etana searched until he found a long branch and thrust it down into the pit, but the eagle was too weak to cling to it. Etana was perplexed. But he was eager to fulfil his destiny, so he prayed for inspiration. He began to hurl small stones into the pit. Seeing the eagle quail, Etana spoke. "Do not fear. I do not intend to harm you. I am trying to make a ramp so you can come out of this pit."

The eagle cowered in the corner as stones and rubble poured into the pit. Then Etana gathered brushwood and mountain plants, whatever grew in that wild place, and he threw all that down too. The ramp grew, though slowly. At last Etana, reaching down, could touch the top of the pile with his hand. "Come up," he urged the eagle. "Come up to where I can take hold of you. Working together, we will bring you out of this pit."

The eagle shuffled on to the ramp. He struggled upwards until Etana could reach it with his outstretched hand. Grasping the eagle by his ruined wing, he drew him out of the pit.

Etana found food and water for the eagle. He fed him tiny morsels and sheltered him from the sun. He rubbed oil on his bare flesh to encourage his plumage to regrow. He cared for the eagle as the midwife cares for the newborn. Like the birth attendant watching over the mother-to-be, he remained at the eagle's side for nine full months, bringing food, helping him build strength. Over nine months his broken body healed. His plucked feathers regrew. He gathered strength until once again he could soar high in the sky.

Then the eagle said to Etana, "When I prayed for mercy, Lord Shamash said he would send a man to save me. You are the man. As you have been his instrument to grant my prayer, he decreed that I shall be the instrument to help you. What is it that you need from me?"

Etana said, "I have prayed for a child to inherit my kingdom and rule the great city-state of Kish. Without a child to secure my line, I risk being forgotten. I have prayed and prayed for a child, as indeed has my wife, but the gods have remained silent. No child has come to us. But last year I had a dream, and in my dream, Shamash spoke. The sun god's message was one of hope. He said that my prayers and sacrifices had not gone unnoticed. He told me to follow his instructions. He sent me, alone, into the mountains. He told me to search for the deep pit. In it I found you. I was following the great god's commands when I rescued you and tended you. Now your feathers have regrown and your strength has been restored. Now that you can fly again, I ask you to help me find the plant of birth. Once the plant of birth is in my hand, my line will be secure. As I helped you, help me now, that the will of Shamash may be fulfilled."

The eagle agreed that the god's word must be obeyed. He rose into the air and flew around the mountain, searching for the plant of birth. He could not find it. He returned to Etana, saying, "The plant of birth is not growing on the earth. The herb you need must grow in the land of the gods. Climb onto my back, between my wings, and take hold of my feathers. I will carry you on my back to where the plant of birth can be found."

Etana settled himself as best he could between the great wings of the eagle and clutched the feathers of his shoulders. The eagle rose into the sky, heading for the realm of the sky god.

When they were already one mile above the earth, the eagle said, "Look down, my friend. How does the land look to you now?" Etana looked down and said, "The land looks like a hill. The sea is no bigger than a pond!"

When they were two miles above the earth, the eagle said, "Look down, my friend. How does the land look to you now?" Etana looked down and said, "The land looks like a garden. The sea is no bigger than a ditch!"

When they were three miles above the earth, the eagle said, "Look down, my friend. How does the land look to you now?" Etana looked down and said, "I am looking for the land, but I cannot see it. My eyes cannot even pick out the wide sea!

My friend, I am afraid! I cannot go any higher! Please, let me go down!"

The eagle heard his words, and shrugged Etana off his back. Etana fell for one mile. The eagle dipped down and caught him on the tip of his wing.

A second time the eagle shrugged Etana off his back. Etana fell for another mile. The eagle dipped down and caught him on the tip of his wing.

A third time the eagle shrugged Etana off, and he fell for another mile. Again the eagle dipped down and caught him on the tip of his wing. Now Etana was just above the earth, so the eagle shrugged him onto solid ground once more. Etana returned to Kish.

Night after night, Etana dreamed that the people of the city were lamenting because he had no child. Night after night, his queen dreamed that the people of the city were lamenting because they had no child.

Then Etana dreamed a new dream. It put courage back in his heart. He returned to the mountains and told the eagle his dream.

"My friend, now the god has shown me a favourable dream. In my dream, you and I were entering the gate of the gods. We bowed before Sin, Shamash and Ishtar. Then I saw a house with an open window. I looked through the window and saw a young woman adorned with a crown. She was immensely beautiful. She sat on a throne with lions crouched beneath it. When I approached the throne, the lions sprang up and roared at me. I was afraid, but I did not let my fear overwhelm me. Take me again upon your back. I will not let my fear overwhelm me. Let us rise high enough to find the plant I need, the plant of birth."

The eagle agreed that it was a favourable dream. Once again he took Etana on his back, between his great wings. Etana clutched the shoulder feathers. They rose one, two, three miles above the earth. Etana looked down and saw how small the kingdom was, how small the sea was. But this time he did not lose heart. The eagle carried him higher still, until they reached the gate of the gods. Etana and the eagle bowed before Sin, Shamash and Ishtar. The gates were open to them, and they went in.

The tablet is broken at this point, so we do not know whether Etana received the plant of birth, or whether his quest was successful.

But we do know that Etana's name appears in the Sumerian king list, which states that he was succeeded by his son Balih. Until the rest of the tablet is found and read, let us trust the interplay between story and history, and hope that Etana's story had a happy ending.

A GLOSSARY OF NAMES & PLACES IN THE TEXT

Spelling of proper names changed over time and varies a lot between translators. Where different versions are used in different stories, both are given here. (A= Akkadian form of a name, B= Babylonian form of a name, S= Sumerian form of a name.)

Abzu (S) Male ancestor of the gods; also the deep sweet waters, home of Enki; also Enki's temple in Eridug.
Adab City to the east of Suruppag.
Adad Storm god.
Aga Lord of Kish.
Agushaya Epithet for Ishtar in her warrior aspect, given by Ea.
An (S) The supreme deity, the air god.
Anshar (B) Father of the great gods.
Antu (B) The wife of Anu in later mythology.
Anu (A) The supreme deity, the air god.
Anuna gods Collective name for the major gods.
Anzu/Anzud (A) A mythical bird: half eagle and half lion.
Apsu (A) *See* Abzu.
Arali Desert lands, possibly a name for the underworld.
Aratta City far to the east of Sumer.

Aruru A birth goddess, a fierce deity and 'mother of all'. Sister of Enlil.

Asag A powerful being, adversary of Ninurta.

Atrahasis (A)/Utnapishtim (A)/Ziusudra (B) Survivor of the Flood

Balih King whose name is found in the Sumerian King List, son of King Shulgi.

Belili An old woman in whose house Dumuzi sought shelter.

Belet-ili/Mami/Ninhursag/Ninmah (B) Goddess who created humans.

Bibbu (B) Butcher of the underworld.

Birhur-tura A member of Gilgamesh's royal guard.

Damkina (B) Wife of Ea, mother of Marduk.

Dilmun A beautiful land: present-day Bahrain.

Du-asaga An as-yet unidentified city.

Dumuzi/Dumuzid (S) Shepherd god, husband of Inana, brother of Gestinana (S).

Duttur A deity associated with keeping animals and pastoralism (*definition uncertain*).

Ea (A) God of wisdom, god of the deep sweet waters.

E-ana/Eanna Inana's temple in Uruk.

Ebih A mountain range northeast of Sumer.

Ekur Enlil's temple in Nibru /Nippur.

Elam A region to the east of Sumer, now part of Iran.

Ellil (A)/Enlil (S) Father of the gods, god of earth.

Enegir An as-yet unidentified city.

Enheduanna High priestess of Ur, daughter of King Sargon, the first named author in history.

Enki (S) God of wisdom, father of Dumuzi.

Enkidu Friend/servant to Gilgamesh.

Enkimdu A farmer.
Enlil (S) *See* Ellil.
Enmerkar King of Unug, father of Lugalbanda.
Ennugi (B) God associated with agriculture and irrigation.
Ensag Lord of Dilmun.
Ensouggirana Lord of Aratta.
Ereshkigal Queen of the Underworld, sister to Inana.
Eridu/Eridug City in southern Sumer, cult centre of Enki.
Etana King whose name is found in the Sumerian King List.
Ezina Goddess of grain.
Galla Demons of the underworld.
Ganzer Outer gate of the underworld.
Geme-Sin A cow.
Gerra (A) A fire god.
Gestinana Sister to Dumuzi.
Gestindudu Gestinana's friend.
Gibil God of fire.
Gilgamesh (B)/Gilgameš (S) Hero king of Unug, son of Lugalbanda and the goddess Ninsun (B).
Gimil-Ninurta A poor man living in Nibru/Nippur. His name means 'Ninurta's Revenge'.
Hamazu Legendary city in what is now Iran.
Humbaba (B)/Huwawa (S) Guardian of the Cedar Forest in present-day Lebanon.
Huwawa *See* Humbaba
Igigi gods Collective name for the lesser gods.
Igisigsig Father of Sukaletuda.
Inab An as-yet unidentified location.
Inana (S) Goddess of love and war, goddess of Unug, associated with the planet Venus. *See also* Ishtar.

Ishkur God of rain.

Ishtar (A and B) Goddess of love and war, associated with the planet Venus.

Isimud Servant/vizier (sukkal) to Enki.

Isin City to the north of Nibru/Nippur.

Kalkal (B) Enlil's gatekeeper.

Kiritab An as-yet unidentified location.

Kish City in the north of Sumer, near Babylon.

Kubires An as-yet unidentified location.

Kulaba Temple area of Unug/Uruk.

Larsa City to the southeast of Unug/Uruk.

Lilith A female spirit or demon.

Lugalbanda King of Unug, son of Enmerkar, father of Gilgamesh.

Lugalnirgal Father of the woman Ninkuzu.

Lulal Son of Inana.

Lulubi Mountains Northeast region of the Zagros or Zubi Mountains.

Mami *See* Belet-ili.

Marduk (B) Son of Ea and Damkina, god of Babylon, killer of Tiamat.

Martu Leader of a nomadic people.

Mashu Mountains Sacred twin-peaked mountain, possibly in the Taurus Mountains.

Mrs A A woman involved in an argument with a neighbour.

Mummu (B) Counsellor to Apsu.

Nammu (B) Mother of Enki.

Nammur (B) Servant/vizier (sukkal) to Ereshkigal.

Namtar A plague god, servant of Ereshkigal.

Nanna (S) Moon god, husband of Ningal, father of Inana and Utu.

Nanna-Sin/Nanna-Suen (A) Moon god, husband of Ningal, father of Inana and Utu (A).

Nanse A marsh goddess associated with fish and birds.

Nergal Warrior god; later, husband of Ereshkigal.

Neti Gatekeeper of the underworld.

Nibru (S) City in northern Sumer.

Ningal Mother of Inana, wife of Nanna.

Ningirida Goddess worshipped at Enegir.

Ninhursag *See* Belet-ili.

Ninkasi Goddess of beer and brewing.

Ninkura Granddaughter of Ninhursag and Enki.

Ninkuzu A woman involved in an argument with a neighbour.

Ninlil Goddess, wife of Enlil, worshipped at Tummul.

Ninmah *See* Belet-ili.

Ninmena Goddess who represented the deified crown.

Ninmush Mountain where Utnapishtim's boat grounded after the Flood. Possibly Pir Omar Gudrun in Iraqi Kurdistan.

Ninsar Daughter of Ninhursag and Enki.

Ninshiliha (B) Cleaner of the underworld.

Ninshubur Sukkal (servant/friend) of Inana.

Ninsun (S)/Ninsur (A) Goddess, 'Lady Wild Cow', mother of Gilgamesh.

Ninsur *See* Ninsun

Nintu (S) Mother goddess, also goddess of pregnancy.

Ninurta God of war and agriculture, son of Enlil.

Nippur (A) City in northern Sumer.

Nisaba Goddess of the scribal art, accounting and grain.

Nungal Goddess of prisoners; daughter of Ereshkigal.

Nusku (B) Enlil's chamberlain.

Qingu (B) Tiamat's supreme commander, killed by Ea to make humans.

Qasutabat (B) Sweeper of the underworld.

Sagburu Wise woman who defeated a wizard.

Saltu Mirror image of Ishtar, 'Discord', created by Ea.

Sargon King of Akkad, known as Sargon the Great, father of Enheduanna.

Serida (S) Wife of the sun god Utu.

Shamash (A) Sun god.

Shamhat A temple woman.

Shara Son of Inana.

Sharur An animate mace belonging to Ninurta.

Shulgi King of Ur, whose name is found in the Sumerian King List.

Sin (A) Moon god.

Siduri Divine wise woman associated with winemaking and brewing.

Sirtur Mother of Dumuzi.

Subir A land in northern Mesopotamia.

Suen (S) Moon god.

Sukaletuda A gardener's boy, whose name means 'Spotty youth'.

Suruppag City south of Nippur, north of Uruk.

Tiamat (B) Female ancestor of the gods.

Tummal City between Nibru and Suruppag, cult centre of Ninlil.

Unug (S) City in the south, near the Euphrates, ruled by Gilgamesh and previously by his father Lugalbanda; cult centre of Inana, also known as Uruk.

Ur City in the south, near the Persian Gulf, one of the earliest city states.

Urim Sumerian term associated with Ur.

Ur-Nammu King of Ur, whose name is found in the Sumerian King List.

Ur-shanabi (B) Ferryman who carries Gilgamesh across the ocean to Utnapishtim.

Uruk (A) *See* Unug.

Utnapishtim *See* Atrahasis.

Uttu Goddess of weaving, great-granddaughter of Ninhursag and Enki.

Utu (S) Sun god, brother of Inana.

Zangara God of dreams.

Ziusudra *See* Atrahasis.

Zubi Mountains Possibly the Zagros Mountains, which extend from Iran into Turkey and Iraq.

A GLOSSARY OF MYTH & FOLKLORE

A selective glossary for comparative interest, featuring terms from other key ancient cultures of the world.

Aaru Heavenly paradise where the blessed go after death.

Ab Heart or mind.

Abiku (Yoruba) Person predestined to die. Also known as ogbanje.

Absál Nurse to Saláman, who died after their brief love affair.

Achilles The son of Peleus and the sea-nymph Thetis, who distinguished himself in the Trojan War. He was made almost immortal by his mother, who dipped him in the River Styx, and he was invincible except for a portion of his heel which remained out of the water.

Acropolis Citadel in a Greek city.

Aditi Sky goddess and mother of the gods.

Adityas Vishnu, children of Aditi, including Indra, Mitra, Rudra, Tvashtar, Varuna and Vishnu.

Aeneas The son of Anchises and the goddess Aphrodite, reared by a nymph. He led the Dardanian troops in the Trojan War According to legend, he became the founder of Rome.

Aengus Óg Son of Dagda and Boann (a woman said to have given the Boyne river its name), Aengus is the Irish god of love whose stronghold is reputed to have been at New Grange. The famous tale 'Dream of Aengus' tells of how he fell in love with a maiden he had dreamt of. He eventually discovered that she was to be found at the Lake of the Dragon's Mouth in Co. Tipperary, but that she lived every alternate year in the form of a swan. Aengus thus plunged into the lake transforming himself also into the shape of a swan. Then the two flew back together to his palace on the Boyne where they lived out their days as guardians of would-be lovers.

Aesir Northern gods who made their home in Asgard; there are twelve in number.

Afrásiyáb Son of Poshang, king of Túrán, who led an army against the ruling shah Nauder. Afrásiyáb became ruler of Persia on defeating Nauder.

Afterlife Life after death or paradise, reached only by the process of preserving the body from decay through embalming and preparing it for reincarnation.

Agamemnon A famous King of Mycenae. He married Helen of Sparta's sister Clytemnestra. When Paris abducted Helen, beginning the Trojan War, Menelaus called on Agamemnon to raise the Greek troops. He had to sacrifice his daughter Iphigenia in order to get a fair wind to travel to Troy.

Agastya A rishi (sage). Leads hermits to Rama.

Agemo (Yoruba) A chameleon who aided Olorun in outwitting Olokun, who was angry at him for letting Obatala create life on her lands without her permission. Agemo outwitted Olokun by changing colour, letting her think that he and Olorun were better cloth dyers than she was. She admitted defeat and there was peace between the gods once again.

Aghasur A dragon sent by Kans to destroy Krishna.

Aghríras Son of Poshang and brother of Afrásiyáb, who was killed by his brother.

Agni The god of fire.

Agora Greek marketplace.

Ahura-Mazda Supreme god of the Persians, god of the sky. Similar to the Hindu god Varuna.

Ajax Ajax the Greater was the bravest, after Achilles, of all warriors at Troy, fighting Hector in single combat and distinguishing himself in the Battle of the Ships. He was not chosen as the bravest warrior and eventually went mad.

Ajax of Locris Another warrior at Troy. When Troy was captured, he committed the ultimate sacrilege by seizing Cassandra from her sanctuary with the Palladium.

Aje (Igbo) Goddess of the earth and the underworld.

Aje (Yoruba) Goddess of the River Niger, daughter of Yemoja.

Akhet Season of the year when the River Nile traditionally flooded.

Akwán Diw An evil spirit who appeared as a wild ass in the court of Kai-khosráu. Rustem fought and defeated the demon, presenting its head to Kai-khosráu.

Alba Irish and Scottish Gaelic word for Scotland.

Alberich King of the dwarfs.

Alcinous King of the Phaeacians.

Alf-heim Home of the elves, ruled by Frey.

All Hallowmass All Saints' Day.

Allfather Another name for Odin; Yggdrasill was created by Allfather.

Alsvider Steed of the moon (Mani) chariot.

Alsvin Steed of the sun (Sol) chariot.

Amado Outer panelling of a dwelling, usually made of wood.

Ama-no-uzume Goddess of the dawn, meditation and the arts, who showed courage when faced with a giant who scared the other deities, including Ninigi. Also known as Uzume.

Amaterasu Goddess of the sun and daughter of Izanagi after Izanami's death; she became ruler of the High Plains of Heaven on her father's withdrawal from the world. Sister of Tsuki-yomi and Susanoo.

Ambalika Daughter of the king of Benares.

Ambika Daughter of the king of Benares.

Ambrosia Food of the gods.

Amemet Eater of the dead, monster who devoured the souls of the unworthy.

Amen Original creator deity.

Amen-Ra A being created from the fusion of Ra and Osiris. He champions the poor and those in trouble. Similar to the Greek god Zeus.

Ananda Disciple of Buddha.

Anansi One of the most popular African animal myths, Anansi the spider is a clever and shrewd character who outwits his fellow animals to get his own way. He is an entertaining but morally dubious character. Many African countries tell Anansi stories.

Ananta Thousand-headed snake that sprang from Balarama's mouth, Vishnu's attendant, serpent of infinite time.

Andhrímnir Cook at Valhalla.

Andvaranaut Ring of Andvari, the King of the dwarfs.

Angada Son of Vali, one of the monkey host.

Anger-Chamber Room designated for an angry queen.

Angurboda Loki's first wife, and the mother of Hel, Fenris and Jormungander.

Aniruddha Son of Pradyumna.

Anjana Mother of Hanuman.

Anshumat A mighty chariot fighter.

Anubis Guider of souls and ruler of the underworld before Osiris; he was one of the divinities who brought Osiris back to life. He is portrayed as a canid, African wolf or jackal.

Apep Serpent and emblem of chaos.

Apollo One of the twelve Olympian gods, son of Zeus and Leto. He is attributed with being the god of plague, music, song and prophecy.

Apsaras Dancing girls of Indra's court and heavenly nymphs.

Aquila The divine eagle.

Arachne A Lydian woman with great skill in weaving. She was challenged in a competition by the jealous Athene who destroyed her work and when she killed herself, turned her into a spider destined to weave for eternity.

Ares God of War, 'gold-changer of corpses', and the son of Zeus and Hera.

Argonauts Heroes who sailed with Jason on the ship Argo to fetch the golden fleece from Colchis.

Ariki A high chief, a leader, a master, a lord.

Arjuna The third of the Pandavas.

Aroha Affection, love.

Artemis The virgin goddess of the chase, attributed with being the moon goddess and the primitive mother-goddess. She was daughter of Zeus and Leto.

Arundhati The Northern Crown.

Asamanja Son of Sagara.

Asclepius God of healing who often took the form of a snake. He is the son of Apollo by Coronis.

Asgard Home of the gods, at one root of Yggdrasill.

Ashvatthaman Son of Drona.

Ashvins Twin horsemen, sons of the sun, benevolent gods and related to the divine.

Ashwapati Uncle of Bharata and Satrughna.

Asopus The god of the River Asopus.

Assagai Spear, usually made from hardwood tipped with iron and used in battle.

Astrolabe Instrument for making astronomical measurements.

Asuras Titans, demons, and enemies of the gods with magical powers.

Atef crown White crown made up of the Hedjet, the white crown of Upper Egypt, and red feathers.

Atem The first creator-deity, he is also thought to be the finisher of the world. Also known as Tem.

Athene Virgin warrior-goddess, born from the forehead of Zeus when he swallowed his wife Metis. Plays a key role in the travels of Odysseus, and Perseus.

Atlatl Spear-thrower.

Atua A supernatural being, a god.

Atua-toko A small carved stick, the symbol of the god whom it represents. It was stuck in the ground whilst holding incantations to its presiding god.

Augeas King of Elis, one of the Argonauts.

Augsburg Tyr's city.

Avalon Legendary island where Excalibur was created and where Arthur went to recover from his wounds. It is said he will return from Avalon one day to reclaim his kingdom.

Ba Dead person or soul. Also known as ka.

Bairn Little child, also called bairnie.

Balarama Brother of Krishna.

Balder Son of Frigga; his murder causes Ragnarok. Also spelled as Baldur.

Bali Brother of Sugriva and one of the five great monkeys in the *Ramayana*.

Balor The evil, one-eyed King of the Fomorians and also grandfather of Lugh of the Long Arm. It was prophesied that Balor would one day be slain by his own grandson so he locked his daughter away on a remote island where he intended that she would never fall pregnant. But Cian, father of Lugh, managed to reach the island disguised as a woman, and Balor's daughter eventually bore him a child. During the second battle of Mag Tured (or Moytura), Balor was killed by Lugh who slung a stone into his giant eye.

Ban King of Benwick, father of Lancelot and brother of King Bors.

Bannock Flat loaf of bread, typically of oat or barley, usually cooked on a griddle.

Banshee Mythical spirit, usually female, who bears tales of imminent death. They often deliver the news by wailing or keening outside homes. Spelled *bean sí* in Gaelic.

Bard Traditionally a storyteller, poet or music composer whose work often focused on legends.

Basswood Any of several North American linden trees with a soft light-coloured wood.

Bastet Goddess of love, fertility and sex and a solar deity. She is often portrayed with the head of a cat.

Bateta (Yoruba) The first human, created alongside Hanna by the Toad and reshaped into human form by the Moon.

Bawn Fortified enclosure surrounding a castle.

Beaver Largest rodent in the United States of America, held in high esteem by Native American people. Although a land mammal, it spends a great deal of time in water and has a dense waterproof fur coat to protect it from harsh weather conditions.

Behula Daughter of Saha.

Benten Goddess of the sea and one of the Seven Divinities of Luck. Also referred to as the goddess of love, beauty and eloquence and as being the personification of wisdom.

Bere Barley.

Berserker Norse warrior who fights with a frenzied rage.

Bestla Giant mother of Aesir's mortal element.

Bhadra A mighty elephant.

Bhagavati Shiva's wife, also known as Parvati.

Bhagiratha Son of Dilipa.

Bharadhwaja Father of Drona and a hermit.

Bharata One of Dasharatha's four sons.

Bhaumasur A demon, slain by Krishna.

Bhima The second of the Pandavas.

Bhimasha King of Rajagriha and disciple of Buddha.

Bier Frame on which a coffin or dead body is placed before being carried to the grave.

Bifrost Rainbow bridge presided over by Heimdall.

Big-Belly One of Ravana's monsters.

Bilskirnir Thor's palace.

Bodach The term means 'old man'. The Highlanders believed that the Bodach crept down chimneys in order to steal naughty children. In other territories, he was a spirit who warned of death.

Bodkin Large, blunt needle used for threading strips of cloth or tape through cloth; short pointed dagger or blade.

Boer Person of Dutch origin who settled in southern Africa in the late seventeenth century. The term means 'farmer'. Boer people are often called Afrikaners.

Bogle Ghost or phantom; goblin-like creature.

Boliaun Ragwort, a weed with ragged leaves.

Book of the Dead Book for the dead, thought to be written by Thoth, texts from which were written on papyrus and buried with the dead, or carved on the walls of tombs, pyramids or sarcophagi.

Bors King of Gaul and brother of King Ban.

Bothy Small cottage or hut.

Brahma Creator of the world, mythical origin of colour (caste).

Brahmadatta King of Benares.

Brahman Member of the highest Hindu caste, traditionally a priest.

Bran In Scottish legend, Bran is the great hunting hound of Fionn Mac Chumail. In Irish mythology, he is a great hero.

Branstock Giant oak tree in the Volsung's hall; Odin placed a sword in it and challenged the guests of a wedding to withdraw it.

Brave Young warrior of Native American descent, sometimes also referred to as a 'buck'.

Bree Thin broth or soup.

Breidablik Balder's palace.

Brigit Scottish saint or spirit associated with the coming of spring.

Brisingamen Freyia's necklace.

Britomartis A Cretan goddess, also known as Dictynna.

Brocéliande Legendary enchanted forest and the supposed burial place of Merlin.

Brokki Dwarf who makes a deal with Loki, and who makes Miolnir, Draupnir and Gulinbursti.

Brollachan A shapeless spirit of unknown origin. One of the most frightening in Scottish mythology, it spoke only two words, 'Myself' and 'Thyself', taking the shape of whatever it sat upon.

Brownie A household spirit or creature which took the form of a small man (usually hideously ugly) who undertakes household chores, and mill or farm work, in exchange for a bowl of milk.

Brugh Borough or town.

Brunhilde A Valkyrie found by Sigurd.

Buddha Founder of buddhism, Gautama, avatar of Vishnu in Hinduism.

Buddhism Buddhism arrived in China in the first century BCE via the silk trading route from India and Central Asia. Its founder was Guatama Siddhartha (the Buddha), a religious teacher in northern India. Buddhist doctrine declared that by destroying the causes of all suffering, mankind could attain perfect enlightenment. The religion encouraged a new respect for all living things and brought with it the idea of reincarnation; i.e. that the soul returns to the earth after death in another form, dictated by the individual's behaviour in his previous life. By the fourth century, Buddhism was the dominant religion in China, retaining its powerful influence over the nation until the mid-ninth century.

Buffalo A type of wild ox, once widely scattered over the Great Plains of North America. Also known as a 'bison', the buffalo was an important food source for Native American tribes and its hide was also used in the construction of tepees and to make clothing. The buffalo was also sometimes revered as a totem animal, i.e. venerated as a direct ancestor of the tribesmen, and its skull used in ceremonial fashion.

Bull of Apis Sacred bull, thought to be the son of Hathor.

Bulu Sacrificial rite.

Bundles, sacred These bundles contained various venerated objects of the tribe, believed to have supernatural powers. Custody or ownership of the bundle was never lightly entered upon, but involved the learning of endless songs and ritual dances.

Bushel Unit of measurement, usually used for agricultural products or food.

Bushi Warrior.

Byre Barn for keeping cattle.

Byrny Coat of mail.

Cacique King or prince.

Cailleach Bheur A witch with a blue face who represents winter. When she is reborn each autumn, snow falls. She is mother of the god of youth (Angus mac Og).

Calabash Gourd from the calabash tree, commonly used as a bottle.

Calchas The seer of Mycenae who accompanied the Greek fleet to Troy. It was his prophecy which stated that Troy would never be taken without the aid of Achilles.

Calpulli Village house, or group or clan of families.

Calumet Ceremonial pipe used by Native Americans.

Calypso A nymph who lived on the island of Ogygia.

Camaxtli Tlascalan god of war and the chase, similar to Huitzilopochtli.

Camelot King Arthur's castle and centre of his realm.

Caoineag A banshee.

Caravanserai Traveller's inn, traditionally found in Asia or North Africa.

Carle Term for a man, often old; peasant.

Cat A black cat has great mythological significance, is often the bearer of bad luck, a symbol of black magic, and the familiar of a witch. Cats were also the totem for many tribes.

Cath Sith A fairy cat who was believed to be a witch transformed.

Cazi Magical person or influence.

Ceasg A Scottish mermaid with the body of a maiden and the tail of a salmon.

Ceilidh Party.

Cerberus The three-headed dog who guarded the entrance to the underworld.

Chalchiuhtlicue Goddess of water and the sick or newborn, and wife of Tlaloc. She is often symbolized as a small frog.

Changeling A fairy substitute-child left by fairies in place of a human child they have stolen.

Channa Guatama's charioteer.

Chaos A state from which the universe was created – caused by fire and ice meeting.

Charon The ferryman of the dead who carries souls across the River Styx to Hades.

Charybdis *See* Scylla and Charybdis.

Chicomecohuatl Chief goddess of maize and one of a group of deities called Centeotl, who care for all aspects of agriculture.

Chicomoztoc Legendary mountain and place of origin of the Aztecs. The name means 'seven caves'.

Chinawezi Primordial serpent.

Chinvat Bridge Bridge of the Gatherer, which the souls of the righteous cross to reach Mount Alborz or the world of the dead. Unworthy beings who try to cross Chinvat Bridge fall or are dragged into a place of eternal punishment.

Chitambaram Sacred city of Shiva's dance.

Chrysaor Son of Poseidon and Medusa, born from the severed neck of Medusa when Perseus beheaded her.

Chryseis Daughter of Chryses who was taken by Agamemnon in the battle of Troy.

Chullasubhadda Wife of Buddha-elect (Sumedha).

Chunda A good smith who entertains Buddha.

Churl Mean or unkind person.

Circe An enchantress and the daughter of Helius. She lived on the island of Aeaea with the power to change men to beasts.

Citlalpol The Mexican name for Venus, or the Great Star, and one of the only stars they worshipped. Also known as Tlauizcalpantecutli, or Lord of the Dawn.

Cleobis and Biton Two men of Argos who dragged the wagon carrying their mother, priestess of Hera, from Argos to the sanctuary.

Clio Muse of history and prophecy.

Clytemnestra Daughter of Tyndareus, sister of Helen, who married Agamemnon but deserted him when he sacrificed Iphigenia, their daughter, at the beginning of the Trojan War.

Coatepetl Mythical mountain, known as the 'serpent mountain'.

Coatl Serpent.

Coatlicue Earth mother and celestial goddess, she gave birth to Huitzilopochtli and his sister, Coyolxauhqui, and the moon and stars.

Codex Ancient book, often a list with pages folded into a zigzag pattern.

Confucius (Kong Fuzi) Regarded as China's greatest sage and ethical teacher, Confucius (551–479 BCE) was not especially revered during his lifetime and had a small following of some three thousand people. After the Burning of the Books in 213 BCE, interest in his philosophies became widespread. Confucius believed that mankind was essentially good, but argued for a highly structured society, presided over by a strong central government which would set the highest moral standards. The individual's sense of duty and obligation, he argued, would play a vital role in maintaining a well-run state.

Coracle Small, round boat, similar to a canoe. Also known as curragh or currach.

Coyolxauhqui Goddess of the moon and sister to Huitzilopochtli, she was decapitated by her brother after trying to kill their mother.

Creel Large basket made of wicker, usually used for fish.

Crodhmara Fairy cattle.

Cronan Musical humming, thought to resemble a cat purring or the drone of bagpipes.

Crow Usually associated with battle and death, but many mythological figures take this form.

Cu Sith A great fairy dog, usually green and oversized.

Cubit Ancient measurement, equal to the approximate length of a forearm.

Cuculain Irish warrior and hero. Also known as Cuchulainn.

Cutty Girl.

Cyclopes One-eyed giants who were imprisoned in Tartarus by Uranus and Cronus, but released by Zeus, for whom they made thunderbolts. Also a tribe of pastoralists who live without laws, and on, whenever possible, human flesh.

Daedalus Descendant of the Athenian King Erechtheus and son of Eupalamus. He killed his nephew and apprentice. Famed for constructing the labyrinth to house the Minotaur, in which he was later imprisoned. He constructed wings for himself and his son to make their escape.

Dagda One of the principal gods of the Tuatha De Danann, the father and chief, the Celtic equivalent of Zeus. He was the god reputed to have led the People of Dana in their successful conquest of the Fir Bolg.

Daikoku God of wealth and one of the gods of luck.

Daimyō Powerful lord or magnate.

Daksha The chief Prajapati.

Dana Also known as Danu, a goddess worshipped from antiquity by the Celts and considered to be the ancestor of the Tuatha De Danann.

Danae Daughter of Acrisius, King of Argos. Acrisius trapped her in a cave when he was warned that his grandson would be the cause of his ultimate death. Zeus came to her and Perseus was born.

Danaids The fifty daughters of Danaus of Argos, by ten mothers.

Daoine Sidhe The people of the Hollow Hills, or Otherworld.

Dardanus Son of Zeus and Electra, daughter of Atlas.

Dasharatha A Manu amongst men, King of Koshala, father of Santa.

Deianeira Daughter of Oeneus, who married Heracles after he won her in a battle with the River Achelous.

Deirdre A beautiful woman doomed to cause the deaths of three Irish heroes and bring war to the whole country. After a soothsayer prophesied her fate, Deidre's father hid her away from the world to prevent it. However, fate finds its way and the events come to pass before Deidre eventually commits suicide to remain with her love.

Demeter Goddess of agriculture and nutrition, whose name means earth mother. She is the mother of Persephone.

Demophoon Son of King Celeus of Eleusis, who was nursed by Demeter and then dropped in the fire when she tried to make him immortal.

Dervish Member of a religious order, often Sufi, known for their wild dancing and whirling.

Desire The god of love.

Deva A god other than the supreme God.

Devadatta Buddha's cousin, plots evil against Buddha.

Dhrishtadyumna Twin brother of Draupadi, slays Drona.

Dik-dik Dwarf antelope native to eastern and southern Africa.

Dilipa Son of Anshumat, father of Bhagiratha.

Dionysus The god of wine, vegetation and the life force, and of ecstasy. He was considered to be outside the Greek pantheon, and generally thought to have begun life as a mortal.

Dioscuri Castor and Polydeuces, the twin sons of Zeus and Leda, who are important deities.

Distaff Tool used when spinning which holds the wool or flax and keeps the fibres from tangling.

Divan Privy council.

Divots Turfs.

Dog The dog is a symbol of humanity, and usually has a role helping the hero of the myth or legend. Fionn's Bran and Grey Dog are two examples of wild beasts transformed to become invaluable servants.

Dōshin Government official.

Dossal Ornamental altar cloth.

Doughty Persistent and brave person.

Dragon Important animal in Japanese culture, symbolizing power, wealth, luck and success.

Draiglin' Hogney Ogre.

Draupadi Daughter of Drupada.

Draupnir Odin's famous ring, fashioned by Brokki.

Drona A Brahma, son of the great sage Bharadwaja.

Druid An ancient order of Celtic priests held in high esteem who flourished in the pre-Christian era. The word 'druid' is derived from an ancient Celtic one meaning 'very knowledgeable'. These individuals were believed to have mystical powers and in ancient Irish literature possess the ability to conjure up magical charms, to create tempests, to curse and debilitate their enemies and to perform as soothsayers to the royal courts.

Drupada King of the Panchalas.

Dryads Nymphs of the trees.

Dun A stronghold or royal abode surrounded by an earthen wall.

Durga Goddess, wife of Shiva.

Durk Knife. Also spelled as dirk.

Duryodhana One of Drona's pupils.

Dvalin Dwarf visited by Loki; also the name for the stag on Yggdrasill.

Dwarfie Stone Prehistoric tomb or boulder.

Dwarfs Fairies and black elves are called dwarfs.

Dwarkanath The Lord of Dwaraka; Krishna.

Dyumatsena King of the Shalwas and father of Satyavan.

Ebisu One of the gods of luck. He is also the god of labour and fishermen.

Echo A nymph who was punished by Hera for her endless stories told to distract Hera from Zeus's infidelity.

Ector King Arthur's foster father, who raised Arthur to protect him.

Edda Collection of prose and poetic myths and stories from the Norsemen.

Eight Immortals Three of these are reputed to be historical: Han Chung-li, born in Shaanxi, who rose to become a Marshal of the Empire in 21 BCE. Chang Kuo-Lao, who lived in the seventh to eighth century CE, and Lü Tung-pin, who was born in 755 CE.

Einheriear Odin's guests at Valhalla.

Eisa Loki's daughter.

Ekake (Ibani) Person of great intelligence, which means 'tortoise'. Also known as Mbai (Igbo).

Ekalavya Son of the king of the Nishadas.

Electra Daughter of Agamemnon and Clytemnestra.

Eleusis A town in which the cult of Demeter is centred.

Elf Sigmund is buried by an elf; there are light and dark elves (the latter called dwarfs).

Elokos (Central African) Imps of dwarf-demons who eat human flesh.

Elpenor The youngest of Odysseus's crew who fell from the roof of Circe's house on Aeaea and visited with Odysseus at Hades.

Elysium The home of the blessed dead.

Emain Macha The capital of ancient Ulster.

Emma Dai-o King of hell and judge of the dead.

Eos Goddess of the dawn and sister of the sun and moon.

Erichthonius A child born of the semen spilled when Hephaestus tried to rape Athene on the Acropolis.

Erin Term for Ireland, originally spelled Éirinn.

Erirogho Magical mixture made from the ashes of the dead.

Eros God of Love, the son of Aphrodite.

Erpa Hereditary chief.

Erysichthon A Thessalian who cut down a grove sacred to Demeter, who punished him with eternal hunger.

Eshu (Yoruba) God of mischief. He also tests people's characters and controls law enforcement.

Eteocles Son of Oedipus.

Eumaeus Swineherd of Odysseus's family at Ithaca.

Euphemus A son of Poseidon who could walk on water. He sailed with the Argonauts.

Europa Daughter of King Agenor of Tyre, who was taken by Zeus to Crete.

Eurydice A Thracian nymph married to Orpheus.

Excalibur The magical sword given to Arthur by the Lady of the Lake. In some versions of the myths, Excalibur is also the sword that the young Arthur pulls from the stone to become king.

Fabulist Person who composes or tells fables.

Fafnir Shape-changer who kills his father and becomes a dragon to guard the family jewels. Slain by Sigurd.

Fairy The word is derived from 'Fays' which means Fates. They are immortal, with the gift of prophecy and of music, and their role changes according to the origin of the myth. They were often considered to be little people, with enormous propensity for mischief, but they are central to many myths and legends, with important powers.

Faro (Mali, Guinea) God of the sky.

Fates In Greek mythology, daughters of Zeus and Themis, who spin the thread of a mortal's life and cut it when his time is due. Called Norns in Viking mythology.

Fenris A wild wolf, who is the son of Loki. He roams the earth after Ragnarok.

Ferhad Sculptor who fell in love with Shireen, the wife of Khosru, and undertook a seemingly impossible task to clear a passage through the mountain of Beysitoun and join the rivers in return for winning Shireen's hand.

Fialar Red cock of Valhalla.

Fianna/Fenians The word 'fianna' was used in early times to describe young warrior-hunters. These youths evolved under the leadership of Finn Mac Cumaill as a highly skilled band of military men who took up service with various kings throughout Ireland.

Filheim Land of mist, at the end of one of Yggdrasill's roots.

Fingal Another name for Fionn Mac Chumail, used after MacPherson's Ossian in the eighteenth century.

Fionn Mac Chumail Irish and Scottish warrior, with great powers of fairness and wisdom. He is known not for physical strength but for knowledge, sense of justice, generosity and canny instinct. He had two hounds, which were later discovered to be his nephews transformed. He became head of the Fianna, or Féinn, fighting the enemies of Ireland and Scotland. He was the father of Oisin (also called Ossian, or other derivatives), and father or grandfather of Osgar.

Fir Bolg One of the ancient, pre-Gaelic peoples of Ireland who were reputed to have worshipped the god Bulga, meaning god of lighting. They are thought to have colonized Ireland around 1970 BCE, after the death of Nemed and to have reigned for a short period of thirty-seven years before their defeat by the Tuatha De Danann.

Fir Chlis Nimble men or merry dancers, who are the souls of fallen angels.

Flitch Side of salted and cured bacon.

Folkvang Freyia's palace.

Fomorians A race of monstrous beings, popularly conceived as sea-pirates with some supernatural characteristics who opposed the earliest settlers in Ireland, including the Nemedians and the Tuatha De Danann.

Frey Comes to Asgard with Freyia as a hostage following the war between the Aesir and the Vanir.

Freyia Comes to Asgard with Frey as a hostage following the war between the Aesir and the Vanir. Goddess of beauty and love.

Frigga Odin's wife and mother of gods; she is goddess of the earth.

Fuath Evil spirits which lived in or near the water.

Fulla Frigga's maidservant.

Furies Creatures born from the blood of Cronus, guarding the greatest sinners of the underworld. Their power lay in their ability to drive mortals mad. Snakes writhed in their hair and around their waists.

Furoshiki Cloths used to wrap things.

Gae Bolg Cuchulainn alone learned the use of this weapon from the woman-warrior, Scathach and with it he slew his own son Connla and his closest friend, Ferdia. Gae Bolg translates as 'harpoon-like javelin' and the deadly weapon was reported to have been created by Bulga, the god of lighting.

Gaea Goddess of Earth, born from Chaos, and the mother of Uranus and Pontus. Also spelled as Gaia.

Gage Object of value presented to a challenger to symbolize good faith.

Galahad Knight of the Round Table, who took up the search for the Holy Grail. Son of Lancelot, Galahad is considered the purest and most perfect knight.

Galatea Daughter of Nereus and Doris, a sea-nymph loved by Polyphemus, the Cyclops.

Gandhari Mother of Duryodhana.

Gandharvas Demi-gods and musicians.

Gandjharva Musical ministrants of the upper air.

Ganesha Elephant-headed god of scribes and son of Shiva.

Ganges Sacred river personified by the goddess Ganga, wife of Shiva and daughter of the mount Himalaya.

Gareth of Orkney King Arthur's nephew and knight of the Round Table.

Garm Hel's hound.

Garuda King of the birds and mount Vishnu, the divine bird, attendant of Narayana.

Gautama Son of Suddhodana and also known as Siddhartha.

Gawain Nephew of King Arthur and knight of the Round Table, he is best known for his adventure with the Green Knight, who challenges one of Arthur's knights to cut off his head, but only if he agrees to be beheaded in turn in a year and a day, if the Green Knight survives. Gawain beheads the Green Knight, who simply replaces his head. At the appointed time, they meet, and the Green Knight swings his axe but merely nicks Gawain's skin instead of beheading him.

Geisha Performance artist or entertainer, usually female.

Geri Odin's wolf.

Ghommid (Yoruba) Term for mythological creatures such as goblins or ogres.

Giallar Bridge in Filheim.

Giallarhorn Heimdall's trumpet – the final call signifies Ragnarok.

Giants In Greek mythology, a race of beings born from Gaea, grown from the blood that dropped from the castrated Uranus. Usually represent evil in Viking mythology.

Gillie Someone who works for a Scottish chief, usually as an attendant or servant; guide for fishing or hunting parties.

Gladheim Where the twelve deities of Asgard hold their thrones. Also called Gladsheim.

Gled Bird of prey.

Golden Fleece Fleece of the ram sent by Poseidon to substitute for Phrixus when his father was going to sacrifice him. The Argonauts went in search of the fleece.

Goodman Man of the house.

Goodwife Woman of the house.

Gopis Lovers of the young Krishna and milkmaids.

Gorgon One of the three sisters, including Medusa, whose frightening looks could turn mortals to stone.

Graces Daughters of Aphrodite by Zeus.

Gramercy Expression of surprise or strong feeling.

Great Head The Iroquois believed in the existence of a curious being known as Great Head, a creature with an enormous head poised on slender legs.

Great Spirit The name given to the Creator of all life, as well as the term used to describe the omnipotent force of the Creator existing in every living thing.

Great-Flank One of Ravana's monsters.

Green Knight A knight dressed all in green and with green hair and skin who challenged one of Arthur's knights to strike him a blow with an axe and that, if he survived, he would return to behead the knight in a year and a day. He turned out to be Lord Bertilak and was under an enchantment cast by Morgan le Fay to test Arthur's knights.

Gruagach Mythical creature, often a giant or ogre similar to a wild man of the woods. The term can also refer to other mythical creatures such as brownies or fairies. As a brownie, he is usually dressed in red or green as opposed to the traditional brown. He has great power to enchant the hapless, or to help mortals who are worthy (usually heroes). He often appears to challenge a boy-hero, during his period of education.

Guebre Religion founded by Zoroaster, the Persian prophet.

Gugumatz Creator god who, with Huracan, formed the sky, earth and everything on it.

Guha King of Nishadha.

Guidewife Woman.

Guinevere Wife of King Arthur; she is often portrayed as a virtuous lady and wife, but is perhaps best known for having a love affair with Lancelot, one of Arthur's friends and knights of the Round Table. Her name is also spelled Guenever.

Gulistan *Rose Garden*, written by the poet Sa'di.

Gungnir Odin's spear, made of Yggdrasill wood, and the tip fashioned by Dvalin.

Gylfi A wandering king to whom the Eddas are narrated.

Haab Mayan solar calendar that consisted of eighteen twenty-day months.

Hades One of the three sons of Cronus; brother of Poseidon and Zeus. Hades is King of the Underworld, which is also known as the House of Hades.

Haere-mai Maori phrase meaning 'come here, welcome.'

Haere-mai-ra, me o tatou mate Maori phrase meaning 'come here, that I may sorrow with you.'

Haere-ra Maori phrase meaning 'goodbye, go, farewell.'

Haji Muslim pilgrim who has been to Mecca.

Hakama Traditional Japanese clothing, worn on the bottom half of the body.

Hanuman General of the monkey people.

Harakiri Suicide, usually by cutting or stabbing the abdomen. Also known as seppuku.

Hari-Hara Shiva and Vishnu as one god.

Harmonia Daughter of Ares and Aphrodite, wife of Cadmus.

Hatamoto High-ranking samurai.

Hathor Great cosmic mother and patroness of lovers. She is portrayed as a cow.

Hati The wolf who pursues the sun and moon.

Hatshepsut Second female pharaoh.

Hauberk Armour to protect the neck and shoulders, sometimes a full-length coat of mail.

Hector Eldest son of King Priam who defended Troy from the Greeks. He was killed by Achilles.

Hecuba The second wife of Priam, King of Troy. She was turned into a dog after Troy was lost.

Heimdall White god who guards the Bifrost bridge.

Hel Goddess of death and Loki's daughter. Also known as Hela.

Helen Daughter of Leda and Tyndareus, King of Sparta, and the most beautiful woman in the world. She was responsible for starting the Trojan War.

Heliopolis City in modern-day Cairo, known as the City of the Sun and the central place of worship of Ra. Also known as Anu.

Helius The sun, son of Hyperion and Theia.

Henwife Witch.

Hephaestus or **Hephaistos** The Smith of Heaven.

Hera A Mycenaean palace goddess, married to Zeus.

Heracles An important Greek hero, the son of Zeus and Alcmena. His name means 'Glory of Hera'. He performed twelve labours for King Eurystheus, and later became a god.

Hermes The conductor of souls of the dead to Hades, and god of trickery and of trade. He acts as messenger to the gods.

Hermod Son of Frigga and Odin who travelled to see Hel in order to reclaim Balder for Asgard.

Hero and Leander Hero was a priestess of Aphrodite, loved by Leander, a young man of Abydos. He drowned trying to see her.

Hestia Goddess of the hearth, daughter of Cronus and Rhea.

Hieroglyphs Type of writing that combines symbols and pictures, usually cut into tombs or rocks, or written on papyrus.

Himalaya Great mountain and range, father of Parvati.

Hiordis Wife of Sigmund and mother of Sigurd.

Hoderi A fisher and son of Okuninushi.

Hodur Balder's blind twin; known as the personification of darkness.

Hoenir Also called Vili; produced the first humans with Odin and Loki, and was one of the triad responsible for the creation of the world.

Hōichi the Earless A biwa hōshi, a blind storyteller who played the biwa or lute. Also a priest.

Holger Danske Legendary Viking warrior who is thought to never die. He sleeps until he is needed by his people and then he will rise to protect them.

Homayi Phoenix.

Hoodie Mythical creature which often appears as a crow.

Hoori A hunter and son of Okuninushi.

Horus God of the sky and kinship, son of Isis and Osiris. He captained the boat that carried Ra across the sky. He is depicted with the head of a falcon.

Hotei One of the gods of luck. He also personifies humour and contentment.

Houlet Owl.

Houri Beautiful virgin from paradise.

Hrim-faxi Steed of the night.

Hubris Presumptuous behaviour which causes the wrath of the gods to be brought on to mortals.

Hueytozoztli Festival dedicated to Tlaloc and, at times, Chicomecohuatl or other deities. Also the fourth month of the Aztec calendar.

Hugin Odin's raven.

Huitzilopochtli God of war and the sun, also connected with the summer and crops; one of the principal Aztec deities. He was born a full-grown adult to save his mother, Coatlicue, from the jealousy of his sister, Coyolxauhqui, who tried to kill Coatlicue. The Mars of the Aztec gods. In some origin stories he is one of four offspring of Ometeotl and Omecihuatl.

Hurley A traditional Irish game played with sticks and balls, quite similar to hockey.

Hurons A tribe of Iroquois stock, originally one people with the Iroquois.

Huveane (Pedi, Venda) Creator of humankind, who made a baby from clay into which he breathed life. He is known as the High God or Great God. He is also known as a trickster god.

Hymir Giant who fishes with Thor and is drowned by him.

Iambe Daughter of Pan and Echo, servant to King Celeus of Eleusis and Metaeira.

Icarus Son of Daedalus, who plunged to his death after escaping from the labyrinth.

Ichneumon Mongoose.

Idunn Guardian of the youth-giving apples.

Ifa (Yoruba) God of wisdom and divination. Also the term for a Yoruban religion.

Ife (Yoruba) The place Obatala first arrived on Earth and took for his home.

Igraine Wife of the duke of Tintagel, enemy of Uther Pendragon, who marries Uther when her first husband dies. She is King Arthur's mother.

Ile (Yoruba) Goddess of the earth.

Imhetep High priest and wise sage. He is sometimes thought to be the son of Ptah.

Imam Person who leads prayers in a mosque.

Imana (Banyarwanda) Creator or sky god.

In The male principle who, joined with Yo, the female side, brought about creation and the first gods. In and Yo correspond to the Chinese Yang and Yin.

Inari God of rice, fertility, agriculture and, later, the fox god. Inari has both good and evil attributes but is often presented as an evil trickster.

Indra The King of Heaven.

Indrajit Son of Ravana.

Indrasen Daughter of Nala and Damayanti.

Indrasena Son of Nala and Damayanti.

Inundation Annual flooding of the River Nile.

Iphigenia The eldest daughter of Agamemnon and Clytemnestra who was sacrificed to appease Artemis and obtain a fair wind for Troy.

Iris Messenger of the gods who took the form of a rainbow.

Iseult Princess of Ireland and niece of the Morholt. She falls in love with Tristan after consuming a love potion but is forced to marry King Mark of Cornwall.

Isis Goddess of the Nile and the moon, sister-wife of Osiris. She and her son, Horus, are sometimes thought of in a similar way to Mary and Jesus. She was one of the most worshipped female Egyptian deities and was instrumental in returning Osiris to life after he was killed by his brother, Set.

Istakbál Deputation of warriors.

Izanagi Deity and brother-husband to Izanami, who together created the Japanese islands from the Floating Bridge of Heaven. Their offspring populated Japan.

Izanami Deity and sister-wife of Izanagi, creator of Japan. Their children include Amaterasu, Tsuki-yomi and Susanoo.

Jade It was believed that jade emerged from the mountains as a liquid which then solidified after ten thousand years to become a precious hard stone, green in colour. If the correct herbs were added to it, it could return to its liquid state and when swallowed increase the individual's chances of immortality.

Jambavan A noble monkey.

Jason Son of Aeson, King of Iolcus and leader of the voyage of the Argonauts.

Jatayu King of all the eagle-tribes.

Jesseraunt Flexible coat of armour or mail.

Jimmo Legendary first emperor of Japan. He is thought to be descended from Hoori, while other tales claim him to be descended from Amaterasu through her grandson, Ninigi.

Jizo God of little children and the god who calms the troubled sea.

Jord Daughter of Nott; wife of Odin.

Jormungander The world serpent; son of Loki. Legends tell that when his tail is removed from his mouth, Ragnarok has arrived.

Jorō Geisha who also worked as a prostitute.

Jotunheim Home of the giants.

Ju Ju tree Deciduous tree that produces edible fruit.

Jurasindhu A rakshasa, father-in-law of Kans.

Jyeshtha Goddess of bad luck.

Ka Life power or soul. Also known as ba.

Kai-káús Son of Kai-kobád. He led an army to invade Mázinderán, home of the demon-sorcerers, after being persuaded by a demon. Known for his ambitious schemes, he later tried to reach Heaven by trapping eagles to fly him there on his throne.

Kaikeyi Mother of Bharata, one of Dasharatha's three wives.

Kai-khosrau Son of Saiawúsh, who killed Afrásiyáb in revenge for the death of his father.

Kai-kobád Descendant of Feridún, he was selected by Zál to lead an army against Afrásiyáb. Their powerful army, led by Zál and Rustem, drove back Afrásiyáb's army, who then agreed to peace.

Kailyard Kitchen garden or small plot, usually used for growing vegetables.

Kali The Black, wife of Shiva.

Kalindi Daughter of the sun, wife of Krishna.

Kaliya A poisonous hydra that lived in the jamna.

Kalki Incarnation of Vishnu yet to come.

Kalnagini Serpent who kills Lakshmindara.

Kal-Purush The Time-man, Bengali name for Orion.

Kaluda A disciple of Buddha.

Kalunga-ngombe (Mbundu) Death, also depicted as the king of the netherworld.

Kama God of desire.

Kamadeva Desire, the god of love.

Kami Spirits, deities or forces of nature.

Kamund Lasso.

Kans King of Mathura, son of Ugrasena and Pavandrekha.

Kanva Father of Shakuntala.

Kappa River goblin with the body of a tortoise and the head of an ape. Kappa love to challenge human beings to single combat.

Karakia Invocation, ceremony, prayer.

Karna Pupil of Drona.

Kaross Blanket or rug, also worn as a traditional garment. It is often made from the skins of animals which have been sewn together.

Kashyapa One of Dasharatha's counsellors.

Kauravas or Kurus Sons of Dhritarashtra, pupils of Drona.

Kaushalya Mother of Rama, one of Dasharatha's three wives.

Kay Son of Ector and adopted brother to King Arthur, he becomes one of Arthur's knights of the Round Table.

Keb God of the earth and father of Osiris and Isis, married to Nut. Keb is identified with Kronos, the Greek god of time.

Kehua Spirit, ghost.

Kelpie Another word for each uisge, the water-horse.

Ken Know.

Keres Black-winged demons or daughters of the night.

Keshini Wife of Sagara.

Khalif Leader.

Khara Younger brother of Ravana.

Khepera God who represents the rising sun. He is portrayed as a scarab. Also known as Nebertcher.

Kher-heb Priest and magician who officiated over rituals and ceremonies.

Khnemu God of the source of the Nile and one of the original Egyptian deities. He is thought to be the creator of children and of other gods. He is portrayed as a ram.

Khosru King and husband to Shireen, daughter of Maurice, the Greek Emperor. He was murdered by his own son, who wanted his kingdom and his wife.

Kia-ora Welcome, good luck. A greeting.

Kiboko Hippopotamus.

Kikinu Soul.

Kimbanda (Mbundu) Doctor.

Kimono Traditional Japanese clothing, similar to a robe.

King Arthur Legendary king of Britain who plucked the magical sword from the stone, marking him as the heir of Uther Pendragon and 'true king' of Britain. He and his knights of the Round Table defended Britain from the Saxons and had many adventures, including searching for the Holy Grail. Finally wounded in battle, he left Britain for the mythical Avalon, vowing to one day return to reclaim his kingdom.

Kinnaras Human birds with musical instruments under their wings.

Kinyamkela (Zaramo) Ghost of a child.

Kirk Church, usually a term for Church of Scotland churches.

Kirtle One-piece garment, similar to a tunic, which was worn by men or women.

Kist Trunk or large chest.

Kitamba (Mbundu) Chief who made his whole village go into mourning when his head-wife, Queen Muhongo, died. He also pledged that no one should speak or eat until she was returned to him.

Knowe Knoll or hillock.

Kojiki One of two myth-histories of Japan, along with the *Nihon Shoki*.

Ko-no-Hana Goddess of Mount Fuji, princess and wife of Ninigi.

Kore 'Maiden', another name for Persephone.

Kraal Traditional rural African village, usually consisting of huts surrounded by a fence or wall. Also an animal enclosure.

Krishna The Dark one, worshipped as an incarnation of Vishnu.

Kui-see Edible root.

Kumara Son of Shiva and Paravati, slays demon Taraka.

Kumbha-karna Ravana's brother.

Kunti Mother of the Pandavas.

Kura Red. The sacred colour of the Maori.

Kusha or Kusi One of Sita's two sons.

Kvasir Clever warrior and colleague of Odin. He was responsible for finally outwitting Loki.

Kwannon Goddess of mercy.

Labyrinth A prison built at Knossos for the Minotaur by Daedalus.

Lady of the Lake Enchantress who presents Arthur with Excalibur.

Laertes King of Ithaca and father of Odysseus.

Laestrygonians Savage giants encountered by Odysseus on his travels.

Laili In love with Majnun but unable to marry him, she was given to the prince, Ibn Salam, to marry. When he died, she escaped and found Majnun, but they could not be legally married. The couple died of grief and were buried together. Also known as Laila.

Laird Person who owns a significant estate in Scotland.

Lakshmana Brother of Rama and his companion in exile.

Lakshmi Consort of Vishnu and a goddess of beauty and good fortune.

Lakshmindara Son of Chand resurrected by Manasa Devi.

Lancelot Knight of the Round Table. Lancelot was raised by the Lady of the Lake. While he went on many quests, he is perhaps best known for his affair with Guinevere, King Arthur's wife.

Land of Light One of the names for the realm of the fairies. If a piece of metal welded by human hands is put in the doorway to their land, the door cannot close. The door to this realm is only open at night, and usually at a full moon.

Lang syne The days of old.

Lao Tzu (Laozi) The ancient Taoist philosopher thought to have been born in 571 BCE a contemporary of Confucius with whom, it is said, he discussed the tenets of Tao. Lao Tzu was an advocate of simple rural existence and looked to the Yellow Emperor and Shun as models of efficient government. His philosophies were recorded in the Tao Te Ching. Legends surrounding his birth suggest that he emerged from the left-hand side of his mother's body, with white hair and a long white beard, after a confinement lasting eighty years.

Laocoon A Trojan wiseman who predicted that the wooden horse contained Greek soldiers.

Laomedon The King of Troy who hired Apollo and Poseidon to build the impregnable walls of Troy.

Lava Son of Sita.

Leda Daughter of the King of Aetolia, who married Tyndareus. Helen and Clytemnestra were her daughters.

Legba (Dahomey) Youngest offspring of Mawu-Lisa. He was given the gift of all languages. It was through him that humans could converse with the gods.

Leman Lover.

Leprechaun Mythical creature from Irish folk tales who often appears as a mischievous and sometimes drunken old man.

Lethe One of the four rivers of the underworld, also called the River of Forgetfulness.

Lif The female survivor of Ragnarok.

Lifthrasir The male survivor of Ragnarok.

Liongo (Swahili) Warrior and hero.

Lofty mountain Home of Ahura-Mazda.

Logi Utgard-loki's cook.

Loki God of fire and mischief-maker of Asgard; he eventually brings about Ragnarok. Also spelled as Loptur.

Lotus-Eaters A race of people who live a dazed, drugged existence, the result of eating the lotus flower.

Ma'at State of order meaning truth, order or justice. Personified by the goddess Ma'at, who was Thoth's consort.

Macha There are thought to be several different Machas who appear in quite a number of ancient Irish stories. A particularly well-known 'Macha' is the wife of Crunnchu. The story unfolds that after her husband had boasted of her great athletic ability to the King, she was subsequently forced to run against his horses in spite of the fact that she was heavily pregnant. Macha died giving birth to her twin babies and with her dying breath she cursed Ulster for nine generations, proclaiming that it would suffer the weakness of a woman in childbirth in times of great stress. This curse had its most disastrous effect when Medb of Connacht invaded Ulster with her great army.

Machi-bugyō Senior official or magistrate, usually samurai.

Macuilxochitl God of art, dance and games, and the patron of luck in gaming. His name means 'source of flowers' or 'prince of flowers'. Also known as Xochipilli, meaning 'five-flower'.

Madake Weapon used for whipping, made of bamboo.

Maduma Taro tuber.

Mag Muirthemne Cuchulainn's inheritance. A plain extending from River Boyne to the mountain range of Cualgne, close to Emain Macha in Ulster.

Magni Thor's son.

Mahaparshwa One of Ravana's generals.

Maharaksha Son of Khara, slain at Lanka.

Mahasubhadda Wife of Buddha-select (Sumedha).

Majnun Son of a chief, who fell in love with Laili and followed her tribe through the desert, becoming mad with love until they were briefly reunited before dying.

Makaras Mythical fish-reptiles of the sea.

Makoma (Senna) Folk hero who defeated five mighty giants.

Mana Power, authority, prestige, influence, sanctity, luck.

Manasa Devi Goddess of snakes, daughter of Shiva by a mortal woman.

Manasha Goddess of snakes.

Mandavya Daughter of Kushadhwaja.

Man-Devourer One of Ravana's monsters.

Mandodari Wife of Ravana.

Mandrake Poisonous plant from the nightshade family which has hallucinogenic and hypnotic qualities if ingested. Its roots resemble the human form and it has supposedly magical qualities.

Mani The moon.

Manitto Broad term used to describe the supernatural or a potent spirit among the Algonquins, the Iroquois and the Sioux.

Man-Slayer One of Ravana's counsellors.

Manthara Kaikeyi's evil nurse, who plots Rama's ruin.

Mantle Cloak or shawl.

Manu Lawgiver.

Manu Mythical mountain on which the sun sets.

Mara The evil one, tempts Gautama.

Markandeya One of Dasharatha's counsellors.

Matali Sakra's charioteer.

Mawu-Lisa (Dahomey) Twin offspring of Nana Baluka. Mawu (female) and Lisa (male) are often joined to form one being. Their own offspring populated the world.

Mbai (Igbo) Person of great intelligence, also known as Ekake (Ibani), which means 'tortoise'.

Medea Witch and priestess of Hecate, daughter of Aeetes and sister of Circe. She helped Jason in his quest for the Golden Fleece.

Medusa One of the three Gorgons whose head had the power to turn onlookers to stone.

Melpomene One of the muses, and mother of the Sirens.

Menaka One of the most beautiful dancers in Heaven.

Menat Amulet, usually worn for protection.

Mendicant Beggar.

Menelaus King of Sparta, brother of Agamemnon. Married Helen and called war against Troy when she eloped with Paris.

Menthu Lord of Thebes and god of war. He is portrayed as a hawk or falcon.

Mere-pounamu A native weapon made of a rare green stone.

Merlin Wizard and advisor to King Arthur. He is thought to be the son of a human female and an incubus (male demon). He brought about Arthur's birth and ascension to king, then acted as his mentor.

Merrow Mythical mermaid-like creature, often depicted with an enchanted cap called a cohuleen driuth which allows it to travel between land and the depths of the sea. Also known as murúch.

Metaneira Wife of Celeus, King of Eleusis, who hired Demeter in disguise as her nurse.

Metztli Goddess of the moon, her name means 'lady of the night'. Also known as Yohualtictl.

Michabo Also known as Manobozho, or the Great Hare, the principal deity of the Algonquins, maker and preserver of the earth, sun and moon.

Mictlan God of the dead and ruler of the underworld. He was married to Mictecaciuatl and is often represented as a bat. He is also the Aztec lord of Hades. Also known as Mictlantecutli. Mictlan is also the name for the underworld.

Midgard Dwelling place of humans (Earth).

Midsummer A time when fairies dance and claim human victims.

Mihrab Father of Rúdábeh and descendant of Zohák, the serpent-king.

Milesians A group of iron-age invaders led by the sons of Mil, who arrived in Ireland from Spain around 500 BCE and overcame the Tuatha De Danann.

Mimir God of the ocean. His head guards a well; reincarnated after Ragnarok.

Minos King of Crete, son of Zeus and Europa. He was considered to have been the ruler of a sea empire.

Minotaur A creature born of the union between Pasiphae and a Cretan Bull.

Minúchihr King who lives to be one hundred and twenty years old. Father of Nauder.

Miolnir *See* Mjolnir.

Mithra God of the sun and light in Iran, protector of truth and guardian of pastures and cattle. Also known as Mitra in Hindu mythology and Mithras in Roman mythology.

Mixcoatl God of the chase or the hunt. Sometimes depicted as the god of air and thunder, he introduced fire to humankind. His name means 'cloud serpent'.

Mjolnir Hammer belonging to the Norse god of thunder, which is used as a fearsome weapon which always returns to Thor's hand, and as an instrument of consecration.

Mnoatia Forest spirits.

Moccasins One-piece shoes made of soft leather, especially deerskin.

Modi Thor's son.

Moly A magical plant given to Odysseus by Hermes as protection against Circe's powers.

Montezuma Great emperor who consolidated the Aztec Empire.

Mordred Bastard son of King Arthur and Morgawse, Queen of Orkney, who, unknown to Arthur, was his half-sister. Mordred becomes one of King Arthur's knights of the Round Table before betraying and fatally wounding Arthur, causing him to leave Britain for Avalon.

Morgan le Fay Enchantress and half-sister to King Arthur, Morgan was an apprentice of Merlin's. She is generally depicted as benevolent, yet did pit herself against Arthur and his knights on occasion. She escorts Arthur on his final journey to Avalon. Also known as Morgain le Fay.

Morholt The knight sent to Cornwall to force King Mark to pay tribute to Ireland. He is killed by Tristan.

Morongoe the brave (Lesotho) Man who was turned into a snake by evil spirits because Tau was jealous that he had married the beautiful Mokete, the chief's daughter. Morongoe was returned to human form after his son, Tsietse, returned him to their family.

Mosima (Bapedi) The underworld or abyss.

Mount Fuji Highest mountain in Japan, on the island of Honshū.

Mount Kunlun This mountain features in many Chinese legends as the home of the great emperors on Earth. It is written in the *Shanghaijing* (*The Classic of Mountains and Seas*) that this towering structure measured no less than 3300 miles in circumference and 4000 miles in height. It acted both as a central pillar to support the heavens, and as a gateway between Heaven and Earth.

Moving Finger Expression for taking responsibility for one's life and actions, which cannot be undone.

Moytura Translated as the 'Plain of Weeping', Mag Tured, or Moytura, was where the Tuatha De Danann fought two of their most significant battles.

Mua An old-time Polynesian god.

Muezzin Person who performs the Muslim call to prayer.

Mugalana A disciple of Buddha.

Muilearteach The Cailleach Bheur of the water, who appears as a witch or a sea-serpent. On land she grew larger and stronger by fire.

Muloyi Sorcerer, also called mulaki, murozi, ndozi or ndoki.

Munin Odin's raven.

Murile (Chaga) Man who dug up a taro tuber that resembled his baby brother, which turned into a living boy. His mother killed the baby when she saw Murile was starving himself to feed it.

Murtough Mac Erca King who ruled Ireland when many of its people – including his wife and family – were converting to Christianity. He remained a pagan.

Muses Goddesses of poetry and song, daughters of Zeus and Mnemosyne.

Musha Expression, often of surprise.

Muskrat North American beaver-like, amphibious rodent.

Muspell Home of fire, and the fire-giants.

Mwidzilo Taboo which, if broken, can cause death.

Nahua Ancient Mexicans.

Nakula Pandava twin skilled in horsemanship.

Nala One of the monkey host, son of Vishvakarma.

Nana Baluka (Dahomey) Mother of all creation. She gave birth to an androgynous being with two faces. The female face was Mawu, who controlled the night and lands to the west. The male face was Lisa and he controlled the day and the east.

Nanahuatl Also known as Nanauatzin. Presided over skin diseases and known as Leprous, which in Nahua meant 'divine'.

Nandi Shiva's bull.

Nanna Balder's wife.

Narcissus Son of the River Cephisus. He fell in love with himself and died as a result.

Narve Son of Loki.

Nataraja Manifestation of Shiva, Lord of the Dance.

Natron Preservative used in embalming, mined from the Natron Valley in Egypt.

Nauder Son of Minúchihr, who became king on his death and was tyrannical and hated until Sám begged him to follow in the footsteps of his ancestors.

Nausicaa Daughter of Alcinous, King of Phaeacia, who fell in love with Odysseus.

Necromancy Communicating with the dead.

Nectar Drink of the gods.

Neith Goddess of hunting, fate and war. Neith is sometimes known as the creator of the universe.

Nemesis Goddess of retribution and daughter of night.

Neoptolemus Son of Achilles and Deidameia, he came to Troy at the end of the war to wear his father's armour. He sacrificed Polyxena at the tomb of Achilles.

Nephthys Goddess of the air, night and the dead. Sister of Isis and sister-wife to Seth, she is also the mother of Anubis.

Nereids Sea-nymphs who are the daughters of Nereus and Doris. Thetis, mother of Achilles, was a Nereid.

Nestor Wise King of Pylus, who led the ships to Troy with Agamemnon and Menelaus.

Neta Daughter of Shiva, friend of Manasa.

Ngai (Gikuyu) Creator god.

Ngaka (Lesotho) Witch doctor.

Niflheim The underworld in Norse mythology, ruled over by Hel.

Night Daughter of Norvi.

Nikumbha One of Ravana's generals.

Nila One of the monkey host, son of Agni.

Ninigi Grandson of Amaterasu, Ninigi came to Earth bringing rice and order to found the Imperial family. He is known as the August Grandchild.

Niord God of the sea; marries Skadi.

Nirvana Transcendent state and the final goal of Buddhism.

Nis Mythological creature, similar to a brownie or goblin, usually harmless or even friendly, but can be easily offended. They are often associated with Christmas or the winter solstice.

Noatun Niord's home.

Noisy-Throat One of Ravana's counsellors.

Noondah (Zanzibar) Cannibalistic cat which attacked and killed animals and humans.

Norns The fates and protectors of Yggdrasill. Many believe them to be the same as the Valkyries.

Norvi Father of the night.

Nott Goddess of night.

Nsasak bird Small bird who became chief of all small birds after winning a competition to go without food for seven days. The Nsasak bird beat the Odudu bird by sneaking out of his home to feed.

Nü Wa The Goddess Nü Wa, who in some versions of the Creation myths is the sole creator of mankind, and in other tales is associated with the God Fu Xi, also a great benefactor of the human race. Some accounts represent Fu Xi as the brother of Nü Wa, but others describe the pair as lovers who lie together to create the very first human beings. Fu Xi is also considered to be the first of the Chinese emperors of mythical times who reigned from 2953 to 2838 BCE.

Nuada The first king of the Tuatha De Danann in Ireland, who lost an arm in the first battle of Moytura against the Fomorians. He became known as 'Nuada of the Silver Hand' when Diancecht, the great physician of the Tuatha De Danann, replaced his hand with a silver one after the battle.

Nunda (Swahili, East Africa) Slayer that took the form of a cat and grew so big that it consumed everyone in the town except the sultan's wife, who locked herself away. Her son, Mohammed, killed Nunda and cut open its leg, setting free everyone Nunda had eaten.

Nut Goddess of the sky, stars and astronomy. Sister-wife of Keb and mother of Osiris, Isis, Set and Nephthys. She often appears in the form of a cow.

Nyame (Ashanti) God of the sky, who sees and knows everything.

Nymphs Minor female deities associated with particular parts of the land and sea.

Obassi Osaw (Ekoi) Creator god with his twin, Obassi Nsi. Originally, Obassi Osaw ruled the skies while Obassi Nsi ruled the Earth.

Obatala (Yoruba) Creator of humankind. He climbed down a golden chain from the sky to the earth, then a watery abyss, and formed land and humankind. When Olorun heard of his success, he created the sun for Obatala and his creations.

Oberon Fairy king.

Odin Allfather and king of all gods, he is known for travelling the nine worlds in disguise and recognized only by his single eye; dies at Ragnarok.

Oduduwa (Yoruba) Divine king of Ile-Ife, the holy city of Yoruba.

Odur Freyia's husband.

Odysseus Greek hero, son of Laertes and Anticleia, who was renowned for his cunning, the master behind the victory at Troy, and known for his long voyage home.

Oedipus Son of Leius, King of Thebes and Jocasta. Became King of Thebes and married his mother.

Ogdoad Group of eight deities who were formed into four male-female couples who joined to create the gods and the world.

Ogham One of the earliest known forms of Irish writing, originally used to inscribe upright pillar stones.

Oiran Courtesan.

Oisín Also called Ossian (particularly by James Macpherson who wrote a set of Gaelic Romances about this character, supposedly garnered from oral tradition). Ossian was the son of Fionn and Sadbh, and had various brothers, according to different legends. He was a man of great wisdom, became immortal for many centuries, but in the end he became mad.

Ojibwe Another name for the Chippewa, a tribe of Algonquin stock.

Okuninushi Deity and descendant of Susanoo, who married Suseri-hime, Susanoo's daughter, without his consent. Susanoo tried to kill him many times but did not succeed and eventually forgave Okuninushi. He is sometimes thought to be the son or grandson of Susanoo.

Olokun (Yoruba) Most powerful goddess who ruled the seas and marshes. When Obatala created Earth in her domain, other gods began to divide it up between them. Angered at their presumption, she caused a great flood to destroy the land.

Olorun (Yoruba) Supreme god and ruler of the sky. He sees and controls everything, but others, such as Obatala, carry out the work for him. Also known as Olodumare.

Olympia Zeus's home in Elis.

Olympus The highest mountain in Greece and the ancient home of the gods.

Omecihuatl Female half of the first being, combined with Ometeotl. Together they are the lords of duality or lords of the two sexes. Also known as Ometecutli and Omeciuatl or Tonacatecutli and Tonacaciuatl. Their offspring were Xipe Totec, Huitzilopochtli, Quetzalcoatl and Tezcatlipoca.

Ometeotl Male half of the first being, combined with Omecihuatl.

Ometochtli Collective name for the pulque-gods or drink-gods. These gods were often associated with rabbits as they were thought to be senseless creatures.

Onygate Anyway.

Opening of the Mouth Ceremony in which mummies or statues were prayed over and anointed with incense before their mouths were opened, allowing them to eat and drink in the afterlife.

Oracle The response of a god or priest to a request for advice – also a prophecy; the place where such advice was sought; the person or thing from whom such advice was sought.

Oranyan (Yoruba) Youngest grandson of King Oduduwa, who later became king himself.

Orestes Son of Agamemnon and Clytemnestra who escaped following Agamemnon's murder to King Strophius. He later returned to Argos to murder his mother and avenge the death of his father.

Orpheus Thracian singer and poet, son of Oeagrus and a Muse. Married Eurydice and when she died tried to retrieve her from the underworld.

Orunmila (Yoruba) Eldest son of Olorun, he helped Obatala create land and humanity, which he then rescued after Olokun flooded the lands. He has the power to see the future.

Osiris God of fertility, the afterlife and death. Thought to be the first of the pharaohs. He was murdered by his brother, Set, after which he was conjured back to life by Isis, Anubis and others before becoming lord of the afterworld. Married to Isis, who was also his sister.

Otherworld The world of deities and spirits, also known as the Land of Promise, or the Land of Eternal Youth, a place of everlasting life where all earthly dreams come to be fulfilled.

Owuo (Krachi, West Africa) Giant who personifies death. He causes a person to die every time he blinks his eye.

Palamedes Hero of Nauplia, believed to have created part of the ancient Greek alphabet. He tricked Odysseus into joining the fleet setting out for Troy by placing the infant Telemachus in the path of his plough.

Palermo Stone Stone carved with hieroglyphs, which came from the Royal Annals of ancient Egypt and contains a list of the kings of Egypt from the first to the early fifth dynasties.

Palfrey Docile and light horse, often used by women.

Palladium Wooden image of Athene, created by her as a monument to her friend Pallas who she accidentally killed. While in Troy it protected the city from invaders.

Pallas Athene's best friend, whom she killed.

Pan God of Arcadia, half-goat and half-man. Son of Hermes. He is connected with fertility, masturbation and sexual drive. He is also associated with music, particularly his pipes, and with laughter.

Pan Gu Some ancient writers suggest that this God is the offspring of the opposing forces of nature, the yin and the yang. The yin (female) is associated with the cold and darkness of the earth, while the yang (male) is associated with the sun and the warmth of the heavens. 'Pan' means 'shell of an egg' and 'Gu' means 'to secure' or 'to achieve'. Pan Gu came into existence so that he might create order from chaos.

Pandareus Cretan King killed by the gods for stealing the shrine of Zeus.

Pandavas Alternative name for sons of Pandu, pupils of Drona.

Pandora The first woman, created by the gods, to punish man for Prometheus's theft of fire. Her dowry was a box full of powerful evil.

Papyrus Paper-like material made from the pith of the papyrus plant, first manufactured in Egypt. Used as a type of paper as well as for making mats, rope and sandals.

Paramahamsa The supreme swan.

Parashurama Human incarnation of Vishnu, 'Rama with an axe'.

Paris Handsome son of Priam and Hecuba of Troy, who was left for dead on Mount Ida but raised by shepherds. Was reclaimed by his family, then brought them shame and caused the Trojan War by eloping with Helen.

Parsa Holy man. Also known as a zahid.

Parvati Consort of Shiva and daughter of Himalaya.

Passion Wife of desire.

Pavanarekha Wife of Ugrasena, mother of Kans.

Peerie Folk Fairy or little folk.

Pegasus The winged horse born from the severed neck of Medusa.

Peggin Wooden vessel with a handle, often shaped like a tub and used for drinking.

Peleus Father of Achilles. He married Antigone, caused her death, and then became King of Phthia. Saved from death himself by Jason and the Argonauts. Married Thetis, a sea nymph.

Penelope The long-suffering but equally clever wife of Odysseus who managed to keep at bay suitors who longed for Ithaca while Odysseus was at the Trojan War and on his ten-year voyage home.

Pentangle Pentagram or five-pointed star.

Pentecost Christian festival held on the seventh Sunday after Easter. It celebrates the holy spirit descending on the disciples after Jesus's ascension.

Percivale Knight of the Round Table and original seeker of the Holy Grail.

Persephone Daughter of Zeus and Demeter who was raped by Hades and forced to live in the underworld as his queen for three months of every year.

Perseus Son of Danae, who was made pregnant by Zeus. He fought the Gorgons and brought home the head of

Medusa. He eventually founded the city of Mycenae and married Andromeda.

Pesh Kef Spooned blade used in the Opening of the Mouth ceremony.

Phaeacia The Kingdom of Alcinous on which Odysseus landed after a shipwreck which claimed the last of his men as he left Calypso's island.

Pharaoh King or ruler of Egypt.

Philoctetes Malian hero, son of Poeas, received Heracles's bow and arrows as a gift when he lit the great hero's pyre on Mount Oeta. He was involved in the last part of the Trojan War, killing Paris.

Philtre Magic potion, usually a love potion.

Pibroch Bagpipe music.

Pintura Native manuscript or painting.

Pipiltin Noble class of the Aztecs.

Pismire Ant.

Piu-piu Short mat made from flax leaves and neatly decorated.

Po Gloom, darkness, the lower world.

Polyphemus A Cyclops, but a son of Poseidon. He fell in love with Galatea, but she spurned him. He was blinded by Odysseus.

Polyxena Daughter of Priam and Hecuba of Troy. She was sacrificed on the grave of Achilles by Neoptolemus.

Pooka Mythical creature with the ability to shapeshift. Often appears as a horse, but also as a bull, dog or in human form, and has the ability to talk. Also known as púca.

Popol Vuh Sacred 'book of counsel' of the Quiché or K'iche' Maya people.

Poseidon God of the sea, and of sweet waters. Also the god of earthquakes. His is brother to Zeus and Hades, who divided the earth between them.

Pradyumna Son of Krishna and Rukmini.

Prahasta (Long-Hand) One of Ravana's generals.

Prajapati Creator of the universe, father of the gods, demons and all creatures, later known as Brahma.

Priam King of Troy, married to Hecuba, who bore him Hector, Paris, Helenus, Cassandra, Polyxena, Deiphobus and Troilus. He was murdered by Neoptolemus.

Pritha Mother of Karna and of the Pandavas.

Prithivi Consort of Dyaus and goddess of the earth.

Proetus King of Argos, son of Abas.

Prometheus A Titan, son of Iapetus and Themus. He was champion of mortal men, which he created from clay. He stole fire from the gods and was universally hated by them.

Prose Edda Collection of Norse myths and poems, thought to have been compiled in the 1200s by Icelandic historian Snorri Sturluson.

Proteus The old man of the sea who watched Poseidon's seals.

Psyche A beautiful nymph who was the secret wife of Eros, against the wishes of his mother Aphrodite, who sent Psyche to perform many tasks in hope of causing her death. She eventually married Eros and was allowed to become partly immortal.

Ptah Creator god and deity of Memphis who was married to Sekhmet. Ptah built the boats to carry the souls of the dead to the afterlife.

Puddock Frog.

Pulque Alcoholic drink made from fermented agave.

Purusha The cosmic man, he was sacrificed and his dismembered body became all the parts of the cosmos, including the four classes of society.

Purvey To provide or supply.

Pushkara Nala's brother.

Pushpaka Rama's chariot.

Putana A rakshasi.

Pygmalion A sculptor who was so lonely he carved a statue of a beautiful woman, and eventually fell in love with it. Aphrodite brought the image to life.

Quauhtli Eagle.

Quern Hand mill used for grinding corn.

Quetzalcoatl Deity and god of wind. He is represented as a feathered or plumed serpent and is usually a wise and benevolent god. Offspring of Ometeotl and Omecihuatl, he is also known as Kukulkan.

Ra God of the sun, ruling male deity of Egypt whose name means 'sole creator'.

Radha The principal mistress of Krishna.

Ragnarok The end of the world.

Rahula Son of Siddhartha and Yashodhara.

Raiden God of thunder. He traditionally has a fierce and demonic appearance.

Rakshasas Demons and devils.

Ram of Mendes Sacred symbol of fatherhood and fertility.

Rama or **Ramachandra** A prince and hero of the *Ramayana*, worshipped as an incarnation of Vishnu.

Ra-Molo (Lesotho) Father of fire, a chief who ruled by fear. When trying to kill his brother, Tau the lion, he was turned into a monster with the head of a sheep and the body of a snake.

Rangatira Chief, warrior, gentleman.

Regin A blacksmith who educated Sigurd.

Reinga The spirit land, the home of the dead.

Reservations Tracts of land allocated to the Native American people by the United States Government with the purpose of bringing the many separate tribes under state control.

Rewati Daughter of Raja, marries Balarama.

Rhadha Wife of Adiratha, a gopi of Brindaban and lover of Krishna.

Rhea Mother of the Olympian gods. Cronus ate each of her children, but she concealed Zeus and gave Cronus a swaddled rock in his place.

Rill Small stream.

Rimu (Chaga) Monster known to feed off human flesh, which sometimes takes the form of a werewolf.

Rishis Sacrificial priests associated with the devas in Swarga.

Rituparna King of Ayodhya.

Rohini The wife of Vasudeva, mother of Balarama and Subhadra, and carer of the young Krishna. Another Rohini is a goddess and consort of Chandra.

Rōnin Samurai whose master had died or fallen out of favour.

Rubáiyát Collection of poems written by Omar Khayyám.

Rúdábeh Wife of Zál and mother of Rustem.

Rudra Lord of Beasts and disease, later evolved into Shiva.

Rukma Rukmini's eldest brother.

Rustem Son of Zál and Rúdábeh, he was a brave and mighty warrior who undertook seven labours to travel to Mázinderán to rescue Kai-káús. Once there, he defeated the White Demon and rescued Kai-káús. He rode the fabled stallion Rakhsh and is also known as Rustam.

Ryō Traditional gold currency.

Sabdh Mother of Ossian, or Oisin.

Sagara King of Ayodhya.

Sahadeva Pandava twin skilled in swordsmanship.

Sahib diwan Lord high treasurer or chief royal executive.

Saiawúsh Son of Kai-káús, who was put through trial by fire when Sudaveh, Kai-káús's wife, told him that Saiawúsh had taken advantage of her. His innocence was proven when the fire did not harm him. He was eventually killed by Afrásiyáb.

Saithe Blessed.

Sajara (Mali) God of rainbows. He takes the form of a multi-coloured serpent.

Sake Japanese rice wine.

Sakuni Cousin of Duryodhana.

Salam Greeting or salutation.

Saláman Son of the Shah of Yunan, who fell in love with Absál, his nurse. She died after they had a brief love affair and he returned to his father.

Salmali tree Cotton tree.

Salmon A symbol of great wisdom, around which many Scottish legends revolve.

Sám Mighty warrior who fought and won many battles. Father of Zál and grandfather to Rustem.

Sambu Son of Krishna.

Sampati Elder brother of Jatayu.

Samurai Noblemen who were part of the military in medieval Japan.

Sanehat Member of the royal bodyguard.

Sango (Yoruba) God of war and thunder.

Sangu (Mozambique) Goddess who protects pregnant women, depicted as a hippopotamus.

Santa Daughter of Dasharatha.

Sarapis Composite deity of Apis and Osiris, sometimes known as Serapis. Thought to be created to unify Greek and Egyptian citizens under the Greek pharaoh Ptolemy.

Sarasvati The tongue of Rama.

Sarcophagus Stone coffin.

Sarsar Harsh, whistling wind.

Sasabonsam (Ashanti) Forest ogre.

Sassun Scottish word for England.

Sati Daughter of Daksha and Prasuti, first wife of Shiva.

Satrughna One of Dasharatha's four sons.

Satyavan Truth speaker, husband of Savitri.

Satyavati A fisher-maid, wife of Bhishma's father, Shamtanu.

Satyrs Elemental spirits which took great pleasure in chasing nymphs. They had horns, a hairy body and cloven hooves.

Saumanasa A mighty elephant.

Scamander River running across the Trojan plain, and father of Teucer.

Scarab Dung beetle, often used as a symbol of the immortal human soul and regeneration.

Scylla and Charybdis Scylla was a monster who lived on a rock of the same name in the Straits of Messina, devouring sailors. Charybdis was a whirlpool in the Straits which was supposedly inhabited by the hateful daughter of Poseidon.

Seal Often believed that seals were fallen angels. Many families are descended from seals, some of which had webbed hands or feet. Some seals were the children of sea-kings who had become enchanted (selkies).

Seelie-Court The court of the Fairies, who travelled around their realm. They were usually fair to humans, doling out punishment that was morally sound, but they were quick to avenge insults to fairies.

Segu (Swahili, East Africa) Guide who informs humans where honey can be found.

Sekhmet Solar deity who led the pharaohs in war. She is goddess of healing and was sent by Ra to destroy humanity when people turned against the sun god. She is portrayed with the head of a lion.

Selene Moon-goddess, daughter of Hyperion and Theia. She was seduced by Pan, but loved Endymion.

Selkie Mythical creature which is seal-like when in water but can shed its skin to take on human form when on land.

Seneschal Steward of a royal or noble household.

Sensei Teacher.

Seriyut A disciple of Buddha.

Sessrymnir Freyia's home.

Set God of chaos and evil, brother of Osiris, who killed him by tricking him into getting into a chest, which he then threw in the Nile, before cutting Osiris's body into fourteen separate pieces. Also known as Seth.

Sgeulachd Stories.

Sháhnámeh *The Book of Kings* written by Ferdowsi, one of the world's longest epic poems, which describes the mythology and history of the Persian Empire.

Shaikh Respected religious man.

Shaivas or Shaivites Worshippers of Shiva.

Shakti Power or wife of a god and Shiva's consort as his feminine aspect.

Shaman Also known as the 'Medicine Men' of Native American tribes, it is the shaman's role to cultivate communication with the spirit world. They are endowed with knowledge of all healing herbs, and learn to diagnose and cure disease. They are believed to foretell the future, find lost property and have power over animals, plants and stones.

Shamtanu Father of Bhishma.

Shankara A great magician, friend of Chand Sadagar.

Shashti The Sixth, goddess who protects children and women in childbirth.

Sheen Beautiful and enchanted woman who casts a spell on Murtough, King of Ireland, causing him to fall in love with her and cast out his family. He dies at her hands, half burned and half drowned, but she then dies of grief as she returns his love. Sheen is known by many names, including Storm, Sigh and Rough Wind.

Shesh A serpent that takes human birth through Devaki.

Shi-en Fairy dwelling.

Shinto Indigenous religion of Japan, from the pre-sixth century to the present day.

Shireen Married to Khosru. Her beauty meant that she was desired by many, including Khosru's own son by his previous marriage. She killed herself rather than give in to her stepson.

Shitala The Cool One and goddess of smallpox.

Shiva One of the two great gods of post-Vedic Hinduism with Vishnu.

Shogun Military ruler or overlord.

Shoji Sliding door, usually a lattice screen of paper.

Shu God of the air and half of the first divine couple created by Atem. Brother and husband to Tefnut, father to Keb and Nut.

Shubistán Household.

Shudra One of the four fundamental colours (caste).

Shuttle Part of a machine used for spinning cloth, used for passing weft threads between warp threads.

Siddhas Musical ministrants of the upper air.

Sif Thor's wife; known for her beautiful hair.

Sigi Son of Odin.

Sigmund Warrior able to pull the sword from Branstock in the Volsung's hall.

Signy Volsung's daughter.

Sigurd Son of Sigmund, and bearer of his sword. Slays Fafnir the dragon.

Sigyn Loki's faithful wife.

Símúrgh Griffin, an animal with the body of a lion and the head and wings of an eagle. Known to hold great wisdom. Also called a symurgh.

Sindri Dwarf who worked with Brokki to fashion gifts for the gods; commissioned by Loki.

Sirens Sea nymphs who are half-bird, half-woman, whose song lures hapless sailors to their death.

Sisyphus King of Ephrya and a trickster who outwitted Autolycus. He was one of the greatest sinners in Hades.

Sita Daughter of the earth, adopted by Janaka, wife of Rama.

Skadi Goddess of winter and the wife of Niord for a short time.

Skanda Six-headed son of Shiva and a warrior god.

Skraeling Person native to Canada and Greenland. The name was given to them by Viking settlers and can be translated as 'barbarian'.

Skrymir Giant who battled against Thor.

Sleipnir Odin's steed.

Sluagh The host of the dead, seen fighting in the sky and heard by mortals.

Smote Struck with a heavy blow.

Sohráb Son of Rustem and Tahmineh, Sohráb was slain in battle by his own father, who killed him by mistake.

Sol The sun-maiden.

Soma A god and a drug, the elixir of life.

Somerled Lord of the Isles, and legendary ancestor of the Clan MacDonald.

Soothsayer Someone with the ability to predict or see the future, by the use of magic, special knowledge or intuition. Known as seanagal in Scottish myths.

Squaw A Native American woman or wife (now offensive).

Squint-Eye One of Ramana's monsters.

Squire Shield- or armour-bearer of a knight.

Srutakirti Daughter of Kushadhwaja.

Stirabout Porridge made by stirring oatmeal into boiling milk or water.

Stone Giants A malignant race of stone beings whom the Iroquois believed invaded their territory, threatening the Confederation of the Five Nations. These fierce and hostile creatures lived off human flesh and were intent on exterminating the human race.

Stoorworm A great water monster which frequented lochs. When it thrust its great body from the sea, it could engulf islands and whole ships. Its appearance prophesied devastation.

Stot Bullock.

Styx River in Arcadia and one of the four rivers in the underworld. Charon ferried dead souls across it into Hades, and Achilles was dipped into it to make him immortal.

Subrahmanian Son of Shiva, a mountain deity.

Sugriva The chief of the five great monkeys in the *Ramayana.*

Sukanya The wife of Chyavana.

Suman Son of Asamanja.

Sumantra A noble Brahman.

Sumati Wife of Sagara.

Sumedha A righteous Brahman who dwelt in the city of Amara.

Sumitra One of Dasharatha's three wives, mother of Lakshmana and Satrughna.

Suniti Mother of Dhruva.

Suparshwa One of Ravana's counsellors.

Supranakha A rakshasi, sister of Ravana.

Surabhi The wish-bestowing cow.

Surcoat Loose robe, traditionally worn over armour.

Surtr Fire-giant who eventually destroys the world at Ragnarok.

Surya God of the sun.

Susanoo God of the storm. He is depicted as a contradictory character with both good and bad characteristics. He was banished from Heaven after trying to kill his sister, Amaterasu.

Sushena A monkey chief.

Svasud Father of summer.

Swarga An Olympian paradise, where all wishes and desires are gratified.

Sweating A ritual customarily associated with spiritual purification and prayer practised by most tribes throughout North America prior to sacred ceremonies or vision quests. Steam was produced within a 'sweat lodge', a low, dome-shaped hut, by sprinkling water on heated stones.

Syrinx An Arcadian nymph who was the object of Pan's love.

Taiaha A weapon made of wood.

Tailtiu One of the most famous royal residences of ancient Ireland. Possibly also a goddess linked to this site.

Tall One of Ravana's counsellors.

Tamsil Example or guidance.

Tangi Funeral, dirge. Assembly to cry over the dead.

Taniwha Sea monster, water spirit.

Tantalus Son of Zeus who told the secrets of the gods to mortals and stole their nectar and ambrosia. He was condemned to eternal torture in Hades, where he was tempted by food and water but allowed to partake of neither.

Taoism Taoism (or Daoism) came into being at roughly the same time as Confucianism, although its tenets were radically different and were largely founded on the philosophies of Lao Tzu (Laozi). While Confucius argued for a system of state discipline, Taoism strongly favoured self-discipline and looked upon nature as the architect of essential laws. A newer form of Taoism evolved after the Burning of the Books, placing great emphasis on spirit worship and pacification of the gods.

Tapu Sacred, supernatural possession of power. Involves spiritual rules and restrictions.

Tara Also known as Temair, the Hill of Tara was the popular seat of the ancient High-Kings of Ireland from the earliest times to the sixth century. Located in Co. Meath, it was also the place where great noblemen and chieftains congregated during wartime, or for significant events.

Tara Sugriva's wife.

Tartarus Dark region, below Hades.

Tau (Lesotho) Brother to Ra-Molo, depicted as a lion.

Taua War party.

Tefnut Goddess of water and rain. Married to Shu, who was also her brother. She, like Sekhmet, is portrayed with the head of a lion. Also known as Tefenet.

Telegonus Son of Odysseus and Circe. He was allegedly responsible for his father's death.

Telemachus Son of Odysseus and Penelope who was aided by Athene in helping his mother to keep away the suitors in Odysseus's absence.

Temu The evening form of Ra, the Sun god.

Tengu Goblin or gnome, often depicted as bird-like. A powerful fighter with weapons.

Tenochtitlán Capital city of the Aztecs, founded around 1350 CE and the site of the 'Great Temple'. Now Mexico City.

Teo-Amoxtli Divine book.

Teocalli Great temple built in Tenochtitlán, now Mexico City.

Teotleco Festival of the Coming of the Gods; also the twelfth month of the Aztec calendar.

Tepee A conical-shaped dwelling constructed of buffalo hide stretched over lodge-poles. Mostly used by Native American tribes living on the plains.

Tepeyollotl God of caves, desert places and earthquakes, whose name means 'heart of the mountain'. He is depicted as a jaguar, often leaping at the sun. Also known as Tepeolotlec.

Tepitoton Household gods.

Tereus King of Daulis who married Procne, daughter of Pandion King of Athens. He fell in love with Philomela, raped her and cut out her tongue.

Tezcatlipoca Supreme deity and Lord of the Smoking Mirror. He was also patron of royalty and warriors. Invented human sacrifice to the gods. Offspring of Ometeotl and Omecihuatl, he is known as the Jupiter of the Aztec gods.

Thalia Muse of pastoral poetry and comedy.

Theia Goddess of many names, and mother of the sun.

Theseus Son of King Aegeus of Athens. A cycle of legends has been woven around his travels and life.

Thetis Chief of the Nereids loved by both Zeus and Poseidon. They married her to a mortal, Peleus, and their child was Achilles. She tried to make him immortal by dipping him in the River Styx.

Thialfi Thor's servant, taken when his peasant father unwittingly harms Thor's goat.

Thiassi Giant and father of Skadi, he tricked Loki into bringing Idunn to him. Thrymheim is his kingdom.

Thomas the Rhymer Also called 'True Thomas', he was Thomas of Ercledoune, who lived in the thirteenth century. He met with the Queen of Elfland, and visited her country, was given clothes and a tongue that could tell no lie. He was also given the gift of prophecy, and many of his predictions were proven true.

Thor God of thunder and of war (with Tyr). Known for his huge size, and red hair and beard. Carries the hammer Miolnir. Slays Jormungander at Ragnarok.

Thoth God of the moon. Invented the arts and sciences and regulated the seasons. He is portrayed with the head of an ibis or a baboon.

Three-Heads One of Ravana's monsters.

Thrud Thor's daughter.

Thrudheim Thor's realm. Also called Thrudvang.

Thunder-Tooth Leader of the rakshasas at the siege of Lanka.

Tiki First man created, a figure carved of wood, or other representation of man.

Tirawa The name given to the Great Creator (*see* Great Spirit) by the Pawnee tribe who believed that four direct paths led from his house in the sky to the four semi-cardinal points: north-east, north-west, south-east and south-west.

Tiresias A Theban who was given the gift of prophecy by Zeus. He was blinded for seeing Athene bathing. He continued to use his prophetic talents after his death, advising Odysseus.

Tirfing Sword made by dwarves which was cursed to kill every time it was drawn, be the cause of three great atrocities, and kill Suaforlami (Odin's grandson), for whom it was made.

Tisamenus Son of Orestes, who inherited the Kingdom of Argos and Sparta.

Titania Queen of the fairies.

Tlaloc God of rain and fertility, so important to the people, because he ensured a good harvest, that the Aztec heaven or paradise was named Tlalocan in his honour.

Tlazolteotl Goddess of ordure, filth and vice. Also known as the earth-goddess or Tlaelquani, meaning 'filth-eater'. She acted as a confessor of sins or wrongdoings.

Tohu-mate Omen of death.

Tohunga A priest; a possessor of supernatural powers.

Toltec Civilization that preceded the Aztecs.

Tomahawk Hatchet with a stone or iron head used in war or hunting.

Tonalamatl Record of the Aztec calendar, which was recorded in books made from bark paper.

Tonalpohualli Aztec calendar composed of twenty thirteen-day weeks called trecenas.

Totec Solar deity known as Our Great Chief.

Toxilmolpilia The binding up of the years.

Tristan Nephew of King Mark of Cornwall, who travels to Ireland to bring Iseult back to marry his uncle. On the way, he and Iseult consume a love potion and fall madly in love before their story ends tragically.

Triton A sea-god, and son of Poseidon and Amphitrite. He led the Argonauts to the sea from Lake Tritonis.

Trojan War War waged by the Greeks against Troy, in order to reclaim Menelaus's wife Helen, who had eloped with the Trojan prince Paris. Many important heroes took part, and form the basis of many legends and myths.

Troll Unfriendly mythological creature of varying size and strength. Usually dwells in mountainous areas, among rocks or caves.

Truage Tribute or pledge of peace or truth, usually made on payment of a tax.

Tsuki-yomi God of the moon, brother of Amaterasu and Susanoo.

Tuat The other world or land of the dead.

Tupuna Ancestor.

Tvashtar Craftsman of the gods.

Tyndareus King of Sparta, perhaps the son of Perseus's daughter Grogphone. Expelled from Sparta but restored by Heracles. Married Leda and fathered Helen and Clytemnestra, among others.

Tyr Son of Frigga and the god of war (with Thor). Eventually kills Garm at Ragnarok.

Tzompantli Pyramid of Skulls.

Uayeb The five unlucky days of the Mayan calendar, which were believed to be when demons from the underworld could reach Earth. People would often avoid leaving their houses on uayeb days.

Ubaaner Magician, whose name meant 'splitter of stones', who created a wax crocodile that came to life to swallow up the man who was trying to seduce his wife.

Uile Bheist Mythical creature, usually some form of wild beast.

Uisneach A hill formation between Mullingar and Athlone said to mark the centre of Ireland.

uKqili (Zulu) Creator god.

Uller God of winter, whom Skadi eventually marries.

Ulster Cycle Compilation of folk tales and legends telling of the Ulaids, people from the northeast of Ireland, now named Ulster. Also known as the *Uliad Cycle*, it is one of four Irish cycles of mythology.

Unseelie Court An unholy court comprising a kind of fairies, antagonistic to humans. They took the form of a kind of Sluagh, and shot humans and animals with elf-shots.

Urd One of the Norns.

Urien King of Gore, husband of Morgan le Fey and father to Yvain.

Urmila Second daughter of Janaka.

Usha Wife of Aniruddha, daughter of Vanasur.

Ushas Goddess of the dawn.

Utgard-loki King of the giants. Tricked Thor.

Uther Pendragon King of England in sub-Roman Britain; father of King Arthur.

Utixo (Hottentot) Creator god.

Vach Goddess of speech.

Vajrahanu One of Ravana's generals.

Vala Another name for Norns.

Valfreya Another name for Freyia.

Valhalla Odin's hall for the celebrated dead warriors chosen by the Valkyries.

Vali The cruel brother of Sugriva, dethroned by Rama.

Valkyries Odin's attendants, led by Freyia. Chose dead warriors to live at Valhalla. Also spelled as Valkyrs.

Vamadeva One of Dasharatha's priests.

Vanaheim Home of the Vanir.

Vanir Race of gods in conflict with the Aesir; they are gods of the sea and wind.

Varuna Ancient god of the sky and cosmos, later, god of the waters.

Vasishtha One of Dasharatha's priests.

Vassal Person under the protection of a feudal lord.

Vasudev Descendant of Yadu, husband of Rohini and Devaki, father of Krishna.

Vasudeva A name of Narayana or Vishnu.

Vavasor Vassal or tenant of a baron or lord who himself has vassals.

Vedic Mantras, hymns.

Vernandi One of the Norns.

Vichitravirya Bhishma's half-brother.

Vidar Slays Fenris.

Vidura Friend of the Pandavas.

Vigrid The plain where the final battle is held.

Vijaya Karna's bow.

Vikramaditya A king identified with Chandragupta II.

Vintail Moveable front of a helmet.

Virabhadra A demon that sprang from Shiva's lock of hair.

Viradha A fierce rakshasa, seizes Sita, slain by Rama.

Virupaksha The elephant who bears the whole world.

Vishnu The Preserver, Vedic sun god and one of the two great gods of post-Vedic Hinduism.

Vision Quest A sacred ceremony undergone by Native Americans to establish communication with the spirit set to direct them in life. The quest lasted up to four days and nights and was preceded by a period of solitary fasting and prayer.

Vivasvat The sun.

Vizier High-ranking official or adviser. Also known as vizir or vazir.

Volsung Family of great warriors about whom a great saga was spun.

Vrishadarbha King of Benares.

Vrishasena Son of Karna, slain by Arjuna.

Vyasa Chief of the royal chaplains.

Wairua Spirit, soul.

Wanjiru (Kikuyu) Maiden who was sacrificed by her village to appease the gods and make it rain after years of drought.

Weighing of the Heart Procedure carried out after death to assess whether the deceased was free from sin. If the deceased's heart weighed less than the feather of Ma'at, they would join Osiris in the Fields of Peace.

Whare Hut made of fern stems tied together with flax and vines, and roofed in with raupo (reeds).

White Demon Protector of Mázinderán. He prevented Kai-káús and his army from invading.

Withy Thin twig or branch which is very flexible and strong.

Wolverine Large mammal of the musteline family with dark, very thick, water-resistant fur, inhabiting the forests of North America and Eurasia.

Wroth Angry.

Wyrd One of the Norns.

Xanthus & Balius Horses of Achilles, immortal offspring of Zephyrus the west wind. A gift to Achilles's father Peleus.

Xipe Totec High priest and son of Ometeotl and Omecihuatl. Also known as the god of the seasons.

Xiupohualli Solar year, composed of eighteen twenty-day months. Also spelt Xiuhpōhualli.

Yadu A prince of the Lunar dynasty.

Yakshas Same as rakshasas.

Yakunin Government official.

Yama God of Death, king of the dead and son of the sun.

Yamato Take Legendary warrior and prince. Also known as Yamato Takeru.

Yashiki Residence or estate, usually of a daimyō.

Yasoda Wife of Nand.

Yemaya (Yoruba) Wife of Obatala.

Yemoja (Yoruba) Goddess of water and protector of women.

Yggdrasill The World Ash, holding up the Nine Worlds. Does not fall at Ragnarok.

Ymir Giant created from fire and ice; his body created the world.

Yo The female principle who, joined with In, the male side, brought about creation and the first gods. In and Yo correspond to the Chinese Yang and Yin.

Yomi The underworld.

Yudhishthira The eldest of the Pandavas, a great soldier.

Yuki-Onna The Snow-Bride or Lady of the Snow, who represents death.

Yvain Son of Morgan le Fay and knight of the Round Table, who goes on chivalric quests with a lion he rescued from a dragon.

Zahid Holy man.

Zál Son of Sám, who was born with pure white hair. Sám abandoned Zál, who was raised by the Símúrgh, or griffins. Zal became a great warrior, second only to his son, Rustem. Also known as Ním-rúz and Dustán.

Zephyr Gentle breeze.

Zeus King of gods, god of sky, weather, thunder, lightning, home, hearth and hospitality. He plays an important role as the voice of justice, arbitrator between man and gods, and among them. Married to Hera, but lover of dozens of others.

Zohák Serpent-king and figure of evil. Father of Mihrab.

Zukin Head covering.

COLLECTOR'S EDITIONS
FLAME TREE
A wide range of new and classic fiction, including short story anthologies, Collectable Classics, Gothic Fantasy collections and Epic Tales of mythology.
•
Available at all good bookstores, and online at flametreepublishing.com
FLAME TREE PUBLISHING